Office Plays - The Collection

OFFICE PLAYS

SECRETS AND LIES

LOVE AFTER HOURS

ANNA ELLIS

Contents

Office Plays

ANNA ELLIS

Chapter One

BRIENNE

H E HAS AN AMAZING ass.

Those pants really show it off. It's tight and firm, like a Jon Snow ass that you want to grab with both hands when he's thrusting into you.

I shake my head to get rid of the image.

That beautiful ass belongs to the controller of Hever Construction. My boss.

He's just walked by my office with Agatha, one of the new receptionists. I'm pretty sure he's going to fire her.

I'm not sure that's a bad thing. There hasn't been this much turmoil in the eight years I've worked for Hever, even after old Mr. Hever died and his sons attempted to take over. Not that Agatha is responsible for all of it, but receptionists are sort of gatekeepers. I've had whole construction crews come tromping through the finance department on the hunt for the executive to sign their paychecks.

It's me who had to sign them, actually. The crew thought it was fine to clock out at eleven thirty in the morning and that I could provide them with their paychecks right then and there.

It doesn't work that way.

Plus, the men left drywall dust all over my desk.

It's not just that—Agatha spends half the day in the washroom touching up her already perfect make-up and the other half in the kitchen making disgusting green smoothies while the phones ring unanswered. She's not even nice to the people when she does answer the phone.

So I don't feel *too* bad for her. But out of respect, I drag my gaze away from Ian's posterior as they walk by. But before I can manage to do that, Ian glances over his shoulder with a hint of a smile.

Did he catch me staring?

My face aflame, I drop my head, pretending to be fascinated by the neatly piled stacks of paperwork on my desk. It's never-ending, but nothing is urgent. I'm still not sure why Ian asked me to work late tonight.

"It will be quiet tomorrow night. Being here alone means you can really get a head start on some of those overdue account files," Ian had suggested yesterday.

I had been too busy mentally comparing him to Michael Fassbender to respond.

Then Ian had dropped his hand on my shoulder, giving it such a brief squeeze I thought I had imagined it. "You don't have plans for Friday night, do you, Brienne?"

I had been forced to admit to him that no, I didn't have plans.

No plans for Friday night. No plans for the long Victoria Day weekend.

Other than my Netflix, of course. And the cold bottle of wine waiting for me in my fridge.

Ian shuts the door behind him, leaving me alone among the empty pods of desks.

There is a lot of paperwork I could be doing. The fall-out from the new owners taking control has been stressful for all of us and I'm well aware that things have fallen a bit behind. The drama has been never-ending lately with the new hires, terminations and even one executive being escorted out by security. Hever is a small company and its employees are quite close. Things have thankfully quieted down this week. I thought the tension of wondering if we were all going to lose our jobs had dissipated until Ian marched Agatha by my desk right into his office.

It was company legend that the former administrative assistant who Agatha replaced–the elderly, but still stunning Mrs. Busey–had been sleeping with old Mr. Hever for as long as she'd worked there. There are stories of the two of them getting it on in his office, the boardroom, in the staff washroom and even in the back of one of the dump trucks.

The last time I saw Mr. Hever, he couldn't stop staring at my breasts, in a strangely flattering, non-offensive way. He was a sweet man with an uncommonly high libido for someone his age.

That's the type of office I work in.

Any office romance, as brief as it may be, usually happens between the hours of nine to five. There are a lot of coffee breaks, and exceptionally long lunches.

There's a lot of sex that goes on in this office.

My friend Callie always says that we spend at least eight hours a day in this office so why not make it as exciting as we can?

Callie is one who likes as much excitement as she can get if you know what I mean.

I pull my email back up onto my screen after the door shuts. I haven't had a chance to finish my *Who Would You Rather...* question from Callie yet.

Callie Champlain works in the engineering department and is my best friend. She likes to send me these trivial questions at least once a day, usually regarding who I would rather have sex with.

If Mr. Hever had a high libido then Callie's is off the chart.

Most of her *What if* questions are funny—would you rather Bruno or Len from *Dancing with the Stars*? Obama or Justin Trudeau? Channing Tatum or Chris Pratt? Sometimes she switches it up asking the juvenile *Marry, Kill or Fuck,* but most of the time she does her best to get me thinking about who I'd want to have sex with.

The questions also don't let me forget how long it's been since I've had sex.

It's been a while.

I'm not opposed to casual sex; I've just never had many opportunities. I may be thirty-five years old, but I'm pretty inexperienced, sexually. I've had an acceptable number of partners (seven) but as far as variety and trying different things, I've always been pretty vanilla. Callie is a lot more adventurous than I ever have been. Plus, I've got Eli and there's nothing he likes better than straight-up sex. No whips, chains or weird positions for him.

Not that I really have him now. But we were together for six years, six years of the most tumultuous, heart-breaking, yet amazing love affair you can imagine. And I can imagine a lot; I devour romance novels like a bag of chips. Eli is my Mr. Darcy; my Rochester, my Edward Cullen. As hot as Gideon Cross, but not creepily possessive as Christian Grey.

It's over between us now, or at least I'm trying desperately to convince myself it is.

I've even instructed my lawyer to move ahead with the divorce.

I wrench my thoughts away from Eli and back to Callie's *What would you rather...?* question.

I'd rather have sex with Henry, but only during his first marriage, as that was before he first began sampling the maids and beheading his wives. He was inexperienced and Katherine of Aragon (his first wife btw) wouldn't have given him much action so he would be begging for sex. After Anne Boleyn, he got a little misogynist and demanding. Prince William on the other hand, while the sexier of the two, even with his receding hairline, would expect every woman to cater to his every need, and I expect he might be a selfish lover.

Because this is a gossipy type of place, and Callie is my best friend, I give her a postscript on the afternoon events.

Ps. Snake-bastard called Ag into his office. Have you heard anything?

Pressing Send, a resigned sigh escapes as I eye the files and paper piled on my desk. Was Ian trying to punish me for something? There's nothing pressing enough here to warrant overtime on the Friday of a long weekend.

I'm the senior accountant of Hever Construction, in charge of everything financial, and the unofficial Assistant Controller since Ian doesn't have the personality or the compassion necessary to deal with personal staff issues. I've lost track of how many times

I receive the little side wave, *"Brienne will deal with it,"* in that haughty, yet extremely sexy British accent. And of course, I take care of it for him because if just being around him makes my knees weak, actually conversing with him is utter torture.

What are you still doing there? Callie demands via email.

Snake-bastard wanted me to stay late. Not sure why...

Suddenly I realize how eerily quiet it is on the floor. I can even hear the hum of the overhead fluorescents. Pulling out my cell phone, I'm about to turn on iTunes when a loud voice startles me.

It has to be Ian. Is he yelling at poor Agatha? I may not like her but no one deserves to be yelled at.

I hear a sharp *crack* and a cry.

A female cry.

I leap to my feet. What the hell is he doing to her? I'm on the other side of my desk, on the way to Ian's office when I notice exactly what he's doing to her.

"Oh, god."

I turn, about to run back to my desk, but I have, I *have* to look again.

Ian's office has those cheap, plastic slat blinds that are opened with a cord and the blind for one window isn't completely closed. Even with the door closed, I can see into Ian's office.

Where Agatha is naked and bent over his desk.

Naked and bent over the desk.

There may be hookups going on in the workplace, but nothing like this.

I shouldn't be seeing this.

But I am.

And I take another look.

On third glance, I can see Agatha is not just bent over the desk, but *strapped* down, her torso prone on the surface with her arms tied underneath by cords. And Ian is standing behind her bare ass holding a ruler, like some bizarre re-enactment of a *Fifty Shades* scene.

And Ian is looking right at me.

It's like all the air is sucked out of my body. I can't move. I can't even blink.

Ian brings the ruler down on Agatha's ass, which is as rosy as a beefsteak tomato, and I gasp, the sharp sound of wood on skin breaking the spell.

Luckily Agatha's cry masks my own.

"I told you to be quiet," Ian demands. I slap my hands over my mouth before I realize he's speaking to Agatha.

As well as not pulling the blinds, it appears he's left the door ajar. No wonder I can hear everything.

I need to sit down. I shouldn't be watching. I should leave.

How do I get out of here without Ian noticing me?

Why is he still looking at me?

I'm still standing in front of my desk watching them. Why am I still watching?

Because in the office Ian is caressing the welt on Agatha's ass as gently as if he's smoothing on moisturizing cream. Her legs are long and tanned, spread wide and strapped to the desk. Her head faces the wall, so at least *she* can't see I'm watching this.

Naked and strapped to the desk.

His fingers disappear between her legs.

I have to stop watching.

Ian is still staring at me.

It's like he's daring me, but I'm not sure for what. Does he expect me to run screaming out to the elevator? Does he think I'm going to walk in and ask to participate?

Does he want me to join in?

Ian is watching me while his hand is busy between Agatha's legs. The sight of it is enough to send a jolt between my own legs. When Ian delivers another stinging slap of the ruler, I steal closer to his office.

It's like I have no control over my body. My feet move on their own accord, the cheap gray carpet rough under my bare feet.

One step...two...I stop when Ian turns away. My breath catches in my throat as he crouches on the floor behind Agatha. His jacket is off, his shirt is still neatly tucked into his pant and he slides his fingers between Agatha's legs, slowly, like he's giving a demonstration on the best way to finger fuck someone.

I can't be watching this. I can't be getting excited by watching this.

But I am. Everything is tingling from the waist down and I already feel the wetness between my legs.

It's been too long since I've had a hand other than my own between my legs.

I bite my lips to stop the moan from escaping. Ian's tongue—I see his tongue snake between her legs. I know exactly when it touches her pussy because her sudden cry fills the room.

Ian spreads Agatha's cheeks with his hands as he positions himself for better access and to no doubt give me a better view. Agatha's cries become louder.

I want to push Agatha off the desk. I want to feel Ian's hands on me, his mouth.

The quiet moan escapes, like the creak of a floorboard.

Ian lifts his head. "If you're not quiet, I will punish you," he growls.

I slap my hand over my mouth again.

"Is that what you want?"

"Yes! Please punish me!" Agatha gasps.

Ian stands, ignoring Agatha's groan of disappointment as he strides out of sight.

I need to go.

I need to leave. I'll get my bag and turn off my computer and...

Ian's back and this time he's holding a short braided handle with strips of leather dangling from it.

What... the...hell...?

He has a flogger in his office.

The inter-office hookups are one thing but I never expected anything like this!

The leather dangles across Agatha's ass. With a flick of Ian's wrist, the straps fly between her legs.

"Is this what you want?" Ian demands. He brings back his hand, striking her bare ass with the leather.

Once, twice...five times, and with each blow, Agatha cries out louder than before. My hand is still over my mouth, or Ian would hear my gasps as well.

Is this what goes on after hours? Is this a new thing, or have I just been *completely* oblivious for years?

Ian finally drops the flogger and swiftly unties Agatha's arms and legs. Without giving her a chance to stand, he flips her over to her back and yanks her legs up and over his shoulder so that she's lying on her upper back on the desk. It looks uncomfortable.

Until Ian buries his face between her legs.

Oh.

I can hear everything—Agatha's moans and gasps of pleasure, the sounds of Ian's mouth against her wetness.

Even my own panting breaths.

Ian's hips thrust as he assaults Agatha with his lips, his tongue. I have an urge to touch the hardness in his pants.

"Don't stop," Agatha begs. "Please—oh, yes!" The yes is a drawn-out wail and her hips buck in his hold.

But Ian stops and lifts his head. "I don't want to hear you."

Agatha whimpers as Ian returns to his ministrations, this time with his hands cupping her ass, one of his thumbs probing between her legs. Her cries and moans sound strangled, her hands pressed against her mouth.

But Agatha can't quiet the scream a moment later as she comes, her orgasm causing her body to shake and quiver as Ian fights to hold her up.

He made her scream.

Agatha has barely earned her release when Ian pushes her to the floor by her hair. His pants are undone and his cock is out before I know what's happening. Agatha is on her knees and takes him eagerly in her mouth.

That's when Ian glances back out the window at me. At me, with my hand down my own pants.

I've never masturbated at work before.

It doesn't take me long because it has been *so long* since I've felt this excited and sexy and in dire need of a man. I'm so wet. My fingers surround my clit and I rub quickly, frantically.

Ian watches me, his hips thrusting against Agatha's open mouth. Her hands press against his ass, feeding more of his cock into her mouth.

A soft cry escapes me as I feel my own orgasm begin. My legs feel weak but I can't stop watching him, having him watch me. I've never wanted a man to have so much power over me, but right now I want Ian to know how much he's exciting me.

Suddenly I come with a sharp cry, my legs buckling.

Ian grabs Agatha's head with both hands. His face contorts, but I'm gone before he comes, rushing to the washroom at the other end of the floor.

What the hell just happened?

My cheeks are pink with pleasure and my blue eyes are sparkling.

Never have I given Ian any indication I would be so aroused by something like that. Never would I have imagined being so excited. I don't know what to feel—embarrassed? Satisfied? Frustrated?

Still excited?

I wait to come out until I hear the soft ping of the elevator.

Ian stands at the door of his office, with Agatha nowhere in sight. His jacket is on, his pants still snug around his hips.

I freeze in the aisle between the cubicles, unable to play it cool.

"Will you work late next Friday as well?"

My refusal is on my lips as I nod my consent.

Chapter Two

ABBY

"**G**OOD MORNING."

It's Tuesday morning, the day after the long Victoria Day weekend and as usual Brienne and Callie are huddled together in the kitchen with Sadie and Delia, all waiting for their turn for the Tassimo to produce their caffeinated beverages. The four jump apart at my arrival, almost like they are talking about me.

"What's going on?" I ask warily, opening the fridge. The collection of brightly coloured lunch bags and Tupperware full of leftovers fill the shelves, except the bottom, which is full of beer and pop cans.

I've never seen anyone drink the beer but every week or so, it gets replaced with another brand.

"Good stuff! Better than the smut on your T.V. shows," Callie giggles her blue eyes shining with delight. "It's office smut."

Callie is always happy and smiling about something but today she's even more excited. Sometimes I wonder if she's ever unsure of herself.

Her confidence makes me envious as well as draws me to her. It's impossible not to want to be Callie's friend.

"Who is it this time?" I ask. For Callie to be this excited, it has to be about sex. I expect to hear something about Rebecca in HR and Paul the Safety guy. Everyone sees the two of them making moony eyes at each other and gossip is rife about the longer-than-usual lunch hours they take. There's more action happening in the offices of Hever Construction than in an episode of *The Bachelor*. And definitely enough to keep the gossip mill running at all hours of the day.

"Keep it down," Brienne moans, clutching her mug with both hands. "I shouldn't have said anything but I *had* to tell you!"

"Ian and *Agatha*!" Sadie tells me with a frantic clapping of her hands. Sadie is young, cute, and thin, in an athletic rather than anorexic way, which also makes me envious. Like Callie, she's very enthusiastic about things, especially things of a sexual nature.

She wasn't always like this. When she began working here, Sadie was the original babe in the woods, so innocent and trusting that she missed all the obvious signs about her boyfriend's infidelities until he left her to marry another woman.

"What about Ian and Agatha?" I ask, shooting a glance at Brienne. For some reason, Brienne thinks Ian is the cat's meow. He's too sophisticated to be my type, but I agree he is extremely good-looking with a nice ass.

"You sure it wasn't *Alma*?" Callie asks Brienne skeptically. "They look the same. Pretty and skinny with all that dark hair. And cute shoes. They both have good shoes."

"They do look alike," Delia points out, popping her pod into the machine. Instantly the smell of hazelnut begins to seep out. "I thought they were sisters."

I roll my eyes. "I'm sure clients love it when they come through the front door at Hever to find matching Barbie dolls waiting behind the front desk."

"They aren't sisters," Sadie jumps in. "And they're not Barbie dolls."

"They are very pretty," Delia frowns. "It's unfortunate if that's the reason they got the job. I thought we got rid of that sort of thing when the brothers left."

"We've always had sexy receptionists, at least for as long as I've worked here," Brienne offers, always the peacemaker. "Maybe old Mr. Hever made that part of the job description. I wouldn't put it past him."

"I really hope no one will be calling me Old Delia behind my back," Delia sighs., stepping back from the machine with her #1 Best Mom cup in hand and gesturing that it's my turn.

"You're not old." Brienne smiles down at her. "Just small." At nearing fifty, Delia may be the oldest of us working at Hever and also the shortest.

"Old enough to be her mother," Delia looks pointedly at Sadie. "And probably the Double A's at reception."

"Yes, but I'm old enough to be Sadie's mom too." Callie laughs, the contagious sound filling small the room and bringing smiles to our faces. "If I had started having sex when I first wanted to."

"You wanted to have sex when you were *ten?*" Brienne asks in horror. "I didn't even know what a penis looked like when I was that age."

"Maybe eleven," Callie concedes. "I was very advanced for my age."

"Agatha," Sadie interjects before Callie starts on one of her stories. "It wasn't Alma."

"I think I can tell them apart," Brienne assures her. "I am going to check out her shoes next time, though, if they're as nice as you say."

Mothers and shoes and apparent sexism in the office? My head is beginning to spin from all the subject jumping. "Hang on a second. Will someone *please* tell me what all the excitement is about?"

And then my eyes widen as Brienne fills me in about what happened Friday afternoon in Ian's office, with Sadie and Callie, and even Delia adding details and questions.

"He really tied her to the desk? And spanked her." I blink with disbelief. "Alma?"

"With a ruler," Brienne nods, wide-eyed. "And this flogger thing. Straight out of *Fifty Shades*. So hot!"

Now that the image is firmly entrenched in my mind, I can appreciate that it might have been very exciting to watch if that's what a person is into.

I've never watched people having sex, other than Ben trying to get me into porn. Seeing Alma spread over the desk, Ian crouched behind her—

"Agatha," Sadie says quickly. "It was Agatha, not Alma."

"Really?" Callie quirks an eyebrow. "You seem quite adamant about that."

As Callie stares expectantly, Sadie is forced, somewhat reluctantly, to admit that she was with Alma Friday afternoon during the time frame Brienne was playing Peeping Tom.

They were Brienne's words, not mine.

"What's she like?" Delia whispers, hunching her shoulders as if to keep her gossiping a secret. "Neither of Agatha or Alma have been very friendly towards us since they started."

"Well, obviously because you're too nice," Callie laughs. "They like *forceful* people. You need to tell them what to do, and how to do it, like Ian, the snake bastard. Then they'll be nice to you."

"I'm not looking for spanking tips." It surprises me that Delia even mentions spanking. She always seems above Callie's frequent comments.

Callie winks at her. "Don't knock it until you try it."

"Alma's not like that. Not that I know her very well," Sadie is quick to say. "But she doesn't seem the type to be into something like that."

"How would you know this?" I wonder. "How would anyone know what a person is into? I could be into group sex with leprechauns and you'd never know. I'm not," I assure them, as I'm greeted with four dumbfounded expressions. "I'm really not."

"No, I don't think you are," Sadie shakes her head. "But hearing that come out of your mouth..."

These women have apparently judged my book by the conservative cover. I mask a sigh, recognizing once again that I need to loosen up.

"Who would look the type?" Callie wonders in all seriousness. It takes her a moment of musing to realize we're looking expectantly at her. "Not me! Not that I see anything wrong with it, but not if someone's watching. Unless, of course, you like that sort of thing." Callie looks sideways at Brienne. "*You* seemed to like it."

"I've never seen anything like it," Brienne whispers reverently. "The way he...and then he..."

"I shouldn't be hearing this," I say, my hands covering my ears. "I haven't even had my coffee yet."

It's not surprising they think I'm as dull as my navy jacket if I say things like that.

"I'm not sure I should have heard it the first time," Delia agrees.

"I shouldn't have said anything," Brienne moans.

"Of course you should have," Callie corrects her. "It's us. You tell us everything."

It's true. Brienne is very open about her life, especially her misery over her ex, Eli. Or is he her ex-husband yet? In my opinion, the marriage was doomed before it began. You don't marry a musician whose longest relationship was the length of his European tour. And you definitely don't marry a man who considers sleeping with groupies a part of the band's marketing plan.

No matter how sexy he may be.

"No wonder Ian never gave me the time of day," Callie grins smugly. "I bet he could tell I would never be into that shit. If there's flogging going on, I'll be the one with that stick."

I have an image of Callie's curves encased in a black vinyl catsuit, whip in hand. I have to give my head a shake to remove the visual.

"Ian's hot," Sadie announces. "And the thought of him being into all that Christian Grey stuff–wow. Do you think he's got a red room of *love*?"

I read the books, saw the movies and have to admit they did well casting him. Christian Grey in those jeans...

"Those books are not the end all of erotica," Brienne says dismissively. "There's so much more out there. Much better stuff."

"Like what happens here?" Callie laughs.

"Please don't say anything," Brienne begs, glancing around to make sure no one has slipped into the kitchen. We're still alone.

"Don't worry," Sadie assures her. "What happens in the kitchen, stays in the kitchen. Or Ian's office."

"Well, that's a good thing," Callie tells us, with her exaggerated gestures and a big voice. "Because the other night when I was here late—let me tell you, I'm glad this little kitchen can't talk."

I glance around at the tiny counter space and picture her perched precariously on the edge, her legs twined around a man's waist, her hands clutching the cupboards above as he thrusts into her, hard and fast with Callie begging for more.

What would be like if Ben and I were here after hours? We would come into the kitchen–Ben would pull up my skirt and bend me over the counter, thrusting hard and fast and I would...

I swallow my sudden excitement. Lately, despite my reserved outlook, sex is all I'm been able to think about.

For a moment, I want to tell the others about the kitchen sex that I had with Ben during Easter dinner when our families were gouging themselves with turkey at the table in the next room. I've never done anything like that before. I've also never let Ben finger fuck me under the table while his mother sat across from us.

Not sure I'll do that again. It was fun, but having my moth-er-in-law right across the table from me as I came took away a bit of the excitement.

Maybe I'm not as dull as I think I am.

That little scene happened a few weeks ago and I've been waiting with bated breath for Ben to try something else. I want him to. I really hope he knows I want him to because I can't seem to bring myself to tell him about it.

"Talk about a den of debauchery," Delia sighs. I start, thinking I've spoken aloud about Easter before realizing the conversation is still on Callie.

Callie shrugs. "Not my favourite place to get busy in, but it'll do in a pinch."

"And I'm sure you know all the places," Brienne says half-re-provingly, half-admiringly.

"Places for what?" a deep voice interrupts.

Michael, Jason, and Carl enter the kitchen and the energy changes. Callie has a new audience, and I can't help but notice there is more than a few heated glances between her and Michael. But as sexy as Michael is, in a brainy, geeky sort of way, he's never struck me as Callie's type. Plus, he's got a long-time girlfriend, and if there's one thing about Callie is that she doesn't go for the attached type. There's some integrity beneath the impressive chest measurements.

"Places to play," Sadie gushes in response to Michael's query. "Callie was just telling us–"

"Nothing of importance," Brienne smoothly cuts in. "How are you guys this morning? Did you watch *Outlander* Sunday night?"

"I've seen a few episodes," Jason admits. He's the IT guy for the company and quite possibly has an I.Q. greater than the rest of us put together. "But *Game of Thrones* is more my thing."

"Oh, I love that!" Sadie exclaims. "You know nothing, Jon Snow!"

"Can't say either show is my thing," Carl says. He's one of the project managers and works closely with Delia, who looks after the accounts. It's not surprising then, to see the two put their heads together in a private conversation.

I've noticed them together a lot lately.

And I notice the way Callie runs her eyes down Michael's long frame as he talks. But it's not the usual predatory way Callie appraises men. She has a happy smile on her face, not a hungry one. She just likes to watch him.

But Jason seems to like to watch Callie, even though Sadie won't stop chattering to him.

"I met the new boss this morning," Carl announces when there is a break in the television debate.

"Julian Donovan," Jason supplies. Hever Construction was bought by a consortium about six weeks ago, but the new president has yet to make an appearance in the office. "He seems competent enough to run the company."

"There's a glowing endorsement," Michael laughs.

"I've only met the man once. He hasn't earned any sort of endorsement from me."

"But what's your impression of him?" I ask.

Jason shrugs. "He seems competent. He complimented me on my work ethic, gave me a few new responsibilities. I can't find fault with him yet."

"It almost sounds like you expect to."

"I hope not. The senior Mr. Hever was capable of running this company at a profit, but his sons almost bankrupted it."

"It wasn't that bad, was it?" Sadie asks.

"Pretty bad," Brienne agrees with Jason and Delia nodding as well.

"I was worried for a while," I admit. "I still am. Donovan could swoop in and fire the lot of us. Don't forget, Ben works here, too."

"You worry about everything, Abs. I heard Donovan's hot," Callie says lasciviously.

"And that would prevent him from firing us?" I ask ruefully.

"No. It just makes him more interesting," Callie winks at me. "You know Ben is safe and you are the number one lawyer in the place, so you're not going anywhere. You need to stick around and help him fire other people! What did you think of the boss man?" she turns to Carl.

"Not sure if I can help you there," Carl grins at her. "Seeing as I'm not inclined to judge men on their hotness."

"Oh, come on, give us something. Rebecca said he's rocking the tall, dark and handsome thing."

"He seems tall," Carl muses. "I'd say he has nice eyes. Blue, I think."

"They were blue. I thought he was attractive," Jason concedes. "For a man. Like Carl, I'm not inclined to judge a man on his attractiveness, but if I were, I would go so far as to say Julian Donovan is hot."

"There you go. That wasn't so difficult, was it?" Delia teases. "Make the poor girl happy."

"And you're not interested in a hot man walking the floors of this place?" Callie demands.

"I doubt he'll be walking around my desk," Delia tells her.

"You girls have got enough handsome men around here to distract you," Michael says with mock arrogance, earning him a slap on the shoulder from Callie.

"There are quite a few," Brienne says dreamily.

"Ugh! Stop mooning over snake bastard!" Callie cries.

"Would you rather her moon over her ex-husband?" I point out.

"I'm not mooning over anyone!" Brienne protests, her cheeks pink.

"Who or what is a snake bastard?" Carl turns to Delia.

"Ian. Our fearless leader."

Carl nods in agreement.

"Not your favourite, is he?" Delia asks.

"I wouldn't think he should be anyone's favourite," Carl says carefully, with a questioning glance at Brienne.

Brienne shrugs her narrow shoulders. "What can I say? I have horrible taste in men."

"Have you noticed how much he resembles Michael Fassbender?" Jason points out.

"That's what I thought!" Brienne exclaims; in her excitement she waves her arms, almost knocking my just-brewed cup of coffee out of my hand. "Sorry, Ab. But doesn't he look like him?"

"I can't see it," I confess. "Not that I watch many movies these days."

"He's in quite a few good movies," Jason ruminates. "Michael Fassbender, not your snake bastard. You should watch *Shame* if you're so interested. He does a full-frontal nude scene."

"Are you telling Brienne to watch a movie to see a naked man?" Sadie cries with delight.

"In case she might be interested in learning more about him," Jason says with all seriousness.

"Oh, I think she's learning a lot about him," Callie says under her breath to me. "And definitely wants to know more."

Just like I'd like to know if my husband has anything more in store for me.

Chapter Three

SADIE

I'M SO GLAD BRIENNE told us about Ian and Agatha because I was biting my tongue not to blurt the news about *me*. I really don't want to tell anyone until I know for sure what's going on. Was Friday a thing? A one-time event or the beginning of something? What does it mean? What does it mean about *me*?

The email arrives just as I'm back at my desk. I'm the sole member of the marketing team for Hever and therefore have my own space on the third floor near the engineering department. I can call out to Callie from my desk and wave to Abby in her corner office across the floor.

My position also allows me to see how Carl's face lights up whenever Delia is on the floor. The two of them are drawn to each other like ants to a cookie in the sand. It's sweet. Office romance can be fun, not that either of them would call it such. They are *friends,* Delia would insist.

Are we friends?

As soon as I log in, I see the email. I see the three emails already sent and waiting for me. And like Carl, I can't hide the smile from spreading over my face, or the rush I feel, the giddiness of knowing someone likes me.

Are you at your desk yet?

I need to see you.

Can we talk? 5 mins? Same place as before? I have *to see you.*

My fingers fly over the keys as I respond. *I'll be right down.*

I feel like my smile is a flashing neon sign, like one of those lights that beam high into the sky. It's as if I'm announcing to all what happened on Friday.

Friday was a revelation. While Brienne was confiding in us about Ian and Agatha this morning, all I could think about was what happened to *me* on Friday afternoon, right here at work. I didn't tell them about it. I couldn't even hint at it, so I made a big deal about Brienne's story, flushed with relief that no one had found out about me.

I'm not sure what they would say. Even after a long weekend of running through every second of what happened, I still don't know what to say about it.

It's not me. It's not my normal behaviour. But I couldn't help myself.

I quickly arrange my desk to look like I've stepped away for a moment and then rush down the stairs to the main floor. As my shoes clatter down the stairs, a pang of worry shoots through my heart. What if she says it was all a mistake? What if she says she doesn't want to see me? What if her husband found out?

I see her standing amid the shelves in the supply closet at the end of the hall, the dim light masking her slim figure and I step forward, wanting those green eyes to turn their light on me.

I'm having my own office romance.

With Alma.

Alma, along with Agatha, is one of the new administrative assistants for Hever. The two of them sit behind a tall desk, facing the doors on the main floor. They take care of all the little things not assigned to a specific team or person. Management boasts about the Double As, seemingly more proud of the women's stellar appearance than how they fulfill their job functions.

It may not be an office romance. It might be nothing.

I don't know what it is.

"Hi," I whisper.

I've only known her for two weeks but I haven't been able to stop thinking about her.

It had begun on her first day. I had walked into the office to see her sitting there with Agatha, both smooth and glossy with their Victoria's Secret model figures and expertly applied makeup.

I only wear lipstick when I go out at night.

"You're new," I had said, with surprise. I don't think I sounded rude—I had been trying to be friendly.

But Agatha had looked down her patrician nose at me. "You're observant." Then she turned away.

I had been left with my mouth hanging open. I never knew how to handle rude people and had been two seconds away from rushing away from the desk when Alma spoke up.

"Good morning. I'm Alma. First day."

I'll never forget the lurch of my stomach as our eyes met, the warmth of her smile. I had stumbled through my introductions and made some inane small talk.

I don't even remember what I said.

I had spent the night waiting excitedly for the next morning.

"Morning, Sadie," Alma said as soon as I walked in the door.

I'd stop and talk to her in the morning and would leave early to make sure she would still be at her desk. I accidentally on purpose ran into her in the kitchen that afternoon.

By the next day, we were emailing and met for coffee again. The day after we went for lunch.

She told me a few things about her husband and how excited she was to be working here. I told her about my heartbreak over Evan.

We became friends.

But it began to be something more than the usual friendship for me.

I couldn't think straight when she looked at me with those green eyes. When she touched my arm, I felt it in every part of my body. Her lips were so perfectly formed, like a lush little bow and I found that I couldn't stop wondering what it would be like to kiss her.

Since Evan and I broke up, I've only been with one person, my neighbour Laurel. Before her, I had never been attracted to women. Was Alma the start of a new phase for me? Did Evan hurt me so much that I was giving up on men?

How can I tell anyone about Alma when I don't understand it myself?

To make it even worse, she's married. I should understand cheating, being the victim of it myself. I should walk away before anyone else gets hurt.

Instead of walking away, I head to the supply closet.

After I shut the door to the supply closet behind me, the first thing I see Alma's beautiful face creased with worry. I have an urge to kiss away the furor on her brow.

"I didn't know if you'd come," she says, wringing her hands.

"Why wouldn't I? Is everything all right?" I ask quickly, automatically moving forward to touch her wrist but stopping myself at the last minute. What if she thought Friday was a mistake?

That day, the day this began, I had been standing by Alma's desk when she had laughed. She rarely laughed. She would smile and sometimes the smile would reach her eyes. I think Alma's sadness was what first drew me to her. But on Friday, she had laughed aloud at something I said and before I knew it, I had reached out and brushed those laughing lips with my fingers.

The sound of her laughter had died at my touch as quickly as the light vanished from her eyes.

I screwed up, I thought with a groan.

But before I could yank my fingers away, the tip of her tongue had darted out, and she licked my middle finger. It had only been a cat-like flick but it was like a shot of pure adrenaline to my groin.

I think I might have moaned aloud.

And without a word, Alma took my hand and led me here, to the supply closet at the end of the hall.

In the dark room, smelling like toner and cleaning supplies, I leaned into her, and she leaned into me and it was the sweetest kiss ever.

And then it became more than sweet and we ended up christening the supply closet.

I'm still confused about what happened. It had been intense. It had been like nothing I'd ever experienced. I liked it; I'm confused but I want it to continue. I want to feel Alma's touch again, and again and...

But what if Alma regrets the whole thing? What if she called me down here to tell me it's over–whatever this is?

But seeing her shoulders sag with relief at my words, I know she's as scared at the thought of not being together again, as scared as I am. "I couldn't stop thinking about you all weekend," Alma whispers with a tremulous smile.

"Me too," I tell her, fighting my giddiness.

"You don't think it was a mistake?" she asks, twisting her fingers together. Twisting her ring on her finger.

"Do you?" I ask carefully. "You're..." I point to her hand.

Alma yanks her hand away so quickly I wonder if she's pulled off her wedding ring. "I don't want to think about him. He means—I've been so happy these last two weeks. I've never felt like that before."

"But you're married," I remind her.

"He doesn't understand me. He never has."

"Why do you stay with him?" This isn't the conversation I want to have with Alma, but I need to ask. I have to be able to justify what we did, what I want to do again.

Alma drops her eyes. "I can't leave him. He would never let me. I can only find happiness in others. Like you." She lifts her gaze to me and my heart breaks to see tears in her eyes. "Please don't tell me you think this is a mistake. I couldn't bear it."

"I don't," I tell her hurriedly, reaching out for her hand. "It wasn't. I can't stop thinking about you."

"I'm so glad." Alma grabs my outstretched hand and clutches it with both of hers, bringing it to her lips to kiss it. She pulls me towards her.

"I've never done this before," I tell her as I let myself be tugged forward, eager yet nervous.

"I thought you said you'd been with a woman," Alma says sharply. That was what started things. I had confided to her about what happened with my neighbour Laurel over Christmas. How I was so lonely and miserable about my break-up with Evan and Laurel...Laurel took my mind off Evan. Off all men.

Not forever. Just for now.

Before Laurel, I had no more than a passing curiosity in another woman. But now...

Before Laurel, I had no idea a woman's touch could be so exciting, so sensual. For a few weeks, I couldn't get enough of her until she met someone else. I had told Alma about it last week; how I was disappointed it was over, even though I knew it couldn't have been anything serious. Laurel helped me get my mind off Evan. I got to experiment, something I had never done before.

And now Alma and I...

"I have, but not like this. Not at work. And you're married..."

"Stop talking about that," Alma snaps and I pull back at her uncharacteristic tone. "Sadie, this has nothing to do with him. It's about us. You and me." Her hand slides around my waist. "It's okay. Please believe me."

"I want to."

"And I want you."

She kisses me before I can say anything else. I sink into her lips. I'm overwhelmed by the touch of her mouth on mine; all soft lips slick with lipstick. Her perfume surrounds me.

"I missed you," Alma says. She pulls me forward to the low counter at the back.

I'm still unsure about all of this, except that I loved how Alma had made me feel on Friday and so I let her take control. I'm not in the mood to talk any longer and from the looks of things, Alma isn't either.

I boost myself up onto the counter and one of my shoes falls off. Alma gently removes the other one and runs her hand from my foot, up to my calf to my knee, then slips her hand under the fabric of my skirt.

With both hands, Alma pushes up my skirt and I lean back on my elbows. Her fingers stroke my mound through a scrap of fabric I call underwear. Between the two of us, my panties don't last long, dangling from one ankle as Alma's fingers stroke my already wet pussy.

"I can't stop thinking about you, Sadie," Alma whispers, her voice husky in the quiet room, her fingers beginning to explore. "I touch myself all the time, wishing it was you. I need to have my mouth on you. I can't seem to breathe unless you're near me. Not seeing you this weekend was torture."

She slides a finger inside me, and then another, thrusting gently, hypnotized by the rhythm.

"Please..." I moan, pushing my hips forward to the edge of the counter, desperate for more.

I see the white of Alma's teeth in the dim light. She pulls her fingers out of me, ignoring my groan of disappointment, my gasp as her thumb caresses my clit for a brief second. Bending one of my legs, she places it on the counter, leaving me open and vulnerable.

And wanting.

Alma gazes at me breathlessly perched on the counter, a hungry look in her green eyes. I have the same look in mine.

Alma strokes my foot as she presses her lips against my ankle. Slowly, tortuously she kisses her way up along my leg until those lips reach my inner thigh.

I can't stop the moan that escapes when the time she drops the final kiss on the sensitive skin of my thigh, so tantalizingly close that I can feel her breath. She traces her tongue from the spot to where the soft curls cover my mound, blowing on them as her fingers retrace the path of her lips. Then she opens me with her thumbs, and I can feel her breath against the folds as she lingers, poised like a statue, waiting for me to beg for her touch.

I wait as long as I can. "Please..." I whimper.

"What do you want?" she whispers, her lips so close.

"You. Please...touch me..."

She flicks her thumb against my clit like she's sending a text. "Like that?"

"No...oh, god, Alma. Your mouth–please!"

She must hear the desperation in my voice. I know she hears it because she wants to hear it. She waits for it.

"Are you sure?" she asks in a low voice, sliding a finger idly between my folds. I gasp, pushing forward until she removes her touch.

"Alma, please!" I beg.

She's still chuckling as her mouth descends onto my pussy, her laugh providing even more of a vibration. I gasp as she begins to devour me.

Alma may appear demure and withdrawn but as I've found out Friday, she's anything but.

Her tongue is everywhere; licking, probing, thrusting inside me; from my clit to even my puckered asshole. It's a new erogenous zone for me, and Alma has gained more confidence and become even more adventurous since Friday.

She plunges her fingers deep inside me, searching for my G-spot. "Do you like that? Is that good?" she asks breathlessly, her mouth hovering above my pussy.

"Good." I draw out the word like a moan as the vowels hitch on my gasp. "More..." I push her head down to indicate how much more I want.

With her fingers thrusting into me, her pinky probing my ass, Alma goes to work on my clit. She alternates with quick flicks of her tongue to lapping it. When she surrounds my clit with her mouth, sucking hard, I almost fall off the counter.

"Oh, god, *yes!*"

For long minutes, she sucks my clit, pausing often to tongue it frantically, all while thrusting fingers in and out of my pussy. I bite down on my hand to muffle my cries. Sensations invade my body as Alma brings me closer and closer to the edge, as I whimper words of nonsense, begging her not to stop. I push down on her head, frantic for more and as I reach the brink, my cries turn into a scream muffled by my own hand as I tumble, plummet, hurtle over the edge to oblivion, leaving me a shaking, whimpering mess.

I'm having an office romance, even though I have no idea what I'm doing. Alma is a married woman and I am not a lesbian.

But I like it, whatever this is.

Chapter Four

JASON

AFTER KITCHEN CHAT, BRIENNE and Delia head into the cubicle pond of the accounting department, while I head upstairs with the others.

Abby goes straight to her office, as does Carl. My desk is on route to the engineering section, so Callie and Michael stop for a moment like they usually do. Sadie leaves us immediately, and I watch her wind her way through the cubicles to her desk.

"She's in a hurry this morning." Callie toys with the TARDIS figurine on my desk as she watches Sadie hurry away. I have a replica Dr. Who Sonic Screwdriver as well, but I keep that in my drawer.

I wonder if it's my place to tell Callie what's going on with Sadie and Alma.

Not that I know for sure. I have a suspicion, which could in part be based on fantasy. What man wouldn't enjoy imagining two women together, especially two as gorgeous as Alma and Sadie?

Alma isn't really my type; too high-maintenance. Sadie, on the other hand, could very well be my type, especially since physically, she's the complete opposite of my ex Amy, and I don't need any more reminders of her.

I decide not to tell Callie what I suspect about Sadie, even though it might mean more time with her at my desk.

"Sadie might have work to do, unlike some people we know," Michael says, glancing teasingly at Callie. Callie is a tall woman, but Michael is so tall, he's able to look down at her.

I wish I was as tall as Michael. I also wish Callie smiled at me like she does to him. She smiles at me, but it's different. According to Michael, there is nothing going on between the two of them. I hate myself for asking, but some things you just need to know.

"I have things to do, too," Callie protests, her blue eyes twinkling at Michael. "But why would I choose to do it right now when I could hang out with the two of you?"

Her smile blinds me, almost as much as the sight of the extra button Callie left undone on her blouse.

The blouse itself is nothing special; cobalt blue that looks amazing with her blonde hair and thin enough so I can see the outline of the lace on her bra. This might be enough to keep me going for the day but Callie left the third button undone so that the V of the material dips all the way down to midway between her cleavage. Any other woman would only leave the top two buttons undone, but not Callie.

I watch the swell of her breast rise and fall when she laughs, the fabric tight over her voluptuous curves. I've never considered myself a breast man before, but right now I can't seem to stop staring at Callie's chest.

I'm not delusional; I realize there is no chance or any sense of being romantically involved with the ladies at work, especially since I ended things with Kim from accounting. Add that to what happened with Amy, and romance shouldn't be anywhere on my radar these days.

Amy and I had three wonderful years together until she decided I wasn't enough for her and she found someone else who could make her happier. Unfortunately, she didn't have to look very far.

I forgave Amy. It was impossible not to and very necessary because six weeks after breaking my heart, my ex-girlfriend became my sister-in-law.

I should have learned from that and given Kim a wide berth, but she looked too much like Amy.

Because of Amy, and now because of Kim, it's better for me to just enjoy friends with the women at work. It's enjoyable to be able to talk with them without wishful thinking about how I might be able to see them naked sooner rather than later.

It's impossible not to like Callie, regardless of how she looks in that blouse. I like the way she always has a smile on her face. The way she protects Sadie encourages Abby, includes Delia and is a source of strength for Brienne. Women are the minority at Hever, and those five have stuck together despite their differences. Delia is old enough to be Sadie's mother. Abby worries about everything and her conservative nature is the complete opposite of Callie. Brienne is a hopeless romantic.

Callie's not into romance. She's not looking for a relationship unless it's purely a physical one. She wants to have fun, and not hurt anyone.

I could use some fun.

"You wouldn't know what to do with the two of us," Michael is saying to Callie.

"Oh, I'm pretty sure I would," Callie retorts lightly, but with enough conviction in her tone to get my engines running.

Michael laughs, but I don't join in. "You're a funny one, Cal. Look, I'd better get to work. It was a good time on Sunday night," he calls to me as he heads to his desk.

"He's completely clueless a lot of the time," Callie says reflectively as she watches Michael greet others on his way to his desk. I'm not sure if she's talking to me or herself, so I say nothing, letting my eyes drift along the curve of her hip. "So what did you two do on Sunday?" she asks me.

She gives no warning and I'm embarrassed to admit I'm caught with my eyes on her. I don't want her to think of me as some creep who won't stop staring at her, even though I really can't.

"We had–I had a game night," I tell her.

"What kinds of games do you play?" she asks coyly. "Spin-the-bottle?"

"No." I realize too late how awkward I must seem standing behind the desk and abruptly. Then I regret the move, in case Callie will take it as some sort of dismissal.

But my heart soars as she hikes her hip onto the corner of my desk.

Oh, to be that piece of metal!

"*Settlers of Catan*, *Galaxy Trucker*, this one called *Puerto Rico*..." I wait for the glaze of disinterest to waft over Callie's face and am surprised when it doesn't. "You've heard of them?" I ask.

"I love Catan. I play it with my brothers' kids."

"You–really? I wouldn't have thought it."

"I'm a pretty big geek," she tells me casually. She holds up my TARDIS. "I know this stands for Time and Relative Dimension in Space. My father likes to say he named me after Callista Masana in the *Star Wars* books. Of course he didn't," she laughs when my jaw drops. "I was born about twenty years too early for that."

"I, I think I'm in love," I stammer, not entirely joking.

I'm glad I sat down because I wouldn't have been able to remain standing with the blatantly suggestive look Callie gave me. "Doesn't surprise me with the way you can't take your eyes off my breasts."

"Sorry," I mutter, feeling every drop of blood in my body rushing to my face.

"I'm not," she says with a wink. "I take it you saw something you liked? I did, too."

With that remark, Callie walks away, leaving my brain befuddled as I stare after her. To make it worse, she looks back and catches me staring yet again.

Is it my imagination, or does she give her hips an extra sway?

It takes a few minutes for me to get my mind off of that sway and back to work. In fact, I don't realize I'm staring at a blank computer screen until Kim walks by and points it out.

"Uh, thanks," I tell her, quickly turning on my monitor and hoping Kim will keep moving. I want to continue to analyze Callie's comments, and rewind every word she spoke to me.

"You okay?" Kim asks, hovering by my desk, the same spot which Callie had just been perched. *Don't sit down*, I tell her silently.

She doesn't sit, but she doesn't leave either.

"I'm fine." I attempt a smile, which comes out more like a grimace.

"We haven't talked in a while," she says hesitantly." I kind of miss seeing your face."

What am I supposed to say to that? Explain to Kim how she no longer has any right to see my face because, after months of hearing how she was *thisclose* to breaking up with her boyfriend because he treated her so horribly, they have now moved in together. After I opened my heart and my wallet for her, planning for the day when she needed to flee from him, Kim repaid me by staying with the jerk. Yes, she cheated on him with me, but only because I thought we had a future together.

And then she had the nerve to assume I'd still meet her for an afternoon delight only two days after buying a new bed for the two of them.

Kim is the last thing I need this morning. I have bad luck with women. Kim should have been a casual work fling but I went and developed feelings for her.

She had been the first woman I opened up to after Amy broke my heart and look how that turned out.

I give a practiced shrug. "I don't know what to say to that."

"Say you miss me, too."

I take a moment to consider my words. "I don't think I want to say that."

"Oh, Jason. You're still mad at me." Kim reaches to touch my arm, but I don't want her comfort, her manipulations. My gaze flashes to Callie across the floor, laughing with her supervisor.

"No, I'm not mad. Saying I'm still angry with you would entail that I still have feelings for you, which I don't. Good luck with everything, Kim. I hope you're very happy with him." And with that dismissal, I log on to the system without another glance at her. Thankfully, she doesn't attempt to argue and leaves with a little huffing sound. I do glance up to see her walk away and can't help but notice her hips, while far from non-existent, lack the sexy sway of Callie's.

This time when I look over at Callie, she's smiling at me.

Chapter Five

BRIANNE

I 'M BARELY BACK AT my desk after the morning chats in the kitchenette when my soon-to-be ex-husband calls me.

"Brienne." Eli's voice is like a caress.

I hate talking to him on the phone.

I used to love it. The man should have been a radio announcer. He has the most beautiful voice, and it's sexier when he's excited because the Irish comes out. Normally, Eli has only the faintest hint of an accent–you have to listen closely to hear it. There's nothing there when he sings, but when he's excited about something, or angry, the Irish comes out loud and clear.

Or when he tells me what he's going to do to me in bed.

I wrench my mind off the sight and sounds of Eli in bed. That's over. Over.

"What do you want, Eli?" I ask briskly.

"Someone's in a mood today." I hear the smile in his voice. He used to be quite talented in managing to laugh me out of a bad mood. He was quite talented in a lot of ways.

Over.

"Stop it." I didn't mean to speak aloud.

"I'm not doing anything," Eli laughs.

"It's not—never mind." I sigh, kneading my temple with my thumb. When did it become painful speaking to him? Eli and I had never been friends; we met, went straight to sex. "What is it?"

"Why does it have to be anything? Why can't I pick up the phone to call you when the mood arises?"

I can tell he's smiling, which makes me suspicious. Charming, flirtatious Eli is on the prowl today. "You lost that right when I moved out," I snap.

"I didn't ask you to move out," he's quick to point out.

"Finding you in bed with our neighbour kind of meant I wasn't going to want to live there any longer. With or without you."

"Good song." Eli is a musician, one-fourth of a successful rock band. He is able to tie anything back to music. Knowing so many lyrics is a cool party trick, but annoying when having a serious discussion.

"Bad memories. What do you want, Eli?"

"I'm not trying to upset you."

I can hear his accent; he sounds like I've wounded him by my sharp tones. "Is there something you need, or did you just call to say hi?" I relent. I always give in.

There's a pause. Then, "You know how the mortgage is due once a month..."

"You need money for the mortgage." My sharp tones return with a vengeance. "I don't believe you."

"I've got a royalty cheque coming in next week..."

"I'm not paying the mortgage for you, Eli. It's not my mortgage!"

I can't believe the nerve of him.

Actually, I can.

"I'm not asking you to pay it, Brienne. Just for a little help." Charming, flirtatious Eli vanishes and vulnerable Eli takes his place. Unfortunately, he works almost as well as charming Eli.

"No. Ask one of your girlfriends." *Stay firm*, I order. I've opened my wallet to him in the past and it never ends well. I may get really good sex after I lend him money but rarely do I ever see a penny of it again.

I am in a bit of a drought, however.

"There's no girlfriend, Brienne," Eli says patiently. "My heart still belongs to you. You know that."

I take a few deep breaths, angry he still has the power to affect me; and with such a cheesy, corny line! Why couldn't he just be faithful? Why couldn't he think of me first for once?

"But my wallet sure as hell doesn't belong to you. I paid you my share of the house, Eli. If you can't afford it, you should move out," I tell him, holding on to my hurt and anger with a series of deep breathing exercises, which over the phone, probably sounds like I'm halfway to orgasm.

"But the house has such a good vibe," Eli protests.

"You can find another vibe. You didn't have trouble finding another me."

"Brienne...you know I'll never find another you."

"You're not doing this to me today." And proudly, I hang up on him.

I manage to distract myself by making good work of the pile of papers on my desk until an email pops up on my screen. My daily *Would you rather...?* from Callie.

Would you rather experience multi-orgasms from a hand or an amazing one from oral sex? I read.

Callie thinks I need to find someone to take my mind off Eli. I think she's right but I'm in no mood to try to meet someone. It's too hard, too time-consuming. I wish someone would just drop right into my lap.

Literally.

Lately, Ian has been the focus of more than a few of my fantasies, and even more after Friday. I'm embarrassed to admit this weekend I watched every Michael Fassbender movie I found on *Netflix*. For some reason, though, Callie doesn't approve of my fascination with him. I wonder if that's part of the reason I'm so obsessed. I can't think of a single man here at Hever who would dismiss Callie. To find one who seems to appreciate me for her...

I watched Ian have sex. That does not mean he appreciates me. It doesn't mean anything.

I haven't seen him come in yet this morning. Not that I'm waiting for him, of course. I shouldn't even be able to face him. Watching what he did to Agatha was disturbing...

...and exciting. Disturbing because I found it so exciting.

How do you come up with these questions? I email Callie. *No, I don't want to know.*

Oh, yes you do! I saw Spencer this weekend!

Spencer is a friend of Callie's. I've never met him, but I've heard all the stories, including how he is the best sex Callie has ever had. Unfortunately, Spencer is a pilot who lives in Australia, and she rarely gets to see him.

I thought you seemed happy this morning but I wasn't sure if it was just because of your close proximity to Michael.

Of course Michael. He's as cute as ever. And infuriatingly still in love with his girlfriend!!! Maybe I should move on...

You wouldn't say that if you didn't have someone in mind.

Jason looked pretty cute this morning.

Really? *He always looks that cute, but isn't he a little young for you?*

Age is but a number...

I think that would be 10 numbers! Is Spencer at least born in the same decade as you? How is the man with the talented tongue?

OMG!!!! And yes, he's only 2 numbers beneath me. And I do like him beneath me!

I smile, but don't ask for details. I know Callie will give them to me regardless if I want them or not. I'm not in the mood to be excited about everyone's sex escapades, knowing I have none to share or even the possibility of any to come.

Other than what I had a bird's eye view of on Friday afternoon. I feel guilty about sharing that.

But how could I not? It was too good not to share. I left out the part about how much it excited me; no one needs to know I am no longer the master of my own domain.

I never thought I would quote from a *Seinfeld* episode.

I'm also embarrassed to admit Friday was the most excitement I've had for quite a while. I am officially in a drought. I'm a few years away from being in the prime of my life and I can't find a man to have sex with to save my life.

"Hey, Brienne."

I look up to see Adam smiling at me, coffee cup in hand. "I'm headed to the kitchen for the morning caffeine. Can I get you anything?"

I point to my own mug. "Thanks, but I've already been."

"How was your long weekend?"

"Uneventful. Yours?"

I study Adam as he tells me about some bike trail he found. Adam is cute and athletic and single. Callie has been telling me for weeks he has a thing for me, but I haven't been able to see it, probably because I haven't been able to pull my head out of my own ass—or Eli's ass—to notice things like that. But Adam does stop by my desk quite frequently and he's in the engineering department with Callie so it's not like it's on his way to the kitchen.

Maybe it's time to see what the boys at work have to offer.

As Adam walks away, my attention shifts once again to Ian's office. Lately, it's like I have ADD; I can't even keep my mind focused on anything for longer than five minutes without thinking about Ian.

I notice how Adam glances across the floor at me before he disappears inside the kitchenette. I smile reluctantly. Callie's after me to find someone to take my mind off Eli. She tells me I need to screw my ex-husband out of my system but the idea of allowing another man close to my heart doesn't interest me in the slightest.

But maybe Callie's right. Maybe I do need to screw Eli out of me. Not fall in love with someone, but fall in lust.

If there is one person who could take my mind off Eli, it would be Ian. I can't stop thinking of him and Agatha. He wanted me to watch. I did watch; the whole sordid encounter.

Agatha has only been working at Hever for two weeks. How did she get involved with Ian so quickly?

This fact bothers me more than I care to admit.

"Good morning, Brienne."

Ian's voice makes me jump as I whip my head around to face him. He caught me staring in the direction of his office. How could he walk up to my desk without me noticing? Shouldn't I have some sort of radar?

"Uh, hello. Good morning," I stammer.

"Is there some problem with my office?" Ian asks seriously.

"What?"

"You seem to be staring at the door."

"No! Nothing! No–I was only staring into space, thinking about–" My eyes fly wildly to the papers on my desk to find something that would be important enough to cause such a serious stare. "Last month's travel receipts."

Wrong report.

"Is there a problem with them?" he asks. Is it my imagination or is there the hint of a smile peeking at the corner of his thin, yet serious lips?

What would those lips feel like pressed against mine?

"No, not at all."

"Yet you're staring into space in the direction of my office, thinking about them?"

"Yes," I cast my eyes down in embarrassment. "It's Monday–lots on my mind."

"It's actually Tuesday," Ian points out.

"It is, isn't it?" I say with disappointment. What is with him? I can't even remember the long weekend when he's around.

Ian smiles coolly at me and my mind flashes to that mouth between Agatha's legs. Then I look down again, only to find his crotch in those fitted pants directly at eye level, and I flash to Agatha with her mouth full of him.

"Did you have a nice weekend?" Ian's attempt at a conversation startles me as much as his appearance at my desk a moment ago.

"Um—yes. I did. Thank you. And you?" I ask politely.

"Uneventful."

Does that mean you didn't strap anyone to a table?

I stop myself from saying that just in time.

"It's too bad your weekend wasn't more exciting," I say in a conciliatory voice.

"Do you like your weekends to be exciting?" Ian asks.

"Um—sure." He waits expectantly for me to continue. "Of course. I like excitement."

"Do you?"

"I—yes. I do." I am beyond uncomfortable with Ian standing at my desk but I don't want him to leave. "I like excitement," I say boldly. "And adventure. And new experiences."

"Do you?"

I'm not sure what I do right now. I think I'm trying to make it clear I enjoyed Friday, but that I'd rather be a participant instead of an observer, and I really can't believe I'm doing that. I can't believe I'm actually thinking about how I'd like him to spank me in his office and wondering how I can make that happen.

"I do." I stare into his eyes, willing some mental telepathy to pass between us so Ian will instinctively *know* what I want.

His eyes are grey, with flecks of blue. He has nice eyes. They match his suit, which he wears with a crisp white shirt.

My fingers tingle as I think about unbuttoning his shirt.

"I'll remember that." Ian's eyes run across my face, down my body, gazing at me appraisingly, appreciatively, admiringly. For a moment, I feel like he's stripping me naked and is looking at me sitting at my desk in unmatched undergarments.

I'm going to start wearing my good underwear to work.

"Have a good day, Brienne." When Ian says my name, his lips come together like a kiss. I'm so distracted by his mouth I barely answer as he walks away.

"Oh, fuck," I exhale, pressing my legs together in an attempt to stop the jolt of excitement. But I like excitement, or so I told him.

What have I got myself into?

My eyes skip to Ian's office.

He's staring at me.

Chapter Six

ABBY

I WATCH AS SADIE slips back to her desk, leaving Callie and Michael chatting to Jason. Not that I've been keeping track, but I've noticed her breaks have become more infrequent in the last couple of weeks. Maybe it's Callie's recent influence. I can't help but wonder if Sadie's off meeting someone.

But I would know. I would notice. I doubt Sadie would be able to hide such a thing from me, but I know for a fact Callie would ferret a secret out from her if it had something to do with sex.

Even if Sadie is playing around with a work colleague, it wouldn't be my place to say anything. For one, we're friends, so I would never think to reprimand Sadie, and two, I don't have the authority. I'm the sole representative of the legal department; Sadie works in marketing. Our two departments share the third floor in the Hever building, along with Human Resources, IT, engineering and the project managers. Above us is upper management with their plush offices. Accounting and Brienne and Delia are below us and then shipping/receiving, safety and the massive shop for the construction workers.

I should start hanging out in the shop, I think idly. Maybe the sight of sexy men in dirty jeans and work boots will inspire me. But Ben is an on-site project manager. What would think if he found me hanging out in the shop? Not that he's ever been the jealous type.

Did I really need inspiration? Isn't my marriage exciting enough?

Talking to Callie this morning makes me wonder. It's not like I want to be like Callie–okay, maybe part of me does. Part of me wishes I'd stop overanalyzing every sexual encounter and remark I hear. Why can't I just relax and enjoy things?

Am I exciting enough for Ben? Is he looking for more? I know he loves me, still wants me. But does he need more from me?

And am I able to give more?

I keep thinking about what Brienne told us about Ian and Agatha. There is absolutely no way I would be interested in trying something like that. It's not my thing, plus I have a very low pain tolerance. But trying new positions might be okay. Ben is always making suggestions, but I hesitate, not sure if it would be comfortable. Not sure if I would like it, and if I didn't, how could I tell him that?

I need to loosen up. I need to talk to Ben more, tell him what I want.

This morning was a perfect example. I had woken up feeling unusually aroused, probably due to the latest novel Brienne pressed me to read. She loves romance novels and in the last year, has been lending me more and more. Lately, though, they've been becoming more sexually explicit. Is Brienne trying to tell me something? Does everyone think I need more excitement in my life?

When I finally turned out my light last night, Ben had already been asleep. I had given some thought to waking him up.

I didn't.

And then when I woke up this morning, Ben was already rushing off to work. I should have woken him up last night, told him I'd like to have sex. But I couldn't bring myself to because I felt too embarrassed. I thought maybe he wouldn't want to.

We've been together for almost fifteen years. How can I possibly be embarrassed to tell him I want to have sex? I doubt he would ever say no. My husband has a healthy libido, one I normally share, even though I can't seem to bring myself to talk to him about it.

I need to spend more time with Callie to loosen up. And if I can't do that, maybe I can channel my inner Callie.

As if she knows I am in need of her, Callie pops her head into my office later in the morning. She works with a group of men amid the maze of engineering tables at the other side of the floor and unless she's swamped by a project, she'll stop into my office at least once or twice a day.

Sometimes I think it's just for the bag of peanut M&M's I hide in my drawer.

"Can you believe what Bri told us about snake bastard?" Callie asks, plopping herself in the chair across my desk.

Since it's after eleven, I pull out the bag of candy and pass it to Callie. "I really can't believe something like that goes on after office hours," I say, trying not to sound so disapproving.

Callie laughs. "You have no idea what goes on during office hours!"

"Whips and tying people up?"

"Well, no, I think Ian took it a little too far," Callie concedes. "But there are so many hookups around here. Office plays, I call them."

"Just because you–"

"Oh, it's not just me! I'm just the one you hear about because I tell you things. Do you know Jason–your sweet little Jason–and Kim from accounting used to meet every Tuesday at 2:30 in the shop?"

"He's not my little Jason," I say, trying to cover up my shock. Now I won't be able to stop thinking about him and Kim, entwined in some secret corner.

"He has no idea how hot he is. You agree, right?"

"I don't think–"

"Abby, saying some young guy is hot will do nothing to your marriage! And Ben is cool enough not to give two shits about whatever you say."

"I know but I–"

"Have you ever found another man attractive?" Callie asks curiously. "Since you've been married."

"No," I reply in a firm voice. "Never."

"Seriously?"

"No." But as Callie gazes at me with an incredulous expression, I find myself softening. "I'm not like you."

"No one is like me, but you're a woman and you have every right to look. I'm not telling you to *do* anything but there's no harm in looking, you know."

"I realize that but..." I trail off, not wanting to tell Callie my secret but tempted to unburden myself. Not that it would help appease the guilt. "There was someone at the law firm," I say reluctantly. "Before I was married."

"Was he hot?"

"*He* was married. There was an attraction. I was with Ben but things weren't going well because I was under so much stress and Cooper understood what I was going through."

"Cooper," Callie says dreamily. "Did something happen?"

"You don't have to sound so excited about it."

"Abby, I may love you like a sister but you have to realize you are the last person anyone would *ever* suspect of carrying on like that!"

"I know. *I know.* I'm so boring." I hang my head but Callie's quick laugh pulls it back up.

"Are you kidding? You're *in love*. Not only that, you're in love with your *husband*. I don't think there's anything boring about that."

"Really?" I ask her in amazement. "But you–"

"Have never been in love," Callie says matter-of-factly. "I don't think it's possible for me. But it doesn't mean I'm not in awe of anyone who can sustain a relationship. There's a lot of temptations out there and if I wonder if you find other men attractive, it's really because I want to know how you resist the temptation."

"I've never been tempted," I tell her simply. "Except once with Cooper, and there were extenuating circumstances there. But if you saw him..." My thoughts trail off into a memory of Cooper Garrison. Tall, blonde and good-looking, with a sexy South African accent; all nice attributes but it was how *nice* he was that won me over. He listened, and showed concern. He supported me with difficult clients and encouraged me during presentations.

Cooper was as nice as Ben and a little more attractive, a fact I hate to admit.

"If you *knew* him," I continue wistfully. "But we never acted on it–except this one night. It was only a kiss, and it was after we won a big case. He might have kind of grabbed my breast, but that's it. And feeling his hand there woke me up to what I was doing, and I pushed him away. That was the only time. And I've never told anyone, not even Ben."

"It wouldn't do any good to tell Ben," Callie says. "I can't see it happening again."

"Because I'm–"

"–in love with your husband," Callie finishes for me. "Never be embarrassed about that."

"I think Ben might be getting bored of me," I lean forward and say in a hushed voice. "I don't know what to do about it."

"Seduce him," she says simply, reaching across for more chocolate. "What do you usually do?"

"Whatever I do, I doubt you'd call it seduction," I tell her ruefully. "I need to make things more exciting. I think that's what Ben wants."

"What has he said?"

"Nothing but..." I lean forward again, and Callie joins me. Our faces are only inches apart when she sticks her hand in the bag of candy. "He made me come with his fingers under the table during Easter dinner!"

"What does he usually use–his fork?" Callie laughs.

I sit back in my chair "He's never *done* that before!" I hiss. "His mother was right across the table from me!"

"Way to go, Ben! So what happened then?"

"We went in the pantry and had sex," I tell her, trying to sound as matter-of-fact as she usually does.

"Sounds like my kind of Easter dinner."

"It was...fun..." I slowly smile, thinking of the feel of his hand in my lap, his fingers frantically exploring me.

"And you think he wants more like that? You should have people over more often."

"What if someone knew what we were doing?"

"They would probably be cheering you on," Callie says simply. "Have you ever done it here?"

"No!"

"Why not?"

"Well, because–I don't know," I shrug. "It's never occurred to me to have sex at work."

"You need an office play," Callie says decisively. "It'll do you good."

"Ben's usually off-site."

I had wanted to leave my downtown firm because of the pressure and stress, not because of Cooper, and Ben had helped me get the job here. It's better that I no longer have contact with Cooper, but some days I find myself missing him. We had been friends.

"Why don't you sext him? Tell him what you want to do to him when you get home from work. What do you want him to do to you? Bet he'd love that!"

"I couldn't do that!" I recoil in horror at the thought but then, "Do you think he'd like that?"

"Men want to feel wanted, same as we do. Knowing his wife wants him enough to text him about it would keep him going for days."

"Do you really think so?"

"I *know* so. He'd love it!"

"I'm horrible at texting! I don't know any of the acronyms."

"Spell it *f u c k*. I think you can suffer through it. Give it a try." She takes one last handful of M&M's and stands up. "This has been fun. I like seeing a new side of you."

"Well, you won't be seeing a side of me like Brienne saw of Ian!"

"No, I think that would be too much for you," Callie grins. "One thing at a time."

"Do you think–?" I begin, but can't bring myself to finish the thought. Callie seems to be able to read my mind.

"I don't know if she would. Bri has been surprising me lately. I think this thing with Eli has really done a number on her, and she'd like nothing better than to get to him out of her head. Or maybe that's just me."

"I've never met the man but I can't think good of him after what she's told us."

Callie pauses, crunching the peanut. "I have, and you know what? He's so cool. He's sexy and fun and I get how she's so hung up on him. He's a rock star, for God's sake! But he's bad for her–so bad. I don't think Ian would be any better, but I think she'd realize it sooner and kick him to the curb. She needs someone to help her get over Eli."

"And you think that could be Ian?"

"Well, I sure as hell hope it's anyone else, but I think he's the best bet. Unless you think she'd go for Jason."

"I think you should save him for Sadie," I say slyly. "Once she figures things out."

Callie shakes her head. "I can't see him remaining unattached that long. Sadie needs to get her shit together, and I can see that taking a while. No, it might be better off if I–"

"Leave the poor boy alone!" I cry.

Callie laughs. "Did you not notice how cute he looked this morning? How can I possibly stay away from that? Plus, he kept staring at my boobs! That's like waving a red flag in front of me. I can't *not* go for it."

With the last snatch of M&M's, she heads back to her office.

I think about what Callie said. Not about Jason, although the thought of him engaged in some office play–as Callie so unoriginally calls it–makes me uncomfortable.

It takes a few minutes for me to realize the thought of sex happening right here in the office is making me uncomfortably hot.

Ben and I do have an active sex life. I think it's a perfectly satisfactory one but we've been together for a long time and things might not be as exciting as it once was. Kids can do that to you, I know that, and the pressures of career and responsibilities of having a family. When was the last time Ben and I made out on the couch watching television? Or I woke up in the middle of the night to find his hands on me? Our little playtime during Easter dinner was Ben's way of telling me he wanted a little more excitement and I want to make sure he knows I'm listening.

Maybe Callie is right. Ben deserves to know I still want him.

No time like the present to try, I decide and set about sending my husband an email.

You left early this morning.

He responds immediately, so I can tell he's not busy. *Early meeting. Was there a problem?*

I missed giving you a kiss
You kissed me goodbye
I took a deep breath, feeling ridiculous as I typed. *Not the kind of kiss I wanted to give you*
Abby?
What's the matter? Don't you like your wife expressing herself?;) I hold my breath until he responds, fighting the urge to delete the whole conversation. Give it a try, I order.
Love it!!!! But it's not like you.
Maybe it's time I try something a little different.
Go crazy! What kind of kiss did you want to give me? Well, Ben is definitely on board. I smile widely as I think of how to word my response.
I thought I might wake you up with my mouth on your dick. No, that was crude and totally not me. I try again. *I thought I might wake you up in an interesting way.*
What were you thinking?
You would have to be sleeping on your back
I can sleep on my back!
If you were sleeping on your back, I would slide my hand inside your pants. Softly and slowly, so you wouldn't wake up.
Why wouldn't you want me to wake up?
I like to feel you when you're soft and asleep and hold you in my hand until you wake up. I'd rub your length... That sounds kind of technical but I send it anyway. With a fervent glance to make sure no one is watching me, I eagerly wait for Ben's response.
It wouldn't take me long to get hard. Then what?
I'd lean over and take you in my mouth
Are you sure this is my wife???!!!

Like I said, I missed you this morning! ☺
Well, you've got to finish what you started. What next?
Where are you?
In the office. Nobody here.

Ben says that to reassure me. He means he's in one of the construction trailers on site. I'm not sure where in the city he is, but I can picture him in the cramped space, hearing the men and machines outside, working on the laptop. I'm glad no one is with him. I take a deep breath and type slowly.

I'd wait until you were so hard that your hips would start to move when you get really excited. And you make those sounds in your throat

I like the sounds you make...I like how you moan and your little cries

If you were in my mouth right now I'd moan
I want to be inside of you
I could straddle you...right now.
I'd like that.
You could pretend
I'm pretending

I get up and shut my office door. Am I really doing this?
So am I. I'm straddling you. But I want you to touch me.
My hands are on your tits. Your nipples are so hard!
I'm excited. I'm starting to move up and down. Slowly
Not too slowly. I want you to touch yourself.

Did he mean in the fantasy or reality? Since I'm getting turned on by emailing my husband of all things, I slide one hand under my skirt and type with the other.

The image of me whispering those words to Ben has excited me so much that when I slide my fingers under the elastic of my panties, I'm wet and ready. I spread my legs under my desk and find my clit with two fingers.

I'm touching myself. I have to go faster. You feel so good!

I am. I do. And it does.

Harder. You like it when I do it hard.

Fuck me. Fuck me hard.

Can anyone see what I'm doing? Can anyone tell?

I don't really care right now.

So hard. You're making those noises I love.

Faster. Keep touching yourself. I love watching that

I'm concentrating on getting myself off and can barely read what Ben is typing.

I'm close. Are you almost there?

You feel so good...almost there...

I rub myself recklessly, keeping the image of my husband fucking me in my mind. Thinking of how good his cock feels inside me, his size making it just a little painful but still so good. I've never touched myself during sex but I will next time if it feels this good.

With a low moan, I come.

So good, Ben!

I rest my head on my desk and wait for Ben to respond.

Yeah...

Did he? Is he...? I think he did.

What got into you, Ab?

Not sure. Is it bad?

HELL NO! LOVED IT!!!! Again?

Maybe another day ;)

Definitely tonight though. xo

Chapter Seven

SADIE

MY LEGS ARE STILL quivering forty-five minutes later when Alma sends me another email.

When can we meet again?

I just had sex in the supply closet at work and now Alma wants to do it again?

This is definitely new for me.

I can still taste you

Um...oh, wow. How do you respond to that? Is that a good thing? Should I suggest she chew some gum, or maybe gargle?

I love the way your body feels

My whole body, despite the tingles at the thought of her, is feeling pretty uncomfortable right about now. I might need another release if she keeps it up.

Callie stops by my desk later when I'm eating my lunch. Meeting with Alma took more time than I expected this morning, so I keep working while I eat. Not that I knew how long it would take–how do you schedule quickies in the office?

Especially ones that keep your legs quivering afterward. I give my head a shake to rid the image of Alma's mouth between my legs because the thought is so exciting it makes me want to head down to her desk and pull her back into the closet.

She keeps sending me little emails all morning, with cryptic comments about what I tasted like, what she'd like to do to me. I don't know how to respond, but they do make me smile, even as I shake my head in bewilderment.

"I said I'm worried about Brienne," Callie says, looking at me with a quizzical expression from her perch on the corner of my desk.

I give my head another shake. Alma is becoming quite the distraction. "Because she caught the live version of *Ian Does Agatha*?" I ask, but Callie quickly waves away my question. Leaning back in my chair, I pull out my bottom drawer to rest my legs on. Too late, I realize Alma's kiss left a lipstick stain on my ankle, clearly visible with my legs in full view.

"What's that?" Callie snaps, catching hold of my ankle as I quickly pull my legs off the drawer.

"Nothing."

"Looks like something to me," Callie crows with glee. "Looks like *lipstick* to me!"

"So," I bluff, shaking my ankle loose.

"*So*," Callie mocks. "Details, please. Who was wearing that lovely shade of..." She leans to inspect the colour. "Peachy-pink."

"I don't think that's a real colour." Callie only stares at me with her eyebrow raised expectantly. I shake my head, unable to meet her gaze. "I don't kiss and tell."

"Looks like someone else did the kissing," she presses. "I just want you to tell me about it."

"So why are you worried about Brienne?" I ask. My sudden about-face catches Callie off guard but does the trick.

"Okay, okay, so you're not in the mood to discuss. I get it. But remember, I will get it out of you soon. But you have to let me know—is this some sort of *relationship*?"

"You make it sound like it's a bad thing."

Another wave of her hand. "It's not bad, *per se*. But I had high hopes for you, my little sexy Sadie. I thought you were following in my footsteps."

I honestly don't know what I'm doing with Alma and our interlude this morning didn't help ease my confusion one little bit. It was good; I like how she makes me feel but in the office? It isn't me. It's not something I would normally do.

Or maybe it is.

When Laurel came into my apartment back in December and climbed into the bathtub with me, making love to me with her fingers and her mouth, was that me?

Or was I the person who didn't realize her boyfriend had been cheating on her from almost the beginning of the relationship?

I met Evan when I was living in British Columbia. I had been competing with the Canadian National snowboarding team, preparing for the 2010 Olympics in Vancouver. Evan was a skier, recently cut from the National team and we had met one night in

Whistler at a birthday party. We hit it off and went out a few nights later.

And then the accident happened and I was in the hospital for weeks, with a badly broken leg and a knee that needed extensive repair. My snowboarding career was over. I'd never make it to the Olympics. I'd never see the pride in my father's eyes–himself a former Olympian–as I stood on the medal podium.

That was the most difficult time in my life.

But my relationship with Evan developed because of it. He understood the pain and frustration I was feeling, watching my dreams die, because he felt it too. Together we helped each other through it and after I recovered, we left the mountains of the west coast behind us and ended up in Toronto. I started school, he found a job. Evan helped me get through something I thought I'd never recover from and for that, I would always be grateful.

I'm sure that was the reason I never suspected he was cheating on me the entire time we were together.

I have no idea how many other girls he had been with. I know one lasted almost a year. Even now, months after our break-up, I'm discovering dribs and drabs of how he betrayed me. Friends I thought I could rely on have drifted away, loyal to Evan. The ones I kept in touch with seemed to have a perverse desire to keep me informed of what Evan was doing these days, and who he was doing it with. And they keep telling me about what he did when we were still together.

I've been humiliated, betrayed. I lost the man who I thought was the love of my life. I don't know who I am anymore. Who I'm supposed to be.

This...*thing*...with Alma–I don't understand it. I don't know what Alma wants from me.

She has a husband. I've gone from being the cheated-on to being the one someone cheats with.

That's not me.

I suddenly bury my head in my hands, surprising Callie. "What am I doing?" I moan. "She's got a husband. It's going on at work. I just got promoted and I don't have time to be sneaking around. I didn't even know I liked girls! Laurel was one thing but now she keeps emailing me and sure it was fun but..."

"Please tell me it's not Alma," Callie groans.

"Oh, god. How do you know? Why?"

"I was worried about this."

"*Why?*" Leaning forward I clutched Callie's leg.

"Stop freaking out," Callie grumbles, removing my fingers one by one.

"Of course I'm going to freak out if you say something like that! Why is it a bad thing? Tell me!"

"It's not that bad," Callie says evasively. I glare at her until she relents. "Look, Sadie, I've seen how you are with her since she started working here. You're totally crushing on her, and it's not like you."

"It's not," I tell her, going back to clutching my head, rather than her leg. "I don't know what I'm doing," I tell her morosely. "I think I need some advice."

"I don't go that way," Callie says quickly, raising her hands. "I mean, I have, but not often enough to advise you."

"Not for that," I grumble. "I'm good about that."

"Are you, now?"

I smile proudly at Callie. "No complaints." And then I realize what I've said. "Oh, God! What am I doing?"

"When did it start?" she sighs, dropping her voice and moving closer to me. "I know you've been hanging out with her lately, but I thought you had a bit of a girl crush on her. The way you jumped all over me this morning when I suggested it was her with Ian kind of confirmed it."

"I know it wasn't Alma with Ian because I was with Alma on Friday." I know Alma wouldn't want me discussing things with anyone, but I need some help. "That was the first time we–"

"Got busy?" Callie supplies. "Girl-on-girl busy?"

"Well, there wasn't anyone else with us," I mutter, checking around for anyone listening. I can see Abby eating in her office.

"No, that would be something different entirely," Callie laughs as she shifts her weight on the desk. "You know, I never saw this coming, you playing for the other team."

"I don't know if I really am," I confess. "That's the problem."

"Do you like her?"

I shrug. "I guess. I mean, yes, I like her. She's a nice person but there's something about her that excites me. I've never been interested in women before. I mean there was Laurel, but before her, it was all men." I glance imploringly at Callie. "Does this mean I'm gay?"

"It means you're more of a babe in the woods than I thought," Callie tells me ruefully. "You can like both, you know. There's nothing wrong with that. If someone excites you, then act on it. Explore your feelings."

"That's what you do."

"Yes, but you don't have to be me." Callie smiles at me, a warm, comforting smile that is unlike her usual good-time-girl grin. "The way I live my life isn't for everyone. Sure, I might bug you about being my wing-woman, but that's mainly because I think it might help you get over Evan. I can tell you're still hung up on him."

I shrug in response to Callie's statement. "I still miss him, but it doesn't hurt as much. I'm still royally pissed, but I finally stopped doing voodoo on the stuffed bear he got me."

"Did you really?" Callie wonders with a big smile.

"Burnt some pictures, a CD he made me. Stuck some pins in Teddy. Who knows if it worked, but I felt pretty good afterward."

Callie laughs, a big booming laugh that carries across the cubicles that make up the marketing department. "What a dick."

"Teddy?"

"No, Evan. That's why I'm worried about Brienne. She's still so hung up on Eli and I thought it might help if she..." she waggles her eyebrows suggestively.

"With who?" I demand quickly. I don't know what upsets me more; the thought of Callie suggesting Alma for Brienne, or me.

Callie shrugs, flouncing her perfect blonde hair off her shoulder with the movement. I've been forever jealous of Callie's hair. Every time I see the shelves of hair colour at *Shoppers' Drug Mart* and make my selection, I wonder if *this* will be the time I'm brave enough to go Callie blonde.

"There are lots to choose from. We work in an office full of very horny people if you haven't noticed."

I consider what Callie says. I know I'm not the only one getting some action during working hours. Callie is forever running back to me with stories of *who* and *where* and *what*. Hearing about Ian and Agatha was not the surprising part–it was the alleged depravity of the act.

Who am I to say it is depraved? Just because I've never tried it? There are countless people who would think that what Alma and I are doing is just as depraved.

There might be more people who think it would be exciting to watch. I shift in my seat, struck again with a memory of Alma's mouth between my legs. "Why is that?" I wonder, wrenching my thoughts away from the X-rated version and swinging my legs on my open drawer again. Callie stares pointedly at the lipstick stain and I manage to meet her amused glance with a bland expression. "I mean, what is it about this place that brings out the worst in everyone?"

"I wouldn't say it was the *worst* of us. We're in this place over eight hours a day. Why not have some fun while we're here?"

"I guess that's a good way to look at it."

"Do you know it took me six tries to lose my virginity?" Callie asks conversationally.

"And this has to do with..."

"Six times, with six different guys over one summer. I was eighteen and felt that I really needed to lose my virginity, but it just wouldn't happen."

"Why not?" I'm interested in Callie's story despite the abrupt change of topic.

Callie gives a wave of her hand. "Long story. But funny. I'll tell you sometime. But see, that summer I was denied something I really wanted. I *really* wanted to have sex, for a variety of reasons. But I couldn't. Fate intervened. Since then, I've made a point if I want something, then I go and get it, including sex. With whoever, and whenever I want. As long as the other party is willing."

"I can't see how they wouldn't be," I scoff, glancing enviously at Callie's curves. Brienne and Abby have commented more than once about how I resemble Callie–the hair, the height, the blue eyes. But with my lack of hips and bust and breasts, I'm the little sister version of Callie.

"No, I've never had that problem," she smiles modestly. "So that's how I live my life and I don't expect everyone to agree with me, but I don't really give a shit. I'm sure other people in the office have their own reasons for having quickies in the supply closet downstairs."

"Does everyone use it?" I'm horrified at the thought of anyone walking in and seeing me with Alma, how vulnerable and exposed I was. How wanton and shameless I behaved. I pushed Alma's head between my legs...

"You should really lock the door," Callie advises as if she can read my mind.

I shudder at the thought of there being a communal sex room and vow to tell Alma we need to find another place.

That would mean I'm planning on continuing this.

"I'll give you some suggestions on where to hide out," Callie assures me. "What I'm getting to, is that even though not everyone agrees with how I run my sex life, the one thing everyone agrees with is my theory of how to get over someone: you have sex with another person. You don't have to love them. It's better if you don't. But to get a guy out of your heart, get someone else in your pants. Worked for you, didn't it?"

"I guess," I muse. "I mean, it's helped. I don't think of him as much."

"Because you're fixated on Alma and the wonderful things she does to your body," Callie continues.

"I'm not sure if I feel comfortable with you thinking of the wonderful things she does to my body," I tell her uneasily. Callie laughs.

"Sadie, you don't have to worry. I've been in a constant state of arousal since I was twenty-five. There's nothing you could tell or show me that can change that."

"Really? Is that a problem?" I stare at her in admiration.

"I seem to be handling it pretty well, as long as I can find others to handle me. The solo act leaves a little to be desired."

"Uh-huh." I know I'm looking at Callie as if she's a bomb ready to explode and I guess she is. A sex bomb ready to orgasm at the slightest provocation.

I hide my smile.

"Don't worry, I'm not about to spontaneously climax right here on your desk," Callie says wryly.

"Can you read my mind?" I burst out in disbelief.

"No, but I can read your expression. And I think, with time and encouragement, your mind will be almost as dirty as mine."

"I doubt that."

"I said almost. So, back to Brienne. Alma is helping you get over Evan, right?"

"You want Brienne and Alma...?"

"Don't worry, I won't take her away," Callie gives me a mock frown. "But there's got to be someone in here to set her up with."

"She sounds like she'd like to give spanky Ian a try," I suggest.

"I'm not positive Ian is her best bet, but maybe he's what she needs."Callie bangs her hand on my desk for emphasis. "That's what Brienne needs. Sex with no commitment, sex with nothing in return. Only for a good time. So she'll start thinking with her head around Eli, not with what's between her legs. That's the problem. She's penis-whipped by him."

"Do you think he's that good?" I ask with awe.

"From what Brienne has led me to believe, I think so," she says ruefully. "Or else Brienne just hasn't had any comparison. I know that's not the case, though..."

This time I'm the one who gives a wave. "Yeah, yeah, I know all about the two of you picking up the little boys on the highway..."

Callie gives me a wicked grin. "Good times, good times. You'll have to come next time."

I don't respond. I adore Callie, but even though I'm younger, I doubt I could keep up with her. Kudos to Brienne for doing so.

Callie slides off my desk. "Back to work. Give some thought about how to set them up, will you?"

"I can barely hook myself up, so why would you think I could do anything to help Brienne? Besides, she might be okay on her own," I say but Callie is shaking her head.

"I think we need to work on this and fast. I sense Eli is circling for the kill once more, and I won't have her rocking the boat."

"I think you're mixing your metaphors," I call as she heads back to her own office.

Chapter Eight

JASON

I FIND SOME TIME before the end of the day to go through emails.

Not my own. The other employees' inter-office emails.

It's my least favourite part of my job but it's one of the most important, according to Julian Donovan, who personally assigned me the task when he took over the company. I don't see how reading employee email conversations can constitute an important responsibility, but I'm not about to argue. I like my job too much for that. Management provided me with a list of things to look for, which I have yet to read. I like to think I would know what's inappropriate. I don't appreciate being micromanaged. I also don't like being an office spy.

But I like reading the emails.

Not all of them. Some are tedious. Some aren't worth more than a scan. Some I won't even open because I've learned they will only consist of boring work exchanges.

But some are really interesting.

Take the exchanges between Callie and Brienne. I love the *Would you rather*...game they play and I find out lots of information about them. This may make me appear slightly stalkerish, but I'm not about to do anything about it. I don't even report the misuse of office time. I've only had to report one employee for an infraction and that was because the porn sites he was looking at disgusted even me. There was no need for images of goats on the work computers or any other computer.

Callie and Brienne are discussing multiple orgasms today. How can that not be interesting?

Everything about Callie is interesting.

Who is Spencer? She's talking about Michael...

She's talking about me! *Jason looked pretty cute this morning.*

She thinks I'm cute!

I feel like singing, which never is a good thing.

I'm actually humming as I scroll through the emails sent out this morning, stopping at a few just to say I read them. It's not like I'm going to find anything incriminating–

What's this? *Mouth on your cock*

Abby?

I would never have thought. Ben is a frequent participant in my game nights. In fact, it was only Sunday that I trounced him royally in *Settlers of Catan*, although he was quick to get his revenge when we played *Galaxy Trucker*. I had consumed quite a few pints of Guinness by then as well so it's not surprising Ben beat me.

I thought Ben and Abby were happy together. Then I read on.

Abby sent these emails to *Ben*? Wow. That's the kind of wife I'd like to have. Sexting at work.

I force myself to stop reading them. That email is too private, too intimate. This is a married couple *sexting* at work and for whatever reason, they definitely don't need me reading their personal business.

Plus, thinking about the two of them together, doing what they emailed is getting me excited.

I imagine Abby's mouth on my cock.

No, that's wrong.

Abby is pretty and nice and I wouldn't mind whatever she wanted to do to me, but she's married to Ben, who is one of my friends. And I had enough of being the other man with Kim. Knowing she was cheating on her boyfriend with me always left a bad taste in my mouth.

She gave good blowjobs, however.

Callie would be better.

Callie would slide those lips around my cock, teasing and toying with me, bringing me deep into her throat. She would *enjoy* sucking me, unlike Amy, who always made it seem like she was doing me a favour, even after I made it clear I liked nothing more than returning the favour.

I like the taste of a woman's pussy.

I like sliding my fingers into her for the first time, feeling the warmth and wetness.

I like it when a woman makes noises. I like it when she can't control herself, and she thrusts her hips up, pressing me into her.

I like making love to women. And since I won't be making love to anyone anytime soon, I'll have to settle for fucking them. I like fucking women. And I'm pretty good at it.

Whenever I think about sex, my thoughts end up on Callie. Thinking about her blouse straining against her breasts this morning has made me uncomfortably hard.

It would have been so easy to reach out a hand and flick another button, and then another, until her full breasts spring free into my hands and I bring my lips to her tight nipples, at the same time slipping my hand up her skirt...

"Jason?"

"What?" I snap, throwing up a hand to shield my monitor from prying eyes. I'm glad no one could see my thoughts.

However, what I was thinking about would clearly be evident if I stood up right now.

Sadie stands before my desk with a confused look on her face.

"Sorry, Sadie. My mind—I was distracted and didn't see you."

"It's okay. I didn't mean to bother you." Sadie has her cup in her hand and swings it between her fingers. "I was going for tea and wanted to see if you wanted some. Chai tea drinkers should stick together, and all that." She smiles shyly at me and my face creases in response.

"I'd love to join you," I tell her, as I adjust myself under the desk. I also make sure I shut down the email program before I get up and follow her to the kitchenette.

Chapter Nine

BRIENNE

IT'S AFTER EIGHT AND I'm already in my flannel *Victoria's Secret* pyjamas. I know flannel and *Victoria's Secret* doesn't go together, but the store does a good job with comfort, not just sex appeal. It drove Eli crazy whenever I came home with the bright pink bag, with the artfully arranged tissue poking out the top with something warm and comfy inside, something that would cover as much skin as possible.

I've never been one for satin and lace, plus I get cold easily. I've always thought lingerie was a waste of money because it never lasts long on me and always ends up balled up under the bed where I would invariably fish it out the next time I vacuum.

Maybe that was part of the problem with me and Eli. He liked the sexy satin and lace, stick to the crack of the bum stuff. He wanted excitement. I wanted comfort.

He's a musician. I'm an accountant. Enough said.

But he was my musician. He still is. And even though Callie instructed me to avoid thinking about my ex whenever possible, Eli's call this afternoon made me miss him. It also made me pissed that I miss him.

I flop on the couch, a bag of Miss Vickie's potato chips in my hand. Not the best dinner but at least it will offset my trip to the gym after work. I'm settling in with Netflix, ready for another episode of *Once Upon a Time* when the buzzer of the door interrupts me.

I know it's Eli before I even answer.

"I'm not lending you money," I tell him as I open the door to him, instantly regretting sounding so firm and decisive. Eli is smiling at me, the smile that brings out his dimple and makes him the hot and sexy musician I can't keep my hands off.

"I'm not here for money," Eli says, widening his smile when he sees me. "I miss seeing you in your pj's."

"You hate me in my pyjamas," I grumble, breathing in his manly scent as I shut the door behind him.

Stop smelling him.

"I don't *hate* them," he corrects, heading for the kitchen to help himself to a beer. "I just preferred you *out* of them. Like any other article of clothing. You can't blame me for that."

My heart jumps and I fold my arms across my breasts in an attempt to make it stop. I hear the crack and faint hiss of Eli opening a beer. Why do I still stock my fridge with beer? I hardly ever drink the stuff. Wine is better and beer makes me bloat.

I vow never to stop at the beer store again.

Eli hands me a glass of wine. My hostility fades as I notice he gave me my favourite glass, which has '*wine a little, laugh a lot*' painted on it. Eli bought the set for me years ago, and only one of them is left unbroken.

He clinks the edge of my glass with his beer before making his way into the living room to make himself comfortable on my couch.

"Why are you here?" I demand.

Eli tips the bottle to his mouth and takes a healthy swig. I watch his throat as he swallows, my gaze returning to his mouth.

Dammit, why do I have to find him so attractive, with all of his manly scruff and sharp blue eyes? It would be easier to hate an ugly man. One that didn't make me catch my breath every time he looks at me.

"We've got a gig on the weekend. I was thinking you might want to come to see," Eli says casually, resting his arm on the back of the couch invitingly. I continue standing. I'm afraid of being that close to him. I have proven time and time again that I have no willpower when it comes to my husband.

Ex-husband.

Soon-to-be ex-husband.

"You could have called to tell me about it," I tell him, unable to rid myself of the image of how sexy Eli is on stage. "You didn't have to stop by."

"Are you going to stay all the way over there?" Eli asks, with another rakish smile.

"I'm perfectly fine right where I am."

"I'm sure you are, but I'd love you to be over here," he says, patting the spot on the couch beside him. Too close to him, for my comfort.

"Eli," I warn.

"*Brienne*," he mocks my tone. "I miss you. And I hate that I continually find ways to upset you."

"Should have thought of that before you took that girl back to your room."

"What was I supposed to do? She was a reporter. And we'd been on tour for *six weeks*," he says plaintively like I should understand. "I told you all along how it was. I can't do monogamy."

He did tell me that. When Eli and I got together, he told me upfront he had never been able to remain monogamous to another woman. "I love them, but I just can't do faithful, to anyone. Never have been able to."

And I, drunk on love, lust and the thought of succeeding where no other woman had before, swore to him that I would be fine with that. We would have an open relationship, with the consent to be with others as long we only loved each other. Of course, I assumed I would be the one to fully win his heart and make him keep everything in his pants.

I might have had his heart, but as hard as I tried, I couldn't control his wandering manly bits.

While Eli was more than agreeable to that kind of relationship, it turns out I was not. Bitterness and jealousy eventually overcame the headiness of being with him.

"Besides, she gave us a great review," he continues.

"Of course she did." With an indulgent smile, I finally sit beside him.

"That's better," Eli says in an attempt to draw me closer.

"Stay back," I order, settling against the arm of the couch, ensuring a healthy distance between us. "Eli," I warn as he immediately moves closer.

"I can't help it," he says plaintively and I laugh.

"That's always been your problem."

"But it's you that I love," he insists, moving ever closer, his leg pressing against mine. He set his bottle on the coffee table before scooping up my legs to drape them over his. I keep hold of my glass, clutching it with both hands, with the hope it might act as a barrier to fend off the advances I know are imminent. I take a healthy sip and eye Eli warily.

"And I know you love me too. So why can't we be together?"

"Eli..."

"*Brienne,*" he mocks my tone again.

"It's not that simple."

"You just like making it difficult," he counters, his hands beginning to massage my calves.

Briefly, I close my eyes. His fingers are strong and can easily find my aching muscles. "I don't want to talk about this."

"I don't want to talk about anything at all," he murmurs.

"Why can't I say no to you?" I whimper as his strong hands move up my leg.

"You can if you want," Eli says with a gleam in his eye. He wrestles the glass from my grasp which results in a splash of wine falling onto my pyjama shirt before he sets it on the table. "Oops."

I clearly have no willpower against this man.

He pulls my legs so I'm reclining against the arm of the couch, my legs slung over his. Slowly, he begins to unbutton my pyjama top. Starting at the bottom where the wine dampened the fabric, Eli undoes each button before folding back the material until my bare stomach is visible. When my top is open from just under my breasts, he trails his fingertips across my stomach, leaving a wake of goosebumps.

"Eli, stop," I murmur, with such an obvious lack of conviction he smiles in response.

"I don't think you want me to stop," he says. Holding my gaze, he moves to the remaining buttons. My breath catches as his fingers brush against my breasts and my nipples instantly tighten, responding to his searching fingers. I can't help responding to his touch. It's like I'm a magnet and he is the world's strongest metal that draws me relentlessly to him. "Do you want me to stop?" His warm hand cups my breast.

"I don't know what I want right now."

Eli has hurt me; cheated on me, betrayed my love.

But he never lied about it, and he always came back to me. He never stopped wanting *me*. Loving me.

It's a very lame excuse, and Callie would slap me senseless if she could see me now, letting him play me as expertly as he does his bass guitar, his fingers as comfortable against my skin as he is playing the cords of his favourite song.

My top is pushed to the side, leaving me bare. Eli gazes hungrily at my breasts, his fingers constantly moving across the sensitive skin. I close my eyes briefly, enjoying the sensation, knowing how good it will feel when he replaces his hands with his lips and tongue.

"I know what you want. We're so good together, Bri."

No, we're not, I want to say. *This* may be good for us, but *we're* not good. But then he bends over me, his lips pressed against mine, his tongue slipping into my mouth which opens traitorously at his touch. My entire body is betraying me.

Suddenly, I'm flat on my back on the couch, my wrists pinned above my head and Eli is leaning over me. "You want this, you know you do," Eli whispers huskily, his lips searching my neck, moving lower towards the swell of my breasts.

He slips so easily into our roles; Eli, the strong, alpha male desperate to dominate the passive girl trying so hard to resist.

Some nights I resist more than others. Sometimes I submit right away.

Tonight I have a little fight in me.

"No," I whisper, even though I do want him. I want his hands on me, his mouth. I want to feel his touch so much I'm ready to beg for it. But we both like to play...

"Really?" Eli rears back with a knowing smile on his stubbled face. "You don't want me to touch you here?" He traces patterns on my breasts, each time coming closer to my nipples without touching them. "Or here?" A tiny moan escapes as his thumb brushes against my nipple. "I think you do want it."

I bite my lip and keep my eyes cast down as Eli licks his fingers, surrounding my nipple and pulling gently at it until it becomes a hard rosy bud. With each tug, it feels like there is a string attached to my groin.

And then he uses his mouth.

Blowing gently, his tongue darts out and flicks against my nipple, and I let out a whimper. "Told you," he says before his mouth descends on the delicate skin.

"No," I say with a quaver in my voice. I like it when Eli dominates me when he coerces me with his touch. When he overpowers me, making me beg for it.

It's why I can't get enough of him.

"You still think you can refuse?" he demands, his voice husky with lust.

"Yes. Stop it. I don't want this." I sound mechanical but it is all part of the game. Refusing gets me even more excited.

Eli releases my wrists and with a quick move, yanks down my pants. "I'm going to show you that you can't say no."

"No," I say weakly, but still with a hint of defiance.

My panties are quickly pulled off and his hand burrows between my legs. "Are you sure?" he asks, cupping my pussy, his finger begins to probe my wetness.

"No. Yes. Oh, god," I cry as Eli thrusts a finger inside me.

"You like this. You like it when I touch you like this." I try and stifle my moan as his thumb rubs my clit in slow circles. "What if I use my mouth? Will you still say no?"

"No," I tell him in a strangled voice as he kneels on the floor and pulls my legs apart.

"You don't want me to use my tongue...right here?" he asks as he delicately flicks my clit with his finger.

"Ah! No!" I cry. Soon I'll be begging for it and Eli will laugh and fuck me senseless. But before he does that, I want to enjoy our game. It heightens the anticipation to an almost unbearable level.

Eli pushes my knees towards my chest, leaving me open and vulnerable. "You want me to stop now?" he asks, his face inches from my aching pussy. "You don't want me to do this?"

"No...please..."I whimper, already reduced to begging. "Please, Eli!"

"I could just fuck you now," he says, sliding two fingers in and out of me. "You're so wet. I really want to fuck you now. But you seem to want something else..."

Eli laughs as I push his head between my legs, the sound making wonderful vibrations as he surrounds me with his mouth, sucking hard on my clit as he thrusts into me with his fingers.

I'm already on the brink of an orgasm as he begins to tongue me, rapid-fire lashes of his tongue, his fingers continuing to thrust into me. Panting, crying out at the pleasure as I grab fistfuls of Eli's thick hair. My climax crashes over me as he sucks on my clit, and I call out his name as I come.

"You didn't want that at all," Eli says with a grin when he lifts his head.

"Shut up and fuck me now," I tell him roughly as I'm catching my breath.

"So demanding," he says with a shake of his head, still crouched between my legs. "One minute you don't want it and then–"

"I always want you," I say huskily. "Please...now..."

"Happy to oblige," Eli tells me, rising up. He pushes my legs up bending me at the waist so my legs are resting on his shoulders. He fumbles with the condom wrapper always on hand in his pocket and with no more preamble, plunges his cock into me.

Eli's cock is thick and hard and I gasp with pain as he fills me. But as he thrusts into me, the pain quickly turns to pleasure and I sigh with relief. Sex with Eli is like nothing else in this world. Every time we're together, I want him all the time.

Slowly, deliberately he fucks me with a rolling motion of his hips. I'm pinned to the couch by my legs, unable to move but I reach out to grab his ass to urge him deeper inside me.

"You still want me to stop," Eli asks breathlessly, quickening his pace.

"No," I whisper. "Never."

"I could do this forever," he says, and as I meet his gaze, I see the love in his eyes.

"Eli," I gasp, as he thrusts harder, faster.

"Make yourself come," he orders and I move my hand between us, searching for my clit with my fingers. I rub frantically, desperate for another release as he drives inside me with the cock I can't get enough of. I can tell from his breathing he's close; his green eyes are half-closed with concentration. He grabs the back of my legs, pressing down as he fucks me even harder. I feel another orgasm building quickly, my fingers relentless against my clit, my eyes wide open to watch Eli come.

"Brienne!" he gasps, as with a final thrust, he explodes inside me. My back arches as I climax with a cry, watching his face contort with pleasure.

Eli thrusts gently before releasing my legs. Still inside me, he leans over me and takes my face in his hands. "I love you so much," he whispers, with only a breath between our lips. "It's never like this with anyone else."

My heart flips over and I'm confused more than ever.

Chapter Ten

ABBY

"YOU HAD SEX WITH him!" Callie accuses as soon as Brienne walks into the kitchenette the next morning. I didn't want to miss anything today so I got there early.

"Who?" For a moment, I think Callie is talking about me. How did she know? Then I realize she's referring to Brienne, Brienne who flushes deep-red.

"Oh," Delia sighs, as Brienne hangs her head. "Eli? Again?"

"I can't help it," Brienne pleads, turning to Callie's furious face. "I just couldn't. He stopped by and he smelled so good and it's been *so* long—"

"There are ways to get off other than boning your ex-husband!"

"Is he an ex-husband yet?" Sadie wants to know. Brienne shakes her head reluctantly.

"We haven't signed the papers yet. And I'm not ready to date yet; I can't get my head around meeting anyone else."

"I wasn't talking about sex!" Callie exclaims. "You're perfectly capable of making yourself happy, you know."

I hide my smile. After yesterday's email exchanges with Ben, I am perfectly capable of lots of things.

"Callie, c'mon. It was just sex; I didn't even let him stay the night. I made him go home, even though I kind of wanted him to stay because we would have done it again and it was good...but was just sex. It doesn't mean anything. "

"It always means something with Eli." Callie glowers.

"You keep going back to him," I say slowly. "What's so special about him?" It's something I've never been able to ask her about. Callie talks about sex; Sadie complains about missing it and Brienne easily admits to wanting more, but I'm not one for saying much about it. I listen. But when I see Brienne all aglow today after being with Eli and constantly hear Callie rave about how good so-and-so is, I can't help but feel this is some sort of amazing club I'm not allowed to join.

Today, I've decided to become a full-fledged member. Let's talk about sex today.

Emailing Ben yesterday was probably one of the best things I've ever done for my sex life, next to waxing my lady parts. And waxing is a whole lot more painful.

He couldn't keep his hands off me last night, even going so far as putting the kids to bed early. After they were asleep, while we watched *The Voice*, Ben went down on me on the couch. I had only wanted to make out and got so much more. I didn't even have to fantasize about Adam Levine to make myself come and had to stuff the blanket in my mouth so I wouldn't wake the kids with my cries.

And after that, Ben made love to me when we went to bed, once at night and once again in the morning.

I'm surprised Callie missed my perma-smile this morning. I think I might be aglow as well, but obviously, Brienne has eclipsed me.

Brienne stares into the distance, a besotted expression on her face as she answers my question. "It's like Eli knows exactly what I want, even before I do. He'll try something–some new position or...something...and I'll love it, even though I would never have thought of it myself. I have a difficult time asking what I want."

"Me too," I say quietly.

"Sometimes Eli makes me ask, which is good. I feel uninhibited with him, and sexy and desired," Brienne continues.

"But then you have to remember about the other women," Callie points out.

"I know he's cheated on me, and he can't do commitment, but when I'm with him, it's like I'm the only woman in the world who matters to him. And I can't say no to him," Brienne says simply. "I know it's going to be good and I figure, why not? Why not get some while I can? Sad, I know. I'm hooked on him, and have no desire to meet anyone else to offset it."

"You've got to just jump in," Delia urges. "Try online dating."

Brienne shrugs. I feel bad for her since her morning afterglow has been snuffed out by Callie's disapproval. "I set up my profile on *Kettle of Fish* but all I got were creepy guys looking for someone to dress up as a mermaid."

"I probably have a Little Mermaid costume in my house somewhere," I offer.

"Thanks, but I'll pass. I was always more of an *Aladdin* fan. I loved Jasmine," Brienne tells me with a grin.

Callie shakes her head. "We have got to fix you."

"Because I like Jasmine?"

"Because you can't stop fucking the guys who are totally bad for you!" Callie exclaims.

"No, offence," Sadie cuts in, "but can you say all the guys *you've* been with are good for you?"

"She's got a point," I agree.

"A very good one," Delia adds.

"Since when is this about me?" Callie demands.

"I'm just not sure I need fixing," Brienne explains. "I realize I should have kicked him out as soon as he showed his face, but I didn't. It's been a while," she says bleakly.

"You were horny," Sadie commiserates. "I know what it's like."

"It's more than that. You think with your pussy around Eli," Callie says bluntly. "Sorry, Delly," she continues as Delia makes a *tsk* of disapproval. "Would you rather me call it her vagina?"

"Lady parts will do quite well," Delia says primly.

"Fine. You think with your *lady parts* around Eli," Callie says, enunciating the words. "My thinking is that if your *lady parts*," she grins at Delia, "are kept occupied by someone else, it might not be such a problem. You'll stop thinking about Eli and won't want him as much. Sadie agrees with me, don't you?"

"Sure," Sadie says, averting her eyes.

I raise my eyebrow. "Who is it?"

"You're involved with someone?" Brienne eagerly asks, happy to have the focus taken off her.

"I'm not really involved," Sadie hedges. "I'm not exactly sure what to call it."

"Are your lady parts being occupied by someone?" Delia asks politely. Callie bursts out laughing and even Sadie smiles.

"In a way."

"She's fooling around with Alma in the supply closet," Callie tells us, raising her hands in a gesture of surrender when Sadie turns on her. "You were taking too long to tell them."

"Really?" I ask. Sadie had told us about her experimentation with her neighbour Laurel during one drunken lunch for Delia's birthday, but that's all I thought it was–an experiment. Something I had never done, never really wanted. I'm probably one of the few women who has never been curious about being with a woman.

"Maybe I didn't say anything because I didn't know how to tell everyone!" Sadie says defensively.

"You just say, 'Hey, guys, guess what? Alma and I are carpet–"

"Callista," Delia orders in a *don't mess with the mama* voice.

"–Alma has been exploring another side of me," Callie says sheepishly. "And I'm enjoying it."

"Are you?" I ask. "I mean, I'm sure you are, but I didn't think–"

"Neither did I," Sadie says sadly. "Laurel was trying to distract me from being so miserable, and it kind of helped. But I'm not sure what Alma is. She's *married*."

"I'm not sure that would be the best situation for you to be in," Delia points out.

"I don't think it is either, but I can't help myself."

"Just like me and Eli," Brienne jumps in.

"You both need to be fixed," Callie decides.

"I'm not broken," Sadie snaps. "I'm perfectly happy the way I am."

"Confused and frustrated?" Sadie glares at Callie. "Admitting it is the first step."

Instead of answering, Sadie takes her coffee and she marches out of the kitchenette. "Sadie," Brienne calls after her.

"I don't want to talk about it," Sadie replies before we hear her push open the door to the stairs.

"You've got to lay off her," I say tactfully. "She's young."

"And confused," Delia says sympathetically.

"Maybe she is a lesbian," Brienne muses but Callie shakes her head.

"I'm not an expert on things like this, but I don't think so. I think she's experimenting, which is cool, but I'm worried she's too naive and is going to get hurt."

"By Alma?" I ask skeptically.

"She is married," Delia points out. "You know it can't end well."

"How did you find out?" I wonder. "Did she tell you?"

Callie *would* be the one to confide in for something like that. She grins. "I caught her with lipstick on her ankle."

"So?" Delia says in her clipped voice, sounding very British.

"Why would Sadie have lipstick on her ankle? She doesn't even wear lipstick!"

"Why would she leave it on her ankle?" Brienne points out.

"Think about why she might have lipstick on her legs?" Callie says, her eyes wide.

"Oh," Brienne and I say in unison.

We're silent for a moment, listening to the hiss of the Tassimo and thinking about Sadie. At least I'm thinking about her. With all of her sass and Callie-like exuberance, Sadie is inexperienced in matters of the heart. I think there had been a few other than Evan, but all had ended badly. I tried to think where I would be if Ben and I broke up. He's the only man I have ever been with. Would I be as confused as Sadie? Or as reluctant to try with anyone else like Brienne?

I hope I never have that problem.

And then I can't stop thinking about Sadie with Alma.

What would it be like with a woman? Ben convinced me to watch a porn movie with him once, years ago, and there was a girl-on-girl scene. Watching it didn't really do anything for me, and Ben never suggested it again. But now, years later, I finally get around to wondering what it would be like to be with a woman.

I wonder if Ben would like to hear about what I'm thinking about.

"Well, I would love to fix Sadie up with someone," Callie announces, as she takes her cup from the machine. "Like Delly says, this thing isn't going to end well. Although Alma is really hot. I think she's sexier than Agatha; one of those quiet librarians who get all hot and bothered when they take down their hair?"

"Alma doesn't wear her hair like a librarian," Brienne points out.

"But don't you think she's hot? And I don't play for that team."

"If you were a man, I would take offence at that," says a deep voice with a hint of a Hispanic accent. "But as you are a woman speaking of my wife, I find your comments somewhat arousing."

In unison, the four of us whirl around to face the door, Brienne spilling her coffee. Jason and Michael stand in the doorway, which wouldn't normally be a problem, but today they brought a stranger with them. A very handsome stranger, with the most piercing blue eyes I've ever seen. He's wearing a navy suit, the pants fitted to better display his trim figure, the jacket covering his broad shoulders.

"I like your shirt," Brienne blurts out. It's an interesting shade of pink, worn without a tie. I'm surprised she noticed; I can't bring my gaze past those eyes.

Only Callie remains still. "I'm not sure if talking about what arouses you is the most appropriate thing you could say to a woman in the workplace," she says thoughtfully.

"I'm sure it isn't," he replies with a smile almost as piercing as those eyes. "But neither was your comment. Are we even?"

Callie breaks into a smile. "I like your style. Who are you?"

"I can say the same thing, Ms. Champlain. Lovely to finally meet you."

The fact he knows her name doesn't faze Callie one bit. Some days I'd love just a bit of her self-confidence.

"And you are...?" Callie prompts, still with a winning smile.

"Julian Donovan. Your new boss."

"*You're* Julian Donovan?" Brienne gasps. I'm glad she blurts it out first. "And Alma's your *wife?*"

"You seem alarmed," Julian says, turning his gaze on her. "Ms. Lawson."

"Cool party trick," Callie comments. "Bri's only concerned because we were gossiping around Alma's desk and she can't remember if we said anything about you."

I'm in awe of Callie. The way she can cover for others is nothing short of brilliant.

I wonder which one of us should tell Sadie who Alma's husband is. Delia was right; this thing with Sadie and Alma can't end well.

Chapter Eleven

JASON

Mr. Donovan—Julian, he insists I call him—chats to the girls in the kitchenette until the situation becomes less awkward. Watching him charm them is impressive, although it makes me feel invisible standing beside him. Callie and Brienne are all smiles, but Abby is more wary, especially when Julian turns to her.

"Ms. Park, I wonder if we can schedule a meeting for Friday afternoon," he says politely, but in a way that leaves no room for her to decline. "Late afternoon would be best."

"Of course," Abby tells him, professional enough to know not to ask what the meeting is regarding, although I'm sure she's dying to know. I know I am.

"I'm hopeful it won't take long; I wouldn't want to keep you from any plans you and your husband might have. It sounds like Ben is right on schedule with the St. Albert project."

"I'm available for as long as it takes," Abby says with a frown. "Have you been studying up on names and faces or something?"

Julian gives a mischievous grin, or as mischievous as such a good-looking man can be. "I like to know my people. It makes dealing with them easier if I know the background already. But I don't think you should worry about me checking up on you. I haven't found anything alarming."

Abby's cheeks flush a faint shade of pink and I guess she is thinking about her email with Ben yesterday. Julian might think that was alarming if I brought the correspondence to his attention. Or he might think it was sexy like I did. But that is something we'll never find out because I'm not about to tell him.

Julian finally takes his leave with Michael, leaving me with the ladies.

"Wow," Brienne rolls her eyes. "The big boss man paid us a visit."

The last thing I want to do is to recap the visit and Delia seems to sense that. "How are you this morning, Jason?" she asks, smiling warmly at me. She's so sweet and motherly and it's impossible not to return her smile. "You came at a good time. The machine is finally free."

"We've been here a while," Brienne says.

"And the drop-in by him didn't help," Abby whispers. She actually darts to the door to make sure Julian is out of earshot. "Those *eyes*." She pretends to swoon. "I can't believe he came down here."

"He's welcome to come *all* the way down here whenever he likes." Callie's curves give a little shimmy at her words.

"Julian–Mr. Donovan–seems to be settling in," Delia says. "He seems nice enough."

"And," Brienne prompts with a smile.

"You'll not get me gossiping about him," Delia admonishes her.

"Just give me something," Brienne pleads. "Something little."

Delia shakes her head with a smile. "I'll be heading back to my desk now." But just as she's walking out of the little room, she pauses. "Did you catch the arse on the man?"

Brienne chortles with laughter as Delia leaves. Even I have to smile.

"You're still here?" Sadie appears at the door with a flash of blonde hair and an uncharacteristic scowl. "Hi, Jason. I forgot to put my lunch in the fridge," she explains, doing just that. "I don't want to talk about anything with you."

"To me?" I ask in bewilderment. Sadie is wearing a short skirt, and I can't keep my eyes off her legs.

"No, she's being pissy with me," Callie explains." Sweet Sadie, you know I love you."

"And she doesn't want you to get hurt," Brienne adds. "None of us do."

I keep quiet, setting up the Tassimo for my chai tea latte; not wanting to intrude, but enjoying being around them and the interaction.

"I know," Sadie sighs. "I'll get my head on straight someday."

"You'll figure it out," Abby assures her, gathering her things. "I'd better get back to work preparing for a meeting I know nothing about."

"You'll tell us what's going on, won't you?" Callie grins.

"I have a legal obligation to the company, and would never want to break my confidentiality agreement," Abby says primly, all the while nodding her acquiesces with a smile. "If it has anything to do with you, that is. You haven't harassed any of the boys downstairs again, have you?"

"Not lately. And not so they'd complain," Callie replies. "What about you, Jason?"

She turns to me and my heart freezes. A part of me wakes up, however. "What about me?"

"What would you do if I harassed you?"

I don't know if she's teasing or being truthful and frankly, I don't care. Today Callie is wearing a sweater that makes her breasts look like pillows that I ache to lay my head on. "That would be fine," I answer after a pause.

"Callie, leave him alone," Abby chides. "Do I have to stay and protect him?"

"Why? Jason is a big boy. He can handle himself. I wonder if he could handle me," she muses, with a finger tapping her lips.

Abby shakes her head. "Sorry, Jason," she says apologetically.

"I don't mind," I tell her. And I don't. I stand firm before Callie as she glances appraisingly at me.

"I wonder how big of a boy he is," she says idly.

"I'm five feet, eleven inches, one hundred and seventy pounds and my penis is above average for length and width," I tell her. "If that answers your question about my size."

"What?" Brienne's eyes pop with delight.

"Well, I might have liked to find that out for myself, but great. Good to know," Callie laughs. "Now I'm intrigued."

"I've always been intrigued," I say honestly.

"You don't think I'd be too much for you?" she narrows her eyes, taking in my mussed hair and dark-rimmed glasses. I look like the geek I am–someone happier to spend alone time with my computer than people. I take a deep breath.

"I believe I could handle you."

"What would you do to handle me?" Callie presses.

"I can hold my breath for an impressive ninety-three seconds underwater, which helps, along with the substantial length of my tongue, in oral sex. I've performed this on six females, and all assure me I'm the best they've ever had. Also, I can masturbate up to four times a day, and my recovery rate is remarkable. I've also been told on several occasions that I have extraordinary stamina."

Brienne and Callie share the same shocked expression. Sadie claps her hands with delight. "Holy shit! Can I try?"

"I was under the impression that you were involved with Alma?"

"*What*?" she cries, with a guilty look at Callie and Brienne.

"I never heard anything like *that*!" Callie drawls, sharing a glance with Brienne who isn't as effective as covering her expression. From Callie's response, I gather they both already know. "How's that going for you?"

"It's not–I never–we aren't–do you know *everything* that goes on around here?" Sadie demands.

I shrug. "I would say about ninety percent. I do read emails–"

"You do what?" Brienne pales.

"It's part of my job description, constant monitoring of employees use of emails, search engines and social media for non-work related issues."

"You read our emails?" Sadie cries.

"Holy Christ, it's like Big Brother is watching us!" Callie says with disgust.

"I've never reported any problems with management," I quickly tell them. "And there have been a few inappropriate uses I've found. Did you know there's a manager in engineering who spends at least an hour a day surfing for porn? That's his business and until it affects his performance–"

"Kip," Callie confirms. "If he doesn't look at it he gets bitchy so it's best to let him have it. It's not too bad. I've seen worse."

"What do you call 'bad' porn?" Brienne wonders.

"Kid stuff is the worst. The nasty anal stuff; really kinky whips and stuff. Kip keeps it simple," Callie says. I'm amazed at her matter-of-fact tone. Amazed and somewhat impressed.

"And you know this because..." Brienne asks with a questioning smile.

Callie shrugs. "It gets boring up there once in a while. One time we were watching it and he got so turned on–" I'm disappointed when she realizes I'm avidly listening to every word and clamps her mouth shut. "I probably shouldn't tell you that. But if you know everything, I probably don't have to."

"I don't know about the details about that particular day, no," I tell her slowly, then decide to put everything on the line. "I would like to hear about it."

"What's going on here?" Sadie demands, her gaze switching like she's watching a tennis match. "Do you two want to be alone?"

"Just a minute," Callie says carefully, her finger tapping on her lower lip.

Oh, to be that finger.

"Back to these emails. You read all of our emails?"

"No, I wouldn't have time in the day to do that. I only skim about fifty percent of them. I do particularly enjoy your *would you rather* exchange. They are one of the highlights of the day." Too late I realize I should have kept that information to myself.

Brienne looks horrified. "Are you serious?"

"They're quite tame compared to some of the other exchanges," I'm quick to reassure her. "Just the other day I found a heated conversation between Abby and her husband–"

"Abby!" Callie cries with glee. "Way to go, girl! Sexting the hubby!"

"Is it really called sexting when it's to your husband?" Sadie wonders.

"Yes," Brienne tells her scornfully. "Married people can be sexy, too. That's how babies are born."

"Well, Abby and Ben seem so *content*. Not that sexy. And is it sexting when it's over email?"

"I wondered that myself," I confide. "Which is why I'm not classifying or reporting it."

"You have to report Abby?" Brienne gasps.

"Based on the record of the email, I should, so disciplinary measures can be taken. But I know she's your friend and I don't want to get her into trouble."

"Well, isn't that sweet of you," Callie drawls.

"I thought it was a nice thing to do," I agree.

"And do you think you deserve a reward for that?"

"Callie," Brienne warns.

Callie shrugs. "What do you want me to do? It is nice of him to cover for Abby and us. Some of the stuff we email back and forth–"

"Which we will *never* do again!" Brienne exclaims.

"Please don't stop on my account," I tell them. "I won't report you."

"Isn't that nice of you?"

"Are you thinking what I think you're thinking?" Sadie asks Callie. I have no idea what she's thinking about because I've actually stopped thinking. Callie is standing before me, running an appraising hand across my chest and down my arm. I might have stopped breathing as well, since I exhale in a gasp when she slides her hand down my arm, tickling my palm with her fingers.

"I can't watch this," Brienne says.

"C'mon," Callie wheedles. "All that talk of holding his breath and recovery rate? You can't say you're not curious."

"Being curious and doing something about it are two very different things," Brienne tells her.

"You're no fun. What do you think?" she turns to Sadie. "Should I take one for the team? Add a little protection for Abby, and for us?"

"There's no need. I'm not about to report…" I stammer. Callie is still holding my hand and brings it slowly to her lips. "But if there's an issue about trusting me…"

"I really think I need to find out how much I can trust you," Callie says earnestly. She nibbles on my middle finger and I instantly harden. Is she serious? Is this really going to happen? This is better than anything I've ever dreamt about.

"Seriously?" Sadie gives a little yelp. "Right now?"

"No, not now," Callie says with disgust. "This afternoon. He's totally got an Andrew Garfield vibe going for him, doesn't he?" My puff of pride must have been noticeable. "Spider-man geek, are you?"

My reply is unintelligible because Callie brings my finger all the way into her mouth and sucks hard on it.

"Why can't I do that?" Brienne wonders sadly.

"You can! Here," Callie offers Brienne my hand. "You can take one for the team. Or we could team up and really blow his mind. Would you like that?"

I'm unable to respond to that or even the simplest question. I might not even know my own name right now.

"So what's going to happen," Callie kisses my finger before dropping my hand. "With all your expertise in this place, you find out the best place where we can be alone. Then you email me the location at about 2 o'clock, and I'll meet you there. You can do your best to impress me. Sound good."

"I won't let you down," I promise eagerly.

Chapter Twelve

SADIE

*C*AN WE MEET TODAY?

I really need to see you

I miss you

I can't stop thinking about you

Last night I touched myself thinking about you

I think my husband suspects

I'm not sure what I'll do if he finds out

I NEED to see you

I need you

Emails like that have flooded my inbox since yesterday. There was a two-page diatribe about how silky my skin is and how much I've changed her waiting for me when I woke up this morning. Alma must have written it late last night.

I'm getting a little concerned.

Actually, it's moved way beyond concern.

Alma seems very interested in me; very invested in this relationship. Even though I'm relatively inexperienced, I'm beginning to
suspect this isn't the norm. Alma's last few emails had been more
than a little demanding. She wants me to agree on a time for us
to meet during the day but work has been really busy. Alma has
only been working here for two weeks so I thought she would
understand; I thought she'd want to make a good impression.
From the sounds of the emails, she doesn't care at all about work.

Only me.

Her need for me is starting to freak me out.

I have never been needy; nothing in my relationship with Evan
suggests I was anything but secure. Evan was a good boyfriend,
other than he was a good liar and had no problem betraying me.
He might have been good at deceiving me but he never made me
feel insecure, so I don't understand where Alma is coming from.

I'm not equipped to deal with an insecure Alma. It's enough
that I had doubts about this before. Alma is married; I had been
cheated on. I wouldn't want to put anyone through the pain I had
endured. But this–it's like she's stalking me. Already she's friended
me on Facebook, is following me on Twitter, and has begun to
make some really inappropriate comments on social media. I'm
becoming uncomfortable and I don't like that feeling.

My strategy is to hide from her. Avoid.

This works until lunchtime.

I'm in the kitchen watching my leftover pasta rotate in the
microwave, wondering about the radioactive waves undoubtedly
leaking out of such an ancient appliance. If people are getting
replaced, maybe we're due for a new microwave. I'm transfixed by
the sounds, and the smell and thinking about the copyediting I still

need to do before the end of the day. I wasn't exactly lying when I told Alma I was too busy to sneak away.

As I smell something other than cheesy pasta—something floral, like perfume, I feel hands on my breasts.

"What the hell?" I jump forward only to find myself pinned against the counter.

"I found you," a voice whispers into my ear. Fingers dip between the buttons on my blouse.

"Alma, what are—not here!" I hiss, craning my neck to look behind me. Alma has a beguiling smile on her face.

"I've missed you so much," she says beseechingly. "There's no one around."

"We're in the kitchen," I protest. One of her arms slides around my waist, the other undoes the middle button of my blouse so her hand can wander more freely along my bare skin.

This feels wrong. I don't like being trapped like this.

Alma's fingers find my nipple as she begins kissing my neck.

"Please don't move," Alma whispers into my neck, her voice tickling in my ear. My neck has always been sensitive. So has the area between my legs which is beginning to feel uncomfortably warm as Alma toys with my breasts, now with both hands.

Having her hands on my breasts is different than a man's. A man would be grabbing and fondling, sometimes painfully in their excitement. Alma is gentle, using her fingertips, softly gliding over the surface of my skin, brushing the soft buds until they form hard peaks.

She takes her hand out of my shirt and brings her fingers to my mouth. "Wet them, please," she suggests in a husky voice.

Despite myself, I obediently open my lips, wetting the tips of her fingers with my tongue and catching my breath as she immediately returns to my nipples. The wetness hardens them even more as she toys with them.

"You shouldn't," I whisper.

"I have to," she tells me, and the thought of Alma wanting me so much she would risk someone walking in on us like this, thrills me. I don't stop her as her hand slips under the waistband of my skirt. I close my eyes and brace my hands on the edge of the counter as Alma quickly finds the wetness between my legs.

"I want to taste you," she says in a husky voice, her finger sliding inside me before beginning to circle my clit. "I want to lick you right there. Do you want that?"

I can barely nod my assent as Alma's fingers quicken their pace around my clit. Her other hand continues to play with my nipple.

"I love the taste of you," she continues to murmur huskily in my ear, her voice exciting me almost as much as her fingers.

Almost.

"I want to make you come with my mouth," Alma tells me. "I want to lick every part of you, and when you come, with your little noises and your cries, you'll push the back of my head so I'll go deeper–do you like when I do that? Do you?"

I make a wordless sound, unable to speak. I've braced myself against the counter, my legs spread as far as my skirt allows them, as Alma rubs wildly between my legs, never losing contact with my clit. Already she knows exactly the touch I need, and already I feel my orgasm build.

"After I make you come with my mouth, my tongue exploring every inch of you, inside and out, I'm going to *fuck* you with my fingers—"

I've never heard Alma use the word, and I try my best to suppress a moan.

"—fuck you so hard and good you'll be screaming for more, and you'll never want another cock inside you ever again. Does that sound good to you?"

I can't answer because I'm having trouble staying quiet and I can't bear to do anything to make Alma stop, take away her fingers—

"I'm going to make you come right now," she tells me. "Aren't I? Do you want to come right here in the kitchen? Right like this?"

"Yes," I cry in a breathless whisper. "Please, don't stop!"

"Come now," she urges, rubbing frantically, and I do. I erupt around her fingers, thrusting my hips forward, my head thrown back in a wordless cry. And as my legs shake and I fight to keep standing, Alma thrusts her fingers inside me, searching for my G-spot. When she finds it, pressing the secret spot, I come again, and Alma yanks her hand out of my shirt to slap over my mouth to quiet my cries.

Later, after it's over and Alma leaves me in peace to eat my lunch, I wonder if this thing with Alma might be a problem.

Chapter Thirteen

CALLIE

I'M STILL NOT SURE why I agreed to meet Jason that afternoon. Horny–yes. Always. Intrigued? Well, if a guy–a non-arrogant, non-asshole of a guy–can recite stats like that about himself, who wouldn't be intrigued? I think that was the most words I've heard come out of Jason's mouth since he's been here. He's always so quiet, shy, Michael's shadow. He is a geek, and geeks have never been my type.

Until Michael.

Not that Michael is anything to me. I just can't seem to stop thinking about him.

Not that it's a problem. I'm sure I can stop thinking about him, anytime I want.

It's just that I *like* to think about him.

Darn pesky girlfriend. If it wasn't for her, and how happy he seems to be with her, I would screw the boy out of my system. And he is a boy–at least eight years younger than me. He looks like he should be asking his mother's permission to stay out at night or ask his older brother the best way to woo a girl.

He could woo me any day.

Stop thinking about him! Michael is too young for me, happily contained with a loving girlfriend. He's a comic book, *Dungeons & Dragons* playing geek. Actually, I don't think he plays *D &D*; the last time we talked, he gave me this in-depth explanation of another game which sounded pretty interesting. I wonder what would it be like if I got Jason to invite me to Sunday night game night?

I know too much about games and comic books and super-heroes, thanks to my father and four older brothers. And *Star Wars*. I get to use my wealth of information to show my nephews how cool I am. It works for guys I'm picking up as well, and Michael is always suitably impressed by my knowledge.

I remind myself that Michael has a *girlfriend*. And if there's one thing I don't do, is mess around with guys who are in a relation-ship. At least not in a good relationship.

There is no hope for me and Michael. Jason, on the other hand...

He's cute, he's hot, I'm horny. Why not?

Another reason I propositioned Jason was to give me something other than Michael to think about for the afternoon. I love the anticipation, the slow build of excitement before I meet someone in the office. I know it's wrong, and I might be fired if management knew what was going on, but it makes me feel so *sexy* to slip away from my desk for twenty minutes; coming back with pink cheeks and a buzz still between my legs.

I spend at least eight hours a day in this place. Why not make it as enjoyable as I can?

"Hi, Callie," Jason startles me. His suggestion was that we meet in the storeroom, next to where the trucks are parked. I was half-hoping Jason would suggest one of the trucks. I have fond memories of those trucks. Greg, from HR, and I were going at it one day—I had straddled him and was riding him for everything I was worth and old Mr. Hever walked through the bay and never noticed a thing because we were so high up.

I wonder if Julian Donovan would notice something like that.

"Hi, Jason," I say, distracted by the possibility of Julian Donovan walking into the storeroom while Jason and I are indisposed.

But then Jason takes my hand and leads me to a pallet of bags of cement in the corner of the cavernous space. Taking off his jacket, he places it on the neatly piled bags and helps me sit on it. My heels fall to the ground with a clatter and Jason places them gently beside the pallet. I'm touched by his gallantry. "What do you like?" he asks in a low voice.

"Why don't we see what you've got?"

"No." Jason's cheeks are pink. "I—uh, like to be told what to do."

"You do, do you? Well, then, right up my alley because I like to tell what to do. Why don't you start by taking off my panties? No, wait," I cry as his hands immediately move to my hips. I jump off the cement bags, forcing him to step back. "I want to see what's in store for me."

"To see if I'm as big as I said?"

"Something like that," I say, my fingers nimbly working the button of his khakis. "But I've been thinking about you since this morning and I want—ah." I draw out the word as slowly as my hand discovers Jason was telling the truth. He's already hard, a stiff length of cock with the tip visible at the waistband of his briefs. "Oh, my."

"I seem to impress people," Jason says modestly, and I bite my lip.

"I should say so. You know, we're going to have to find out whether you've told the truth about everything." Idly, I stroke his cock, loving the way Jason closes his eyes at my touch.

"I was hoping you'd say that," he mutters. "I've wanted to taste you for so long..."

The moisture drains from my mouth and collects between my legs. "I wouldn't want you to have to wait any longer."

"Thank you." Jason helps me back up onto the stack of cement bags and positions me as comfortably as I can be. "Would you still like me to take off your panties?"

"I think they'll just get in the way," I concede, trying not to sound so eager. Jason's shy and matter-of-fact demeanour is a big turn-on, as is the way Jason looks in those black-rimmed glasses. And the size of his cock...

His fingers find my panties under my skirt and pull them off in a businesslike way, forcing me to wiggle until they are past my hips. The way he strokes my legs as he removes them is heaven. As is the way his hands glide back up to my inner thigh. Just as I think his fingers are moving in, he stops and looks questioning up at me.

"What's wrong?"

"I like to be told what to do," he reminds me.

"Well, I'm telling you to go for it. Only–what would you like to do?"

Jason glances at me lying back on the cement bags, skirt pushed up, exposing my pussy shining pink and hairless. "This is nice. But

I would like to see your breasts first because I think this might take up most of my attention for a while."

"Be my guest," I tell him, pulling up my sweater until my breasts are visible. It's not the most ladylike move, but Jason did ask nicely.

"You don't have to take it off," he stops me as I'm about to yank it over my head. "You look—just like that."

"I look like what?" I whisper. I stroke a finger down my cleavage, smiling as Jason swallows audibly.

"Beautiful," he tells me hoarsely, never taking his eyes from my finger.

"You can touch them if you like," I invite. Men have always loved my breasts but I've never had one with such a fixated fascination. It must be Jason's personality. He seems very intense.

Reaching out with his hand, he traces the edge of my bra with his fingers; across my breast, down into the valley and up the other side. Slowly, confidently, his fingers never slipping under my bra.

And then he retraces this route with his tongue.

My breath escapes as Jason slides his hand around my waist and moves closer. I widen my legs so he's able to stand between them. His mouth travels across my breasts once, twice...three times...

"More," I gasp. "You can touch more of them."

Automatically his thumb moves to my nipple and circles it, hard and tight under my bra. He brings his other hand from my waist to cup my other breast.

"You can...mouth..."

I'm already having trouble speaking and he's only just begun.

Jason pushes my bra down allowing my breast to escape and follows with his mouth. Instead of going straight for the nipple, he traces patterns with his tongue, moving ever closer to the sensitive bud without ever touching it.

I lean back onto my arms, enjoying Jason's caresses. He seems to want to take his time, and I kind of want to let him.

No part of my breasts is left unexplored but I'm ready for more. I push his head towards my nipple. "More, please," I instruct huskily.

Instantly obliging, Jason laves his tongue slowly against my nipple, sending a jolt of desire between my legs. When he takes it in his mouth, rolling it around with his tongue, I clutch his head, my fingers sinking into his thick hair.

"These are wonderful," Jason mumbles as he kisses a trail to my other breast. "Better than I imagined."

"You imagined me? What was I doing?" Jason looks up at me, his tongue on my nipple. His eyes are a dark brown behind his glasses. "You can talk and touch, can't you?" I tease. "You can touch other things."

With a shy smile, he keeps one hand on my breast while the other slides up my leg. Like before, he stops right at the edge of the warmth. "What did you imagine me doing?" I repeat.

"Lots of things. Everything. I imagined what you looked like when I would bring you to orgasm."

"You think you can do that?" I ask hoarsely, nudging my hips forward in an attempt to move his hand closer to my heat.

"Yes."

"Do you like to do that?"

"Oh, yes. It's my favourite thing."

"To make women come?"

Jason nods and leans forward. At the last second, I realize he's trying to kiss me and move my head so his lips fall onto my neck. "I don't kiss," I mutter. "You can touch my pussy now."

He nuzzles the skin beneath my ear as his fingers begin to explore me, moving between the folds, a finger sliding deep into my wetness. I gasp as his thumb rubs my clit. "I want your mouth there now," I tell him.

Obediently Jason spreads my pale legs on the cement bags and bends his head between them.

"Oh...my..." I whisper, at the touch of Jason's tongue against my bare skin. He lifts one of my legs to rest it on the bag, leaving me open and vulnerable.

The touch of Jason's tongue elicits a moan from deep within, one I do my best to stifle. He licks me with soft, sure strokes, delving inside before travelling to my clit to circle questioningly around it. I clutch the back of his head with one hand and cover my mouth with the other.

The only noise in the room is the faraway hum of a fan and the sound of Jason lapping at my wetness. And my sudden gasp as he sucks hard on my clit.

Bags of cement make for an uncomfortable surface to lie back on, but all is forgotten as I clutch Jason's curly hair and greedily press my hips against his mouth. I feel, rather than hear him groan, sending vibrations through me.

"That's...good," I moan. "Don't stop."

"Never," he says into my pussy, a simple word never sounding so good.

I want to forget myself, let myself go but part of me is still conscious of being in the storeroom, lying on a pallet of cement mix. That part of me manages to muffle most of my cries, but I can't do anything to stop the soft moans and gasps.

Jason tucks his hands under me and lifts my hips off the cement bags. His dark eyes seem to be smiling at me.

His tongue is everywhere and I cry out with delight.

With both hands squeezing my cheeks, Jason tongues me thoroughly, leaving nothing untouched, always returning for a suck on my clit before moving off again. He drags his tongue between my lips, circling the edge of my opening before plunging inside. Tickling my perineum, he uses the tip against my ass, before moving back to my clit.

I feel like Canada when the Europeans first arrived–explored, discovered, plundered.

Setting me gently on the cement, Jason adds fingers to his administration, dipping deep within me. His tongue flicks a rhythm against my clit before sucking it hard. And then even harder as his fingers thrust inside me.

He's searching for my G-spot, and when he presses deep inside me, he finds it.

"Oh, God!" I cry out, forgetting where we are, conscious of the sensations racing through my body. I clutch Jason's hair as his mouth, his tongue, and his fingers claim me. My cries are loud and harsh and fill the room and I can't think of quieting myself. "I'm coming! Oh, God, Jason, now, please–" I arch my back as I crash over the edge.

Jason relentlessly continues his licking and sucking, his fingers thrusting fast inside me. I'm bucking against him, his hair gripped tight in my hand. He doesn't stop; he never falters. He's insistent, inexorable like he's demanding every ounce of pleasure I can supply. He–

"Oh, fuck, don't–this is so good," I gasp. "More–again! I'm–again!"

And then I come a second time, even more intense than the first.

"You screamed my name," he says quite proudly when he finally lifts his head.

"I didn't know that," I tell him, dazed by the power of my orgasms. I lie back against the uncomfortable bags. "You deserve to have your name screamed."

"That's how I imagined it."

"Glad I lived up to your fantasy. You certainly did." I lift myself onto my elbows. "Now, would you like your turn?"

"Do you need a minute?" he asks solicitously.

"No, I'm good," I tell him, touched again by his concern. I struggle to sit up and reach out my hands to him. "Condom?"

Jason pulls the foil wrapper out of his pocket. "I've found it handy to leave a few at work," he says sheepishly.

I hop off the pallet before he can help me, and land on shaky legs. I grab him by the hips, to keep my balance and because I can't wait to get my hands on him. "First time for everything. If you're lucky, there'll be a second." I peel down his briefs until his cock juts out. "Holy fuck," I murmur. "Now I'm the one who wants to taste that." I still his hand that's about to roll on the condom and grip his cock.

Bending my head, I tease the tip, swirling and licking it with flickers of my tongue. As I ease him all the way into my throat, Jason groans deeply, his hands clamping on the sides of my head.

I play with him, listening to his groans as I suck, use my teeth. I'm having fun finding out what he likes, loving how much he's enjoying it. But soon the ache between my legs is back and I can't wait any longer for him to be inside me.

I straighten up and turn to face the pallet. "From behind, please," I say politely, hiking up my skirt. "Hard. And fast."

"Just as I imagined," Jason says in a strangled voice. He rolls the condom on in record time. I smile as he positions himself behind me, grasping my hips with a warm hand as he guides his cock into my waiting pussy.

I gasp as he enters me slowly, moaning softly as he slides in. He fills me completely, with more than a hint of pain as he slowly thrusts, allowing my pussy to stretch to accommodate. And I want to accommodate all of him.

"Is this okay?" he whispers, pausing in his thrusts.

"Oh, god, *yes!*"

That's when he really starts to go to town. Jason's thrusts are firm and measured like he's taking his time.

This is so impressive.

I push back against him and he slows his thrusts, pulling back so only the tip is inside me, before slamming back against me.

"Oh, god," I cry. "Just like that."

I brace myself with my arms on the bags, the sounds of my cries and moans mixing with the slap of his legs against mine.

But I want it–I need it faster, and harder–and I grip the side of his leg, the other searching for whatever handhold I can find on the pallet. Jason understands my unspoken need and begins to fuck me faster, less measured, more frantically, like he can't control himself. He reaches around and his thumb rubs my clit. I cry out.

I rest my head on my arms as he fucks me, loving the sensation of his cock tight inside me. He keeps his thumb on my clit the entire time and soon I start to build again.

"Don't stop!" I cry. "Just like–don't stop!"

I bite my lips against my cries as the thundering sensations roar through me.

"Yes! Yes," I cry, unable to stop myself as I come hard, gripping him tightly with every muscle I can.

Almost immediately as I'm still quivering, my eyes tightly closed, Jason bucks against me and with the barest groan erupts inside me.

"That," I manage to get out between gasps for breath, "was impressive."

Chapter Fourteen

BRIENNE

THE NEXT DAY I'M at my desk reading my daily *Would you rather*...from Callie. Apparently, she trusts Jason enough to continue our email game.

Would you rather have satisfactory, but not earth-shaking sex with someone you know, with the possibility of a repeat performance, or amazing, mind-blowing sex with a stranger you will never see again?

I have a feeling this question might be for Jason's benefit.

I wonder how things went with the two of them.

Did it surprise me to see her in action in the kitchen yesterday? Not really. When Callie sees what she wants, she doesn't hesitate about going after it.

Am I jealous? I think so.

Even though I had perfectly good sex Tuesday night, *and* made Eli leave when we were finished. I wanted nothing more than to crawl into bed with him after it was over but I made him leave. It was the least I could do to salvage a shred of my self-respect.

I would love to be so confident when dealing with men. I would love to be able to tell Ian I will be in his office tomorrow after work and that I expect a good spanking.

Is that really what I want?

I've always been curious about experimenting but never knew how to begin. I've never been able to ask my partner–how do you ask someone to spank you when you're not sure if you'll like it? Not to mention how you are unable to say the words without breaking into a blush the colour of a ripe tomato. I remember when I was with a boyfriend in my twenties and we had talked about trying to spice things up. One night after we both had a fair amount to drink, I tentatively suggested he tie my hands. I had to ask three times before he understood what I was asking him to do, and by the time he had found something to use, most of my excitement had dried up. Plus, he tied them too tight and I lost all circulation. It wasn't a good experience.

With Eli, I always went along with what he suggested. It was always good with Eli; hence the reason I kept allowing him into my pants even with all he's done to me.

Do I really want Ian to bend me over his desk and spank me until I tell him how bad I've been? Do I want to allow myself to be that vulnerable and out of control in such a situation?

"And how is your afternoon so far?"

My reverie shattered, I whip my head up to see Ian standing before my desk.

Not again.

This is the second time he's walked up to me without me noticing. If I'm so obsessed with him, you'd think I'd be able to sense him coming; maybe hear or smell him.

He does smell nice.

"Hi." The heat has already risen to my cheeks and Ian looks down at me with an amused expression.

"How is your day?" he asks again.

Ian has never once asked me how my day was.

That, even more than my daydreams about his desk, sparks something new in me.

"Fine, thank you," I reply. "And yours?"

"Tolerable. Looking forward to our meeting?"

My mouth drops open. "Ah..." I blink up at him, horrified, yet excited that he would come right out and discuss how he asked me to stay late. For what I don't know; to watch? Hopefully to participate, but I'm not really sure...

"The planning meeting for the proposed strip mall north of the city," Ian supplies, his lips curling up at my discomfort. I'm not sure if I've ever seen him smile and the sight of it produces a funny feeling in my stomach. "Did you forget?"

"Of course not," I tell him quickly, glancing down at my appointment book on my desk. I'm one of the few in the office that writes things down as well as slots them into my phone and my organizational abilities have never paid off more. There in the little square with today's date is a notification about the meeting. *Strip meeting. 3 pm.* "I'm all ready." I grab a file and hope it's the correct one.

"I'm glad to see you didn't forget," Ian's eyes seem to give me a secret meaning. But why would he do that? "You look different today," he adds curiously.

I had sex the other night. It's on the tip of my tongue and I have to press my lips together to stop myself from blurting it out. I can't imagine what he'd say. Callie would have had no problem telling anyone that, but I have proven time and time again that I'm not her, even if I did have sex Tuesday night with a total of two very satisfying orgasms. Instead, I shrug my shoulders and stand up. "I'm the same as always."

"No," he says decisively, staring at me intently. "I don't think you are. Or maybe I'm just seeing you differently."

"I'm sure you saw me differently on Friday." I gasp when I realize I've said that out loud.

Ian's reaction is instantaneous. His eyes droop and a lascivious smile spreads across his face. "Yes, well. Agatha had a few questions and was in need of a firm hand that day."

"You don't like to be questioned?" I ask, holding my breath.

"I enjoy using a firm hand," he corrects, his grey eyes holding my own. "And I suspect you would like to question me."

"I might," I say flippantly. Is this really happening? Am I behaving like an idiot, or am I propositioning my boss? My boss, who likes to spank and tie up and made Agatha whimper with delight. I hold his gaze and slowly run the tip of my tongue across my lower lip.

Ian avidly watches the progress of my tongue, and I bite my lip for good measure. If it works for Anastasia Steele...

"We should really be going," he finally points out, tapping his watch with a finger. "We shouldn't keep them waiting."

"I'm ready whenever you are. Sir," I tack on, not meeting his eyes.

What the hell am I playing at?

"I don't like to be kept waiting," he tells me. "I see excessive tardiness as an excuse for discipline."

"I understand," I whisper, bringing my eyes back up see catch his expression. He looks hungrily at me, his eyes idly devouring my face, my body. It excites me when Ian looks at me like that. It won't happen again," I promise.

"Can you be sure of that?" he asks sternly.

"No," I say boldly. There's a hint of a smile on my face as I follow him into the meeting room.

I flash a smile at Abby and Delia and take my seat beside Ian. Agatha rushes in at the last minute and primly takes the seat on the other side of Ian. Is she late because she wants to be disciplined again? Am I going to have to watch it again?

I don't think so. If something is going to happen with me and Ian, *I'm* going to be the recipient, not Agatha.

I sound jealous, even in my own head.

After a quick glance, I refuse to look at Agatha again because I'm picturing Ian's hand resting firmly against her supple thigh, close enough to feel the heat from between her legs.

The simple touch of Ian's hand would excite her, remind her of Friday. He tied her to the desk. She would be thinking about the way he yanked up her legs and buried his mouth between them.

I'm getting excited just thinking about it. I can't imagine what Agatha is going through with Ian right there beside her. And with his hand on her leg.

Maybe his hand isn't on her leg. Ian doesn't participate much in the meeting, but as plans are laid out for the new strip of stores, and parking is discussed as well as how the traffic will be affected, I can't stop the niggling at the back of my head.

It's like someone is watching me.

We are sitting in a U around the table, facing the front of the room. Ian is on my right, which means he has to look around me to see the presentation at the front. If I turn to glance at him, it will be completely obvious that I am looking at him.

Finally, I can't bear it any longer and I look to my right.

To find Ian staring directly at me.

I meet his eyes with surprise but instead of turning away, or even averting his eyes to make it less obvious he is looking at me, the corners of Ian's thin lips curve up in a mocking smile. He has a wide mouth, and a nice smile when he deigns to use it but there's not much to his lips.

I wouldn't turn away from having those lips pressed against mine, or nuzzling my neck...or teasing me between my legs...

Instead of turning away, Ian drops his gaze to my own mouth, and then lower, to where the V of pale skin isn't covered by my blouse. The tip of his tongue pokes out of his mouth.

I can't wait until tomorrow.

Chapter Fifteen

JASON

F RIDAY MORNING I GO to work with a smile on my face. I can't wait to see Callie.

Yesterday was a revelation. Having someone like Callie–having *Callie*–so helpless at my touch, crying out for me, was nothing short of amazing. Not to mention a huge ego boost. I feel like Superman today. No, Spiderman after he saves Mary Jane; Iron Man after he saves the world. The Hulk, after he has fun smashing things.

Why would someone like Callie Champlain be interested in a geek like me?

But when I enter the kitchen and find the girls grouped together as always, Callie makes a point of smiling at me, giving me a wink that swells my chest with pride.

I don't notice the knowing look between Brienne and Sadie, or how Abby rolls her eyes. I beam at Callie.

"And how are you this morning, Jason?" Delia distracts me with her question.

"I'm well, thank you. And you?"

I don't hear what she says because at that moment Michael walks in.

And then it's like I'm completely invisible.

My heart sinks as I see the way Callie smiles at Michael.

Why have I never noticed it before? It's like Callie is lit from within when Michael is near. Why did I never see? How could I ever think I had a chance with her?

"Jason?" I blinked at Sadie beside me. "I asked if you're okay?"

"Fine," I tell her with resignation. Sadie glances over at Callie sharing a laugh with Michael.

"Ah," she says with understanding.

"It doesn't matter," I mutter, turning away.

"It does," she argues, her slim fingers catching my shirt. "You thought...and she...you..."

"You don't have to spell it out."

"She's an idiot," Sadie declares. "I mean, she's my friend, but he's already got a girlfriend. Not that she's looking for anything serious you know. You *do* know that, right? Callie just likes to have fun."

"I did get that impression, yes," I sigh. "It doesn't matter. I don't know why I ever thought–"

"Because you're a great guy," Sadie tells me stoutly. "And the two of you hooked up. So why wouldn't you think? If it's any consolation, it sounds like it was pretty fantastic."

"She told you that?" I ask sharply.

"No," she says, suddenly refusing to meet my eyes. "I mean, I just got the impression that she enjoyed herself with you. That's all. Of course, she wouldn't talk about it."

"Yes, she would." I'm not sure if the thought of Callie discussing me with the others upsets me or gives me heart. I know she enjoyed herself; if there is one thing I know what to do, is pleasure a woman.

"She would. But it was all good," Sadie assures me. "*Really* good." She gives me a shy smile. "Kind of makes me look at you in a new light."

"I'm not sure how to respond to that."

Sadie shrugs. "Be flattered, I guess."

I am flattered. I've always liked Sadie but now she has a special place in my heart. Unfortunately, Callie seems to be taking up the majority of the space at the moment.

"Sadie, I think there's something you should know." I glance around the others chatting and laughing together. "You've always been so nice to me and I don't know if the others have told her yet–do you know who Alma is married to?"

"No–who? And why does it matter?"

"She's married to Julian Donovan," I tell her.

Chapter Sixteen

SADIE

I GO STRAIGHT TO Alma's desk after kitchen talk is over. "We need to talk," I tell her ominously. I feel ominous. How *dare* she not tell me?

"Good morning, Sadie," Alma says with a carefree smile. "Happy Friday."

"Is there somewhere we can talk?" I ask, flicking my eyes to Agatha. How much does she know? She has her own secrets to keep.

"Don't mind me," Agatha says, rising from her perch behind the counter. "I've got to run something up to Mr. Donovan's office. Back in a few minutes."

I watch as she walks away, waiting until I can no longer see her, before turning to Alma. Even then, I wait until I hear the chime of the elevator before speaking. "Does she know you're married to the boss?"

"Who?" Alma asks innocently.

"You. Married to Julian Donovan."

"Is that a problem?"

I throw up my hands. "It's not bad enough that you're *married* but that you're married to my *boss*! Don't you think that's a problem? I could be fired!"

"And I could be divorced, so we'll have to be discrete."

"We won't be anything, Alma," I tell her seriously.

Her face falls. "You're breaking up with me?"

"There's no breaking up. I don't know what this is, but it's not something you need to break up. We just need to end it."

"I don't want to," she whispers.

I don't either, is on the tip of my tongue, but to say that would give her hope. "I can't do this anymore. Sneaking around at work; you married to my boss! Why didn't you tell me?"

"I didn't think it was important."

"Not important!" I cry, louder than I mean to. Alma jumps up from around the other side of the desk and grabs my arm.

"Not here," she hisses. "Let's go to the closet."

"We're not doing anything," I tell her, allowing myself to be dragged along.

"No, that's fine. Just let me explain where we can have some privacy."

I'm quiet until we're back in the supply closet, the scene of our earlier dalliances. Alma leads me to the back table and I hop up on it. "I should have told you," she begins. "But I was afraid you'd react like this. Julian and I don't have a conventional marriage."

"What's that supposed to mean?"

"We're not often together. We live separate lives, so to speak."

"What's that supposed to mean?" I repeat. "I don't understand. You're married. To him."

"Yes, but–"

"That's all I need to know." I move to slide off the table but Alma stops me, standing between my legs with her hands warm on my thighs. Even as angry as I am at her deceit, I can't stop thinking about those hands moving a little farther up my legs.

"You knew I was married before!"

"Not to my boss! Look, Alma, this has been fun–" I'm not imagining it; Alma's hands are sliding up my legs, cupping my pussy with one hand, as nimble fingers unbutton my jeans. "No! Stop!"

"You liked it when I came to you in the kitchen," Alma says breathlessly.

"That was different!"

"You'll like it now." I stare in astonishment; she's so quick that my jeans are undone and she's tugging them down my hips before I do anything to stop it.

And I must stop her. Even though I want what she's offering.

"Alma, no," I give a weak attempt to push her hand away, even as I lift myself off the table, allowing her to rid me of my pants quicker than Evan had ever done.

"Sadie, I can't breathe without you," Alma tells me, crouching over my lap, her fingers already pushing the elastic of my underwear to the side. "I don't know how to live without you. Even if it's over, just let me give you this one last time. I need to taste you one last time. Please?" she implores.

She doesn't give me a chance to respond before her mouth is on my pussy; pulling my leg up on the table, I feel her tongue probe questioningly against my lips.

With a frustrated groan, I touch the back of her head. One last time and then it's over. Over.

Alma begins to lick me frantically, desperate to please me. I lean back, bracing against my arms, resigning myself to the fate of a woman desperate to pleasure me.

It could be worse. She could be married to my boss.

"No," I groan.

"I can't stop," Alma says, plunging her fingers into my wetness. "You don't want me to. I can tell." Her mouth is inches from my aching pussy, I can feel her breath. That's when she begins to suck my clit, sucking it so hard and for long, I moan as I push my hips forward against her greedy mouth. Her fingers thrust in and out rhythmically with a knobby sensation a smooth penis lacks. Add the sucking, the feel of her tongue lapping at my clit, it's no wonder I can't control my cries.

Alma knows what I want, what I need. How can I end things with her when she can make me feel this good? I push her head, spreading my legs wider, shamelessly begging for more. She fucks me with her fingers, with her mouth, making me forget anything but her, fucks me until I come with a cry that's part sob of frustration.

"Make me come, Sadie, with your fingers," Alma says, getting to her feet and pressing herself between my legs. She takes my hand and reaches under her skirt. She and Agatha are the only ones who aren't allowed casual Friday. I reach between her legs and find her wet and ready under her panties, her clit hot and swollen. I begin to run my fingers up and down, and Alma grasps my wrists with her hand and guides me. Soon she's frantically using my hand as a toy to pleasure herself, with a grip so tight I can't pull away.

It's over soon; Alma comes with a silent cry, her head falling into the hollow of my shoulder.

"We shouldn't have done that," I say weakly after a moment. Alma sighs, breathing deeply into my neck and I shiver. Then she pulls away.

"You're wrong," she tells me. "We'll continue to do that."

"What?" I must have heard her incorrectly but when I search her face, I see that she's serious.

And has a dangerous glint in her eyes.

"I like fucking you, Sadie, so we're going to keep doing this, whenever I want to. Whenever I call, you come running and you let me do whatever I want to you, wherever I want to. You can't say no any longer."

I stare at her, unable to comprehend what I'm hearing.

"Because if you say no, I'll tell my husband exactly what you're doing to me, and then you should be really scared for your precious job."

And with that, Alma gives me a sweet smile and leaves me in the supply closet, alone to put my pants on.

What the hell am I supposed to do now?

Chapter Seventeen

ABBY

I'M EMAILING MY HUSBAND again.

This is the third time I've done it this week and while I'm still embarrassed to begin, it is getting easier. The thought of what will happen tonight makes it worthwhile.

Last night I gave Ben a blowjob while he was doing the dishes. And because the kids were already tucked into bed, he lifted me onto the counter and made me come with his mouth. Twice.

Our sex life is definitely getting exciting this week. I'm happy about this. I just wish Callie had talked to me sooner and given me the idea. Happily married parents *can* have a great sex life–this week I'm the perfect example of that!

Have you ever wanted to see me with another woman? I begin today's missive. I think it might get his attention.

Yes!! Guess I was right. Definitely got his attention.

Why? What would you want me to do?

I wait impatiently for Ben to respond, glancing continually out the door to make sure no one can see what I'm doing. I'm sure the others in the cubicles would have no clue I could be doing something so outrageous as sending sexy emails to my husband.

Maybe the thought wouldn't be exciting to them.

It is for me.

I'd want to see another woman make you come. I want to see her head between your legs, using her tongue and her mouth to give you pleasure. I want to watch that.

I catch my breath at the image Ben presents me. Me, lying on a bed with a faceless, nameless woman crouched between my legs. I definitely enjoy oral sex with Ben, but now, after hearing about Sadie and Alma, I can't help but wonder how different it would be with a woman.

Would a woman know more about my body? Would she have a gentle touch, or be firm and demanding like a man?

I like it when Ben is demanding.

Are you thinking about it?

I'm not sure if Ben is asking if I'm thinking about being with a woman *right now* or turning his fantasy into a reality in the future. Knowing how well Ben knows me, I suspect it's the former, but I surprised him once already this week.

I can't stop thinking about it, I type breathlessly. Which is the truth. *It excites me.*

How excited are you?

I'm closing the door. And I am, getting up from my desk and giving the door a click to make sure it's closed properly.

Are you touching yourself?

I smile as I read Ben's response, my hand sliding under the desk like the other day. This is something I never thought I would ever do. Masturbating in my office, knowing my husband was doing the same thing. I know for sure because we showed each other what we did last night.

Yes.

Me too.

Is it good?

Yes. Not as good as you.

I spread my legs as much as I can under the desk and arch my pelvis as I rub my clit with my fingers, crouching over my desk to hide what I'm doing.

I need to fuck you again tonight.

How?

I want you on top. I want you to touch yourself while I fuck you.

I'd rather you touch me.

I'll do it first. I'll use my mouth again. Did you like that?

I hear a sound in the room and realize it came from me. I'm not sure if it's because of what Ben wrote, or how my fingers feel against my clit.

Yes.

Are you wet? Do you want me now?

So much

I want to do it on your desk...

I think of what Brienne told us about Ian then, of Agatha bent over his desk. I don't think Ben is picturing that, though.

I'd lay you on the desk...you'd wrap your legs around my waist. And then I'd fuck you...hard. Hard enough to make you scream.

I screamed the other night

Remembering the feel of Ben's mouth on me, tonguing me with abandon, I bring myself to swift orgasm; not as intense as the one my husband brought me to, but satisfactory enough to make me let out a deep sigh as I come. I wanted to scream right then

My turn…

The smile is fixed on my face as I wait for Ben to respond, which he does after he finishes his solo act. *This is getting to be a habit*

Are you complaining?

NO WAY! See you at home tonight. Love you

I'm humming as I send my own email, concentrating on thoughts of my husband that I don't hear the knock on my door until it's repeated loudly.

"Come in?" I call breathlessly, thanking every god out there that I was so quick to come today. Especially when Julian Donovan opens the door and smiles at me with those blue eyes.

"Got a second, Ms. Park?" he asks politely.

"Of course." I wave a hand at the chair on the other side of my desk, not getting up because I'd have to adjust my skirt which is still hiked up over my thighs. I hope my cheeks aren't flushed.

I suspect they are.

"What can I do for you, Mr. Donovan? I thought our meeting wasn't until three o'clock?"

"Julian, please," he says, leaning so casually in the chair I wonder if this is a social visit. And I then wonder why he would be paying a social visit to me.

"Abby," I tell him unnecessarily.

"Abby, we seem to have a situation happening here at Hever."

"What kind of situation?" I ask when he pauses.

"It's a delicate situation, especially discussing it with you. It seems that there is inappropriate behaviour going on in the office."

My heart stops beating. *He knows about my emails to Ben.*

Chapter Eighteen

BRIENNE

ALL DAY, I'VE BEEN deliberating if I should wait for Ian to say something. If he asks me to stay, should I? What do I want from him? All day I'm in an internal debate; will curiosity win out?

And then I get so busy, I lose track of time as one by one my colleagues call goodbye to me. Finally, I'm the only one left.

"Brienne?" Ian calls from the door of his office. He's one of the few who doesn't wear jeans to the office and I'm glad. I'm sure he could fill out a pair of Levis like no other, but I like him looking more professional. "Do you mind coming in here for a moment?"

My mouth dry, I stand, pausing behind my desk for a long moment before I move.

"Don't make me ask you again?" Ian says quietly. "I don't like repeating myself. I see that as an excuse for discipline."

My feet seem to have a will of their own as they begin to move towards his office. He smiles arrogantly when I stand before him, silently appraising me, his eyes crawling over my body like he's stripping me naked.

It's an odd sensation, but one I don't find unpleasant.

"I'd like you to come in," he invites, stepping back so I can enter his office.

This time I don't hesitate and he shuts the door behind me. I hold my breath as he stands before me, silently appraising me with his grey eyes. What do I do? What does he expect of me?

Is this what I really want?

"Are you sure about this?"

It's Ian asking, not the voice in my head.

"You have to trust me not to hurt you, not to do anything you can't bear. The safe word is red; if you say that I'll stop immediately. Do you understand?"

"Yes," I tell him softly.

"Please take off your clothes." It may be the least romantic beginning to an interlude I've ever heard, but the words send a tremor through me nonetheless. I quickly pull off my cardigan and the long-sleeved T-shirt I'm wearing underneath; I'm easing my jeans down my hips before I deign to look him in the eye again. And then I'm standing before him in my second-best matching set of bra and panties.

For some strange reason, I didn't think Ian deserved my best set, the pale pink lacy bra with matching thong. I do buy more than flannel pyjamas at *Victoria's Secret*.

"Everything," Ian orders in a quiet voice.

Suddenly I know exactly what Anastasia in *Fifty Shades* felt like; excited but scared, aroused but fearful. The not-knowing is the worst part. I reach behind me and unhook my bra, letting it fall onto the floor before I daintily remove my panties.

I'm standing naked in my boss's office.

There's a heavy silence between us. I have no idea what to say; what could I say in this situation? Just when it's getting too awkward and I'm ready to grab my clothes and make a run for it, Ian reaches out a hand and cups my breast, moving his thumb over my nipple, which instantly hardens.

I bite back my whimper as a jolt of desire courses through my body. I'll stay. How could there be any question?

"On the desk please," Ian instructs.

"How...?"

"Face down."

This is how it's going to be then. "Have I done something wrong?" I ask meekly as I lean over the side of Ian's desk, leaving my bare ass vulnerable.

"I believe so. Don't you?" he asks, caressing my bottom with a warm hand.

"Yes," I say in a shaky voice. "I've been bad."

"How bad?" he asks, now cupping my buttocks, sliding his hand between my legs. I know he can feel how wet I am. His finger traces my cleft, allowing no more than a tentative, teasing touch. I stare at the door and the window to make sure no one is watching *me*.

Everything is completely closed. We're alone. This is what I wanted.

"I've been very bad," I finally whisper, and close my eyes, readying myself.

Even so, the shock of his hand against my bare ass takes me by surprise, his hand firm and flat against my cheek. As soon as he spanks me, Ian begins caressing the area softly, as if he's trying to remove the sting, and then his hand moves between my legs. I spread them wider, all my weight on the desk, as his finger slides over my clit, rubbing it questioningly.

Slap. This time it's the other cheek and this time his finger darts inside me. I moan quietly, my head resting on my arms.

"No noise," he instructs. *Slap.* His fingers roam freely on my ass, between my legs; longer this time, giving my reddened ass a chance to recover from the sting. *Slap.* It's difficult to keep quiet, when he spanks me and when his hand is between my legs. Pain, and then pleasure.

I can hear my breathing sounding harsh in the quiet office, and bite my lip to stifle my whimpers. The pain isn't that bad. *Slap.*

I suck in my breath. Okay, that one stung a little.

"Stand up, please, " Ian orders. I rise on shaky legs, my ass stinging and my pussy wanting more of his touch. "Turn around."

Ian helps me sit on his desk and the sudden coolness of the metal feels good against my reddened buttocks. Thankfully he allows me to lie down. Without a word, he rolls his chair around to my side and spreads my legs apart with his hands.

Is it over? Will he..?

"Is that it?" I ask hesitantly, resting on my arms. I don't know what to expect, what I want.

Ian looks up at me lying on his desk, wide-eyed and with a sore ass. He reaches up with one hand to touch my breast, dragging his hand back along my stomach, to my thigh.

"Enough for the first time," he says. "You did very well. But I'm not through with you yet."

He bends his head and plunges his tongue inside me without any preparation, nudging my clit with his nose. Drawing my legs onto the desk, I spread them as wide as I can, giving him full access. Wheeling the chair closer, Ian pulls me closer to the edge, leaving his hands clasping my ass as he slowly, languorously begins to tongue me; beginning from my clit to my ass with stops along the way.

I sigh with relief. This is like nothing else I've ever experienced. Ian's mouth...

After only the third trek, I'm beginning to squirm with pleasure and arch my hips to give him more of me, all of me. Ian spends countless minutes focused on just my clit, licking me with just the right amount of pressure to make me moan and whimper. It's impossible to be quiet; the sensations are too much. I feel my orgasm building deep within and expect it to crash over me, but then Ian stops and begins to explore me with his fingers, pausing frequently to suck on my clit, sending exquisite shivers through my legs and forcing me to grab the back of his head so he can take even more of me into his mouth.

When he starts licking my clit again, the pleasure is almost unbearable.

"Quiet," he instructs after a particularly loud moan escapes me. I slap my hand across my mouth.

His fingers thrust inside me—two maybe three—moving slowly but insistently; his tongue mirrors the rhythm against my clit. I can feel a climax swiftly build inside me like none I have ever felt before and then I explode with a cry, the sensations going on and on and I think it might last forever. Ian continues to lick and suck and finger fuck me like a master. I writhe on the desk, coming again and again, unable to stop, not wanting to stop until he lifts up his head.

I lie there and try to catch my breath but then Ian pulls me up by my arms, guiding me to where he sits in the chair with his cock rearing up out of his pants, sheathed for protection and ready to go. Without a word, Ian helps me straddle him. His chair is wide enough so my knees can easily fit on either side of his, and sturdy enough–I hope–for both of our weights.

I gasp at the thickness of his cock as I slide down onto him and Ian grasps my waist. This is not what I expected.

Slowly I begin to move, my legs protesting as I ride him. My pussy is tight around his cock. I let out a strangled cry at a flash of pain as Ian thrusts his hips up and pierces me deeply. He grabs my ass with both hands, helping me find my rhythm as he thrusts into me. My fingers grip the back of his chair and I can't bother to muffle my cries as he fucks me.

"Look at me when you come," Ian instructs me. I want to tell him I can't come like this, but then I'm awash in sensations once again.

"I think...my g-spot," I gasp with delight.

"I should hope so," Ian growls, going even deeper, harder. Strong hands lift me up and down and all I can do is hang on to the chair.

Quickly, too unbelievably quick, I feel another orgasm begin to crash over me and cry out loudly as Ian thrusts into me relentlessly. My back arches, I grip anything–finding out later it was Ian's shoulders, leaving an imprint of my nails through his shirt–as I come once more with a series of harsh shrieks that ring through his office, joined by a growl-like groan as Ian erupts inside me.

Unable to move, I stay where I am, feeling Ian's arms slowly wrap around me.

This was not what I expected.

It was so much better.

Chapter Nineteen

ABBY

T HE OTHERS ARE ALREADY crowded around the Tassimo when I stop by the kitchen on Monday morning.

"You're so late," Delia says with concern when she catches sight of me. "I was getting worried something was wrong."

"Early morning meeting with Julian," I say grimly.

"And how is our fearless leader this fine morning?" Callie asks breezily. She's leaning against the counter, looking intimate with Michael smiling down at her.

I glance at Jason, who has followed me in. He was with me at the meeting. After a quick look at Callie, he refuses to meet her eyes.

"Is everything okay?" Brienne asks seriously.

"Not for some. Ian was terminated this morning," I say, wincing as her face falls with horror.

"What?" she cries with real distress.

"Agatha pressed harassment charges," Jason supplies. "They fired him."

"Wow," Callie says. "Because they had sex in the office?"

"I think it was the nature of the sex," I explain. "Julian was curious if anyone else would come forward." I glance at a white-faced Brienne, who gives her head a shake. I don't want to ask her in front of the others, but Callie has no such qualms.

"Did you think it was consensual?"

"It was!" Brienne cries. "We even talked about it, with safe words and everything."

Silence crashes over the kitchen. "I think Callie was referring to when you witnessed the incident between Ian and Agatha," I finally manage to say.

"You didn't tell me," Callie accuses her.

"I haven't had the chance," Brienne snaps. "And now..."

"Playtoy is gone," Callie says sympathetically.

"I think I'm missing something here," Michael says with confusion.

"It's that Brienne—" Sadie begins, but Delia cuts her off.

"It's of little importance now," she says with a smile. "What matters now is that we'll be getting another controller."

"They should just give you the job," Carl suggests.

"Brienne is more qualified," Delia argues.

"I can't work in that office," Brienne mutters. I'm desperate to find out what happened to her and Ian and I wonder if Jason can sense it.

"I've got to get back to work," he announces once he has his tea. "Just so you all know, though, Julian has asked me to begin monitoring internal emails more closely."

I'm so distracted by thoughts of Brienne and Ian that it takes a moment for Jason's words to sink in. "Monitor what?" I choke.

"Emails. Internal only," he tells me. Why can't he look me in the eye?

"Ab, are you okay?" Delia cries as I clutch the counter to steady myself. My legs can barely hold me up. *Internal emails.*

Ben.

"Oh my God!" I cry.

"No one knows," Jason tells me urgently. "No one has seen them."

"I have to delete them! I have to tell Ben."

"It might be a good idea," Jason says softly.

Without another thought about Brienne, I head for the door and crash into the solid wall of a man standing in the doorway.

"Abby?" It's a familiar voice, with a South African accent, one I never expected to hear again. Slowly, I raise my eyes to his face, his smile still able to warm me despite being chilled from Jason's warning.

"Cooper? Cooper Garrison? What the hell are you doing here?"

Abby's past pays her a visit in Secrets and Lies! Find out more about what her office mates are up to!

Secrets and Lies

ANNA ELLIS

Chapter One

SADIE

"I DON'T THINK IT's going to work," I tell Callie, gnawing on my thumbnail. It's almost bitten down to the quick and I'm glad when Callie slaps my hand away from my mouth.

I stare at the flashing red light on the phone on my desk, signalling a message. Alma has called, requesting my presence.

"Why not?" Callie demands. "The little bitch is *blackmailing* you! It's totally going to work. Why wouldn't it work?"

Callie is on her usual perch on the corner of my desk and I wish she'd keep her voice down. I wish I believed in her plan more, but the truth is I'm still reeling from Alma's threats.

"I like fucking you, Sadie, so we're going to keep doing this, whenever I want to. Whenever I call, you come running and you let me do whatever I want to you, wherever I want to. You can't say no any longer. Because if you say no, I'll tell my husband exactly what you're doing to me, and then you should be really scared for your precious job."

I had no idea that when I started this thing with Alma, she was married to Julian Donovan, the president of Hever Construction, the company I've worked for the last year and a half. I really like my job. I really need my job, and it's not worth losing for some action with Alma in a supply closet.

Even though it was really, really good action.

But when I told Alma two weeks ago that I couldn't continue our relationship, or whatever I can call it, I thought she might be a little upset, but would understand. She's the married one after all, and being the victim of an unfaithful partner in the past, I couldn't live with myself being the one to cause another person that sort of pain. I had known Alma was married, it was wrong of me to let things progress the way I did.

I had clearly been caught up in the moment.

I should have realized something wasn't right when Alma got kind of needy. Possessive. Her way of thinking was that since she knew what buttons of mine to push, she could go around pushing them whenever she wanted to. Wherever she wanted.

Even though there's more action going on in this office than in an episode of *The Bachelorette*, it's still a place of work for me.

Alma didn't see it that way, probably because her husband is the boss. She sees me as her personal playtoy.

That doesn't float well with me.

The whole thing is a big ball of confusion. I still consider myself a heterosexual, even though Alma excites the hell out of me. The first time I was with a woman was my neighbour Laurel, who had done her best to cheer me up over a bad breakup. Evan and I had been together for years, and I had had no clue he was cheating on me nearly the entire time. Laurel had helped take my mind off the pain but I knew the experience was only a one-shot deal.

Three shots, actually.

Alma helped me get over Evan a little more but despite my being grateful, the whole time we were getting busy in the supply closet, I knew deep down Alma wasn't right for me. I finally told her we shouldn't see each other.

But then she turned mean. Not bitchy nasty, like she insulted my shoes or told me I needed to trim the wobbly bits. But mean; cruel and nasty. Vicious, like some sort of vengeance demon. She actually threatened me, turned *hold-the-sex-over-my head* spiteful and heartless. Who does that?

When Alma admitted she was married, I should have run from her, not given her the naked kind of comfort. I should have clued into the *my husband doesn't understand me,* which is the oldest excuse in the book.

Of course her husband Julian doesn't understand her–Alma is a world-class bitch!

But she gives amazing head.

I frown at Callie. "Are you *sure* you want to do this?"

Callie was my first choice to confess my sins to and she didn't disappoint. She came up with a plan that was so out there it might actually work.

Callie grins, her big blue eyes telling me how much she's into this. "From the sounds of it, I won't have to do much but lay back and enjoy myself and I'm *always* up for that. Is she really as good as you say?"

"I haven't had much to compare to," I remind her. "This is a new thing for me."

Callie snorts. "A girl can tell when she's getting good head, even when it's the first time."

"Then she's good," I say reluctantly.

"We'll see if she's better than Jason." Another grin which widens as I clamp my hands over my ears to avoid hearing details.

"I told you I don't want to hear about him!"

Callie actually doesn't usually give specific details; she's more of an all-encompassing statement sort of girl. But she's brought up Jason's name more than a few times, which is unusual. She's normally a love 'em and leave 'em type of girl.

"He's so hot," Callie lowers her voice. "A-*mazing*. I'd say top ten, but don't tell him that or it'll go to his head. And he doesn't need any more help with that."

"Callie!" I hiss. I know she's not talking about the size of his ego.

"So we're all straight? Even though we're still not sure about you," Callie looks pointedly at me and I drop my head.

"I'm going back to boys. Women are too difficult."

"Only the crazy ones. Back to The Plan."

"You don't have to do this," I protest. "I think I'm asking too much."

"You didn't ask, I offered. And believe me, I wouldn't have offered if I wasn't somewhat intrigued."

"Only somewhat?" It's my turn to give Callie the knowing look. She's been after me for details of Alma since I first confessed to what we were doing.

Callie laughs. "Come on, let me do this. It's an *adventure*. I haven't had any fun since Jason."

"And that was over two weeks ago," I tease. "You must be in a drought."

"Oh, please. It was Tuesday."

"This last Tuesday? So it wasn't just a one-time thing?"

I don't know how I feel about that. Jason is a friend, I remind myself. I like talking to him and we have a lot in common. For the last week, we've been meeting for tea in the afternoon, something I haven't shared with Callie. For one thing, she would wonder why it was only *tea* we were enjoying and secondly, I like having something to keep to myself. Since working at Hever, I've shared pretty much all the details of my life with Callie, Brienne, Abby, and Delia and while I love them to death, it's nice having something none of them know about. It's like I have a secret.

A much nicer secret than the one I tried to keep about Alma.

"I thought you didn't want to talk about Jason?" Callie asks suspiciously. She has the best women's intuition I've ever witnessed. If anyone is thinking, talking about her, or even smelling her perfume as she walks by, she knows about it.

"I don't," I say firmly. "Back to The Plan."

"I like how we capitalize it," Callie grins. She may be thirty-eight, ten years older than I am, but she's much more of a kid than I ever was. "So, I've been chatting her up for the last two weeks. You've been avoiding her as much as you can, so I'm sure she's *in the mood.* I'll head to her desk late this afternoon, work my Callie charm and she'll whisk me off to the Closet of Sins, where you'll be hiding out. Take a few pics with your phone—of her giving, not receiving—and then jump out and say boo. We'll convince her you'll go to Julian and tell him what she's been doing if she doesn't leave you alone. Problem solved."

"You make it sound so easy."

"It is—for you. I'll be the one enduring this harsh punishment, of being a slave to the desire of another. Hey, make sure she finishes me before you stop it, okay?"

"You're enjoying this way too much," I grimace.

Callie winks. "Anything for a friend, Sadie. Anything at all."

Callie's plan starts out well. By five o'clock, I've hidden among the shelves in the darkened supply closet, waiting for Callie and Alma. I can't help but gaze at the table at the back of the cramped room; the table where Alma perched me, her head between my legs, making me beg for more. The feel of her tongue, her fingers inside me...

Luckily, I hear the door open before I get too carried away.

I'm kneeling on the floor behind a stack of boxes, hidden from Alma's view, but it also means I can't see them. I can hear them, though.

"I've never been with a woman before," I hear Callie say.

I grimace; anyone who knows Callie knows that's complete bullshit.

But apparently, she's convinced Alma. "It can be so much more than with a man," Alma says in her husky voice. "I find women softer, more sensitive."

I hear the scrape of table legs as Callie backs against it, the sounds of lips meeting in an urgent kiss. I can't see it, but I can hear it all. I check my phone again—lots of battery.

Biting my nails seems to drown out the sounds they are making.

I hear a low moan and wonder if my little vibrating ducky at home has lots of power. I might need something after this.

I picture Alma's hand between Callie's legs, exploring her wetness. She had never been really interested in my breasts. Alma has always been clear that she wants pussy and lots of it. Callie has one thing right—there's not much she has to do. Alma loves being in control. She likes to dominate, the giver rather than the receiver. That way she can do what she wants, decide how she wants it and can stop when she wants to.

She liked to make me beg. I wonder if she'll try that with Callie.

Low, breathy moans. Murmuring voices. I crane my neck in an attempt to see what's going on. From the sounds of it, something is definitely going on. Is Alma fingering her? Rubbing Callie's clit with firm and unyielding fingers?

Despite everything, I can't help but wish Alma was touching me.

Are Alma's fingers inside Callie? Thrusting deep with a knobbiness a penis can't produce?

Callie cries out. Did she come already? Is it over?

If I move to another set of shelves, I can see what's going on. Do I really want to watch?

"Sit up here," I hear Alma invite Callie. As Callie settles herself on the same table I sat on, I crawl forward, my hands and knees gathering grit from the floor. If I stay low and peer around the boxes of toner, I can watch them.

My mouth falls open as the two women come into view.

Callie is sitting on the table, leaning back on her elbows, her skirt hiked up around her waist. As I watch, Alma positions one of Callie's long legs on the table beside her and kneels down.

She had me in the very same position. I sat there, just like Callie is, with Alma's head between my legs.

I know when Alma begins to tongue her because Callie cries out.

As I watch them, I can almost feel what Alma is doing to Callie; long slow strokes between her folds, deliberately avoiding her clit until the need is almost painful. Exploring every inch of her with her tongue, her fingers until finally when the ache is becoming unbearable, focusing on her clit. Quick firm flickers, long slow circles around the nub, the blood vessels becoming engorged until the sensitive skin reacts to the faintest touch.

And then Alma will suck her clit.

I know exactly when she begins to suck Callie because she gasps aloud and pushes Alma's head deeper between her legs.

"Do you like that?" I hear Alma's muffled voice ask.

Her voice will be sending vibrations into Callie's pussy.

"Yes," Callie groans. "God, don't stop."

"I want to make sure you're enjoying it."

"Oh, god, *yes!*" Alma is teasing her; she'll be giving Callie timid flicks of her tongue, making her beg for more."

"What do you want me to do?" Alma asks. I picture the smile on Alma's face. She has Callie right where she wants her.

"Fuck me," Callie groans. "Fuck me with your mouth. Don't ever stop..."

"Say please."

"Fuck! *Please* fuck me now!"

I should be taking pictures of this. I should be taking a video because I might want to watch this again.

This is better than any porn movie I've ever watched because I know what it feels like to have Alma's mouth against my pussy, her fingers thrusting inside me while her tongue...

I've never wanted her mouth on me so much.

I push the red triangle and my phone begins recording. Will it pick up Callie's frantic cries of pleasure? Will it hear Alma's groans as she begins to touch herself under her skirt?

"Oh, god that's *so* good! Right there—don't stop! Oh god, don't—right there!"

I copy Alma's movements; with a shaky hand I keep recording but the other begins fumbling under my own skirt. I never imagined this would be so arousing. I don't think Callie will last much longer but the heaviness between my legs is becoming a problem and I need to do something about it right now...

I push my fingers into my panties, finding the warm wetness. I imagine my fingers are Alma's tongue as I frantically rub my clit. I'm almost there already; my hips jerking forward in time with my heavy breaths.

I have to be quiet, I order myself, stifling a moan. I wish it really was Alma's mouth against my pussy, sucking my clit.

"Oh, god!" Callie cries. Both hands are on the back of Alma's head. She's close, but so am I. So close.

I try to keep my hand steady as I feel the waves build, racing through my legs. Eyes closed, head thrown back, I explode with a quick, intense orgasm.

I slap my hand still holding the phone over my mouth as I come quick and hard, hearing Callie's cries echoing the noises I want to be making.

Whoever watches this video is going to know the exact moment when I came.

The thought makes me want to press stop, but I focus back on the activity before me and record Callie's own orgasm. I find that she's surprisingly quiet when she comes; her back arched, a wordless cry on her lips as she climaxes.

Alma stands up, a gloating smile on her face.

"I knew you'd like that," Alma tells her.

"You have no idea," Callie says breathlessly. "More than I thought I would."

"I want your fingers on me. I'm going to dream about you tonight," Alma croons, pressing her body between Callie's legs, and gliding her hand under her skirt. "I'm going to make myself come thinking about you, right beside my husband in bed..."

"About that husband of yours," Callie begins briskly.

This is my cue. I just don't know how Callie is able to do it now; I'm still having difficulty controlling my own breathing. But I silently get to my feet and step out around the shelves while Callie's hand is trapped by Alma's hand under her skirt.

Alma is probably beside herself with excitement. I know she has quick orgasms but she's not getting one this time.

"Boo," I say.

Chapter Two

ABBY

"SO THEN WHAT HAPPENED?"

I can't believe Sadie came up with this idea to get back at Alma. Actually, I know she didn't—this is Callie's plot through and through. There's no way Sadie would have come up with such a way to get back at Alma; she's not that devious.

Speaking of devious...

I haven't been able to look Jason in the eyes for the last few weeks. Knowing he has read the emails I sent Ben has made conversations decidedly uncomfortable between us. Finding out one of Jason's responsibilities is to monitor inter-office email was a bit of a shock for all of us, but especially me. I had recently gotten into the habit of sending my husband Ben sexy scenarios via email, and Jason had access to them all.

It was like Jason was in our bedroom while Ben and I were intimate.

Jason had read about my desires; he knew what excited me. Did he–could he–know that what I had described to Ben had turned me on so much that I had secretly masturbated in my office? Not so secret–Ben obviously knew what I was doing during our sexting, but it's not that I wanted it to be common knowledge.

Is it called sexting when it's through email?

Finding out Jason had read our emails hasn't seemed to bother my husband; Ben was over at Jason's last night at one of their game nights, talking and laughing with no thoughts to the fact Jason read all about his wife touching herself at work.

"She was pissed," Callie says with delight and I wrench my thoughts away from my embarrassment and back to Alma. "Like a little hellcat."

"We gave her the weekend to think it over," Sadie adds. "I haven't heard anything from her, which is a good sign."

"I can't believe she was using threats to make you have sex with her," Delia says indignantly.

"Yes," Callie agrees. "She really didn't need to use threats."

"That good?" Brienne asks skeptically.

Callie nods with a big smile on her pretty face. "Not that I'm an expert or anything."

"If you're not, I don't know who is," Brienne sighs.

At that particular moment, Cooper Garrison walks into the kitchen with Michael. Callie immediately brightens when she sees Michael; I still don't understand that relationship. Callie makes it clear that there is no relationship save a friendship, and friends without benefits really isn't Callie's style. But Michael makes no secret that he's happy with his girlfriend, and Callie does nothing to change that, even though I suspect she would be able to persuade any red-blooded man to stray.

Callie just has this way about her. She would never have to resort to sexy emails to keep things exciting with her husband. She did give me the idea, however.

And it did work. Even now that Ben and I only send G-rated emails while at work, things have definitely heated up between us again. We've been married nine years–still happy and in love but kids really can put a damper on the romance part. Since I started the email campaign, relations have been getting steamier. Sex has always been good for Ben and me but lately, he's like a man-inspired. Only last night, after the kids were asleep, Ben made me so distracted that I missed half the episode of *Orange is the New Black*. And then he wouldn't let me rewatch it! Who would have thought he could be so imaginative with–?

"Have a good weekend?" Cooper asks, rudely interrupting my reminiscing. He smiles brightly at me, his South African accent making the words sound erotic.

Exotic, not erotic.

"Sure," I reply shortly. I know it's not Cooper's fault I feel awkward around him. Even though, if I remember correctly, it *was* his fault that we shared a kiss back when we worked together at the law firm. As I remind myself countless times, it was a *long* time ago. Cooper obviously has gotten over the moment and has been nothing but friendly towards me. It was a bit of a shock when he suddenly started working at Hever, taking over the controller position after Ian was terminated because of the sexual harassment charges.

Not that Cooper would be anything more than friendly. Taking a position after the former employee is fired for licentious behaviour means that Cooper isn't going to be doing anything but smiling at me, or any other woman here at Hever.

Not that I was at all worried about something happening between us again.

Not that there was even an *us*. It was just one kiss!

It's strange how one kiss can make everything so awkward.

It's not Cooper's fault that every time I see him, I remember how it felt to be in his arms and I have to go and have sex with my husband at the earliest possible opportunity to wipe away the memory.

Once again, Ben's getting laid tonight.

Cooper narrows his blue eyes at me. Everyone mistakes him for Australian not only because his South African accent sounds similar but because Cooper looks like the poster boy for the land down under. Tall, tousled blonde hair and friendly smiles on a rugged face, with the broad shoulders of a rugby player and the lean hips and taut abs of a surfer.

I wonder if he's got that V-indentation along his hips?

But I prefer the dark good looks of Ben. My husband has amazing green eyes and his body is pretty good, for someone who doesn't exercise other than video games on the Wii.

"So, Abby, what're the thoughts on how I'm doing so far?" Cooper asks, dragging my mind back from the comparisons I keep tormenting myself with.

Good, he thinks the awkwardness is because of the job, not because I can't look at him without wanting to know if he's as good a kisser as I remember.

Maybe I'll reward Ben with a blowjob tonight.

I shrug. "I'm not the best person to say. I don't have much to do with the accounting."

"Yes, but you have friends, and friends talk," he smiles, motioning to Brienne and Delia. Between the two of them, they practically run the department.

"Work is usually not the main priority for our discussions," I tell him. Unless it's about having sex at work.

I don't say that. I don't have sex at work. I can't even email about wanting sex at work now that Jason reads everything.

"Yes, but we're friends," Cooper insists, with the smile that used to drag me from my desk to *Starbucks* for a mocha frappuccino any time of the day. "At least we used to be."

Why does he sound so wistful? I rarely go to *Starbucks* anymore.

I held his gaze for the first time since he surprised me in the kitchen. Cooper's eyes are so blue, a brilliant sky blue.

Ben has beautiful green eyes.

"Are we still friends, Abby?" Cooper asks in a low voice.

"Of course," I say automatically, finally averting my eyes when it's becoming uncomfortable to keep looking at him.

"Really? Every time I see you, you're looking away from me." More than wistful, Cooper's moved on to disappointed. "I miss being able to make you smile. We always had fun together. Remember–"

"I'm married," I mutter because there isn't anything else I can say that would allow me to feel guiltless about talking to him. I glance around to see if anyone is paying attention to how close Cooper is standing is to me; no one is. Callie is holding court by the Tassimo, claiming all the attention.

Except for Cooper. So far, he seems to be immune to her charms, preferring to talk to me.

Cooper needs to remember I'm married.

I need to remember I'm married.

Why the hell did he have to come and work here?

"I know that, and I've apologized over and over again for what happened," Cooper says in a low urgent voice. "Please tell me you're not holding a grudge. Please, Abby. It was once, only once and we had been drinking. I don't know if I can take it if you're still pissed at me. It was a celebration; remember that huge case and the other side were such assholes and–"

"I remember," I cut him off, not wanting to get into reminiscing about the time I cheated on my husband. "I remember *everything*."

"Oh?"

I've said too much. Now Cooper thinks the moment meant something to me when in reality I'm embarrassed it happened at all. "Not that it meant anything to me," I add quickly.

"Of course not," he says smoothly, his face a blank mask so I'm unable to tell what he's thinking. And Cooper and I were good enough friends that I always used to be able to tell when he was stressed or happy or annoyed at his latest girlfriend. "It was just a moment that shouldn't have happened. You're still happily married."

"Are you still with–what was her name?" I ask.

"Irena? No, that never worked out. Neither did Michaela or Peta."

"That's a lot of A's," I say. "Women with names ending in A."

Cooper laughs and I breathe a sigh of relief as the mood between us lightens. "You're right. I never noticed that. I went out with a

Helena once as well. And I think there was a Deanna... I should definitely stay away from women who have names ending in A. Good thing you're not an Abba, or we'd never be able to be friends."

"If I was, I'd be a member of a Swedish pop band from the 70s," I tell him, unable to contemplate the possibility of Cooper staying away from me. When he first started her a few weeks ago, it had seemed like a good idea, but now that we're talking again and it's so easy and nice, I can't help but remember how easy he is to talk to, just to be around.

I just have to think of him as a friend. If Callie can be just friends with Michael then I should be able to manage it with Cooper. Regardless of how soft I remember his lips being.

Cooper smiles at me again and I do my best to erase any thoughts of his lips. "I was so glad when I found out you were still here," he admits. "It was so easy to work with you before; really, you were one of the few associates at the firm I could actually tolerate. Most lawyers are assholes."

"Present company exempted, of course," I say primly.

"Of course. But we've both got MBA's so we're technically not that lawyerly lawyers anymore. We're business/lawyers."

"And business makes us less of an asshole?"

"Well, something must!" His blue eyes light up at my laugh and I feel myself relax a little. "It's nice to have a friendly face here. Someone to have my back. Because, you know, I think there are a few that would like to stick a knife in it." Cooper nods towards Brienne, who is scowling at him. Caught, she looks away.

"Ah," I nod, not wanting to tell tales, but wanting to reassure Cooper because that's what friends would do. "I think there were some extenuating circumstances there. Ian..."

"Were they together?" he asks eagerly. Cooper always did enjoy a good gossip.

"No, but there might have been a possibility."

"And then Brienne found out he was into stuff with the other girl?"

How am I supposed to answer that?

"It's...complicated." I know I can trust Cooper–at least I used to be able to trust him—but I know Brienne wouldn't want her Peeping Tom moment to become common knowledge. People might have picked up that Brienne hooked up with Ian but having everyone know how she stood and watched Ian and Agatha have kinky sex would be worse than Jason reading my emails. "And I'm not sure what happened to the girl is exactly as it sounded. I was under the impression it was more consensual than she let on."

From what Brienne reported, it definitely sounded like Agatha had enjoyed Ian spanking her, but then I hadn't been there. And if I had been, would I have watched like Brienne did?

Cooper cringes. "I hate these cases. It's always he said, she said and no witnesses."

Brienne was a witness.

"I feel bad about how I got the job," Cooper continues. "But what can I do? It's a good job. I get to work with you again." He smiles at me, and I have to fight the grimace that threatens after my stomach flips over.

I wonder if I can get away with texting Ben at work.

Chapter Three

MICHAEL

A s Callie laughs at something Jason says, I have an inexplicable desire to bend her over the counter in the kitchen. I can picture my hands yanking up her skirt to reveal her bare ass, thrusting into her, hard enough to make her whimper, making her give little cries of pleasure.

It's difficult not to let that little fantasy show on my face. Fortunately, I've been getting quite a bit of practice. I'm not sure how any man could look at Callie and not daydream about her.

But I have a girlfriend. I'm very happy with Liana. I'm not in need of any fantasies about Callie or anyone else.

"Did you have fun?" I'm yanked out of my dream where Callie is begging me for *more, please God don't stop,* pulled away from the made-up vision of Callie bent over the counter with her ass in the air, to the reality of her standing beside me asking me an innocent question.

"What?" I have no idea what Callie's talking about. For a bad moment, I think I've spoken my thoughts aloud.

"At Jason's last night," Callie says, drawing me back into the conversation. Her big blue eyes twinkle at me. Those eyes are almost as distracting as her chest measurements. "Weren't you listening? Are you ignoring me?" She presses a hand against her chest, pretending to be offended.

Oh, to be that hand, that I might touch—

Great. She's got me misquoting Shakespeare.

"I asked if you had fun. Jason says he kicked your butt in *Roll for the Galaxy* during game night," Callie continues.

"Sorry. I was too busy concentrating on how lovely you look this morning," I say. Callie makes a face at my cheesy comment. It was pretty bad but the best I could do under the circumstances.

Even after working at Hever with her for the last year and a half, Callie remains a mystery to me. She's a great friend, sexy as hell but sometimes it's almost like she's into me. Like she's interested in me. I find this impossible to believe because–look at her. She's amazingly beautiful, sexy, funny, so sexy...

Did I say that twice?

There is no reason why Callie Champlain would be interested in *me*. No way. And even if she was, I'm with Liana.

Liana keeps me in line. She has her ways of keeping me in line.

But there's still something about Callie that I can't get out of my mind and this means I have these little daydreams about her. And they usually occur at the worst times.

"Are you married, Michael?"

Now I turn to Cooper, the new controller in the accounting department. He's a good-looking guy and seems friendly enough.

I'm an engineer and don't have a lot to do with accounting, but Callie's best friend is Brienne who basically runs the accounting department with Delia, so there's a lot of inter-department mingling in the kitchen in the mornings.

I avoid thinking of the inter-mingling I'd like to do with Callie and answer Cooper's question. "No. Girlfriend, though."

"Co-habitating?" he asks politely. I know he's doing his best to get to know everyone, but I can't help but feel singled out.

"No," I tell him after an uncomfortable pause. "I have my own place."

Even after five years with Liana, I don't want everyone to know my personal business. Not that I'm embarrassed, but it's kind of private.

"Freedom," Carl chimes in, giving me a manly slap on the shoulder. "A wonderful thing."

Carl should talk. He lives with a woman and he has a work wife here. He and Delia are practically joined at the hip.

Delia's not my type, but I can see what Carl sees in her. She's a tiny, sexy little thing that does her best to hide her appeal. What I've noticed about her tits is that they can compare to Callie's but Delia does everything she can to cover them up, and usually with the worst colour combinations. The blouse she's wearing this morning is actually making my eyes ache with the huge, ugly purple rose print.

I can't see anything ever happening with the two of them, despite Carl having an obvious hard-on for Delia.

"I thought you lived with her," Callie says with confusion. She misses Jason answering the same question from Cooper and also doesn't notice the glance Jason gives her when he admits to Cooper that he doesn't have a girlfriend.

I notice it, though.

"No, she likes her space," I shrug, like Liana's refusal to live with me isn't the main source of disagreement between us anymore. It used to be. Now I'm not sure what would be good for us.

But once again, I keep my thoughts to myself. I'm very good at hiding my secrets.

"Do you have kitchen talk every morning?" Cooper asks with interest. I like him better than Ian, who in all the time I've worked at Hever, never said one word to me. "It's like some kind of talk show. *The View* or *The Chat*, whatever it's called."

"You make it sound like all we do is stand around gossiping," Brienne says scornfully. Heads swivel towards her with surprise. Brienne's not the bitchy type but there's no denying that tone is anything but.

"But we do," Callie laughs, defusing the sudden awkwardness. "And it's fun, so feel free to come waste time with us in the morning during an episode of *Office Chat*."

Beside me, Jason stiffens at Callie's invitation to Cooper. He's always had a hard-on for Callie, but recently something must have happened between them for him to display such passive possessiveness. Glances implying he doesn't have a girlfriend–yet. Body language that screams he does not appreciate Callie showing interest in another man.

My phone vibrates and I pull it out to check who's calling me. It's well after nine and none of us have started our work day. Seeing as the new controller is hanging out with us makes me less inclined to go back to my desk.

It's Liana calling. Reluctantly, I let it go to voicemail. Even though I'll probably pay for it later, I don't feel like talking to her right now.

"You need a better title," Cooper is saying to Callie.

"*Office Place Comings and Goings?*" she suggests, which makes Cooper laugh.

Jason frowns.

Not that it's any business of mine. Callie and I are just friends. Jason is a good guy, another good friend of mine. I shouldn't have a problem with the thought of them together.

I shouldn't, but the thought of Jason behind Callie thrusting hard into her and her cries and whimpers reserved for *him* is not a happy one.

"Do you ever take it out of the office?" Cooper asks.

"Take what out?" a bewildered Sadie asks.

Now she would be perfect for Jason, much better than Callie. She's always chattering to Jason about stuff and she's got the long and lean look going for her. I heard she was a champion snowboarder but had to give it up because of an injury. I can picture her riding demon-like down a snowy hill.

I wonder what she would be like in bed.

"Our gossip," Abby explains.

"Or anything else."

Callie laughs at Cooper's teasing innuendo. She's the queen of suggestive remarks, so they have got off to a flying start.

I wonder if Cooper will remain impervious to her charms.

Callie is the queen of office hook-ups, so the thought of her and Cooper shouldn't bother me. Or Jason.

It doesn't bother me. There's no reason for it to bother me. Callie means nothing to me. We're friends.

Even though there is only a tiny, straining button preventing her awe-inspiring cleavage from bursting free and giving me more *more-than-friend* fodder for the daydreams.

Chapter Four

SADIE

"HAVE YOU SPOKEN TO her?" Callie asks me on Tuesday afternoon. She's perched on the corner of my desk, bare legs swinging. It's a slow work day for me. Or maybe it's because I can't still concentrate on anything other than the thought of Alma showing up at my desk with Julian Donovan to fire me for having sex with his wife.

"Do you really think he'd fire you for having an affair with his wife?" Brienne asks, trying to sound positive. She wandered up to my desk with Callie; apparently, it's a slow day for her too. Unlike Callie, Brienne always makes a point of keeping her head lower than the cubicle wall when she stops by. Because of this, I keep an empty recycling bin in my pod and flipped over, it makes an extra seat for her. Brienne leans back against my desk and sips her coffee, looking at the cup like she wishes it contained someone more than a double double. It's been a long week and it's only Tuesday.

"He fired Ian." It's not fair to bring the subject up in front of Brienne, but I don't want a positive spin on things. I want to wallow in my fear and regret and Brienne is being a good friend and refusing to let me.

"Yes, I realize that," Brienne says. "But I'm beginning to think that was a good thing."

"What happened?" I demand, all thoughts of Alma and my situation forgotten. I'm so glad no one sits in the cubicles connected to me. Bill, one of the safety guys is diagonal across the aisle but he won't stay at his desk without headphones, so I never have to worry about him overhearing.

He's also a little strange so the headphones make it easy to keep my distance.

"I got a hold of Ian over the weekend. He finally responded to my emails."

"And..." I'm agog to hear, but Callie shakes her head, obviously abreast of this new change in Brienne's attitude.

To be honest, I never really understood what Brienne has been so upset about. Yes, she had a thumping great crush on Ian, but it was obviously one-sided. Brienne is cute and sweet, but Ian's taste ran to the more sophisticated, showy types, like Agatha, the assistant who got him fired. And then all of a sudden, Ian took notice of Brienne. I'm not cynical but it was convenient timing. I think Ian arranged to have Brienne witness his little office scene with Agatha, which involved non-office behaviour such as tying Agatha to the desk and spanking her before culminating in oral sex for both of them.

Of course, Brienne gave us all the details, making it sound like it was consensual and enjoyable for all involved.

And then because Ian knew watching him had excited her, he then suggested Brienne work late the following Friday. That was when her own interlude with Ian took place. She didn't give us many details about that, but enough so that I can tell things must have gotten pretty hot between the two of them. I think there was spanking involved.

And then Ian was fired Monday morning, for alleged sexual harassment, brought about by Agatha.

I don't know all the details of the case and lawyer Abby can't tell us much, but all I know is that Ian is gone and Brienne is miserable.

What I don't understand is why she is so upset. Yes, she liked him and yes, they had sex–pretty amazing from the sound of it–but truth be told, Ian is an ass. I have no doubt he did something offensive to Agatha. Maybe it wasn't the day Brienne watched them, but I bet it happened another time. It also wouldn't surprise me to discover that Ian set the whole thing up with Brienne to have a defence against Agatha's story.

I'm keeping that opinion to myself, however.

According to Callie, the best way to get over someone is to have sex with someone else, which alleviates any sexual hold the ex may still have on you. I have to admit, it worked for me. Alma did help me get over Evan, but it's been sort of an 'out of the frying pan, into the fire thing'. I don't think I gained much. I may not be obsessed with Evan any longer, but getting involved with Alma didn't do me any favours. I know Brienne was following the same game plan to try and exorcise her ex-husband Eli from her life but I think she picked the wrong guy in Ian.

"So what did Ian say?" I ask Brienne.

"It's what he *didn't* say," Brienne admits.

"Or didn't want to do?" Callie asks pointedly.

"Yes, I did suggest getting together," Brienne tells her defensively. "He said he had a lot going on."

"I'm sure." I glance up at Callie's icy tone in time to see Brienne look away, flushing.

"I made a mistake," she says, hands splayed with surrender. "Yes, he's an ass. Yes, I had sex with him and yes, I want to do it again, but I won't because he's an ass."

"Did you realize this before or after you asked for a booty call?"

"It wasn't a booty call!" Her cheeks redden even more at Callie's derisive laughter. "I asked if he wanted to get a drink."

"Even I know that's a booty call," I say, laying my hand sympathetically on her knee.

"Well, at least one of you has figured things out," Callie tells Brienne before turning to me. "And now, back to the girl problems."

"I don't want to have girl problems anymore." I pout.

"I think you should switch back to boys," Brienne suggests. "At least at the office."

"It's been since Friday and Alma hasn't said a word," Callie says dismissively. "She's not going to say anything to Julian. You're safe, Sadie."

"I wish I could believe it. God, what was I doing with her?" I drop my face into my hands. "I don't even like girls."

"Well, obviously you like something about them." I look up in time to see Callie grin at Brienne.

"You were experimenting," Brienne says, mirroring the sympathy I gave her. It's nice to have good friends at the office and tell you that you're an ass but care about you anyway. "Now you know office place hookups aren't a good thing for you."

"I don't agree with that," Callie argues. "Just not with neurotic, blackmailing women."

"Everything okay?" Jason asks. I must be distracted because he's able to walk up to my desk without me noticing.

I hope he didn't hear that conversation.

"Just great, thanks." Callie smiles brightly at him and instantly Jason forgets Brienne and I are in the building.

"How's your day?" Jason asks Callie.

"Super." I watch with interest as Callie runs her gaze over Jason, who practically preens like a peacock under her appraisal. "You? Busy?"

"Not bad."

"I'm glad." There's a pause; Jason looks expectantly at Callie.

"Maybe we can talk later," Callie suggests, giving him the kind of smile I suspect she uses to give the brush off. I'm not sure how many men Callie actually brushes off, but I think I'm witnessing one now. "But now we really have to discuss..." she nods her blonde head sagely in my direction. "Girl stuff."

"Oh, sure. I don't want to interrupt. I just saw you, and I thought—you looked upset, Sadie, and I wanted to make sure everything was okay," Jason tells us, looking so adorable despite the inopportune interruption that I have to smile at him.

"Thanks, Jason. I'm fine. It's just..." I trail off. I suspect Jason knows everything that goes on at Hever but I'm not about to discuss my personal business with him just in case he doesn't. He's a great guy, a good friend, but I could tell him the building was on fire right now and he would continue to gaze at Callie with those puppy dog eyes.

"Alma hasn't been at work this week," he says, surprising me.

"She hasn't?"

"There's talk of her leaving," he adds. "But I'm not positive about that."

"Is it–do you know–why?" I stammer. Jason smiles shyly at me, and I'm struck by how attractive he is. His brown eyes shine behind his glasses, thick hair tumbling onto his forehead. His good looks aren't obvious but seem to have grown on me lately.

"I'm not sure," he admits. "But I'll let you know if I hear anything else."

"I'm not sure if I want to know how you find out what you do," Callie says. But Jason holds my gaze a moment longer before turning to her.

"Then I won't tell you," he grins briefly at Callie, taking a step away from my desk. "I'll let you get back to your chat."

"See you later," Brienne smiles at him.

"Thanks, Jason," I say. Callie only smiles knowingly and watches him walk away.

"What's going on there?" Brienne wonders, getting up from her seat to peer around the cubicle divider to make sure he's out of earshot. Callie shrugs. "He was yours for the taking."

"What do you mean?" I ask with confusion. Brienne nods at Callie. "Oh. Have you–are you? Still? You and Jason–more than once?" Callie shrugs again.

"Only twice. Well, three times but we heard someone come in so it didn't end well. It did for me, but...he's *really* talented."

"And he really likes you," Brienne says disapprovingly.

"No, he doesn't. He's a big boy; he knows what we're doing," Callie says dismissively. "No commitment. No excuses. Just having fun at work."

"I don't think he does, Callie. That boy is one hundred percent, prime time, in like with you."

"What?" I ask.

"Haven't you ever seen *Top Gun*?" Brienne turns to me. "It's a Meg Ryan line in the movie."

"I didn't even know Meg Ryan was in *Top Gun*!"

Brienne sighs. "Sometimes I forget how young you are."

"Not that young!"

"Don't you think Jason has a thing for Callie?" she demands, dropping her movie trivia. She knows I can't compete. Brienne's life revolves around her *Netflix* subscription, watching movies and television shows I've never even heard of.

"He doesn't!" Callie insists, but Brienne takes no notice of her, waiting for me to answer.

"I don't know," I admit. From what I saw, the way Jason looks at Callie, the way he always looks at her, is the way a smitten man watches his beloved.

But I don't like thinking Jason as smitten with Callie. Apparently, the feeling is mutual.

"I don't want him to like me," Callie says quietly.

"Still getting nowhere with Michael?" Brienne asks with another sigh.

It's obvious to all of us Callie has not-so-hidden feelings for Michael, but she *never* discusses it. She hardly ever makes comments about it, other than the odd remark about how cute he is.

"There's nowhere to go, even if I wanted to," Callie says firmly. "I don't mess around with guys who are already taken."

"I wish I thought of that rule earlier," I say, forlornly.

"Alma isn't a guy," Brienne points out. "That can be your rule for the next time if you're serious about switching teams again."

"I was never on the team," I tell her. "I only played for a couple of games."

"You can play for more than one team, you know," Callie tells me. "There's nothing wrong with that."

I give a dismissive wave of my hand. "Too complicated for me. I'll save that for pros like you."

"Which is what brings me to my observation," Callie announces.

"You're switching teams?"

Brienne and Callie burst out laughing. "Not a chance. I'll play relief whenever possible, but I *like* my team too much to consider a change. No, this is about Jason. I don't agree that he has a thing for me. But I think, with a little encouragement, he could like Sadie," Callie points out, rising to her feet to peer over the wall in the direction of Jason's desk a few rows away. I stand and follow her gaze.

"He's going to see you staring at him," Brienne hisses, still in her seat.

"He's on his computer; he's in the zone," I tell her.

"Probably reading more emails," Callie grumbles. "I don't like monitoring what I type to you."

Jason recently admitted that one of his duties as the resident information technician was to read and monitor all inter-office emails. We only discovered this when he warned Abby her sexy messages to her husband Ben could easily be seen as inappropriate for office hours.

Knowing Abby, I've always wondered just how inappropriate her emails to Ben would be. She's not the type I could ask, either. I know she's happy with Ben, but she strikes me as quite conservative and too serious to even think about sexting in the office.

First time for everything. I'm sure no one who knows me would ever contemplate what Alma and I got up to in the supply closet.

Whatever observation Callie was going to make is interrupted by the sudden appearance of Cooper Garrison stepping from Abby's office in the corner.

"Shit," Brienne hisses, glancing around for someplace to hide.

Cooper advances towards my desk with a grin lighting up his blonde good looks. He epitomizes what I consider a surfer to look like, plus a sexy accent. "So that's where you're hiding, Brienne," Cooper says cheerfully, instantly taking in Brienne crouched behind my chair. I didn't even see her shuffle the recycling bin across my tiny office.

"I'm heading back to my desk now," Brienne says sullenly, jumping to her feet.

"Don't go back on my account. You're entitled to a break. It's quiet today and I'm sure your work is up to date," Cooper says.

I look at him with confusion. He sounds sincere, not sarcastic. Any other supervisor would have been reading us the riot act for wasting time. Brienne stares at him with her mouth slightly agape.

I glance from Cooper to Brienne. *Ah...*

"I better get back to work," Brienne says as Cooper continues to grin at her.

"Let me walk with you," Cooper says quickly, giving Brienne no room for argument. She barely hides her grimace as they say goodbye to us.

Callie peers over the wall to watch them go. "He's hot," she whispers with a nod of approval.

"You're not thinking…"

"No, I have other plans for him."

I'm about to demand to know what these other plans are when Abby rushes over to my desk. "Did he catch her up here?" she wants to know. "I wanted to warn you that he was in my office but I couldn't text you without him seeing it."

"Yes, but it's fine. He seems cool. About everything," Callie tells her.

"Oh. Good. He is…cool," Abby says awkwardly.

"Is he?" Callie asks with a knowing smile.

"What's that supposed to mean?" Abby snaps.

"Nothing," Callie says innocently, raising her hands in surrender. "Good meeting?"

"Yes, just a meeting, Callie," Abby sighs. "Get your mind out of the gutter."

"But it's such a fun place to be!"

I laugh. "I wouldn't mind having him in my office," I tell Abby. "He's hot."

To my surprise, Abby sinks down onto my desk beside Callie. "He is," she confesses. "And I feel so guilty thinking it!"

Chapter Five

ABBY

"You're just thinking it," Callie says. "You're not doing anything about it. Right?"

"Of course not," I say quickly. I'm confident I wouldn't betray Ben—again—with Cooper, but that doesn't stop the thoughts running through my mind about what it would be like to do so.

"How's your sex life?" Callie asks in her usual blunt way. "The guilt should help with that."

"What do you have to feel guilty about?" Sadie asks in bewilderment.

"Nothing," I sigh. "I haven't done anything, I'm not about to do anything."

"But you're thinking what it would be like to," Callie points out.

"How do you know these things?" I demand, and Callie laughs and gently slaps my leg.

"Oh, Abs, I know, because I'm a woman. And so are you-you're a woman who just happens to know how good of a kisser Cooper Garrison is!"

"Do you have to remind me?" I mutter with a roll of my eyes.

"Just how good is he?" Sadie wants to know.

"Ah. You've intrigued the young one," Callie mocks.

"Will you stop with the young stuff?" Sadie protests. "What does my age have anything to do with wanting to know how good of a kisser Cooper is? He's hot!"

"He is," I admit with another sigh. "And he's a really good kisser. But that's all we did–just a kiss. Nothing more. And only once, and we were both drinking."

"Methinks the lady protests too much," Callie says with eyebrows raised.

"Okay, that's from *Macbeth*. Enough with the quoting today," Sadie cries.

I look at her painfully, unable to let the massacre of the Bard's pass uncorrected. "It's actually from *Hamlet* and the correct quote is *The lady doth protests too much, methinks.*"

"I like my way better, thanks," Callie says cheerfully. "Stop trying to change the subject."

"I'm not trying to change the subject, but I don't want to talk about it. There's nothing to talk about," I tell her, standing up. I hope they don't see how my eyes track Cooper and Brienne as they reach the stairwell together. How can it take them so long to walk across the floor? "Nothing at all."

"Uh huh,' Callie grins. "You going to text Ben now?"

"I'm going back to work," I retort. Callie laughs as I stalk back to my office.

Callie has too much woman's intuition, I decide as I close the door to my office and sink into my chair. Plus, she's too easy to talk to.

I confessed to Callie about Cooper, back when we worked together at the law firm. Too much stress, lack of sleep and a huge win for our team brought me together with Cooper and in a moment of weakness, I kissed him. Or he kissed me—I really don't remember. We kissed each other when I was happily married to Ben. I've never been able to tell Ben about what happened and I thought I would never have to. I left the firm soon after to come work for Hever, leaving Cooper and my guilt behind me. Who would ever imagine that Cooper and I would end up working together again?

Did Cooper follow me to Hever? Did he track me down, thinking something could happen between us again? Did he want something to?

I gently bang my head on the surface of my desk, trying to banish these thoughts from my head. I know it's silly for me to think this way about Cooper; that he's obsessed with me, about how much our kiss meant to him that he's come to find me after so many years.

"That's stupid, not silly," I mutter to myself. "It was only a kiss."

Deep down I know Cooper turning up at Hever is nothing more than a coincidence. He found an opportunity and he took it and it means nothing to him that I was already working here.

But what if it wasn't?

"I can't believe I found you again," Cooper says, *staring intently into my eyes.*

"It's been seven years," I tell him weakly, *confused with how fast my heart is beating. I can't look away from his eyes, his lips...*

"And I've thought of you every single day." His hand grips my shoulder, sliding up to curve around the base of my neck. *"Abby, please tell me you feel the same way?"*

"Cooper, my husband..."

"I've waited so long for you." He moved closer to me and I felt his breath on my neck. Almost against my will, I arch my neck, my hair falling back to give him a clear path to the sensitive skin that even now is aching for his touch.

"I gave you no indication..." I say weakly.

"You wanted me. You still do. You can't deny it."

He's right. I can't deny it. I want him with every part of my body. Cooper's hand presses my legs apart so he can stand between them, the heat of his body making me arch closer.

"I can't," I moan as his lips press against my skin. Both his hands are on my legs now, pushing up my skirt.

"Saying no isn't an option," he tells me huskily. *"I've wanted this for far too long. We both have. You can't deny it."*

"No..."

I don't know if I'm saying no to his touch, or that I can't deny it. But he takes away any opportunity for me to clarify as his lips trail up my jaw to my mouth. Any more protest, weak or otherwise, is stifled as he kisses me. Cooper kisses me like I've dreamed of him kissing me for so long. My lips part willingly and his tongue darts into my mouth. So consumed with the feel of his mouth against mine that I don't realize my skirt is around my waist. Cooper pulls my hips towards him, his hand roughly pushing my panties aside as he thrusts into me.

"Cooper," I moan into his mouth as his cock fills the ache inside me.

"I need you," he groans. *"I have to have you."*

I cry out as he thrusts deeper, pulling my hips against him. I move with him willingly, knowing that this is wrong–I shouldn't be doing this–but unable to stop.

Unwilling to stop. I want him. I've always wanted him.

"Abby, I want you so much. I've always wanted you..."

"Yes! Please, Cooper," I beg, clutching his arms, his legs, trying to draw even more of him into me. The guilt vanished, all I want is the pleasure of having his cock so far inside me that–

"Abby?"

My head whips up so fast that I'm afraid I've given myself whiplash. "What?" I snap. My door is open and Callie stands there.

"You okay?" Callie asks, her tone of concern contrasting with her knowing smirk. "I wake you up?"

"No," I tell her, trying to steady my breathing. I tell myself it's because Callie's sudden appearance has frightened me, not because my little daydream about Cooper has turned me on so much I'm out of breath and halfway to orgasm. "You could knock, you know?"

"I did," Callie says with an innocent smile. "You didn't answer. I didn't want you to be caught napping at your desk."

"I wasn't–thanks," I tell her, deciding that Callie thinking I was sleeping is easier than confessing what I was doing. "What do you need?"

"M&M's," Callie grins and I groan.

"You woke me for chocolate?"

"Is there a better reason?"

"I expect you can come up with a few." I pull out the bag of candies I keep in my drawer and offer them to Callie, impressed with my recovery. I've never been so deep into a daydream that I've missed hearing something as loud as a knock on my door. Maybe it wasn't a daydream—maybe I was sleeping. Maybe it was a dream, instead of a daydream, something I had no control over. How can I control what my subconscious is doing? I have no knowledge of how or why it creates the situations in my mind.

Is dreaming about Cooper better or worse than merely fantasizing about him?

"You okay?" Callie is standing in front of my desk, in the same spot imaginary Cooper stood while he fucked me. "You seem a little off."

"You just woke me up," I tell her, giving my head a shake. "I can't believe I fell asleep."

"Uh-huh. Well, I'll leave you to your beauty sleep. Thanks for the candy fix."

"Anytime," I tell her, trying for enthusiastic but not quite making it. Callie shuts the door after her, and I let my head fall back onto the desk.

What am I doing? I'm happily married to Ben and I can't stop thinking about what it would be like to be fucked by Cooper right here in my office.

I don't want that.

My head doesn't want that. The rest of my body is another story.

I drop my hand under my desk, trying to summon thoughts of my husband rather than Cooper, trying to make myself feel less guilty as I touch myself.

Chapter Six

MICHAEL

"YOU NEVER TALK ABOUT your girlfriend."

Callie stops by my desk on her way back from Abby's office. It's a slow day and I know she's been doing the rounds. I can't help but notice she's been away from her desk for a while.

There's always the possibility that Callie could have been with someone else rather than visiting her friends, but I don't want that image in my mind right now. It's difficult enough to look her in the eye when she's perched on my desk, once again with only a few straining buttons preventing me from getting an eyeful of heaven.

"What do you want to know?" I ask, leaning back in my chair providing a little distance from her bare legs swinging off my desk. Does she have any idea how hot she is sitting there like that? It's all I can do not to grab her and pull her onto my lap and...

"Is she pretty?" Callie asks. "Jason says she's pretty."

"Then why are you asking me?" I laugh.

"You can tell a lot about a man by the way he describes his wife. Or his girlfriend."

"You've had experience with this?"

"Have you ever noticed how Carl talks about his girlfriend? He's never really that complementary and the tone of his voice suggests to me that he's really not that happy with her," Callie explains, twirling my pen between her fingers. I wish she would keep her hands off my stuff because all I can think of is what it would be like to have her hands on my dick.

I have to stop thinking about her like that. Callie is a *friend*. I have a *girlfriend*.

"If Carl's not happy with his girlfriend then that bodes well for Delia since they seem to be so into each other," I surmise.

"They are cute together," Callie says affectionately. "Carl follows Delly around like a big little puppy, watching her ass like a schoolboy."

"I happen to know grown men also watch women's asses. It's not just a schoolboy thing." I make a point of keeping my eyes no her face and not letting them drift down to the curve of her hip balanced on the very edge of my desk.

"Really? I've never noticed." Callie gives me a knowing smile that suggests she knows exactly how often I check out her ass. How can I not?

I have a girlfriend.

"Do you think anything is going on with the two of them?"

Callie shakes her head before I even finish the question.

"Delly's like me—you don't do something like that. You don't mess with a relationship. She and Aidan are good together. Tight. She's not going to let a silly crush get in the way of her marriage.

Cheating never works out. It's like a huge slap of disrespect to your partner."

It's like Callie's disapproving words are designed to make me feel guilty. It's not wrong to look and fantasize. I'm not doing anything else.

But I want to, and this fact makes me feel guilty, and today it puts me on the attack.

"Are you saying you respect all the men you fling with?" As soon as Callie's face falls, I feel like clutching at the words to pull them back into my mouth. I've held in my comments about her office play escapades for so long but the possibility of her and Jason, my fantasizing and her disapproval over the thought of Carl and Delia, is too much.

"The men I *fling* with?" Callie's eyebrows rise scornfully.

"Sorry, I shouldn't have said that," I say quickly. "It's none of my business what you do in your personal time. Or even during working hours."

"No, it's not. I'm not doing anything wrong. It's consensual, I'm not breaking any rules and I never mess around with someone who's married," Callie says defensively. "How do you know about it anyway?"

"I've heard...there might be rumours..." I stammer.

"What do the rumours say? That I'm some sort of slut?" Callie sounds suddenly bitter and hurt and I hate I've made her feel that way. "Is that what you think?"

"Of course not!" I exclaim. "The opposite, actually. The guys—it's an honour. To help Callie pass the time at work."

"They should know better," Callie says, and right away I know she's cut off the possibility of any repeat hookups with those in the office.

"So what you do think about the guys you...you know. Do you like them? Respect them?"

Callie blinks at the question and pauses before answering. "Why wouldn't I? There are no secrets about it; I'm not lying to anyone. I'm on the up and up and everyone knows not to expect anything from me. Plus, I'm very choosy."

"You don't want to expect something from them? There's got to be someone..." I trail off, unable to stop my mind from the thought of her choosing *me*.

"Like what? Relationships don't work for me. They never have. I'm thirty-eight and too set in my ways now to try again. Besides, there's no one available who I'd be interested in." Callie refuses to meet my eyes at the blatant lie.

It's comments like that which make me think she might be interested in me. The way I catch her looking at me. The way she's always touching me. I may have been with Liana for five years, but I was single before that and I know the signs.

Actually, I really don't. I've been in three serious relationships, including one that spanned from high school to university and there weren't many pick-ups in between.

It can be said Callie is definitely more experienced than I am. I might have a wider variety of experiences, but in terms of sheer numbers, she's got me beat.

"Sex is sex. Everyone wants it, needs it. Some more than others," she adds with a sexy grin. "I don't think there's any reason to get worked up about having it."

"Do you know what the best sex is?" I ask quietly.

"When I'm on top?" she jokes. I smile, trying to ignore the way my cock throbs at the thought of Callie on top, bare breasts swinging in my face...

I have a *girlfriend.* I have to stop thinking about Callie like that. But it's not doing any harm.

It's not like I'm going to tell Liana about Callie. I make it a point never to mention her name when we're together. Liana is very jealous, sometimes obsessively so. And if Liana ever found out I'm friends with Callie, there would be punishment.

And not the kind I enjoy.

"When you're in love with the person," I tell her. "That's the best sex."

"That sounds like one of those daily quotes from Facebook," Callie scoffs.

"Have you ever been in love?" I wonder.

"Of course!" I continue to stare at her until her shoulders slump. "It was a long time ago. It didn't work out

"What happened?" Callie and I talk about a lot of things but we've always steered clear of personal intimacies. I should have stopped at her confession that she likes to sleep around.

Callie stares at her hands, her fingers twisting together. Then she gives herself a shake. "Hey, I asked about your girlfriend first, remember?" She turns suddenly shrewd eyes on me. "What's she like?"

Point taken. Callie doesn't like talking about her past. I'm intrigued, but at least smart enough to bide my time until I can find out more.

Unfortunately, I want to talk about my relationship with Liana even less than Callie wants to talk about hers.

"Do you have a lot in common?" she persists.

I stare into the dregs of coffee in the cup on my desk. How to answer this? The most truthful answer would be no, we don't have much in common unless you count the fact she loves to spank me, often with riding crops or paddles and once with my belt, and I like to let her do it.

There's not much I want to tell people about Liana.

I've never told anyone I'm the submissive in a BDSM relationship. It's not the kind of thing you discuss at the office.

Chapter Seven

SADIE

I'M IN THE KITCHEN on the first floor with Abby when Julian Donovan appears. "Ladies," he says, with a heart-stopping smile. "How are we this morning?"

"We are fine," Abby replies because I can't seem to come up with a suitable reply. Julian Donovan's blue eyes seem to pierce through me, and I have the sensation that he knows everything I've done with his wife.

And likes the thought of it.

I don't understand why I think that. Maybe it's just the way he smiles at me, with those blue eyes hooking me in and not letting go.

Why on earth would Alma cheat on *that*?

"How is our new controller making out?" Julian asks, those eyes taking in both of us. I turn back to the Tassimo and pull out my empty chai tea package before inserting a coffee for Abby.

I wonder whether Abby has the same sensation as I do, that Julian seems to be slowly peeling my clothes off, one layer at a time. I would think that such a sensation would be creepy, or offensive, but I'm not feeling either right now.

In fact, I'm feeling this twinge between my legs that I haven't felt in a while, at least not because of a man.

This gives me hope that there still might be penises I want to see in this world.

Like the one right in front of me.

"Okay?" I squeak, in answer to Julian's question. Where did that bit about his penis come from? Julian is *married*, to my former lover of all people, who threatened to have her husband fire me; the same man whose penis I'm thinking about.

This is messed up.

"You don't sound confident at all," Julian says with a smile.

"Neither one of us is in the accounting department, so we might not be the best ones to ask," Abby explains, shooting me a confused glance. I gaze at her with innocent eyes over the rim of my teacup as I take a sip.

She's confused; how does she think I feel?

"Yes, but you're the lucky ones here with me now," Julian says, his voice deep with a hint of a South American accent. It makes me think of salsa and mojitos and dark, sexy men pressed against me on the dance floor. I snowboarded in Chile when I was seventeen and experienced none of those things at that time. I have no idea why I associate them with Julian now.

"Lucky," I echo, finally finding my voice.

Julian smiles at me, making me wonder what I ever saw in Alma. Why does he have to own the company I work for? And be Alma's husband?

"Cooper seems to be settling in well," Abby elaborates as I stand, trapped in Julian's blue gaze. "He's organizing a gathering after work to get to know some of us."

I sense Abby's immediate discomfort because I come to the same conclusion: will Julian take that as an invitation to join us?

"That sounds like a fantastic idea," Julian says and my heart sinks and leaps at the same time. There's no way I would survive a social outing with him. I can barely string two words together in the kitchen. "If I wasn't afraid of ruining the party, I would join you."

"Oh, you wouldn't ruin it," ever-polite Abby tells him quickly and Julian laughs. I can't find my words again, so I set my tea down and busy myself making Abby's coffee.

"I doubt that. That smells great." He sniffs appreciatively at the coffee, with another glance at me.

"Help yourself," I manage to get out.

"I always do." His smile is part cocky, part charming and all sexy. "I think I will while I'm down here," Julian says, leaning against my arm as he reaches into the cupboard where we keep the packages for the Tassimo, almost causing me to spill Abby's coffee as I stir in the sugar for her. He selects one of my chai tea lattes and smiles at me.

"This is what you're having, isn't it?" I can only nod, still feeling the warmth in my arm. I hand Abby her coffee and snatch up my own cup and clutch it like a lifeline. I haven't been this affected by a man in a long time. Forget about the coffee–Julian smells incredible. "It looks so good."

Not once did he glance at my teacup.

"I know no one wants the big boss along," he says heartily, turning back to Abby. "I hope you have a great time and bond with each other so you're even more productive. Speaking of which," he turns those eyes back to me. "Would you be able to meet with me, Sadie, to discuss some marketing ideas I have?"

"Um, sure. Of course," I stammer. A one-on-one meeting might be worse than a social gathering. *Why* did I ever get involved with Alma?

"Great. I'll have Alma check my schedule and get in touch with you. Probably not until Thursday. I'm out of the office most of the day today."

"Alma?" I squeak and with a jerk of my hand, a wave of tea slops over the rim of my cup onto my arm, splashing on the floor. Thankfully it's cooled enough so I do my best to try and pretend it never happened until Abby takes pity and pulls a piece of paper towel off the roll and mops me up.

"One of the receptionists?" Julian asks with a puzzled smile. "I thought you knew each other. I'm sure Alma's mentioned you."

"Oh, sure, *that* Alma. I don't know her *that* well..." I bluff.

Abby to the rescue once more. "We heard she's your wife," she says with a coy smile.

"That she is. We've been married for almost ten years now. I don't mind her staying at home but for some reason, she wanted to work here. Keep an eye on me, I suppose." He grins rakishly at us.

Maybe you should keep an eye on her, I feel like screaming. And then I have an image of Julian watching Alma and me together and clamp my mouth shut before I can accidentally blurt out something I really shouldn't.

"I have to admit I do enjoy sharing the workplace with her," Julian continues. "You must know what it's like," he nods at Abby. "With both you and Ben working here."

"It's great," Abby tells him.

"It's nice when you know the people your partner talks about at work, isn't it?" My mouth drops open but thankfully Julian has created enough chaos for me for one morning. He asks Abby about Ben while his tea finishes brewing. "I'd better be off. Abby, have a great day and good luck with the project manager meeting. Give 'em hell for me. And Sadie," his blue eyes glance searchingly at me, lifting his cup in a farewell. "I'll be seeing you soon."

He's out the door before I can find my voice again.

"What the hell was *that*?" I whisper hoarsely, slumping against the counter.

"Do you think he knows?" Abby asks with a wide-eyed expression.

"I don't know! I have absolutely no idea. Oh, god," I moan, clutching at my head. "I don't like being the other woman. What was I thinking? And you wouldn't believe the improper thoughts I was having about him! Thank god he can't read minds or he'd fire me for sure!"

"No one can fire you for improper thoughts," Abby says. Then, "What kind of thoughts."

"The dirty kind!" I hiss.

"He's very attractive," Abby muses, leaning on the counter with me and sipping her coffee. Both of us stare blankly into the distance, thinking about Julian. "Those eyes..."

"Did you feel like he was stripping the clothes off you with his eyes?" I demand and Abby laughs, breaking the spell he had over us.

"No! He must have been looking at you a little more than me."

"It wasn't just me thinking that then. He shouldn't do that–those eyes are like a weapon. I could barely string a sentence together!" I give my head a shake and then sip my tea. I spilled more than half of it on myself and the cup is almost empty.

"That could have been guilt," Abby points out.

"Maybe," I muse. "Maybe I'm just a bad person because there wasn't a lot of guilt I was feeling there! He's seriously hot. Can you believe I was wondering about his penis?" Abby laughs even harder this time. "I think I'm definitely off girls now. Julian Donovan has cured me!"

"I don't think you needed 'curing,'" Abby corrects. "You were experimenting. And I'm kind of glad you've got it out of your system. You don't need the drama of Alma."

"Me too, but me crushing on him would be just as bad!"

Abby nods solemnly. "Definitely not the best idea."

"I'm just full of them these days," I tell her gloomily. "I don't know what I've been thinking. Ever since Evan broke up with me it's like I can't think straight."

"He broke your heart," Abby says sympathetically. "You needed time to get over it. Are you still thinking about him?"

"No, I think I'm finally over it. I haven't checked out his Facebook page in a while. Do you have any idea how much it hurt when he de-friended me?"

"I can't even de-friend this annoying girl I met in Europe years ago," she tells me. "There's no way I could de-friend an ex."

"Well, Evan sure could. Must have something to do with how easily he found it to cheat on me for all those years."

"Jerk."

"And then I go be the other woman to a married woman!" I roll my eyes, the guilt rising. "Now I feel guilty?"

"It's over now," Abby soothes. "And no one knows. Well, not too many people."

"And you don't think he has any idea?" I ask hopefully.

Abby frowns. "I saw what you meant about the way he looked at you, but I think that might be because he's a flirt. He's a charming man. But I don't think he knows," Abby says decisively. I can't tell if she truly believes that or is just trying to make me feel better.

"You can't be sure."

"No, but he didn't give any indication…"

"'*It's nice when you know the people they talk about*'" I quote Julian's words. "He's saying right there that she's talked about me."

"He might not have been talking about you." Like Brienne earlier, Abby's attempts to reassure me aren't working.

"Who's talking about you?" a voice interrupts. I glance up in horror to see Jason enter the kitchen and he stops short when he sees my expression. "What's wrong? I didn't do anything!" he cries.

"Sorry," I tell him, unable to hide my worry. "It's not you."

"But why–ah," he nods, a look of understanding crossing his features. "I just saw Julian Donovan. Was he in here?"

"Does everyone know?" I moan, clutching at my head and almost spilling what's left of my tea.

"I know nothing," Jason says stoically, his gaze flitting to Abby.

"There's nothing to know," Abby nods grimly at him.

"But I can see how you might be a little nervous speaking to the president of the company," Jason continues. "He can be somewhat intimidating, as nice as he is."

I look at Jason trying so hard to pretend he doesn't know what's going on and smile, feeling my shoulders relax for the first time this morning. "Intimidatingly nice," I echo. "That's our boss."

"Technically, though, I think Cooper is our boss. Or yours, at least. I really don't report to anyone."

"Must be nice."

"It is. It gives me a degree of responsibility and accountability I've never had before. Plus, it's nice to have a one-on-one relationship with the head of the company."

"Better than having a one-on-one with the wife of the head," I mutter, and Abby elbows me. "I need some more caffeine."

"I'll get you another," Jason says and starts the Tassimo for me.

Chapter Eight

ABBY

I'M MARVELLING AT SADIE'S ability to get into the worst situations when Delia comes into the kitchen, followed as always by Carl. This morning, they both have matching smiles on their faces as they share an inside joke.

"And here's the office husband and wife," Sadie says under her breath.

"They're cute together," I murmur, watching how Carl gets a cup down for Delia and how she smiles up at him. Carl is tall and rangy and has always reminded me of Mark Harmon, from *NCIS*. Whenever I see him I can't help the little wish that Ben will be in as good as shape as Carl when he's his age. Which isn't that long.

Delia touches Carl's hand as she takes the cup. His gaze is almost a caress. I've never really watched the two of them together; they seem intimate, familiar with each other. I know they've been friends for years but...

I wonder...

No. I slap down the thought. Not Delia. She's married, happily married and with kids. She'd never...not even with Carl. I can't see her cheating on her husband...

You did, a little voice inside me says.

It was just a kiss, I argue with myself.

"Abby?"

I look up to see Callie staring at me. "You okay? You look a little...odd."

"Lots on my mind," I tell her, waving away her concern.

"Do tell," she asks, taking her turn with the coffee maker. As always, I marvel at Callie's continual good mood. Does nothing ever bother her? She has no husband, no responsibilities; I had always pitied Callie that she was missing out on so much but now I wonder if I was wrong. How can she feel she's missing out on anything? She embraces life to the fullest and it's like nothing gets her down. Maybe she's got it right.

Not that I would ever give up Ben or my babies.

No one depended on her. She didn't have to feel guilty about not being home on time or spending time with friends. I love my life but this morning, I envy Callie more than a little.

I shake my head. "It's fine." And it is. I can deal with these thoughts of Cooper. I'm strong, with enough willpower not to fall again. Enough willpower to stop tormenting myself with thoughts of one moment in time.

Enough of Cooper.

"Did you tell Benny boy about drinks Thursday night?" Callie wants to know.

"I did. He thinks it's a great idea."

"Of course he did. He gets to see *me*." She flings her hair around her shoulders and I laugh.

"I think you should just ask for an invite to games' night instead of trying to cozy up to my husband."

"But I like your husband," she says, full lips pouting provocatively. "He's the only one here I haven't cozied up to!"

"Not very discriminatory, are you?"

Callie winks, her blue eyes twinkling. "I like variety."

How can anyone be so happy all of the time? Maybe it's all the sex she has.

"You sure like something," I grumble.

"You're just jealous," Callie says breezily, blowing to cool her coffee before moving aside for Carl to take his turn.

"Nope," I say, putting any thoughts of Cooper firmly out of my mind. "I'm perfectly happy being a one-man woman."

"Oh, I know that. But wouldn't it be nice to see a little more of your husband at work?" Callie asks coyly.

"Those emails pushed the boundaries enough," I tell her firmly.

Callie laughs. "Never enough."

"Don't you ever…" I begin, before stopping myself. It's none of my business whether Callie feels like she needs more out of life. She's a grown woman who can make her own choices, make her own decisions.

"Ever what?"

"Want…more. Love. A life with someone –"

"What you have?" Callie interrupts. "You think I need kids and the white picket fence to make me happy?"

"No." I shake my head. "Actually, I was wondering how you're happy all the time. Nothing ever seems to get you down."

"I don't let anything get me down," she corrects, serious for once. "If I start, then things begin to bottle up and everything starts to affect me and before you know it, I'll be the freaked-out lady in the fuzzy slippers eating food from the cat dish."

"Sounds... unpleasant." I grimace.

"Yep," Callie says cheerfully. "So you fake it til you make it."

"What's that supposed to mean?"

"Pretend you don't have a thing for Cooper until it's the truth."

"I wasn't–why are you bringing up Cooper?" How does she do this? Callie is not a mind-reader, yet she always seems to know what I'm thinking about. "We weren't even talking about him?"

"Oh, Abs," Callie sighs. "How long have we been friends? How many times do I have to tell you it's okay to look at other men and still be in love with your husband? Ben isn't going anywhere and he'll still love you even if you think Cooper is hot."

"I don't—"

Callie nods sagely. "Good. You're learning. But you don't have to lie to me."

"I really don't understand you," I tell her with bewilderment.

"Imagine how men feel," she says with a cackle.

"You sound like you need a cauldron with that laugh," Delia calls over to us with a frown. "What are you two plotting?"

"Nothing that you would approve of, my dear Delly," Callie says affectionately.

"Oh, to be young and fancy-free," Delia heaves a sigh.

"You're not that decrepit," I point out.

"I feel like it this morning. Anyway, I'm back to work," she says, Carl moving in beside her, ready to escort her back to her desk.

"Already? We have no time to gossip?" Callie mock whines.

"We can do that tomorrow night," Delia assures her.

"Do you still drink tequila?" Callie wonders.

Delia gives her a surprised glance. "Doesn't everyone?"

"Not me," I shudder. "Nasty stuff." My stomach rolls over at the mention of it. The last time I drank was...

The last time I drank to excess was the night I kissed Cooper.

That was seven years ago. I must have gotten drunk since then.

There's no way I should be going to a bar with him where alcohol will be served.

Ben will be there. I don't know if that will make it better or worse.

"Delly's hard-core," Callie cheers. "She's an animal!"

"Yes, she can be," Carl says to Delia, in a voice just loud enough for me to overhear.

"Shh," Delia frowns at him, but it's clear that's a smile she's hiding.

Callie and I stare at each other as Delia and Carl leave the kitchen with their coffee cups, huddled close together.

"What the hell –?"

"Do you think—?"

"Definitely," Sadie says, breaking her conversation with Jason to join ours.

"I'd say so," Jason says, before looking apologetic. "If you want my opinion, that is."

"*Really?*" Callie breathes, staring after them. "Not Delia."

"Maybe not," Sadie cautions.

"Are we all suspecting the same thing?" I ask. "Extra-marital, after-hours?"

"It could be during hours," Callie says. "It's been known to happen. But not Delia. I can almost guarantee it."

I notice she doesn't glance at Jason when she says that. I know what happened between them because she told me and I suspect Jason would like it to happen again by the way he is looking at her, like a little boy in love with his babysitter.

Maybe not a babysitter. There's an age difference between them but not enough to suggest a creepy babysitting angle. Like a crush on his teacher; much better.

"But *Delia*?" I wonder. "She's..."

"She's only forty-eight; not eighty-four," Callie points out.

"I know but—"

"I want to still be getting it on when I'm forty-eight," Sadie says, inciting a groan of disapproval from both Callie and me.

"How old are you?" I cry.

"You're such a child," Callie groans.

"I'm twenty-seven," Sadie protests.

"And forty-eight is twenty years away, not two hundred," Callie points out. "It'll be here before you know it."

"I just meant I want to have someone to be getting it on with when I'm her age," Sadie backpedals, and I groan again.

"There's no respect from today's youth," I tell her.

Brienne bustles into the kitchen, looking uncomfortable with Cooper, who follows her in and is clearly making an attempt to talk to her.

I try not to be obvious as I stare at them in wonder. Cooper and *Brienne*? It's not the first time I've seen them together and he's always trying to engage her when we're together. Maybe...

This should solve everything. This will take this guilty weight off my shoulders. This will make it so much easier to deal with Cooper in a professional manner.

Then why do I feel jealous of the way Cooper is smiling at Brienne?

Chapter Nine

MICHAEL

I'M LATE TO WORK this morning, thanks to Liana. By the time I make it to the kitchen for my coffee, the group has dispersed. I have a pang of disappointment that I've missed Callie.

She's not at her desk either.

I'm wondering where she could be as I sit down, and realize a moment too late that it's not a good idea.

Liana used the crop on me again last night and some of the welts are still tender. I prefer the crop to the paddle but sometimes it's easier to sit down after she paddles me.

Last night she punished me again for missing her phone call on Monday morning. Liana likes to have reasons for what she does, to justify the pain she causes me. Usually, they're pretty stupid reasons, like missing a phone call, or the wine I served her not being cold enough.

I don't like that aspect of our relationship.

We both get satisfaction from being in a BDSM relationship and I wish Liana would just accept that rather than feeling the need to create excuses for tying me up and giving me a few whacks. I've never spoken to her about this because Liana takes the dominant role very seriously and rarely considers my feelings outside the bedroom. Inside the bedroom, I've got everything I need, even though I never expected to need or want it. But other than sex, things are pretty one-sided with the two of us.

I was never looking for this kind of relationship. I never expected to be involved with something like this. I also had the wrong idea that men were never submissive. Liana convinced me of that pretty quickly.

She convinced me of a lot of things, in very short order. I met her in a bar, trying to drown my sorrows after a bad breakup. Less than an hour later she chatted me up, I was tied up and tied down and having the best sex of my life. Now, five years later, the sex is still exciting, but I'm beginning to wonder if that can make up for everything between us feeling out of sorts.

Right on time, my phone rings. "Did you get to work okay?" Liana asks with her customary greeting.

"I doubt I'd be talking to you if I didn't."

Liana clicks her tongue at me, a sure sound of her disapproval. "That's no way to talk to me." Her tone changes into her dominatrix's voice. The excitement begins to churn within me when I hear it.

"No, it isn't. I apologize." I instantly revert to my submissive side, my voice low and softer, speaking quietly into the phone so I'm not overheard.

"You'll have to be punished."

My cock hardens in my pants, and I slid my chair closer to my desk. Sex is what brings us together, what keeps us together, despite everything else that may be wrong. "Of course."

"I thought after last night you would have had enough punishment for missing my call on Monday. I expect you to be at your desk when I call, and to be polite," Liana instructs. "Is that too much to ask?"

"No, of course not."

After last night...

"Are you hard?" Liana asks, her voice sounding silky like she's caressing me over the phone. My brain switches off; any thoughts about how healthy the relationship might be is now gone.

The woman has an incredible sexual hold over me, one I'm not considering breaking anytime soon.

"Yes." I glance around to make sure no one can overhear me.

"Did you enjoy tonguing my pussy last night?" Liana asks. "When I straddled your face and you made me come with your mouth?"

I stand in her bedroom, my hands grasping one of the posters on Liana's huge bed, counting the lashes of the crop. "Nine...ten," I groan.

"Is that enough? Do you need another reminder?"

"No, miss. I've learned my lesson." I drop my arms to my sides, muscles aching already. I'm tense from the pain, ready for the release Liana will allow me to have, but unsure when she'll give it to me. Something tells me she has more in store for me tonight.

"Lay down on the bed," Liana orders, regardless of the welts on my tender ass. Some nights she'll rub my reddened cheeks, substituting

soft hands and lips with blows. Pain and pleasure; that's how it's been with us.

Tonight, I sense it's more about pain. And her pleasure.

I've always wondered how Liana can possibly get away with these conversations when she's at work. She's a dental hygienist, which is such an incongruous career choice for such a foul-tempered little vixen.

Actually, maybe not. Liana likes to cause pain, so who better to work for than a dentist?

"I always enjoy it when you're satisfied," I tell her, dropping my own voice to a tone of respect and obedience, exactly what would make her happy.

Her hips straddling my shoulders, her pussy grinding into my mouth as she bucks above me with the force of her orgasm. I'm not allowed to touch her with my hands, despite my longing to flip her over onto her back and fuck her senseless. She's not ready for that yet; she gets to decide when I can fuck her. She's only had one orgasm, and I'm sure my task is not complete. I continue with my tongue, sucking hard on her clit as she writhes above me.

"I want you to do that again tonight," she instructs me. "But I want you to stick your tongue in my ass, as well, and then your finger. I know you like fucking my ass; it'll be like you're getting me ready. Ready for your thick cock. Do you think you could do that? Would you like that?"

"Yes." My throat thickens with desire.

Liana on all fours, tight ass in the air, telling me what to do and how to do it. Deciding on how I am allowed to fuck her. I have no control over my own pleasure and it's how I want it.

Liana is long and lean with sinewy muscles carved out by her enjoyment of whips and spanking. She's also the most sexually adventurous woman I've ever met; definitely, the most adventurous I've ever been with. She will let me do anything–as long as it's something she suggests. Thinking about my mouth on her pussy, making her cry out...I love how vocal she is when she comes. Thinking about sliding my cock into her tight orifice—I'm rock hard, just thinking about it. Maybe I'll take a trip to the men's room.

"I know what you're thinking," she says, still using her voice. "You are not allowed to waste yourself. You are not allowed to come until I tell you so."

"Of course," I stutter only slightly.

"I don't want you jerking off, touching yourself at all. You can think of me, think about all the things I'll let you do to me, but in no condition are you allowed to touch yourself. And of course, no one is supposed to touch you, either," she instructs. Along with being intense and tightly wound, Liana is also pathetically jealous. It's her only vulnerability; the only way I could hurt her if I wanted to.

"No one would," I assure her.

"I'm sure there are lots of women there at work with you who would like you to lick their pussies," she says, sounding more like a jealous girlfriend than a dominatrix and doing a great job of deflating my hard-on.

But then I see Callie.

"There's no one here who would want that," I lie. I'm sure Callie would welcome oral sex from me. She might even look forward to it; beg for it.

The image of Callie begging me to touch her revs up the engines again. For once I'm glad Callie stays at her own desk instead of coming over.

"I don't believe you," Liana says. "You're mine. They need to realize it."

"Everyone knows we're together," I assure her.

"Do they know what we do together?" she asks, her voice thickening with desire. As much as Liana likes to dominate me, she loves reminding me of our roles. "Do they know how I *spank* you? What toys do I use? How you'll do *anything* for me?"

"No, no one knows about that." I keep my eyes on my desk, not wanting to look up to see if Callie is watching me. I can feel her eyes on me, making the hair at the back of my neck prickle, but also making me reluctant to continue my conversation with Liana.

While I've never been ashamed of being a submissive, it's the last thing I want Callie to know about me. What would she think of me?

Why does that matter? I'm with Liana.

"I think it might be a good idea if you told them," Liana says coolly. "If I want you to, you'll tell them, won't you?"

"Liana," I warn, breaking role. She's taking this too far today.

"Michael," she barks in her no-nonsense, *don't mess with me* voice. "Are you really arguing with me?"

"No," I say in a low voice, my shoulders hunching from her tone.

"Are you ashamed of how you love me?"

"Of course not."

"Then why would you feel ashamed if people knew about it? How you want me to tell you what to do? How you ask me to punish you?"

"It's none of their business," I tell her stiffly.

"You're right. But I might want you to tell them. You'll do that for me if I ask, won't you Michael?"

"Of course," I say quietly, feeling like a puppet who has no control over my strings.

"Would you like me to punish you tonight?" she asks, switching to her sexy voice. Visions of the paddle, and me bent over the bed dance in my head. Of my cock in her mouth between slaps of the crop, my balls nestled in her hand.

Of fucking her just the way she wants it, in whatever new and outrageous position she's devised.

"Yes," I tell her, my own voice thick with desire.

When I finally get off the phone, I glance over to Callie's desk. She's smiling at me.

Chapter Ten

CALLIE

JASON CALLS ME THAT afternoon. "How about coffee?"

I can tell he's trying his best to sound casual but I know Jason and he's anything but. His attempts make him sound a bit desperate.

I could think it's sweet, the way he's trying if I was so inclined. But for some reason, I'm not.

For the first time in a long time, I'm not in the mood for an office hookup.

"Sure," I tell Jason. "I'll meet you in the kitchen downstairs."

"The—kitchen?"

"For coffee. And to talk," I say firmly, wondering what I'm doing. I can tell Jason is wondering too.

"Okay?"

"Five minutes." I hang up before he can question me, and head downstairs before I can see him move from his desk.

This is because of Michael. Lately, things seem different between us. I've always had a crush on him. I admit to the infatuation, even though I am much too old to feel that way. Maybe that's why I like him. Being around Michael makes me excited, happy, almost giddy sometimes. I miss him when he's not around. Weekends have slowly become torture for me because it's forty-eight hours without him. Not only that, but I picture him with *her*, the girlfriend.

I know nothing about her. Michael doesn't even have a picture of her on his desk and it's been so long since I've been in a relationship that I don't know if that's normal or not.

I picture her with blonde hair. Small, with tiny, jutting breasts and a waist Michael can span with his hands. He would hold her delicately, afraid to break her...

There would be no breaking me. He could be rough, or gentle; I'm up for anything, anytime.

Except not with Jason.

And not with anyone else here at Hever.

I've got it bad for Michael.

I hate thinking of him having sex with her, but other things cause me grief; that she knows how Michael takes his coffee in the morning; picturing them watching television together and fighting over the remote. Sharing the last cookie in the bag. Holding each other in bed.

It's been so long since I've let anyone hold me in bed. These days, it's sex, and then out. It's been a long time since I've had someone in my bed; someone that I've wanted to take home.

What's *wrong* with me?

It was Michael's comment that brought this on. I had already been concerned that I was too caught up in the headiness of what

I was feeling for Michael. I know it's not reciprocated; could never be, but I was all right with that.

"Have you ever been in love?" The pity in his voice when he thought I had never experienced the emotion.

"The best sex is when you're in love with the person."

I haven't thought about love in years. It wasn't something I felt I needed or wanted, or to be truthful, felt like I deserved. I had been in love once–that life-altering myriad of emotions that make you see things differently. Like when the waves in the lake stop lapping at the shore and the water is perfectly, exquisitely clear so that the rocks and the pebbles and even the tiny fish at the bottom are visible in the depths.

I had that with Devon. And I lost it.

"I don't think it's a good idea for us to meet anymore," I tell Jason as he's standing before me in the kitchen with an expression of hope and confusion mixed on his face, making him appear younger than his thirty years.

"Is it–is there something I did? Something I could have done better?"

"No. God, no," I chuckle, the memory of his mouth between my legs, of *him* between my legs making my stomach clench in a way I'm all too familiar with.

His tongue was everywhere.

With both hands squeezing my cheeks, Jason tongued me thoroughly, leaving nothing untouched, always returning for a suck on my clit before moving off again. He dragged his tongue between my lips, circling the edge of my opening before plunging inside. Tickling my perineum, he used the tip against my ass, before moving back to my clit.

I felt like Canada when the Europeans first arrived–explored, discovered, plundered.

Setting me gently on the cement, Jason added a finger to his administration, dipping deep within me; and then two. His tongue flicked a rhythm against my clit before sucking it hard. And then even harder as his fingers thrust inside me.

Searching for my G-spot, and when he pressed deep inside me, he found it.

"Oh, God!" I cried out, forgetting where we were, conscious of the sensations racing through my body. I clutched Jason's hair as his mouth, his tongue, and his fingers claimed me. My cries were loud and harsh and filled the room and I couldn't think of quieting myself. "I'm coming! Oh, God, Jason, now, please–" I arch my back as I crashed over the edge.

Jason relentlessly continued his licking and sucking, his fingers thrusting fast inside me. I bucked against him, his hair gripped tight in my hand. He didn't stop; he never faltered. Insistent, inexorable, like he demanded every ounce of pleasure I could supply. He–

"Oh, fuck, don't–this is so good," I gasped. "More–again! I'm–again!"

And then I came a second time, even more intense than the first.

"You screamed my name," he said proudly when he finally lifted his head.

What am I doing turning him down? Maybe just once more...

"It's me," I tell him, the words sounding disappointingly lame even to my ears.

"I don't understand. I thought—"

"I don't either," I confess. "Michael said something about needing love—"

"You want a relationship?" Jason jumps as eagerly as a kid on a trampoline onto the idea. "Because I'd be okay with that."

Oh no. "You're sweet," I tell him wistfully, reaching a hand to his shoulder to take the sting out of the words. I run my hand down his chest, over his heart. "It would never work out between us."

"I don't see why it wouldn't. We're both attractive, have similar interests, and a more than healthy libido that would keep us occupied," he insists.

"That's true but—"

"Is it the difference in our ages?" he interrupts. "Because I don't see an issue with that either."

Jason may only be using his logical side to argue it with me, but I'm seeing neediness and it strengthens my resolve, despite our mutual attractiveness. I've never understood being needy. Maybe it's because there are so many memories of *me* being the one begging for another chance clogging my brain.

"It's not that, Jason," I tell him irritably. "I like being friends with you but that's all it can ever be."

"So you're breaking up with me?"

I throw up my hands. For an intelligent man, this is turning out to be much more difficult than I thought it would be. "There's nothing to break up. There's no–there's nothing. We hooked up a few times which was good for both of us."

"That's why I don't understand..."

"I don't think I want to do that anymore. Just...sex. I don't think it's for me." The words sound foreign even to me, and from the look on Jason's face, I can see he's surprised. And that he doesn't really believe me. "I'm serious," I continue. "Lately–it was good between us, don't get me wrong, but I don't know. I don't understand it."

"I don't either." He clearly wants to say more but has too much pride to argue further.

"I know you're pissed off," I tell him with more exasperation than I need to. "I knew you were expecting–"

"It's not that!"

"Maybe you got too hung up on me. God knows that's happened before." I try for a playful smile but Jason remains glum. "You should look further than me. Someone younger, even age isn't the issue here. Sadie, maybe."

"There's something going on with her and Alma." Jason sounds even more forlorn, which makes me feel more hopeful, rather than offended at the thought of him preferring Sadie. I hope he does.

"Oh, that's over," I assure him. "It wasn't anything. Sadie is back to boys now."

"Are you sure about that? I saw Alma at Sadie's desk before I came down here."

After I storm out of the kitchen to find Sadie, she's not even at her desk. I head downstairs to Brienne instead.

I forgo my usual spot on her desk and pull over a chair. "I just turned down Jason."

"But I thought..."

"I know. He's amazing. I told him he should go for Sadie. I don't think he was opposed to the idea."

"What the hell has happened to you?" Brienne is wide-eyed.

"I don't know," I wail. "Maybe I'm hormonal. Michael said–"

"Well, there you go."

"What's that supposed to mean?"

"Callie, you've always had a thing for Michael, but lately it's been different. And he seems different around you, too. Like he's woken up after a long nap."

"What's that supposed to mean?" I repeat irritably. The last thing I want is any encouragement about my feelings for Michael. I think about him too much to begin with. He's the first person I think about when I wake up in the morning and the last before I go to sleep, no matter who I might be sharing my bed with. I make decisions based on what he would think and gauge my comments based on what he would say...

I've got it bad for him and I don't know what to do about it. *Girlfriend, girlfriend, girlfriend* seems to flash on his forehead when he's around me, and that's something I don't mess around with.

"I think he likes you," Brienne tells me gleefully.

"Don't say that," I groan. "He's not allowed to like me. He has a girlfriend."

"But what if he didn't?"

"But he *does*."

"And what if things were to change?" Brienne persists, leaning forward. "I've always respected your decision not to attract him because he has a girlfriend–"

"What do you mean 'attract'?"

"You know how peacocks fluff up their tail feathers when they're trying to mate. Well, I guess only men do that..."

"You're comparing me to a peacock?" I laugh.

"No. Well, kind of. You don't actually have to do anything to attract men. They sort of just flock to you. But I've seen you pile on the smiles, use the chest and guys don't stand a chance. I'm saying that you haven't tried to work your magic on Michael, and I respect that. But what if you did just to see what would happen?" Brienne asks eagerly.

"Well, you know as well as I do what would happen," I tell her with a cockiness I don't feel. I *don't* know what would happen if I made a play for Michael. I don't know how strong his feelings for this girlfriend are. They've been together for five years...

"Does he seem happy with her?" Brienne asks. I hesitate. "I don't think he is."

"I thought it was just wishful thinking on my end..."

"What if he's not happy with her? What if he feels the same way about you? What if you're missing out on something great with him? You just turned down sex because of this guy–how many Jasons are you going to have to turn down before you get so desperate–"

I slap at Brienne's leg and she wheels her chair away with a giggle.

"That sounds like a *would you rather*!" I snap my fingers, thinking of the fun questions I would always ask Brienne. "Even though I could email you this one because it's a non-dirty version."

"What fun are they?" Brienne makes a face. "I miss my dirty *would you rather questions.*"

"I know, but I don't want to get you in trouble. Or I don't want Jason to be in the situation that he would have to report us."

"You like him," Brienne sighs.

"I never said I didn't, only that I don't want to have sex with him anymore. Well, the more I think about it, the more that I do, but I'm not going to. So—question," I say, changing the topic from Jason because I need to stop thinking about him or I just might recant my decision and drag him off to the closet to screw his brains out. And since I suspect he has a great many brains... I clear my throat. "Would you rather be one of those big, beautiful birds, like a swan that sits around doing nothing, or some cute little birdie like a sparrow or swallow—"

Brienne interrupts with another childish giggle. "You said swallow."

"It's been a long time since I've swallowed," I sigh. "It's a good thing when a guy does you without insisting you go down on him. Not that I wouldn't, but it's nice not to be an obligation."

"When it is ever an obligation for you?"

"You're right; never. And I hate guys telling me what to do. I like being in charge."

"I can totally see you with a whip when you say things like that," Brienne tells me but I shake my head.

"I don't want to go that far. I talk a good game, but at the end of things, when I've got what I want, I want him to take me however he wants to and not to have to keep instructing him about how and when and why."

"Is there ever a why?"

"Maybe why not?"

We laugh together. Brienne means the world to me. I've never had a friend like her. "So you think I should go fluff up my tail feathers?" I ask slowly.

"I think this might be a good time to ask why not."

Chapter Eleven

SADIE

I HAVE MY HEAD down, working at my desk when I smell her perfume. I never found out what it was but it smells expensive like it should have Nicole Kidman promoting it in a commercial. The scent brings with it a wave of unwelcome desire. Alma's smell would often cling to my clothes after we—

"Hello, Sadie."

My shoulders hunch and it takes a moment for me to look up. "Hi, Alma."

She's smiling but it doesn't reach her eyes. Fake, pretend with her face tight and pinched around her eyes.

I still think she's beautiful, but the appeal has lessened. Thank goodness for that. It's just the memory of her touching my body I have to get past.

"You don't have to look so scared to see me. You're perfectly safe," Alma says wryly. "I'm not about to try and seduce you. Again. Ever."

I can't help but grimace. This is what I've been dreading. I hate confrontations and I'm expecting the worst from Alma. She's a very passionate woman who enjoys getting her own way. And I took that away from her.

"I'm sorry," I tell her automatically.

"Are you really?" Alma wants to know. "What exactly are you sorry for? For playing some game with me? For the stunt with Callie? I thought better of you, Sadie."

"It wasn't a game," I say stiffly. "Not with you." I don't want to be sucked in by the hurt in her voice but I'm too soft-hearted for the comment not to hit the mark.

"Then what was it? I thought you cared about me. I thought we had something special."

I meet Alma's eyes, expecting to see the shimmer of tears, but all there is iciness. Her eyes look like they did after she brought me to orgasm—smug, self-satisfying. And that makes me angry.

"What about you?" I cry defensively, my voice too loud. Heads turn and I slink into my chair. "I'm not talking about this with you."

"Don't you owe me at least that?"

"I don't owe you anything," I mutter. "You threatened me."

"I didn't mean it," Alma says dismissively. "Come into the kitchen."

"I'm not going anywhere with you!" I can see Jason's head pop up over the cubicle wall a few rows over. This discussion shouldn't take place in public. "Ok. The kitchen."

"Nice to know you can still listen to reason," Alma says smugly, stepping back from my desk. "Don't worry, I'll keep my hands to myself."

"It's not that," I protest.

"Or maybe you don't want me to keep my hands to myself."

I scowl at the haughty expression on Alma's face and push my chair back to stalk past her to the kitchen.

I'm glad it's ending like this, with me still pissed off at her. I'm tired of missing her.

I don't like admitting I do.

"So what would you like to talk about? How you threatened to have your husband fire me if I don't become some sort of love slave?" I demand, feigning politeness as we face off in the kitchenette. It's bigger than the one on the first floor but has no microwave or coffeemaker. Only a table, an uncomfortable-looking couch, and a water cooler fill the room. And now Alma and I, both with our arms folded in front of our chest, ready to brawl.

I have a sudden, vivid image of touching those breasts. Alma's nipples are small and pink and she likes it when—

Stop it!

"Has anyone seen the video?" Alma says flatly. I quickly shake my head. "So I don't have to worry about it turning up on YouTube?"

"I would never do that!" I tell her, stung at the implication.

"I didn't think you'd record me with someone!"

"*You're* trying to be the victim here? You blackmailed me! You lied to me and then you threatened to get me fired! What am I supposed to do? Lie back and take it?"

"But I thought you liked lying back and taking it from me?" Alma purrs, suddenly switching from the scorned woman to the seducer, trying to catch me off guard.

It almost works.

"Stop it."

"Stop what?"

"Stop whatever it is you're trying to do. I don't want to play games with you."

"But that's what I like to do, Sadie. I thought you knew that. I play games. I like to play with you. You wanted some excitement, a new experience, another notch on your belt."

"I did not!"

"Well, I knew you weren't looking for any sort of relationship with me." Alma rolls her eyes, which annoys me.

"What were you looking for? You have a husband, you know."

"Who knows all about this."

"What? He knows?" My heart stops at the thought, of talking to Julian and him aware of everything that happened with his wife. My face flames.

"Well, not about you, not at first," Alma concedes. "He knew I was...involved...with someone here, and he was fine with it."

"Seriously? But why?"

"Sadie. You're so young and naive."

"I'm not that young!"

"I think you might have an old-fashioned view of marriage. It's not all like the shows on television. Julian and I are very happy together–despite what I led you to believe–but we do enjoy an unconventional marriage."

"You play around. And he's okay with that?"

"Of course he is. He has other pursuits as well. Sometimes we enjoy them together."

I can't think of anything to say. I have a new impression of Alma and I can't figure out if it's better or worse than what I thought of her before.

"What did you come to talk to me about?" I finally ask.

"To tell you that you over-reacted."

"You came to tell *me* that? After you threatened to have me fired if I didn't do what you wanted?"

"I wouldn't have said anything to Julian," Alma brushes off my incredulous expression like she's removing a crumb from her sweater. "It was just a game. Besides, Julian has had his eye on you for a while. He thinks you have a lot of potential."

"What's that supposed to mean?"

"What do you think, Sadie? You're a smart girl."

"I don't want to play games with you, Alma. I don't want to play *that* game."

"But what about other games?"

I'm shaking my head before she finishes. "No. Absolutely not."

"Oh, come on, Sadie. We were good together and you know it. I was the best you've ever had." Alma steps closer, surrounding me with her heady fragrance. I stare into her eyes, hardly daring to breathe as she touches my arm, running light fingers to my hand before she takes it and pulls it towards her mouth. "Wasn't it good for you?" she whispers, sliding one of my fingers between her lips.

"Alma," I try and warn her, but it comes out as a pathetic whisper. The touch of her tongue on the tip of my fingers sends a jolt of desire between my legs. When she sucks it, I almost groan aloud.

"You liked it, didn't you? You liked my mouth on you...between your legs. The way you taste, Sadie..." Alma closes her eyes as she sucks hard on my finger. "Why don't we give it another try? Tomorrow afternoon..."

"I don't..." I can't say no. The words won't come. I'm too distracted by the feel of my finger caught in her warm mouth, the memories of what else her mouth could do to me...

"We could use Julian's office. He wants a meeting with you, after all."

I stare at Alma, feeling her tongue caressing my finger. "Julian...?"

"Of course. This would make him very happy."

"You're saying..." My brain is foggy, I can't comprehend what Alma is trying to say.

"*Yes*, Sadie. Think about it," she tells me, releasing my hand with a tiny smile. "I'll be in touch."

She leaves me then, standing alone in the kitchen. It's only when the door closes behind her, that I finally groan aloud. What have I gotten myself into?

Chapter Twelve

CALLIE

I GO IN TO work early on Thursday morning.

This is my little secret. It's not like I don't have work to do in the office; I have tons. Despite my proclivity for fooling around during the day, I'm actually a very hard worker and have never been accused of letting my part of the team down. The engineers work together and I don't want anyone to have a reason to out me for all my office hookups. If the work doesn't get finished during the day, I make a point of coming in early.

I've never told anyone about my early mornings. No one even knows I have the key, other than Julian Donovan, who gave it to me. He also told me about the senior engineering position that's going to be available. From the sounds of things, I'm in the running but so is Michael.

And when I get to my desk, who do I find at his?

"What are you doing here?" Michael demands, but the smile on his face suggests my early appearance is a good thing.

"I can ask you the same thing." Trying to hide my own smile, I tuck my purse into the drawer on my desk. Michael's thick hair has been slicked back; by the time I see him in the morning, his hair is dried and already falling forward into his eyes. He's not much for products or for personal grooming. He's clean, with no visible stains on his clothing and he smells good, a mixture of soap and deodorant. I've gone out with metrosexuals before and I prefer a man who takes less time getting ready than I do, and I'm pretty quick.

I think I prefer Michael for just about everything. The realization lessens my good mood.

Michael shrugs. "I'm having trouble sleeping and this project still needs some work. I've been here early the last few mornings."

"You've got a dirty little secret," I muse, avoiding my concern over his lack of sleep. He doesn't need me to worry about things like that. He has a girlfriend; that's her job.

Lately, I've been wondering if she's up to the task. Michael hasn't looked happy for the last few days and I can't help wondering if she's the cause.

I'm probably just imagining things.

Or maybe they had a fight. It could be that she's denying him sex and he's all bottled up, ready to explode at the slightest touch...

Could I make him explode? With a simple touch, a caress? If I reached out and grabbed him?

"More than one," Michael says grimly.

I walk over to his desk and tip his coffee cup towards me. "No coffee yet?" I ask rather than demanding to know what his dirty secrets are. I find myself somewhat desperate to know.

It's more difficult being friends and wanting more than I thought it would ever be. I'm more than attracted to Michael; I have to be honest about that now. The only question is, what am I going to do about it?

Is it really time to fluff my feathers, as Brienne puts it?

He has a girlfriend. So—nothing. I don't take what's not mine to take. I never have and I never will. But I've never been more tempted.

"I've been here for a while." Michael points to the large Starbucks cup in his trashcan and I laugh, happy to see his face instantly brighten at the sound.

"Feel like escorting me to the kitchen so I can get some much-needed caffeine? I wish there was a Starbucks on my way here. Actually, it might be better if there wasn't." I smile at him as he leaps to his feet. "Less temptation to stop."

"I thought you liked temptation?" he asks with a coy smile.

"It's six o'clock in the morning and you're already flirting with me?" I demand. Why did I bring up temptation? Does he have any idea how I feel, or is this just a game to him?

"Anytime, Callie, anytime," Michael sighs as he holds the doors to the stairwell open for me.

Just as we step through, I hear the chime of the elevator door opening on the floor. "Is anyone else here?" I ask.

"I haven't seen anyone, but I've been hiding at my desk the whole time. There were no cars in the lot when I got here. Why? Expecting someone?"

No, just wondering if we're the only losers who do this. But it is kind of cool being in here alone."

"Very cool. Plus I finally have you all to myself," Michael says in a fake and very bad Dracula accent.

"Whatever will you do with me?" I ask, batting my eyelashes and playing along.

"If only. You have no idea the ideas I have for you," he sighs, sounding surprisingly serious for our playful banter.

"What would your girlfriend think of you flirting with me?" I wonder.

"What's this sudden fascination with my girlfriend?" he counters abruptly.

I glance over as we descend to the first floor. "No sudden fascination," I say simply, even though I'm confused at the expression of annoyance on his face. "Just simple curiosity about your life."

"It's pretty uneventful," he tells me.

"I don't believe you. What's the most boring thing you did last night?"

"Wouldn't you rather know the most exciting?"

"No, because you might think you need to tell me about what you and your girlfriend got up to last night and truthfully, I don't need to know that."

"I wouldn't do that." Michael seems stung at the suggestion.

"You have every right to say whatever you want about her," I tell him. "I have no problem talking about sex."

"I'm aware of that," he says drily. "Like with Jason?"

I stop and turn to Michael in the stairwell. "Do you really want to talk about Jason?"

"I want to know what happened between the two of you, yes."

I open my mouth, debating what to say. I'm attracted to Michael; interested in him. I like him, but I had sex with one of his friends and he wants to know about it.

That tells me loud and clear he's not interested. I keep heading down the stairs, descending almost as quickly as my heart sinks with disappointment. "I don't think you do," I finally say as we reach the bottom.

"So there is something," Michael persists, reaching out to pull open the door for me.

"Was," I correct. "And I don't kiss and tell."

"That's not what I hear."

"Is that so?" I ask with enough ice in my voice to freeze Florida. Michael is taken aback by my tone and I stalk ahead of him into the kitchen.

"No, not really," he says, back-pedalling. "I don't know why I said that."

I load the Tassimo without speaking. I've had sex with more than a few of the Hever employees and I'd be naive not to think people don't talk. If there's one thing I am, it's not naive. I expect the gossip and I've even heard some of it. It's never bothered me in the past; I run my sex life like a man. I go after what I want when I want it. I have a healthy libido and I like to have sex. I've never been ashamed of that fact.

But I've never had a man I'm interested in try and make a joke out of it.

"I'm not a slut," I tell him in a low voice.

"I never said you were!" Michael holds out his hands defensively.

"I like to have sex. There's *nothing* wrong with a woman having a healthy sex drive."

"No, there isn't." He looks bewildered at the change in mood but I'm too angry to care.

"I have sex with a lot of men and none of them are complaining. I fucked Jason," I say, the words sounding harsh in the quiet kitchen. "Is that what you want to know? I like to fuck men, and sometimes women. I don't go for relationships or commitment or anything like that. I just like to fuck. Happy, now? Or do you want details? Do you want to know how Jason went down on me and made me come twice; the second time was so intense I screamed his name? And how he took me from behind and I came a *third* time. This was all in the storeroom, one afternoon and it was really good. Is that what you want to know?"

"I really didn't need to know that," Michael says quietly.

"But you wanted to know. It's not the first time you've asked."

"But now I've heard..." Now it's Michael who is searching for words. "It makes me jealous, all right."

"Jealous." I can't keep the scorn out of my voice because I know he can't be serious.

"I want to be the one doing those things to you. I want to make you come three times. I want you to scream out my name, not anyone else's."

Michael looks astonished like he can't believe he's said that. But he can't be as shocked as I am. For weeks, and months, I've dreamed of Michael telling me he feels the same as I do. But not now. Not like this.

"You aren't allowed to say things like that," I tell him flatly. "You have a girlfriend." And with my heart racing, I head for the stairs without waiting for him.

Michael catches up as I reach the second-floor landing. "Callie!"

"No," I tell him. "There are some lines I don't cross and the girlfriend line is one of them."

"But there are things you need to know."

"Are you still together?" I demand, with one hand on the door handle. Michael doesn't answer; he doesn't have to. "That's all I need to know."

I'm out the door heading to my desk when I hear the noise. I stop short, Michael crashing into me. Luckily, his coffee slops onto the floor instead of on me. I throw up my hand.

"Do you hear that?" Another cry cuts the air.

"Who's here?" Michael demands. I grab his arm as he strides forward. Another cry and a low moan; loud enough for me to recognize the cause of it.

"Someone's having sex!" I cry in a hushed voice, my fingers digging into the fabric of Michael's shirt.

"What?"

"Listen." I press my finger to his lips. "I think they're in the upstairs kitchen."

"Who?" He mouths the word.

I shrug my shoulders, a suddenly gleeful smile on my face. I can't wait to find out who it is. Someone other than me getting busy in the office.

Office romance. Maybe it's Sadie, but if she's with Alma again, after everything I did to get her out of that situation. "That's a guy!" I hiss with excitement as I hear a low growl.

"Who else did you think it was in there?" Michael wants to know. I raise an eyebrow. "Really?" Now he looks excited.

"What do you think they're doing?" I put my mouth close to his ear, breathing in his clean scent as I whisper. Without realizing it, we've angled ourselves closer to the kitchen door, which is shut, but obviously made of very thin wood.

Michael only gives me a look that says clearly, *What do you think they're doing?* without saying a word.

I stifle a giggle. "These walls must be so thin." Another groan escapes the room, and I can't help but feel a jolt of desire between my legs. I've watched my share of pornography over the years, but seeing it in front of me has never turned me on as much as listening. Hearing the moans and cries, the more graphic sounds of the slap of bodies together, the sound of wetness as a cock moves hungrily inside a pussy.

"What do you think he's doing?" I ask again, my lips practically tickling Michael's ear. "Do you think he's on top?" I can picture it; the two faceless lovers, her pinned to the table with her legs tucked up to her chest, hands gripping his ass as he pumps his cock in and out between her legs. "Maybe he's taking her from behind?"

Michael turns to me, his eyes darkening. From excitement, I realize. He's feeling it too. My eyes drift to his lips, thin and curving up at the corners in an ever-present hint of a smile. "Maybe she's on top."

With breasts swinging, I visualize, his hands gripping her hips as she rides him, his mouth trying to capture her erect nipple. My own nipples are standing at attention, a fact Michael would be able to see clearly if he glances at my chest. Instead, his gaze drifts over my face, appearing to avoid looking at my chest with difficulty.

I want him to look. I want him to touch; cupping my full breasts in his hands while his lips tug on my nipples.

I have trouble swallowing.

My shoulder is pressed against Michael's chest, his back against the wall as we listen. Whoever is in there has some serious stamina because they're not giving any evidence they're finishing anytime soon.

"What's your favourite position?" I can't look at Michael when he whispers the question to me because I'm deathly afraid I'm going to kiss him.

"From behind. When he thrusts in hard and I'm not ready for it."

I finally glance up, fearing I've said too much. I didn't say how much I love the feel of a thick cock sliding inside me, going as deep as possible while fingers search for my clit to give me a more intense orgasm. Unlike some women, I can come with straight fucking, but it takes a while and it's less intense. Like sinking into a warm bath rather than plunging into a hot and bubbling hot tub.

I can see the desire in Michael's eyes, mirrored in my own. His lips are open and he's panting slightly. I feel the brush of his finger against my back.

This is not good.

"What about you?" I need to know. I want to know, so when I'm back home tonight I can picture Michael fucking me in that position when I get myself off.

I'm not sure I can wait that long.

"From behind. Grabbing her hips–hard. Really hard."

"I like it hard," I breathe.

A strangled sound escapes from Michael and he leans closer, his hand sliding onto my hip. "I want–"

Loud cries from the kitchen, signalling the end is near, if not arrived. "We have to move," I tell him urgently.

"I can't." I stand there for another long minute, breathing Michael's scent, feeling the warmth of his body, his fingers splayed on my hip. Wanting his hand to move, to touch, to caress...

To feel how much I want him.

And then with a tremendous effort, I step away from him.

Chapter Thirteen

MICHAEL

ALL I WANT TO do is grab my dick and with a few pulls of my hand, rid myself of this painful pressure. I'm already hard; I've been rock-hard ever since I heard that first moan coming from the kitchen. Having Callie's full and luscious-looking body pressed against me is my definition of torture. Wanting my hands on her, knowing I couldn't–unbearable.

This might be worse. I'm afraid I might come in my pants, like some fourteen-year-old confronted with his first sight of bare tits.

Callie's tits...

When she told me how she liked it, I couldn't help but visualize it. I picture bending her over, taking her hard the way I like it, the way *she* likes it. Taking her hard and fast so that her cries erupt into screams as she shouts out my name...

Callie and I rush back to our desks before the couple comes out. There are a few desks between us but it's close enough for me to see her expression when the couple come out.

It's Carl and Delia.

Callie's eyes are about to pop out. I'm sure I look just as shocked.

Carl and Delia. Having sex in the kitchen.

It's like I've wandered into an alternate universe.

Even though I feel like crawling under my desk to hide, I sit hunched over my coffee cup, pretending to be engrossed in the papers on my desk. Neither Carl nor Delia even glance my way as they head directly for the stairs, holding hands and smiling at each other.

Carl and Delia.

As soon as the door shuts behind them, Callie is back at my desk.

"Can you believe that?" she exclaims.

"They're together all the time," I tell her, feeling the need to defend Carl. I can't seem to take my eyes off Callie's chest either, which makes my hard-on even more uncomfortable.

"But Delia's married and Carl has a girlfriend," Callie argues.

"Maybe they couldn't control themselves?'

Callie looks scornfully at me. "It's six o'clock in the morning. If I can control myself around you, then I'm sure anyone can do the same."

It takes a second for what she said to sink in. And Callie didn't realize what she said.

"You have trouble controlling yourself around me?" I ask carefully.

"What are you talking about?"

"You just said 'If I can control myself around you, then I'm sure anyone can do the same.' You said that."

A myriad of emotions flits across Callie's face. I expect her to deny the words that slid out of her mouth, but with a defiant shrug of her shoulders, making her breasts heave and fall, she proves me wrong.

"So? You're a smart boy. I'm sure you can see how I feel about you."

My jaw drops. Literally, drops. "Ah–no? You could–ah, explain. Please."

Her blue eyes widen. "What do you mean?"

"I'm asking you what you mean. You said–"

"I know what I said," she snaps, taking a step back, distancing herself from her confession.

I'm sure you can see how I feel about you.

"Obviously I shouldn't have said anything. You have a girlfriend and I have a big mouth. I made a mistake. Forget I said anything."

"Callie," I grab her wrist as she's whirling away. "I can't forget that."

"Well, you're going to because nothing is going to happen. *Girlfriend*." She jabs an accusatory finger at me.

"What if I said things weren't great with Liana and me," I tell her desperately.

"You're just saying that so you can get a piece of ass."

"If that's true, I would have said it a long time ago."

"Is this some sort of pissing contest between you and Jason?" she demands, her blue eyes narrowed.

"Oh, for Christ's sake!" I explode.

"You're all hot and bothered from listening to the two of them and now you think I'm an easy lay and can help you out with things. You think I'm nothing more than a slut–"

"I don't think of you like that at all," I tell her quickly, grabbing her wrist before she can stalk away again, my other hand sliding around her waist. It's the first time I've touched her, held her like this, in any other way other than friendly.

I'm not thinking of anything friendly right now.

"What do you think of me?" Callie demands.

"I don't know, but I can't stop. I can't stop thinking of you, Callie and I don't know what's going to happen but all I know is that I want to be the one who does that stuff to you."

Unable to control myself I yank her closer, and kiss her, pressing my lips against hers which are still moving in retort. For a brief, glorious moment, she responds; her lips moving under mine, re-laxing and parting just enough for my tongue...

And then she pushes away.

"You have a *girlfriend*!" she cries, wrestling out of my arms.

"What if I didn't?" I counter, struggling to keep hold of her.

"But you do."

"But what if I didn't?"

"Michael," Callie warns, but she's stopped struggling. My arm tightens around her waist. I won't continue to argue, to listen to her protests. She's made it clear she wants me and if I don't have her now, I think I might really explode.

In a quick move, I turn with her still in my arms so that Callie is pinned to my desk. "I don't give a fuck what you did with Jason or anyone else."

I press my mouth against her neck, feeling her body relax again as I nuzzle the sensitive skin below her ear. "I want to taste every inch of you," I whisper, moving from one side to the other, my hands sliding onto her wonderful, generous ass; cupping and squeezing and enjoying the feel of her body in my hands. "I want to be the one who fucks you so hard that you scream out *my* name. I want to be the next cock, the *best* cock you've ever had."

Before Callie says anything, before she can think to stop me or find a reason for us not to do this, I drop to my knees before her. She's wearing a short summer dress, and I reach underneath with both hands and yank down her panties.

"Michael..."

But it's not an admonition and there's no disapproval in her tone. It's a whisper of acceptance, of encouragement, as clear as her hands that find the back of my head as I press my face between her legs.

"Oh, god," she breathes as I find her with my tongue. Callie spreads her legs, pressing herself against the desk to keep her balance, as I probe into her folds, finding her as wet and sweet as I imagine. Her clit is tiny as I flick it with my tongue, kissing it, rolling it between my lips until I hear her gasp. And then I suck it with my mouth, thrusting a finger inside her at the same time.

"We shouldn't," Callie gives one last lack-lustre reprimand. "Your girlfriend..."

"Will not be my girlfriend for much longer," I tell her, feeling suddenly free from the realization that there is nothing holding me to Liana. There was sex, but not now that I have this wonderful, beautiful, sexy woman in my arms, *wanting* me. It's a heady feeling, after years of imagining Liana as my only option.

I'm in control. I'm being dominant. I'm pleasing her the way I want to...

Callie suddenly lifts her leg, slinging it over my shoulder as she presses my head farther between her legs. "Don't stop, Michael, please don't ever stop..."

I can't, even if I want to. Surrounded by her juices, her scent intoxicating me more than any alcohol can, I want nothing more than to pleasure her. And I do; the sound of her cries loud in the open space.

She comes quicker than I expect, with a sudden wail, her hips thrusting forward and I drink from her, willing to continue, wanting to continue, loving how the sound of her calling my name makes me feel.

"Stop it," she says instead, pulling me back by my hair.

"But..." I still have a grip on her ass with one hand, my fingers caught up in the warmth of her and I struggle against her grip to continue.

"I need you to fuck me," she pants. "*Right now.*"

I'm not about to argue with that.

I stand, quickly undoing my pants as I do so. "My bag," Callie instructs. "Condoms." I hand her the purse lying on the floor, yanking my boxers down as she thrusts the foil-wrapped package at me. Sliding it on as quickly as I can, and then she's guiding me inside her, one leg wrapping around my waist and suddenly I'm gripped by her warmth.

"Callie," I groan, my face buried into her neck.

"Fuck me like you want to," she tells me. "Please."

There's no gentleness with my thrusts. I fuck Callie like a man possessed; like a man denied his life's pleasure and finally achieving it. Hard, fast and relentless and it's still not enough. Wrapping my arms around her ass, I pick her up in my arms, slamming her back against the wall behind my desk with the force of my thrusts.

"*Yes!*" Callie shouts. "More, oh, god! Michael, please..."

I can't speak; I can barely breathe. I'm consumed with the sensation of my cock tight inside her pussy, sliding in and out of her, the sound of her cries turning to small shrieks as I pump.

Still, it's not enough.

I set Callie down and pulling out, I spin her to face the wall, yanking out her hips to bend her over. With barely enough time for her to brace her hands on the desk, I'm back inside her once more, thrusting even deeper and harder than before.

"Oh, god..."

I don't know who says it; it could have been either one of us. This is like nothing I've ever felt before. Fucking Callie like this, feeling in control...

I reach around, finding her clit and rubbing it, urging her on with my hips and my fingers. This is fucking fantastic, but it needs to be unforgettable for her as well.

"This is so good," Callie cries, and I grin, reaching around with my other hand to grip her inner thigh, widening her legs so I can thrust even deeper.

I have to fight for control. I want the release, I want to let go inside her but need to hang on for just a moment more.

And then I feel Callie tighten around my cock. As her cries fill the air once more, I explode with a harsh groan of my own.

I stay that way for longer than I need to, holding Callie by the waist as I catch my breath, praying I don't embarrass myself by telling her how much that meant to me.

And how much I want it to happen again.

I don't know if it ever will.

Chapter Fourteen

SADIE

"How are you finding things here?" Julian asks as I sit across from his desk in stupefied wonder. He had Alma schedule an official meeting for us for Thursday afternoon and I'm nervous enough going alone to his office, expecting Alma to be there.

Lying naked on Julian's desk.

But she's not here and I'm confused. Julian is treating this as if this is a real meeting. I don't know what to think.

Or if I'm disappointed.

"Ah, everything is...fine?" I say cautiously.

"Are you sure about that?"

"Everything is great."

"I'm glad to hear it." He moves out from behind his desk, which is the biggest desk I've ever seen. I'm sure Callie would be wondering if Julian is compensating for something.

As he settles himself on the edge of his desk, less than a foot away from me, I can't help but think about it as well. He's such a good-looking man, with the intense blue eyes and the ready smile that shows his charm rather than conceit.

Julian smells amazing.

I perch on the edge of the chair across from his desk, refusing to sink back into the cushions, refusing to relax.

Before Alma, I never considered myself to be adventurous or be willing to experiment. Whatever she did, however, she messed up my mind, I have to give her credit for changing me.

Instead of saying no to the meeting, I agreed. I agreed to find out what Julian wanted with me. What he wanted to do with me.

For the first time in a long time, I know a man is interested in me. Julian Donovan wants me and it's a heady feeling. It almost vanquishes my memories of my time with Alma.

At least until the door to Julian's office opens and Alma slips into the room.

"Oh." The word escapes like a breath of air.

What should I think? Excitement or terror? Desire or fear?

Maybe a little of both?

"Don't be nervous," Alma soothes, sitting beside me on the arm of the chair and running cool fingers along my cheek.

"I'm not nervous."

"You look like you're ready to bolt," she says with a smile. "Doesn't she, Julian? What have you been doing to get her so worked up?"

"I haven't been doing anything," Julian says with a bemused smile.

"We only want you to enjoy yourself. Forget about everything that happened between us and relax. Just feel."

"If I forgot what happened between us I wouldn't be here," I mutter.

Alma's smile widens. "Then you did enjoy yourself with me. You liked what I did." She traces a finger across the V-neck of my shirt, dipping below the fabric on her second trip. "Tell me what you liked."

"You know."

"I want to hear it. I like hearing things, especially what you like. I love listening to you come." She turns to Julian. "She makes the sexiest noises."

"I look forward to hearing it," Julian says.

I sit frozen in the chair. Maybe I expected something like this, but now it's a reality, I'm not sure what to do.

"I want to make you come again," Alma says softly, her fingers delving deeper down my shirt towards my breasts. My nipples push out of the material of my T-shirt, demanding to be touched. "Would you like that?"

I'm physically unable to speak. Panic has drained any moisture from my mouth. Between my legs, however, is another story. I nod.

"And Julian can watch."

"I'd like to make you come as well, sexy Sadie. But first, it would make me happy to watch."

I look at Alma, so confident and beautiful; at her mouth and think of what she can do to me. I glance at Julian, comfortable in this situation. I'm not remotely comfortable. I'm practically panting from the anxiety of this.

But I've never been so turned on.

"Take off your clothes," Alma orders. "Let him see your body."

I obey the request which is really an order because I can't do anything else. I agreed to this, and even if I want to stop it, I'm not sure I know how to.

But I don't want to stop.

This is wrong, this isn't me…these thoughts cloud my mind, but I'm not using my head right now. All the thoughts I'm focused on are coming from between my legs. All I can think of is how much I want to be fucked by both of them right now.

I strip off my clothes quickly, pausing only when I'm down to my undergarments. I'm proud of my body but wish I had larger breasts.

"Beautiful," Julian croons as I unhook and let my bra slide to the floor.

"She is. Perfect," Alma agrees, leaning over to take my nipple into her mouth. She licks and sucks, teasing the sensitive skin and moves to the other side, trailing her tongue between them. "Sit on the desk," she invites, lifting her head from my breast and using her fingers to give me a push. "I need to taste your pussy."

"I need to see you taste her pussy," Julian echoes, and Alma smiles at her husband.

"Are you having fun, Julian, dear?"

"Absolutely," he says, locking his gaze with mine as I settle myself on the glossy surface. "But I want to see her touch herself first."

"Sadie?" Alma asks, spreading my legs with a cool hand. "Touch yourself for Julian. Show him how you pleasure yourself."

"I'd rather you." I'm already aching for Alma's touch and the thought of waiting is almost unbearable.

"Well, I'm not going to unless you do it first," she says sharply. "Please do what you're told."

Obediently, I widen my legs, drawing one up onto the table to give Julian the best view. With hesitant fingers, I feel the wetness as I push my finger between my folds, searching for my clit. I exhale sharply when my fingers find the tiny nub.

"Do you like playing with yourself?" Julian wants to know.

"I'd rather you do it," I tell him.

"You want me to touch you?" he asks, his voice husky. I can see the desire in his eyes and the sight emboldens me.

"Yes," I tell him, adding a finger as I begin to circle my clit. "Both of you."

"At the same time?"

"Yes."

"I think you should ask nicely," Julian reprimands.

"Please?" I ask hesitantly. *"Please."* I quicken my pace, holding Julian's gaze as he walks towards me, touching my inner thighs with cool fingers. He reaches out and cups my breast, rolling the nipple between his fingers as I play with myself.

"I want her first," Alma pouts as she squeezes between Julian and me, crouching on the floor and adding her tongue to the pressure on my clit. I take my hand away, leaning back on my arms as she begins to tongue me.

Long, slow, wet licks reaching into every part of my pussy. Then she attacks my clit with flickers of her tongue, firm enough to make me cry out. Julian keeps caressing my breasts while he watches his wife. I reach for his crotch, excited by the length of hardness straining against the fabric. Biting my lip, I manage to work the zipper so that I can slide my hand into his pants.

He's hard and bigger than I expected. But I've only ever been with one other man, so I don't have a lot to compare to.

Even so, Julian seems pretty big. I glance up at him from under my eyelashes. Peeling his pants away, I gently ease down his briefs until I see the tip of his cock and caress it with shaking fingers. "Oh, god," I moan as Alma increases the pressure on my clit.

"Use your mouth," Julian tells me hoarsely.

It's been a while since I've given a blow job, but I want Julian's cock in my mouth more than anything else. Reaching up, I take it in my mouth, circling the tip with my tongue, scraping my teeth ever so slowly along the length, and hearing Julian's intake of breath.

I moan again as Alma sucks my clit, my own mouth full of Julian. He presses the back of my head so that I take him all the way in until he touches the back of my throat. Alma is making muffled noises, vibrations that add to the pleasure of her tongue. She focuses on my clit, licking in circles, slowly speeding up before flicking just the tip, the sides, and licking my entire cleft.

It's so quick. Already I can feel the rush of sensations racing through my body, towards my core and the release I need. "I'm going to come!" My words are incoherent, my mouth filled with Julian's cock, but Alma understands. She thrusts her fingers inside me at the same time as she sucks on my clit and I explode with a harsh cry, pressing my pussy against her face.

Even before I'm finished, Julian pulls away from me, moving a protesting Alma out of the way so he can stand between my legs. He's rolling a condom onto his cock before I realize what's happing, and then with a swift move, he's sliding into me.

"I'm not finished," a pouting Alma cries.

"Your turn to watch," Julian tells her, pulling out so that he can thrust into me. I cry out and he does it again. His cock fits tightly into my pussy and his deep thrusts mix pain with pleasure. But I'm not complaining. With a sigh, I pull both my legs onto the table as I lay back and allow Julian to have his way with me.

He tucks his hands under my ass, pulling me closer as he drives deep within me. It's been a long time since I've felt a man inside me and never have I felt one like Julian. He's raw and relentless, fucking me without emotion or any tenderness. He keeps his eyes on my face as I cry out from the sensations.

"You like me fucking you?" he grunts, pulling out until only the tip is inside me, before slamming back into me.

"Yes," I pant.

"You like my cock?"

"Oh, god, *yes*!" I cry as he repeats the move. I tuck my knees closer to my chest, desperate to give Julian more of me. "Don't stop—please!"

"Wait—me!" Alma gives a plaintive cry and she grasps my hand, forcing it under her skirt. I can feel how wet and ready she is, and for the first time, I don't want to give her pleasure, so focused on how it feels to have Julian fucking me. But she doesn't allow me to draw my hand away, and instead, begins to rub herself against my hand. I hold two fingers out firmly and let her rub her clit against them.

With my other hand, I reach for Julian's ass so I can somehow draw him even deeper inside me.

"Touch yourself," he tells me once again and instinctively realizing he's close, bring my hand between our bodies, rubbing my clit frantically to help give myself another release before Julian is finished.

"More...harder...don't stop," I gasp. I'm close, so close and I can tell Alma is as well, holding my wrist in a death grip as she rubs against my fingers. Another thrust, as deep as he can go, and then another...

My body tenses, and then I come, the orgasm roaring through my body with such intensity I arch up, freezing in a V position, my mouth open in a wordless scream before I collapse against the table.

I manage to give my fingers a final wiggle and hear Alma's soft cry. And then Julian erupts within me with a wall-shaking growl.

How could I ever think to give up men?

Is Sadin in over her head? Find out in Love After Hours.

Love After Hours

ANNA ELLIS

Chapter One

BRIENNE

ELI ALWAYS LIKES FUCKING me on the couch.

I have to agree because it gives the act a little more spontaneity. A little more urgency, like Eli can't wait to get me into the bedroom and has to have me right then, right there. I like being wanted that much. Who doesn't?

Tonight we're back on the couch with me propped up against the pillow that Callie gave me, the one that says, "Love? No thanks. I'd rather wine." It's hard and slightly uncomfortable against my shoulders but I'm not about to complain.

If I complain, Eli might punish me.

Maybe I should complain.

My pyjama shirt is unbuttoned, the chill air pebbling my nipples. My flannel pants have been flung somewhere across the room and I really don't care if they are hanging off the television or dangling off my orchid. The only thing that matters is what Eli is doing between my legs.

Mouth, fingers, tongue. Fingers, tongue, mouth. On and on and on, the sensations building to a towering spiral until I can't help but cry out, begging for more.

That's when Eli stops.

"Don't stop," I demand in a hoarse voice.

"But I have to," Eli says, his hint of an Irish accent heightening with his excitement. "If I don't stop at the perfect moment, you'll break into pieces as you scream my name, and then I'll have to fuck you." He punctuates his words with slow thrusts of his fingers. "I really want to fuck you, my beautiful Brienne, but I want to play for a while first."

"I can come more than once," I croak, fisting my pyjama shirt. "Please, Eli."

"I'm sure you can." Eli bends his head once more, carving his tongue through my wetness, leaving me aching for more. "But it's more fun this way, isn't it?"

"No!"

But Eli continues his teasing torture, flicks of his talented tongue mixed with his fingers exploring every nook and cranny until I'm almost out of my head with pleasure.

And then, suddenly, Ian is there in my living room.

I stare up at him, thinking how much he looks like Michael Fassbender, remembering the night when Ian had cleverly arranged to have me alone in the office when he had strapped the receptionist Agatha to his desk.

I had seen and heard Ian having his way with her. It had been a total turn-on and the reason why I had agreed to stay late the next

Friday, wondering what else Ian had planned. Turned out he had me planned.

With no preamble, Ian had bent me over his desk and paddled me, my first time stepping into the BDSM zone. Not that it was much, but it was something that left me wanting to explore more.

And then he fucked me stupid.

Stupid was what I was when I reached out to Ian after he got fired and suggested we get together. He said no. I haven't seen or heard from in the weeks after his dismissal from Hever Construction.

So why is Ian suddenly here in my living room while Eli is happily humming between my legs?

"Why...?" I stammer, not even bothering to cover my nakedness. "Ian? Where did you come from?"

"Isn't it better not to know?" Ian says with one of his sexy smirks that makes him look exactly like Magneto.

But even better than having a sexy Magneto in my living room, is having a naked Ian.

And then his cock is in my mouth.

Things speed up, move in warped sideways time. Suddenly I'm at work, the chill of the desk under my stomach. I'm naked, bent over Ian's desk again.

The cheap blinds covering the windows are open and I see a group watching. Callie, and Jason and Sadie, with Delia and Carl, and is that the guy from engineering who watches the goat porn? Abby and Ben stand there entwined in each other's arms, and Michael has his hand down his pants, much like I had when I watched Ian and Agatha.

"You like this?" Eli says from behind me. "You like them watching?"

"I don't know," I say. I try to stand but realize my arms and legs are strapped to the desk. "What are you doing?"

"Trying something new."

Eli brings his hand down on my ass with a slap that rings through the quiet office. I let out a squeak before he does it again, and again.

And then his mouth is back between my legs and I sigh with relief.

"Did you forget about me?"

I crane my neck to see Ian beside the desk, his thick cock in his hand. He grabs a fistful of my hair as I obediently open my mouth. My moan of pleasure from Eli's tongue is muffled by Ian's cock in my mouth. His fingers twist painfully in my hair as he urges me on.

More spanking, more of Eli's mouth, and then with fingers digging into my hips, Eli thrusts his cock into me. My eyes flutter closed, enjoying the sensations of Eli inside me.

There's a flicker of *what's going on* but my body ignores the question, accepting the fact I'm with two men, one who is now lifting me off my feet with his thrusts. I don't feel like digging too deep into the *why* because this feels so good and I don't care what's going on.

It's been weeks since I've been with Eli, Ian, or anyone, and I need this.

I need it so much.

I'm going to come soon, and I think Eli's going to let me this time. And then Ian's going to take his turn and who knows what he's going to do to me.

"Is there room for another in here?"

Because of Ian's grip on my hair, I can't turn my head to see who it is. I recognize the voice but...

"The more the merrier," Eli says with a laugh. "Brienne can take it."

"Of course she can," Ian agrees.

"I hope she can take me."

Ian relaxes his hold enough for me to turn my head slightly, only to be faced with the biggest, most beautiful cock I've ever seen. My body clenches with anticipation at the thought of it coming close to me.

And then I look up to see the cock belongs to Cooper.

I wake with a start.

Chapter Two

SADIE

TUESDAY MORNING I WALK through the front doors of Hever, hoping against hope that Alma isn't at her desk.

Because if Alma is at her desk beside Agatha, then I have to do the rude move, walking past the receptionist's desk with my attention straight ahead of me, or better yet, staring at my phone like I'm reading the answers to the universe rather than the latest Game of Thrones update.

I don't want to talk to Alma. I haven't been able to look at her since the afternoon she and her husband Julian Donovan fucked me on the conference room table.

Not only did I fuck a married woman, but I also fucked her husband. And to make it worse, he's my boss.

I breathe a sigh of relief when I see Agatha alone at the desk. She's busy studying her own phone and doesn't glance up as I walk by. I consider saying a cheery good morning for about a second but decide against it because I really don't like Agatha, and it would look strange when I don't say a word to her when Alma is there.

Alma and I were a *thing* for a few weeks. I call it a thing because I don't know how else to refer to it. We weren't in a relationship; we began as friends, but then she seduced me in the supply closet and that little episode changed things. And then she continued to seduce me in the supply closet, or the little kitchen on the third floor, or once in the washroom on the main floor which no one uses because the guys from the construction sites seem to be too frightened of the tampon dispenser to go near it.

I'd rather they didn't use it. It's the one place in the building where you're almost guaranteed privacy.

Callie gave me the scoop. I've been close friends with Callie since I've worked at Hever, so thanks to her, I know all her tried and true best places for a hookup during office hours. Callie's very open with information like that, as well as who's good at being quiet, and who lasts the longest.

I supplied my own information one afternoon—that Alma can make me come with just her fingers in under three minutes.

Alma is very talented.

Unfortunately, she's also talented at manipulation and stalking. She's also a pretty good liar.

Maybe not a liar. She didn't exactly lie when she didn't tell me she was married to the boss, she just withheld pertinent information. But that's the same as lying in my book.

I knew Alma was married when we started fooling around, which I'm not proud of, but I had no idea that her husband was the new president of Hever Construction where I work as the sole member of the marketing department, a job I'm very good at and don't want to lose.

Alma threatened my job and that's why I won't even look at her anymore.

Plus, it's difficult to look at a woman after she gave you multiple orgasms with her mouth. At least it's difficult not to look at her and want her to do it again.

It's kind of messed up with Alma and me. Friends to lovers, a little blackmail, and then throw in a husband who is also my boss...

I haven't seen Julian in the three weeks since that afternoon, which is a good thing, because I doubt I can look at him without spontaneously combusting from the memory.

It was good. *He* was good; very, very good. So much that while I had briefly considered switching teams because of Alma, Julian made me realize the error of my ways. Not that I don't enjoy women, but after him, there is no way I'm giving up men.

Hot, thick cock thrusting inside me—

Once safely past the receptionist's desk, I punch the button for the elevator. Normally I take the stairs, but my knees are suddenly shaking and it's not because of the brisk walk across the lobby.

Because now I can't stop thinking of Julian's hips pistoning between my legs in a rhythm that was somewhat like a battering ram on a merry-go-round.

It was a lot more enjoyable than it sounds.

Thinking of Julian is starting to affect my work. Either I tear through my assignment at a frenzied pace in the off-chance Julian wants to see me about something, or find myself forgetting the smallest detail because I can't concentrate on anything but how

Julian's fingers felt on my breast. Or how he stared hungrily as Alma made me come right in front of him.

I draw a shaky breath as the elevator chimes. It's going to be one of those days.

The doors slide open and Julian stands there.

Now it's going to be even worse.

"Sadie." His delight at seeing me is evident in his deep voice and the way he cocks his head. At his smile; confident, but not conceited, sexy but not smug.

"I'll take the stairs," I say, backing away.

"Don't be silly." He reaches out a hand to draw me into the elevator, the closed metal box where I will be within reach of his clever hands. "I haven't seen you around much."

The doors close behind me and I breathe in the scent of his cologne.

"I miss seeing you." Julian's voice drops and lust burns in his blue eyes.

"I..." I stammer, suddenly unsure of how or what or who.

"Don't say a word." His arm slides around my waist and tugs me closer. "Just tell me that you enjoyed our time together."

"I..." I can't put together a coherent sentence if my life depended on it. My head swims at his closeness—his lips brushing my ear, my body only a hairbreadth away from his, so near that I feel his warmth. "Yes," I whisper.

His lips sweep against my temple as his arm tightens around me. "I thought you might."

"*Yes.*"

Julian's lips curve into a smile and despite my fascination with his mouth, something about the smile screams *Danger! Danger!*

I'm prepared to ignore the warning.

"Would you be interested in spending more time together?" Julian asks in a low growl of a voice.

"Yes." *Jesus Julia*, can't I come up with some other word?

"I'm glad to hear that." His arm is still around me and his other hand slides up my torso, cupping my breast in a smooth motion, stopping to rest at the V of my simple white blouse. He toys with the button.

I want him to rip it off.

Can he see my nipples are as hard as a rock? Does he know I'm bubbling like a witches' cauldron between my legs?

"I'll be in touch," he whispers. His hand returns to my breast and presses his mouth on mine. It's the first time Julian has kissed me. His lips are firm and demanding, much like a man used to getting what he wants. His tongue slips inside my mouth and I shiver, thinking about where else that tongue has been.

Suddenly Julian releases me and steps back. With a stunned shake of my head, I realize we've reached the third floor. "It's nice to see you again, Sadie," Julian says in a professional voice as the door opens.

"Yes," I say, backing out of the elevator, feeling raw and exposed like I've had a bandage ripped off.

Chapter Three

CALLIE

THE DESKS IN THE engineering department are once again empty at the early morning hour, the shoulder height walls separating them making it difficult to hide.

Is Michael hiding from me?

I'm at work before seven like usual. Before *it* happened, there had been an unofficial race between me and Michael to see who would be first to get into the office. Then we'd go to the kitchen and get our tea and coffee, happily trading little flirtatious comments that could be construed as harmless if you weren't aware of the bloody big crush I had on him.

I can't see how it stayed a secret because if you ask me, we have enough chemistry to blow up a Bunsen burner. Or at least we did. Three weeks ago, we consummated my long-simmering crush, right here in the office and since then, I have no idea what's going on.

I set my purse on my desk with a longing glance. It happened right there at my desk.

It didn't just happen. There were events leading up to it, like tiptoeing across a raging river using wet rocks. There was no doubt as going to fall in, one way or another.

That day, the last slip had been overhearing another couple going at it in the kitchen. It had been Delia and Carl, which is a whole other story, but before we knew that, Michael and I had a whispered discussion about what the unseen couple was doing. Then we started talking about our own favourite positions.

For me, I like from behind. And I like a healthy dose of oral to warm things up first.

It had been a perfect storm. The chemistry between us. My feelings for Michael lowered my willpower. The heated atmosphere in the empty office.

So we had sex.

Which I had vowed would not happen while Michael had a girlfriend but that day, he had told me things weren't good between them. It was like a match hitting a pile of dry kindling; it was the spark I needed to let things get crazy.

I could be upset that Michael lied about his relationship, but the exact words he used have become fuzzy in the past weeks. Did he say things weren't good, implying that he was going to end it, or that he was just going to suck it up and stay with her? Were things really that bad or was that just an excuse to get into my pants?

Or up the skirt I'd been wearing?

I have no idea what Michael's romantic status is now because after we had sex—really good sex, even though it wasn't exactly the mind-blowing, toe-curling episode that I had hoped for—I became persona non grata. I have no idea if Michael has a girlfriend, a boyfriend, or a pet goat that he likes to play with because I haven't talked to him since the sex.

It's hard to be angry with someone you miss so much.

He started ghosting me, which is really difficult to do when we spend over eight hours a day in the same place, but he manages. Not a word, not a smile. He walks out of the kitchen if I'm there, and if he's in there, finds an excuse to leave if I come in. He's even changed his whole bloody early morning schedule, and I knew that he liked those hours of quiet.

It's become obvious to everyone that Michael is avoiding me. I've seen the raised eyebrows, but manage to shut down the questions before anyone can start digging.

I'm going to have to talk to someone about it because not knowing what's going on is slowly driving me crazy.

Because Michael isn't there yet and I don't have to worry about him avoiding me, and because I didn't have time to stop at Starbucks, I head straight for the little kitchen on the third floor.

I'm not entirely surprised to see Delia standing before the coffee maker. I am surprised that Carl isn't with her, though. "Morning, Delia."

Delia turned, her eyes widening. "Callie. You're here early." Her eyes flick to the door like she's waiting for someone.

"Don't mind me," I say with a smirk. "Go about your business. With Carl. Or whoever."

Delia doesn't know that I know about her and Carl. She's married but I know she and her husband have an open marriage. And Delia is almost fifty, which makes me feel good about my own ageing libido.

That makes it sound like my libido is getting tired, which is definitely not the case.

"I'm sorry?" Delia asks with a bemused expression on her pretty face. She doesn't look like she's in her late forties. Her wardrobe, on the other hand, suggests she's not a spring chicken. I think Delia actually dresses older than she is. And her flower-patterned blouses and out-of-fashion skirts hide the figure of a much younger woman.

I give a wave and reach into the cupboard for my mug that some considerate person has washed and put away for me. I've never seen anyone on this floor or mine above do the dishes, but they always seem to get done. "Your secret's safe with me."

"What secret?" Delia asks, a note of wariness creeping into her voice.

"About you and Carl," I whisper his name. "Since it's only the two of us, I thought I'd better tell you."

"Tell me what?" Delia stands with her empty cup in front of the Tassimo, which gives a hiss to indicate that the cup should be ready to catch the coffee. I gesture and Delia gets it there just in time.

"That Michael and I sort of heard, kind of saw, the two of you together."

Delia raises an eyebrow. "You and Michael?"

"Uh uh. You're not getting off that easy. Or maybe it is easy with Carl." I laugh at my crassness, as Delia frowns. "Sorry. Too soon? What's going on with the two of you?"

"There's nothing to tell. Unlike some people, I prefer not to share details."

"Okay, I deserve that but you have to give me *something*. That wasn't the first time, was it?"

Delia drops her gaze with a coy expression. "I don't know what time you're talking about."

"Ah, ha, I knew it! Three weeks ago on Thursday." It's a red letter day for me so I have no trouble remembering the date. "Really early in the morning."

"So that's when you and Michael finally got together?" Delia asks slyly.

"We're not together." I turn to slot my coffee pod in the machine.

"What happened?" There's a concern in Delia's voice, which verifies my suspicion that everyone knew about my thumping big crush on Michael. "Callie?"

"I don't know." I lean against the counter. "I really have no idea. We were friends, and then we crossed the line *only* because Michael gave me the impression things were over with him and the girlfriend so I thought I had a shot. Now—I have no idea. He won't talk to me."

"You wanted that shot, didn't you?" Delia rubs a comforting hand on my back. "Have you tried to talk to him?"

I give a disgusted sniff. "I don't chase men. They chase me."

"And how's that system working out for you?"

My shoulders slump and Delia gives one a squeeze. "I really liked him," I admit in a quiet voice. "And I was so excited because I thought maybe...and then, nothing. He's still with his girlfriend. That has to be it. And he's too embarrassed and guilty to talk to me ever again. I screwed it up."

"How did *you* screw up anything?" Delia asks. "Last time I checked, there's no significant other waiting for you to come home from work."

"I liked being friends with him. If I couldn't have anything else, at least I had that."

"Poor Callie."

But I shrug off her sympathy like I shrug off a jacket. "It's no matter. These things happen. What about you?" I ask in a bright voice. "Carl. You. Kitchen."

Now it's Delia's turn to shrug. "These things happen."

"More than once, I gather." I narrow my eyes at her. "I wondered, how that works with your husband?"

"Adrian is very understanding," Delia says tightly, dropping her spoon in the sink.

"Must be *very* understanding. I think I want a marriage like that."

"Have you ever wanted to get married, Callie?"

I always forget that no one at work knows about my ill-fated and very brief marriage. Some days I wonder why they can't see it. Some days with all the talk of marriage and relationships that swirl around me, I feel like I've pencilled *Divorced* on my forehead in red.

"Once upon a time," I say airily. "But not anymore. I don't think I'm the relationship type."

It's clear that Michael doesn't think so.

Chapter Four

JASON

I KNOW ABOUT MOST everything that goes on in the office.

I knew about Sadie and Alma before Sadie confirmed it, suspected something was going on with Delia and Carl before they began to get touchy-feely. I read the dirty emails going on between Abby and her husband Ben and knew way too much about Ian's office interludes.

But I have no idea what's going on with Callie and Michael.

Across the room, Callie is engrossed in the blueprints spread across her desk when I drop my bag at my desk. Michael's desk is less than six feet away from Callie's but with the new chill between them, the distance could be six kilometres.

Michael is focused on his monitor when I walk up to his desk. "Hey."

"Hey, Jason. How's it going?"

"Good." I wave my tea bag at him. Sadie has got me hooked on drinking chai tea, but I don't like the Tassimo pods since they always taste faintly of coffee. "Time to go to the kitchen?" My gaze flicks to Callie. "We could pick up Callie."

"I've got to finish this," Michael says without meeting my gaze.

He's been working longer hours lately; not unheard of, but I know there's no project due.

There hasn't been a project due since Julian took over.

"Want me to get you anything?" I ask, rather than pressing the issue. Michael and I are friends outside the office, but we don't have the type of relationship where we talk about emotions and feelings. We're not like Callie and her posse.

I like spending time with Callie and her posse. Especially Sadie.

I glance over to her desk at the far side of the floor. Empty.

Is she back with Alma?

I wrench my attention back to Michael. "I'm good," he says, finally glancing up at me.

"I don't believe that, but okay."

Michael's eyes widen. Maybe hanging out with Callie is rubbing off on me. There was a time when I wanted nothing but to have Callie rub me off, but I've gotten past that.

I don't know if I should blame Sadie or thank her for that.

With a last nod, I step away from his desk with my lonely tea bag.

"Jason?" Callie's voice carries across the floor. She must have been watching me. "Wait for me."

"Of course." I can't help but glance back at Michael. He begins to furiously type, his face flushing with anger or sadness. I'm not sure which.

I don't understand female emotions, but I understand men even less.

Out of courtesy for Michael's emotional state, I move away and meet Callie by the stairs. "How are you?" she asks brightly.

I've never seen Callie without a cheerful smile. She's always happy and fun-loving, and those are the traits that draw people to her, along with her cascade of blonde hair and considerable chest measurements.

That's what draws me to her, at least how it started. Now I think she's amazing inside and out.

When I look at Callie that morning, really look at her, I see the ever-present smile but her shoulders are tight and set, and there's a hardness in her eyes that I've never seen before.

"Okay?" I don't mean to make my answer into a question but that's what it is. I need to know what's bothering Callie because it's obviously the same thing affecting Michael, but I don't know if I'm friends enough with her to ask.

I've had sex with her, but I don't know if we're close enough friends for me to inquire into her emotional state.

"I've been here for so long, I'm ready for another coffee. This is my third so far, so I'm a bit twitchy."

Is it me, or is her voice a bit louder than usual? Like she's trying to make sure Michael hears what she's saying.

I glance over my shoulder to find Michael staring after us with an expression of anger on his face.

Who is he mad at?

"What's going on with the two of you?" I ask as soon as Callie steps into the stairwell.

"Two of who?" she asks blithely.

"Two of you—you and Michael. You're not talking, you're avoiding each other."

"Is he avoiding me?" Callie forces a laugh. "I hadn't noticed."

"I don't believe that." I don't catch the sarcasm in her tone until it's too late.

"Always so literal." Callie sighs. "I'm sure Michael thinks everything is fine."

"But you don't."

"I'm not the one with a girlfriend, so it doesn't much matter what I think."

That's the last thing she says until we reach the kitchen leaving me caught up with my thoughts. I can't deny my thoughts are on Callie—her smile, how her breasts gently bounce when she laughs, how her skirt hugs her hips in a way that makes me want to run my hands over her curves. I have touched those curves, and have had a first-hand experience on what else can make those breasts jiggle, and I'm tempted to suggest another tryst in an attempt to cheer her up.

But she's thinking of Michael, and I'm not enough of a sadomasochist to get off on that. If something were to happen with me and Callie again, I want her mind solely on me.

And I'm not sure my mind would be solely on her either.

Chapter Five

BRIENNE

CALLIE HASN'T BEEN HERSELF for the last few weeks.

She used to send me daily emails— *Who would you rather* questions about who I'd want to have sex with, like making me choose between Chris Helmsworth or Chris Evans. Sometimes she'd switch it up asking the juvenile *Marry, Kill or Fuck.* It was all part of her plan for me to think about who I'd want to have sex with, someone other than Eli.

The questions also never let me forget how long it had been since I'd had sex.

Real sex, that is. Dream sex doesn't count.

But it's been a few weeks since she's sent any emails and I think it's more because of her mood than because Jason is now obligated to read any and all inner-office emails. Callie wouldn't care if Jason or anyone else read them, plus she knows that he has such a crush on her, that he'd never do anything to get her in trouble.

I notice the downcast expression on her face as soon as she breezes into the kitchen with Jason, catching the unhappiness in her eyes before she wipes it away with a smile like she's sponged a smear on the counter.

Our morning coffee in the kitchen has lost a bit of its fun with Callie's new pall of sadness. Not that she's told me she's sad. That's part of the problem. She hasn't told me anything.

But Callie's my best friend and I know when something's wrong, even if she's not talking. Plus, Michael's been MIA for kitchen chat so it doesn't take an accountant to figure out the two things are related. I have to get Callie to tell me; not just so I'll stop driving myself crazy trying to figure it out, but because I want to help.

If I focus on Callie, I'll stop trying to figure out what's going on with Cooper.

I steal a glance at him. He was naked in my dream last night, and while I know it was only a dream, I still feel like I've been spying on him. Like I got a glimpse of him in the office shower that he sometimes uses when he rides his bike to work. I have seen him in his bicycle shorts with the tightness...and the bulginess and the...

I jerk my head when I realize I'm staring at him.

Why am I dreaming of *him*? Eli, yes. Ian, understandable, since things were left unresolved between us.

Actually, there's nothing to be resolved. We had sex.

That's it.

It was good and took me out of my comfort zone, but he's not worth me mooning over him.

Take a big step away from your unrequited crush on Ian, I tell myself. But do I want to take a step towards Cooper?

He's holding a Mickey Mouse mug with both hands and laughing at something Abby is saying. I love Abby, but she's not that funny.

So what's going on with *them*?

"...and then Ben said..."

I quickly tune in and out of their conversation. Abby talks about Ben more when Cooper is around like she's trying to drop a twenty-pound hint in every part of the conversation. *I. Am. Married.* Cooper and Abby had been friends back when they both worked in a downtown law firm and when Cooper followed Abby here, getting the job as the controller for Hever Construction, Abby had been out of sorts for a bit.

Turns out Cooper and Abby's friendship had taken a turn into the friends-with-benefits zone, or at least it might have if Abby hadn't put a screeching halt to it.

She loves Ben. Ben loves her. The only hooking up Abby is going to do at work is with her husband.

In a workplace rift with hook-ups and secret lovers, Abby's dedication to her marriage is refreshing.

"What did you do this weekend, Brienne?"

Cooper's question pulls me out of my thoughts, his South African accent sounding sexy even for a Monday morning.

"Not much," I say quickly, wanting Cooper to turn his attention to someone else.

But he doesn't. He stands there with the silly Mickey Mouse mug, staring at me with those green eyes that are trying to see into my soul.

Callie says he's interested in me. Of course, ever since she said that it's all I can think about. Like back in third grade when I didn't see Gary Laughlin for anything else other than his red hair until Stephanie Robins told me she heard he liked me, and then he suddenly became the cutest boy in class.

I'm uncomfortable with how cute Cooper is. Tousled sandy blond hair and green eyes that can pierce one minute and light up with laughter the next.

"I went to a show," I add when it's obvious Cooper isn't giving up. "My husband's band was playing."

"*Ex*-husband," Callie cuts in, making a face at me. "You forgot that part."

"*Is* he your ex-husband yet?" Abby asks sharply.

Callie makes a face at Abby. "Any day now," she says smoothly like it's not the break-up of my marriage that's she's talking about.

Dream or no dream, there wasn't much of a marriage left. Eli had always made it clear that he wasn't one for monogamy, but I was a little slow to pick up that he actually meant it. It had something to do with how he always showed me how much he loved me whenever he was home.

That, and how amazing he was in bed. My gaze flickers to Cooper, hoping he can't read my mind. I couldn't stand it if he ever found out that he played a role in my dream last night. Not a starring role, but definitely a supporting role.

Too bad I woke up or I might have found out if he was star-worthy.

But I'm proud to say that part of my life is now over. "That's why I went to his show," I say proudly. "To give Eli the divorce papers."

"Yay, you!" Sadie cheers.

"Finally!" Callie cries, throwing her arms around me. "I'm so proud of you."

"Did he sign them?" Abby asks with a frown.

"He did," I admit. "Although Eli probably won't pay much attention to them, just like he didn't pay attention to a marriage certificate."

"That just means you get ex-sex," Sadie says, touching her mug of chai tea with mine. "Not that I know anything about that, but it sounds fun, especially if Eli is—"

"Nope, no sex of any kind with Eli," Callie cuts in. "Isn't that right, Bri?"

I don't answer. Callie knows how difficult it is for me to say no to Eli, especially when he really works the sexy Irish charm. But it's clear that Callie also wants me to give Cooper a shot and talking about me and ex-sex isn't good for that.

"So you're divorced?" Cooper asks, trying to sound casual but, even to my ears, failing miserably.

"I am." There's nothing else I can say, but once again, it's like Cooper is waiting. "I'm no longer Mrs. Elias Ford. Not that I ever went by Ford. It's on my license but I never bothered to change it here at work."

"Wait a minute." Cooper frowns. "Elias Ford. Band? He's not the same Elias Ford who's in Fortune 50, is he?"

"You've heard of Fortune 50?" There's a sinking feeling in my stomach.

"Heard of them—I love them! They're a great group. I can't believe you were married to him. I love his voice."

And then until I can escape the kitchen, I have to listen to Cooper rave about my now ex-husband. It doesn't make a good start to Monday and leaves me no time to talk to Callie.

Chapter Six

SADIE

I HAVE NO IDEA why Brienne hasn't jumped Cooper yet.

He's so into her. If a guy looked at me the way Cooper looks at Brienne, I would jump him in a second.

Except with me, I'd probably make a mess of it.

It took me forever to get my heart rate back to normal after bumping into Julian in the elevator. Could I be any more awkward with him? I can't talk to him, I can't look at him without hyperventilating, and when he touched me, I just about spontaneously orgasmed and that was only from a kiss.

I'm a mess.

I tune back into the conversation, hoping to be distracted by the dampness in my panties. If Julian emailed me now I'd go running. Even if Alma—

Would I? After everything, would I still jump when she said how high?

I am a hot mess, one who needs to get laid, preferably with someone who doesn't work at Hever Construction.

"Where's Michael?" I ask, finally realizing that Callie and Jason walked in together, without Michael shadowing them. Now that I've noticed, I think back to the last couple of weeks and I haven't seen them together much lately.

"He says he's busy." Jason glances at Callie, but she's talking to Abby.

"Too busy for Callie?"

Jason shrugs. His shoulders are so wide compared to how narrow his hips are, like a swimmer who'd been at the weights. I wonder what he looks like naked.

Where did that come from?

Jason takes his turn at the Tassimo and then comes back to stand beside me, blowing at the steam before sipping. He has nice lips; full and soft-looking. I wonder why I haven't noticed them before.

I wonder why I notice them now.

There's no point in my noticing anything about Jason. Not only is he completely hung up on Callie, but I would only mess things up. These days, I don't think I'm capable of a normal relationship.

Besides, Jason knows about me and Alma. He might even know about me and Alma and Julian Donovan since he seems to have an ear to everything going on at Hever. At least the hookups.

It's been three weeks since Julian called me into his office for a marketing meeting. The only marketing that went on that afternoon was that Julian left his brand all over me. On the table, up against the window, back in his office, using his desk to brace myself as he pumped into me with enough force that I bruised my knee.

It was a long and drawn-out meeting, with multiple resolutions. Alma assisted with all of the resolutions.

"You okay?" Jason's question pulls me out of my memories of Alma's mouth between my legs as I took Julian's cock in my own.

"Fine," I squeak.

"You've got a funny look on your face."

"I was just remembering something...something I've got to finish today," I manage, feeling my face heat up from both the images of my first ever ménage as well as being caught thinking about it.

"Busy day?"

I smile at Jason, effectively wiping away any thoughts of Julian and Alma. "Always."

Getting involved with Alma proved to be a bad idea, but adding Julian to the mix could very well get me fired.

"I should get back to my desk." I sigh.

"I'll go with you," Brienne says quickly. I wonder if her eagerness has anything to do with Cooper popping another pod in the Tassimo which means he can't follow her back to her desk.

Sometimes I wonder about her.

We say goodbye to Abby, Jason and Cooper. Callie follows us out. "What's going on?" Brienne demands as soon as we're away from the kitchen.

"I should ask you the same thing since you're doing everything you can to put off Cooper," Callie shoots back.

"I'm not trying to put off Cooper," Brienne hisses. "I'm not interested in Cooper."

"You should be," Callie says.

"You really should be," I add.

Brienne throws up her hands, sending a wave of coffee dangerously close to the edge of her cup. "Why are you nagging me? I just want to know what's going on with you," she accuses. "You've been off for weeks now."

"Off?" Callie echoes with a twist of her mouth.

"Off," I agree. "Like, you're sad. But you're never sad about anything, so what gives."

"I'm allowed to be sad."

I meet Brienne's gaze. "You're really not," Brienne says. "It's not like you."

"It could be like me," Callie insists.

"Maybe," I hedged.

"Will you stop agreeing with everything?" Callie bursts out. "I should ask what's going on with you."

We reach the door to the stairwell and I hold it open to spare myself from answering. Callie and Brienne know about Alma—everyone does—but I haven't gotten around to telling them about Alma and Julian Donovan.

I feel like I should call him Mr. Donovan, but once you've had a man's penis inside you, it kind of takes away any pretense of formality.

Penis...cock...the thick, pulsating cock that's going to make me come right here if I don't stop thinking about it.

Brienne follows me and Callie to the door to the stairwell. Her desk is on the same floor as the kitchen but kitchen chat usually continues at her desk. Callie's eagerness to go back to work is another clear sign that something is very wrong.

Callie glances questioningly back at me as her hand hovers over the door handle.

"I'm a mess," I admit.

"Who isn't?" Brienne says with a humourless laugh.

"Tell me about it," Callie adds grimly.

Then, for some reason, we burst out laughing. I wonder if this is one of those times that you have to laugh or you're going to cry.

I don't feel like crying. I didn't much feel like laughing either.

Just as suddenly we stop, and Callie heaves a sigh. "Let's get this over with." She pulls open the door. I'm about to ask what we're getting over with when I hear the voices.

Callie takes two steps up the stairs before she waves a hand to stop us.

"What—?" Brienne gets one word out before Callie smacks a hand over her mouth.

"...Don't care what you want, Alma."

I recognize the voice instantly. So does Callie. *Julian Donovan*, she mouths. Brienne's eyes widen with interest as she leans over the railing to sneak a peek.

Callie pulls her back as I move to the other side of the stairwell and prepare to keep heading down the stairs. Brienne tugs my arm. *Wait.*

I don't want to wait. I don't want to listen to what they say because what if they talk about me?

But why would they say anything about me? It was one time. It was three weeks ago. If they wanted a repeat performance, someone would have been in touch.

Julian was in touch with me this morning.

Despite my reluctance, I listen.

"Not again, Alma. Not with everything going on around here. There's going to be a lawsuit against the controller and we can't suggest an impropriety."

Cooper?

Brienne shakes her head. *Ian.*

"But it was fun." I know Alma well enough to hear the pout in her voice. I can almost picture the petulant expression on her pretty face, the one that demands she get what she wants, whether it be a new pair of shoes or me letting her finger me to a very satisfying orgasm. "Pam wants it, wants me."

Pam? Callie and Brienne whip their heads around to catch my reaction. I don't even bother playing it cool. "Pam?" I hiss with an expression of disgust. Pam from Accounts Received is so sexy that she slithers and has always made it clear she plays for both teams. I think she might be the only person in Hever who gets more action than Callie.

Brienne frowns. She's always made it clear that she doesn't like Pam.

But Pam is forgotten with Julian's next words.

"I think you should cultivate your friendship with Sadie. She's an excellent recruit, someone we can work with. Mould into what we want. What we need."

But I can't hear his next words because as the door to the stair-well opens, Brienne leaps past me to throw her body into it.

"What are you doing?" Callie whispers.

"Too loud." Brienne props her body against the door as the knocking begins. With a shake of her head, Callie pulls her aside, opening the door to a bemused Jason and Cooper.

Two floors down, the door bangs shut behind Julian and Alma.

"What are you doing in here?" Jason demands.

"Did we interrupt a private ladies' meeting?" Cooper asks.

"I think we need one of those, don't we?" Brienne raises an eyebrow at me.

I heave a sigh. "Everything is a mess."

Chapter Seven

CALLIE

AFTER THE LITTLE EAVESDROPPING incident, I follow Jason back to the engineering department but veer right at the last minute and head to Abby's office on the corner of the floor. She must have taken the elevator down to beat us all.

Jason calls after me. "Is everything okay, Callie?"

"Why wouldn't it be?" I say in an oddly high-pitched voice.

"Your desk is this way."

I point to Abby's office. "I need her first. Talk to you later." And then I whip my head around before I can glance at Michael to find out if he's not looking at me.

I knock on Abby's open door. "How's my chocolate fairy godmother?" I sing, trying to sound like my heart hasn't been ripped out of my chest.

Abby reaches into her desk drawer and pulls out a bag of peanut M & Ms without even looking up. "That sounds like I'm made of chocolate."

"Fairy godmother of chocolate?" I offer, pulled in by the tempting aroma of the candy.

"Better." Abby finally meets my gaze as I sit across from her. "What's going on with you and Michael?" she asks.

I internally grimace. "Is that all anyone can ask about? I was about to ask you what was going on with you and Cooper."

"Absolutely nothing," Abby snaps.

"I *know* that, but you're acting weird, especially when he's hanging around Brienne. Which he has been doing quite a lot lately."

The perfect way to get Abby off the scent. "He has been pretty friendly with Brienne," Abby concedes. "But she's been rude to him."

"Remember back in the day, back when kissing tag was the thing?"

"I never played kissing tag."

"Of course you didn't. I had you pegged for more of a Truth and Dare gal."

"I did play that occasionally," Abby admits.

"Well, remember when you could always tell when a boy liked you because he ignored you?"

"I thought it was when they teased you and pulled your hair?"

"Well, Brienne's got things turned around a bit."

"You're saying she likes Cooper?"

"Why shouldn't she like Cooper? He seems like a great guy. Do you know of anyone else who likes Cooper?" I'm much better at getting to the bottom of things than Abby is. A faint blush colours her high cheekbones. "Abby, are you crushing on Cooper?"

"I'm trying not to," she says from between gritted teeth.

"Do you not want Brienne to like Cooper? Hoes before bros and all that."

Abby juts up her chin. "I take offence at being called a ho."

"Okay, friends before Bens? But that doesn't make sense because you have a Ben, and he comes first. Sisters before misters. Chicks before dicks."

"I don't want to stand in the way of Brienne getting..." Abby trails off before she can say the word.

"Dick? Before she gets some fine Cooper dick? I don't know if things will go that way. I think Cooper wants it to, but Brienne is holding back."

"Because of me?"

"I don't know what her deal is, but she better be careful or Cooper's going to get the idea that she's not into him."

"But she's not into him? Not yet."

"But she could be. And why wouldn't she be? Cooper's nice and hot...and nice. Compared to snakedick Ian, and Eli, who is a lot of things, but not nice, Cooper's niceness has got to be the main selling feature."

"He's a great guy." Abby sighs. "And I'd really like him to get together with Brienne because then he wouldn't be a temptation to me."

"He's not a temptation." Abby has confided in me about her marriage a few times; how she's happy but worried that Ben will become bored.

The sexting, or sexy emailing she had set up with Ben last month, had certainly helped with that. But Cooper's arrival seemed to set Abby back. Ben is a fantastic guy and an even better husband.

Abby needs to know nothing will come between them, not even because of a harmless crush on a guy she may have once kissed.

"Cooper would never tempt you because you would never act on it. He can be a fantasy. There's nothing wrong with that."

"I don't know."

"Is Ben the jealous type?"

"Not at all. At least I've never given him anything to feel jealous about."

"Maybe you should."

"Why would I do that?"

"You wanted things to be more exciting. Maybe a bit of jealousy would help Ben step up his game to make sure you're ecstatically happy with him."

"You think I should tell him about Cooper?"

"No! Just drop a few mentions of him. Maybe about how cute you think he is and—"

"I don't think he's cute," she cuts me off.

"Why not? Even Jason thinks he's good-looking."

"Maybe he's a little cute."

"That's like saying Jason Momoa is a little hot."

Abby leans back in her chair. "He doesn't really do it for me."

"Again, why not?" I stick my hand in the bag of candy, fighting the urge to run the smooth chocolates through my fingers. I love putting a few handfuls in a bowl and playing with them. It's relaxing when I'm the only one eating them, but rude when the chocolate is Abby's and who knows who else she shares with.

If she shares with Michael, I'd like to lick them all so he won't touch them.

I sigh to myself. Not even a good gossip-chocolate session with Abby will take my mind off him.

Chapter Eight

JASON

SOMETIMES I WONDER HOW productive I'd be if I worked in a different office.

I know the stats, and I know my work ethic, and I know that I am one of the hardest-working employees that Hever has on staff. Only Delia, and Priya in accounting who never talks to anyone, clock more hours than I do.

It's times like this, when I head over to Michael's desk, that I can't help but wonder what I'd be able to accomplish in a day if I worked at a different place.

"Are you angry with Callie?" I hover over Michael.

I can't read the expression that crosses his face, but it's not a pleasant one. "Why do you ask?"

"Why don't you answer?"

Michael turns back to his monitor even though the screen only shows the hypnotic bouncing ball screen saver. "I'm not mad at her," he says in a careful voice.

"You haven't talked to her in two weeks. Longer. You never go to the kitchen with us anymore. It's Callie," I finish, hands spread wide. "It's Callie."

"I know," he groans, his shoulders slumping. "It's killing me."

"What happened?" I want to know because while I consider both Michael and Callie to be friends, I'm also extremely curious.

"We hooked up," Michael admits in a low voice.

The news is a surprise but not altogether unexpected. Even though Michael has a girlfriend, and Callie has always made it clear that that was one line she would never cross, everyone saw the chemistry between the two of them. Even I saw it, as little as I wanted to see it.

"But you're still with Liana," I point out, leaning against the desk across from Michael's.

Now I'm able to read Michael's expression and it's one of guilt. Guilt and remorse and regret.

How can he be regretful for hooking up with Callie?

"It was one time," Michael says in an urgent whisper. I follow his gaze to where Callie has disappeared into Abby's office. "Things hadn't been good with me and Liana, and I thought they might be over. I let things get out of hand with Callie. I didn't mean to, but hell, it's *Callie*...you know how it is."

"I do," I say proudly.

Michael winces like he's uncomfortable being reminded of my past hookup with Callie. "Callie's amazing and we're good friends but there's always been something more, you know? But Liana..." He swallows and meets my accusatory gaze.

I try not to look accusing or angry, but I can't really help it. Everyone in the office knows Callie doesn't condone cheating, so

Michael must have lied to her, or things got very, very carried away, and I don't want to think about that because I don't want that visual.

"I love Liana." Michael doesn't sound convinced, so he tries again. "I love her. I want things to work out between us."

"Does she know about Callie?"

"God, no," Michael scoffs.

"Would she be upset?"

"Uh, yeah. Yeah, she'd be upset. She's jealous on a good day, but sometimes she can be...possessive. A little dominating."

I've never met Michael's girlfriend, but an image pops into my mind of a Callie-lookalike wearing a black rubber jumpsuit, and holding a whip.

Then another question pops in. *Why* haven't I ever met Michael's girlfriend? We're friends; better friends than the usual work colleagues. He comes over to my place almost once a week for game night, but hardly ever mentions Liana. As well, with all the holiday gatherings where spouses and significant others are welcome, Michael still comes solo.

"Does she dominate you?" I ask.

Surprise flits across Michael's face. "*No*. Why would you even ask that? No."

"You mentioned how she can be dominating. After the incident with Ian and Agatha, I looked up some of the basic tenets of BDSM, and learned some interesting facts about the dominant/submissive relationships."

"It's not like that," Michael says quickly.

"It's common for men to enjoy being emasculated," I continue. "Taking on the submissive role, while allowing partners to act out their dominant desires, is becoming more popular. It's nothing to be embarrassed about."

"I'm not embarrassed, because my relationship with Liana is nothing like that," Michael argues, his voice rising defensively.

So, of course, I know that his relationship is exactly like that.

Chapter Nine

BRIENNE

I ASKED CALLIE IF she wanted to get a drink after work.

I don't tell her the real reason I don't want to go home is that Eli doesn't have a show tonight and after delivering him the divorce papers on the weekend, I have a sneaking suspicion he might drop by my place.

Not to change my mind; he's in agreement that marriage isn't for us. But it doesn't mean he doesn't think it's a good idea to keep up the more carnal relations associated with marriage. I don't want to go home because I'm afraid Eli will show up for sex, and me not being able to say no.

Especially with the dream last night.

I know how the real thing would play out: me dressed in my warm and cozy flannel pyjamas, lounging on the couch, a glass of wine in my hand. Of Eli bursting in, loudly proclaiming his love for me, how if he can't have me, he'll spoil me for anyone else.

Then he makes love to me in a variety of ways, each better than the last, resulting in no less than five toe-tingling orgasms.

I say five because four is my record with Eli.

I can imagine it all in my head, the fantasies making me more aroused than even dreaming about it did, but I still don't want to go home and let it happen.

"What does that say about me?" I ask Callie after I've confessed. There's a bar down the street from the Hever office that employees frequent. I haven't seen any familiar faces yet, but I asked for a booth near the back. There's a group of men at the bar and I know if we're close to them, Callie won't be able to give me her full attention.

It's not because she's a bad friend, but because men can't keep away from her, even if she's in the middle of an in-depth conversation. So I tell the waitress we want a table away from the men, so Callie doesn't have to shame them when they interrupt.

Callie loudly slurps from her straw. She loves fruity, sweet cocktails, with more garnishes the better. Tonight she's ordered a Mai Tai, complete with a hunk of pineapple on the rim of the glass and a paper umbrella stabbing the cherry. "What's wrong with you because you don't want to go home because you're afraid you won't be able to resist your now ex-husband? Nothing. You're making the right move, Bri. And that's coming from me, who thinks sex is more important than...than...this drink right here."

I nod slowly. Callie is my best friend and I know what she's going to say before it comes out of her mouth, because I've heard it countless times before.

"Eli may be good in making your eyes roll back, but he's *bad* for you. End of story. You need to move on."

"I don't think he's ever made my eyes roll back," I muse.

"That's a start. Admitting Eli has a problem. That he's not a perfect pillar of pleasure." She spits out her Ps with a grin.

"I never said he has a problem with pleasure," I say.

Callie groans. "Enough. Get. Him. Out. Of your life! Move on to someone new. One of those gentlemen at the bar who can't stop staring at you, maybe."

"I think they're staring at you."

"They like my boobs, so they have no idea what I look like. You—they like the looks of you." She noisily sucks up the liquid until catches a bit of ice in the straw. "You know what I want to know? I could crook my finger and any of those guys would jump at the chance to buy me a drink, or come home with me." She meets my gaze with a rueful shrug. "I know that makes me sound like a bitch, but it's true."

"It is," I agree. "So who's the lucky guy tonight?"

"That's the problem," Callie moans. "I don't want any of them. Anybody. No one. I am so not in the mood and I don't understand why. That's what I want to know."

"That's not a bad thing," I say nervously. "It's a strange thing, but not bad. Or totally unheard of. Okay, maybe it is a little uncommon for you," I finish after Callie fixes me a look.

Callie stirs her straw around what's left of her drink, her expression more pensive than I've ever seen her.

"What's wrong?" I ask gently.

She stares at the light fixture above us, at the golf game playing on the television above the bar, anywhere but at me. "Michael. Michael is what's wrong."

"I noticed things aren't as friendly as they used to be."

"And that's my fault. I gave in."

I frown, more confused than ever. Callie is no cheater. It's her one hard and fast rule. "But girlfriend? Doesn't Michael have a girlfriend?"

"That's the problem." She sighs and tells me what happened. About how she and Michael had been at work early one morning and had been coming back with coffees when they heard a couple in the kitchen.

How they stood and listened and wondered and whispered, which had ricocheted up the chemistry between them to another level.

"I don't remember the last time I've been so turned on," Callie sighs.

"Delia and Carl," I say with amazement. "I never saw that coming. But I guess I did. I mean, look at them together. They're like an old married couple."

"Except they're not. But it made for a very sexy situation."

Knowing Callie and Michael stood and listened makes me feel a tiny bit better about the time I stood and watched Ian and Agatha. A little bit. Even though watching Ian

"I don't think it was the first time with them," Callie says grimly. "They sounded more like a couple going at it, rather than first-timers if that makes sense."

"Maybe it's because of their age?" Delia is in her late forties and Carl is older than she is. Not that people in their fifties aren't exciting—"Scratch that," I correct myself. "I want to be loud and proud at fifty. Sixty."

"Seventy for me," Callie says. "It was...hot. I don't want to say that because it's *Delia* we're talking about, but it was so hot before

I knew it was her. You know how you get turned on by listening to someone have sex?"

"Not really, no."

"You've had sex when someone's in the next room, right?"

"Only when I'm having sex as well, so that kind of holds my attention."

"Ah. Well, try it sometime. Delia once told me about this resort on the East Coast for swingers—"

"Hang on a sec," I interrupt. "We'll get back to the swingers and next-door sex later. Go back to Michael."

"Michael." Instantly her face droops. "We listened to what was going on in the kitchen, and then after we got back to our desks, it happened. He kissed me."

"*Kissed* you? You don't kiss guys at work."

"He didn't kiss me on the mouth."

"Ah. Okay, so..." I'm not sure what to say. Callie is often open about sex, frequently giving graphic details, but this is Michael we're talking about, which makes it odd. I have a visual image of Michael now that I thought I'd never have.

"Yeah." Callie shakes the ice in her drink and tries to catch the eyes of the waitress to order another round. "It was good. But what was really good was that Michael gave every indication that things were over with him and his girlfriend. That was the only reason I let things happen."

"I know. You don't cheat."

"I don't cheat. I had a mother who cheated; two boyfriends, as well as a husband who did it to me, and I made a vow long ago not to—"

"Hang on a minute," I cry, taking a minute to catch on to what Callie said. "You were *married*? You never told me that!"

Callie waves her hand. "Long story, long ago. Need more alcohol in me before you get that out of me."

"You were married," I repeat with amazement.

"You're missing the point. I've had it happen to me, so I will never be the other woman."

"I know that, but this is big." Callie had an annoyed expression on her face, so I tried to focus on her immediate concern. "Michael lied to you, then."

"He implied. Is that the same as lying?"

"Kind of, when you take it in this context. So you hooked up with him, which is what you've wanted to happen for a long time. What I want to know, is what you're more upset about—that he lied, or that he's staying with his girlfriend?"

"Isn't that the same thing?"

"Did you want the sex to lead to something with him? A relationship?" I ask bluntly before softening his voice. "How much do you like him?"

"A lot." Callie's voice is so low that it's hard to hear her.

"How much?" I probe, my tone gentle now.

Callie sighs and looks around for the waitress. "Where is that girl? I really want another drink, you know."

"Callie?"

She sighs her finger picking at a spot on the table. "I think I might be in love with him."

Chapter Ten

SADIE

I WORK LATE THAT night, refusing Brienne's invitation to join her and Callie at the bar. I have a ton of paperwork sitting on my desk; Julian wants me to come up with a marketing plan that will give us an edge for the lucrative government contract coming up and I want to do my best.

I want to do my best for Julian as well as me, which is sad. I can't get past how good it was with Julian and Alma, how good I want everything to be with him.

"You like me fucking you?" Julian growled, pulling out until only the tip of his cock is inside me, before slamming back into me.

"Yes," I panted.

"You like my cock?"

"Oh, god, yes!" I cried as he repeated the move. I tucked my knees closer to my chest, desperate to give Julian more of me. "Don't stop—please!"

I shake my head to get rid of the image.

I should have gone with Callie and Brienne. It's been a while since we've hung out outside work. It's nice to be friends with co-workers and we've gotten over the awkwardness of moving that friendship outside the office. It would have been nice to tell Callie and Brienne what happened with Julian and Alma and get their take on it.

Even though Callie is all about sex, some part of me thinks she wouldn't approve.

My office phone lights up. I've turned the ringer off again but I can see the number flash on the display.

Julian.

A combination of a squeal and a groan escapes me as I reach for the phone and I quickly glance around to make sure the place is empty. "Hello?"

"Sadie."

My eyes drift shut at his caressing tones and I feel like swooning. "Hi."

"Hi, yourself."

That's when I knew he hadn't called about work. The other times I've spoken to him on the phone, Julian has been profession-al and polite, with an unseen sexy smile marking his words. Now he's...playful?

"Can I help you?" I ask, my voice pert and polite.

"I certainly hope so. Why don't you come down to the confer-ence room and give me a hand with something."

I'm on my feet before I can hang up the phone, and I take two steps away from my desk before I realize I need to save my work.

I'm already so turned on that all I can think of is him. *JulianJu-lianJulian.*

I'm at the stairs before I ask myself what I'm doing.

My steps slow, the *clip-clop* of my heels echoing in the stairwell. The conference room is on the third floor, down the hall from the kitchenette and on the opposite side of the building as the accounting department. Even if someone is working late, no one will see me.

Why am I worried about that? I'm not doing anything wrong.

Am I?

My steps slow even more as I consider what I'm rushing into. I'm going to have sex with a man I barely know; not only do I barely know him, I know enough to know he's married. And he's my boss.

And he wants to have sex with me. Alarms should be going off.

But they're not because this is Hever and things work a little different at this office.

Julian's wife knows all about me, and might well be participating in this little after-hours playtime, so there's no sense worrying about that.

What am I worrying about? Why aren't I rushing into the conference room with my shirt half unbuttoned, ready for some fun?

I stop halfway down the stairs, my hand tightening on the cool metal railing. Is it the sex, or is it Julian?

There is nothing stopping me from having sex with whoever I like. There is no *one* stopping me. I am a free, independent, single woman with not a lot of experience on my sexual resume. Why shouldn't I be jumping into this with both feet?

I take another step down. Ethan had been my first love—emotionally and sexually. I loved him enough for me not to realize that he was bad in bed. Orgasms should be a right, not a privilege doled out whenever he was in the mood.

With Julian, I'm only making up for time wasted with Ethan. I'm twenty-seven years old and I've been with two women and two men.

It's time for a little more experience of the sexual nature. It's time for adventure.

I hurry down the remaining stairs, excitement and apprehension at war within me. There's no reason to be nervous. I may not know Julian very well, but I trust him not to hurt me.

He would never hurt me.

I pull open the heavy door, peeking out before stepping onto the floor. It's dimly lit with safety lights instead of the harsh fluorescents and my shadow looms large as I steal across the floor to the conference room on the far side.

I'm doing this and it's going to be good. It's going to be great.

But as I reach the open door, my steps slow once more. I bite my lip as apprehension wins the battle and forces me to take a deep breath.

I can do this. I will do this.

Julian leans against the table, looking perfectly at home in his dark blue suit and carefully knotted tie. He smiles and motions me forward with a crooked finger, his gaze drinking me in like I'm a tall, frosty beer after a hard day's work. Alma is nowhere in sight. It's just him.

Him and me. In the conference room.

We're going to get it on.

Excitement bounces back and tingles begin in my stomach as I stare at him. I have no idea what to say. Is there a rulebook for this

sort of thing? Meeting your married boss for sex after hours? "Hi."
It takes me clearing my throat twice for the word to be heard.

Julian smiles again, his eyes half closed. I know now that's the
expression when he wants someone.

Right now he wants me.

Slowly, he takes off his jacket, one arm at a time, as if he's savour-
ing it. I know I am. Julian would be perfectly at home on a stage
with the Magic Mike show, taking off one article of clothing at a
time. Placing his jacket on the chair next to him, he smiles wolfishly
as he loosens his tie.

It's now or never. If I'm going to leave, I have to do it now.

Why would I want to leave?

Julian takes a step towards me, looking like a cat stalking prey.
Warm hands cup my face and his thumb caresses my jaw as his dark
eyes stare into mine. "I'm glad you're here, Sadie."

And that's all he says. For those women who think a conversation is an ideal foreplay, they've clearly never been in the same room
with Julian Donovan.

He kisses me then, his mouth hot and hungry. Both of his hands
encircle my throat as his tongue demands and takes.

I stagger, my knees weakened by the force of his kiss and Julian
pushes me against the window beside the door, the glass covered
by plastic slats. The cheap blinds bend under my fingers.

"Do you know much I want you?" Julian mutters against my
mouth.

I can only shake my head mutely, stunned by the onslaught of
passion. When I was with him before, he was cool and controlled.
Alma had been the demanding on.

Now, feeling his hands on my body, his strength as he tightens his grip, I have another moment of apprehension. But then he takes my hand and pulls it to his crotch and I can't help the sigh of satisfaction as I feel his hardness straining against his pants.

My fingers scrabble for his zipper. I want to touch. I need to taste. I have to—

"No," Julian breathes. "Your turn first."

With a twirl of arms, he has me facing the window, my hands crushing the plastic slats. Julian's hand is up my skirt before I catch my breath, pushing and probing, shoving aside the cotton of my underwear to dive deep inside me.

I let out a shaky sigh as he thrusts a second finger into me. "I want to make you scream," Julian hisses into my neck. "It's the only thing I can think about—you and me, me fucking you so hard that you beg for it. Will you beg for it?" His thumb flicks against my clit and I gasp.

I'll beg for anything right now, as long as he keeps doing what he's doing.

"Yes," I say instead.

"Alma says you're so hot for it."

I stiffen. Alma is the last person I want to talk about or hear what she says about me. I think Julian realizes that because he kisses my neck.

"It's better with me," he soothes. "I'm going to make it so good for you." He pinches my clit between his fingers and a whimper escapes from me.

Then his fingers are gone. Before I can turn around, he spreads my legs with rough hands and his mouth is between my legs and his tongue...

"Oh, god," I groan as he licks the length of me, before plunging his tongue inside.

"You like it rough, don't you?" Julian asks, manhandling my hips so that I'm bent over with my hands braced against the cool glass of the window. He pushes my skirt up over my hips, wrinkling the fabric beyond repair, and yanks at my underwear, pulling them off. I shake the cotton boy shorts off my ankle as Julian sucks at my clit.

"Your pussy," he mutters, the rest of his words muffled as his tongue explores me, pulsing, plunging, making me gasp aloud from the sensations.

I lean my head on the window, my fingers clutching the slats with desperation to keep my balance.

When his mouth finds my ass, his fingers thrust inside my pussy so roughly that I cry out.

"You like that, don't you?" he growls. "You're going to come from this, aren't you?"

I think I am. He fucks me with his fingers as his tongue pushes against the puckered skin and I think it's going to be quick. I close my eyes, breathing in heavy pants as Julian brings me closer to the edge.

"Just what is going on here?" a voice demands.

My eyes fly open to see a stranger standing in the doorway, not two feet from me. How did I not hear him? I stand up, try to close my legs, push my skirt down over my hips, but Julian is still crouched behind me, his fingers relentless inside me.

"Julian," I hiss.

"Don't move, Sadie." His hand tightens on my hip with a warning.

"But—" His tongue finds my clit, circling it lazily, before sucking it with an intensity that makes me gasp.

"Don't stop on my account," the stranger says with an arrogant smile on his face. "I'll join in."

My eyes widen as he takes off his well-cut suit jacket and tosses it onto the conference table, but I don't speak because as Julian presses his fingers deep inside me, I come with a sharp cry.

"Beautiful," the stranger applauds. "I love seeing a woman come."

Julian lifts his head. "Sadie, this is my friend Victor. I hope you don't mind if he joins us. I've told him all about you."

My body is still shuddering as Victor grabs a handful of my hair and jerks my head towards his cock, already lunging out of his pants, thick and hard.

"I've told a few of my friends about you," Julian says. "They're all looking forward to meeting you."

Victor pushes his cock into my mouth before I can reply. I have no idea what I'd say, even if I could. Julian's hand is still between my legs, pushing all the right buttons and Victor reaches into my blouse to cup my breast.

I've never been with two men before. Callie would be—

Before I complete my thought, Julian thrusts into me with no warning. My pussy clenches as he pulls out, only to thrust again. My legs buckle with the force and he grasps my hips, his fingers digging into my skin.

"I can't wait to fuck her," Victor says.

"Neither can my wife." Julian laughs as he settles into a rhythm; hard and fast, his fingers moving between my legs to help me along.

I moan around Victor's cock, wondering if Alma is going to make an appearance tonight. The thought of Alma's mouth, her fingers between my legs, makes me even more excited. Julian rubs my clit but Alma would do it differently.

But Alma doesn't have a cock like her husband. I widen my legs, pushing my hips back to meet his thrusts and I'm rewarded with a quick slap on my ass.

I want more. I moan again, this time longer.

"That's what I like to hear." Victor grabs my head with both hands, forcing me to go deeper and he groans in appreciation.

"You like that?" Julian slaps me again. "You're full of surprises, my little Sadie."

"You'll have to keep her around for a while," Victor says.

Julian slaps me harder, then caresses my ass, his fingers leaving my clit to search between my cheeks. My own fingers find my clit as Julian pushes his thumb against the puckered skin. "I have no intention of letting this one go anytime soon," he says.

Blood roars in my head as Julian fucks me roughly from behind, every thrust bringing me closer. Victor says something I can't hear because his hands are clasped against my ears as he fucks my mouth. I don't care what is said; all I want is to come—to come hard, every fibre in my body begging for it.

Victor's hand moves and I hear an animalistic moaning; it takes a second before I realize it's from me.

And then I'm coming with a harsh scream muffled by Victor's cock, my body shivering as it convulses. Julian holds me up as the waves crash over me, never stopping his frantic fucking.

I come again, my fingers rubbing my clit with urgent need.

"Holy shit," Victor says as he pulls out of my mouth. "I want my piece of her."

Julian pulls out and lifts me easily. My body is boneless and sensitive to the touch but as he lays me on my back at the edge of the table, I look at them with unsatiated hunger.

They switch spots, Victor kneeling between my legs. At the touch of his tongue, I cry out.

"You're not done yet, are you my little Sadie," Julian says with a smirk. "How much will it take to satisfy you?"

"More," I pant, pushing Victor's head deeper.

Chapter Eleven

CALLIE

I NEED A GOOD fuck.

It would clear my head, get me out of my Michael funk. I need someone who can make me forget about everything, even for an hour.

I need a fuck friend.

For a moment, I think about Jason.

He's cute in a geeky way, sexy with his swimmer-like body, but more importantly, he can fuck. He can fuck, he can do oral, he can do anything I want him to.

More importantly, he *would* do anything I asked him to. Men, I've found, are easy lays. They always want sex and there are enough single ones out in the world so that it's not that difficult to find a willing one.

I've only been caught twice; two men lied to me about being single. One was engaged and the other was married for twelve years.

After the married one, I became more stringent with my probing questions.

Jason doesn't have a girlfriend.

"Do you know Michael's girlfriend's name?" I ask Brienne, staring at the group of men sitting by the bar. One of them might do the trick, help me take the edge off.

"Lily? LeeAnne? Liana," she decides. "I think it's Liana."

"Pretty name," I muse.

"You okay?" Brienne asks as she signals the waitress for another round.

It would be so easy to grab one of the men at the bar; I could have one with a swing of my hips and a smile. My car is handy, or there was a spot behind the building, in the darkened space away from the garbage bins that is free of smells and the possibility of critters interrupting.

As much as I want it, I don't do anything about it.

I want sex. I'd like to have sex tonight. But the more I think about it, the more the desire wears off.

I don't want sex with just anyone. The thought of a nameless stranger filling my need is turning me off.

This has never happened before.

"Callie? Are you okay?" Brienne repeats when I don't answer.

"I'm good," I say in a cheerful voice. There's no point in confessing more to Brienne tonight. I can see the sympathy in her blue eyes.

"I don't think you are."

I stifle my sigh as the waitress sets our drinks on the table. "What choice do I have?" I demand after she leaves. "Things aren't going to work out for me and Michael, so I'll be fine with it. Relationships aren't my thing."

Brienne leans forward. She's so concerned, so caught up in my drama. "But you think you're in love with him."

Brienne doesn't need to worry about my issues. She has had enough of her own. "Then I'm going to have to be out of love with him. Simple as that."

Maybe.

Not really.

She stirs her vodka cranberry with her finger with a rueful expression. "I've been trying to do that for years with Eli. It's not as simple as you think."

I smile knowingly. She's done so well with Eli, but she's still not over him yet. Hopefully, Cooper will help with that if Brienne would only take my advice and make a move on the man. He's ripe for the taking, at least by her. "Yes, but you were thinking with your women parts and letting them get in the way. I know I can keep the two separate."

I know I can because I've done it before.

"Tell me about your marriage," Brienne urges, leaning her elbows on the table.

I shake my head before she finishes speaking. "There's nothing to tell."

"There has to be something. The fact you were married is something to tell."

I sip my drink and mull over what to tell her, finally deciding nothing is best. It might her crazy but dredging up the past isn't something I want or need to get into tonight. "There's nothing to tell. I was married. And then I wasn't."

"Callie!"

"I can't Bri," I admit with a shrug. "It's not worth getting into it. But believe me when I say I can make myself fall out of love with someone. I've done it before and I can do it again. And then—" I spread out my hands. "We'll just take a little break."

"What if Michael breaks up with Liana?" she asks. "Would you start something with him then?"

Even the words make my heart skip a beat. A Michael who isn't committed a girlfriend, who wants *me*. But then I think about it, think about Michael. It's on the tip of my tongue to say no. No way, because he lied and cheated and I don't want to be with a man like that. But I can't say the word.

Chapter Twelve

JASON

I WAS AT HOME, comfortable in my apartment and about to log on to Hearthstone for an evening of gaming when I realized I left my authenticator at work. I can't leave it at the office since it allows me access to the internal servers for the company, so with a muffled curse, I shut my laptop and head back to Hever.

Julian Donovan has given me full access to all the servers so I can go in and peek at what his employees are doing. He's made me his spy and it's my least favourite part of the job. I'm not exactly sure what he's looking for because he hasn't given me specifics in what to look for.

"I want to know if anything untoward is going on in my company," Julian said a few weeks ago when he presented me with the new responsibility. "Like that situation with Ian Eisley."

Since I don't fully understand the Ian situation, I don't respond. My understanding was that things with Ian and Agatha had been consensual, just like it had been with Brienne.

I don't mention Brienne to Julian, in the hope that he's not aware of that situation. I don't mention a lot of things to Julian. He may sign my paychecks, but I don't trust the man.

The lot is nearly empty when I pull up to the Hever building so it's easy to notice the mountain bike chained to the pole exactly where it had been this morning when I got to work.

It's Sadie's bike. She rides to work almost every day.

She must be working late. But as I park by her bike and hop out, I notice that most of the lights in the building have been turned off.

The conference room on the third floor is ablaze, the light seeping out around the blinds. They hadn't been drawn that morning when I had met with Donovan and a few of the company directors.

It's odd there is a meeting after hours, one that I haven't heard of.

I know everything that goes on in the office.

Maybe Sadie is there. As I pull open the front door, I wonder who she's meeting with. The doors are kept unlocked until nine o'clock, but it's uncommon for anyone other than the caretakers to be here that late.

As I take the stairs two at a time to the fourth floor, I'm hit with an unfamiliar emotion.

Excitement. To see Sadie.

It takes only a few minutes to get to my desk and find the authenticator in my drawer, exactly where I left it. Sadie is nowhere to be found on the floor, which means she's likely downstairs in the conference room. It won't be strange for me to head down and check.

I'll say I saw her bike and wondered if she wanted a ride home because it was so late.

That's not strange. That's something a friend would do. And Sadie is my friend.

The fluorescent lights are off, and the floor is lit only by the yellow safety lights. What kind of meeting is going on? I would think it would be more professional to have the floor lit properly so that—

"Please, more!"

The breathy cry stops me in my tracks.

"I'm going to fuck you so hard that you'll be screaming my name for the next week," growls an unfamiliar voice. "You want this."

"Yes!"

I take a step toward the open door of the conference room, but the sudden cry forces me back two steps.

Who is that? And what are they doing?

The loud, drawn-out moan answers my question.

It's Sadie. Sadie and...someone.

Quietly, I back up to the nearest desk, gripping the edge with white fingers. I don't know what to do. Should I leave without them knowing I've been here? Does Sadie need anything? What are they doing?

Another sharp cry.

I know exactly what they're doing in there.

My cock stiffens at the noise and I picture Sadie bent over, bent backwards, or flat on the table with the unknown man thrusting into her.

Or woman. It could be Alma as well.

"Give it to her good," says a voice. "Oh, that pussy."

It only takes a moment for me to recognize Julian's voice.

Julian Donovan and Sadie. And someone else. There are two men in there with her.

At least.

Instinct screams at me to get out. It will be awkward if anyone sees me. Uncomfortable. What would I say? What would they say?

I should leave before that happens.

But I stand there listening, rooted to the spot by my cock that's decided it wants to be here.

My cock also wants to get in there and join in.

I've done my best to always be respectful in my thoughts of Sadie; considering her as a friend but nothing more, that's changed now.

I want to be the one with her.

I want to be the one thrusting into her, making her gasp with pleasure. I want my mouth on her, my hands on her breasts, my cock buried deep inside her.

I close my eyes as she cries out again.

I never expected her to be so vocal. Would she be like that with me? Could I make her scream? Would she like it better with me?

"Fuck it, I'm going to come!"

Julian's cry snaps me out of my reverie and as I turn to go, things get much louder. Sadie screams, more than once. The third time it's quickly muffled like something is shoved in her mouth.

I can only imagine what's in her mouth.

Then a man's shout, sounding like an animal's roar.

I stand frozen behind the desk. I shouldn't be hearing this. I'm never going to be able to look Sadie in the eye without remembering this. Visualizing it.

Voices talking. Male laughter. Whatever was going on is over now. I glance around, looking for a place where I can't be seen, when Sadie runs out of the office, straight to the washroom.

Without thinking, I sink onto the floor behind the desk, ducking my head as the lights of the conference room click off.

"See you tomorrow, Sadie," Julian calls.

I peek around the corner of the desk, just to make sure.

It's Julian all right, and with him is Victor Barnes, one of the board members who visited Hever earlier today.

Had Julian set this scene up with him then? Did Sadie know what had been planned for her? Was that why she stayed late?

I wait until the door to the stairwell door swings shut before I stand up. I need to leave now before Sadie comes out. I don't want her to know I was here, that I witnessed...

What? What did I witness? I can only imagine, but unfortunately, I have an extremely good imagination.

But some part of me makes me linger until I hear the door to the ladies' room swing open.

"Jason," Sadie gasps. Her eyes are round and terrified.

"Are you okay?" What a stupid question. Of course, she's fine. She's been in an empty office with two men. She's—

She's exhausted, her face pale, eyes red-rimmed. Her hair, tied back in a ponytail, is mussed and frizzy. And she looks so very sad.

"Sadie?"

"Were you here the whole time?" she whispers.

"No." Which isn't a lie, but I can't let her believe I don't know what's going on. "Just a few minutes. I heard...enough...to know I should have left."

Sadie drops her head and heads for the stairs on unsteady legs. "I need to go home."

"Are you all right? What did they do to you?"

"Nothing I didn't want," she says in a defiant voice. "But I didn't know..." Her voice trails off as leans against the wall. I leap to her side.

"Let me drive you home."

She jerks away from my touch on her arm. "You don't want to be around me right now."

I grasp her elbow with a gentle touch. "I always want to be around you. I'm driving you home."

Chapter Thirteen

BRIENNE

As I EXPECTED, ELI is waiting for me when I get home from the bar. Sitting in his truck in the parking lot, like he has all the time in the world.

I do my best to hide my grimace but can't ignore the leaping of my stomach at the sight of him. My head knows he's bad for me, but the rest of my body overlooks that fact.

"Where've you been?" Eli asks with a grin to wipe about any possible sting of possessiveness. Not that he would even consider being possessive...or jealous...or even concerned. Eli's just nosy.

"That's none of your business." I brush by him without a glance on my way to unlock the door. Even though I don't look at him, my body reacts—my breath quickens, everything tightens, even my nipples.

Damn dream the other night.

I've been so *good* with Eli. Good, as in using all the willpower I can muster to stay away, not to call the night after the dream to invite him over. Not to show up at the clubs where his band plays, hoping I'll be the one he goes home with.

I've been good but now he's here...

Eli follows me into the building, waits until I unlock the front door and walks to the elevator. "It was good to see you the other night."

For a heart-stopping moment, I think he's talking about the dream. And then I start to breathe again. "The night you signed the divorce papers?"

"About that."

I whirl around. "No. Don't even go there, Eli. We're divorced. That's not going to change."

His hand on the small of my back is warm. "What if I don't want that?"

I snort but don't step away from his reach. "You should have thought of that sooner."

"We can be divorced if that's what you really want, but I hope we can stay...friends."

The elevator takes this opportune time to show up and with a nudge on my back, Eli escorts me inside. Immediately I realize the space is too small for the two of us, or at least it's too small for someone who clearly wants action and someone who is battling with her body so she won't want it to.

The door closes. "Eli," I warn as he pounces. Or rather slides to me, fitting his body against mine like it was made to go there.

"Brienne," he says in a husky voice, the accent coming out to play. His hands are on my waist and I want them to stay there. If they stay at my waist, then they won't go wandering anywhere else, making it even more difficult to say no.

I'm going to say no. I have to say no.

I let him kiss me.

Eli's lips against mine are soft with the right amount of pressure and his tongue sweeps into my open mouth like a car pulling into the garage. Like it's home. His hands splayed at my sides, long fingers reaching from the waistband of my jeans to under my breasts.

I want his hands to move. I want them to wander and explore and...

The chime of the elevator sounds and Eli releases me. "I think you still want to be friends," he says.

It's the smile that does it. Smug and cocky with a hint of condescending self-satisfaction. He knows I'm going to agree to this because I've always agreed to whatever he's wanted. Eli thinks I'm going to open the apartment door and let him come inside, and then he's going to do all sorts of things to me and I'm going to let him. Not only let him, but I'm going to enjoy it all.

Until the next day when I'll be kicking myself for being so weak.

"I do want to be friends." I quicken my pace so Eli has to hurry to keep up with me. My apartment is halfway down the hall. "I'll always want to be friends with you."

His fingers graze my back and drift down to my ass. Eli's always liked me in these jeans. It's only fitting that he gets to watch my sway as I walk away from him.

If I can. My body tingles with anticipation, but this time I know there's not going to be the sweet release waiting for me.

"I can be a damn good friend to you, Brienne."

My place is only a few doors away. "No, you can't."

"Pardon?"

I made it. I turn and lean against my door, keys in my hand. "You can't be a friend to me or any other woman. You can't handle it. It's because of you that people always say men and women can't be friends. You will always bring sex into your friendships."

"Yeah, but why not? Fun for all." The smirk is back, and the sight of it hardens my heart.

It doesn't do anything for the jolt of desire between my legs, but I'll worry about that later.

"It might be fun for a few minutes—"

"A few minutes? Baby, that hurts." Eli clutches his chest. He reaches around me and rests his hand on mine still clutching the doorknob. "Why don't you open that up?"

"I won't be opening the door until you're walking down the hall. You're not coming in tonight, Eli. Or ever again."

Something inside me gives a cheer of approval at the same time as my women's parts scream with disappointment.

"Bri. Baby. What's going on?"

"I'm not your baby or your Bri. I'm not your wife. And I'm not going to be your fuck friend."

"I only want to make you happy."

"You really don't. Or you do care about my happiness when you're getting me ready to fuck you, but after it's over, you don't care about what's going on in my head. You don't care about making me happy."

He steps away with a frown. "Where's this coming from?"

"This is what I should have told you years ago, but I couldn't come up with enough backbone to let you walk away. But now I'm not letting my pussy do my thinking for me." I rap my knuckles against my forehead. "I'm using this. And my head says you're bad for me. So, go home Eli. And don't come back."

"You don't mean that. You like what we have together. You want it."

I reach down and cup a hand between my legs. "*This* wants it." I touch my head again. "*This* is saying no go. Go home, Eli."

"Brienne."

"Now."

I force myself to stand silently at my door while he peppers me with arguments and then moves on to crooning to me about all the things he wants to do to me. I clench my legs together in the hope that my pussy will stop tightening at the images his words put in my bed.

Spread-eagled on the bed.

His mouth between my legs.

This thick cock inside me, moving with slow, deep thrusts.

Begging for more.

"Stop it," I finally say, wishing my voice sounded firm and strong, rather than a feeble squeak. "It's not going to work. Not this time. Go find someone else."

"But I want you."

And that's the problem. I know he wants me. Eli can work his magic on any number of women, but there's something about me that always draws him back. It's a heady sensation, knowing I'm the woman he wants. The rock star with the panty-melting accent and the eyes that can make you do anything he wants—he wants *me*.

And I want him too.

Or I did.

I put a gentle hand on his chest. "Eli, we're not good for each other. Or, at least you're not good for me. I need someone who I can rely on to come home without smelling like another woman. I need someone who's not going to go out for a night and forget to come home for a week."

"I've always made it up to you."

"But why should you?"

"You knew what I was like."

"I did. And I do. And I'm a lot older and wiser now, and I can't do that any longer." I lean in and kiss his lips softly, once, twice before pulling away with regret. "Please Eli. Go home."

The expressions war on Eli's face. He knows if he keeps pushing, I'll eventually give in. I want him too. But deep down, he loves me.

"Is there someone else?" he asks in a choked voice. "Someone else who can make you happy?"

An image of Cooper replaces all the R-rated visions Eli has produced, and I stop clenching. "I think there is," I say with a smile. "I hope so."

Chapter Fourteen

SADIE

I DON'T KNOW WHY Jason insists on driving me home, but I'm glad he does. My legs tremble like I've run a marathon or snowboarded down Whistler Mountain. There's no way I could have ridden my bike.

It's just because of the sex. The really intense sex I just had. With two men.

I don't say much on the short drive back to my apartment because I don't know what to say to Jason. I don't know what he heard. Did he see anything? I'm too embarrassed to ask him.

Why is he driving me home? Because he suspects I would have difficulty keeping my head in the game long enough to get there? I can't even go thirty seconds before my brain jumps back to the office.

Julian's hands gripping my hips so tightly that he left marks.

Victor, with a fist full of my ponytail, forcing me to take him into my mouth.

Julian offering me to Victor, like I didn't have a say. Like I was some kind of object.

I've never had a sexual experience like that before. And I don't think I want to again.

My body liked it—liked it a lot. Liked it so much that I'm still excited just thinking of what they did to me. But my heart didn't appreciate it.

"This is my place," I say to Jason, indicating where to park.

We don't say another word until we're in my apartment. When I drop my keys on the table, the sound rings through the empty space.

"Why don't you have a shower? Or a bath," Jason suggests.

"I've never done that before," I blurt, unable to meet his eyes.

"That's none of my business."

"I don't understand why you're here. Why do you want to be?"

Jason shrugs and gazes around my apartment. I see it through his eyes—sparsely furnished with IKEA furniture. Framed pictures of my snowboarding exploits still hang on the wall, even though some days it hurts to look at them. A giant pink stuffed flamingo is shoved into a corner of the couch where I had used it as a pillow last night.

"I'm not sure," he finally says. "I want to make sure you're all right."

"I'm fine."

Jason meets my gaze for the first time. "You don't look fine. You look," he pauses, searching for the word. "Spent."

"It was...intense. I'm not used to that."

"Was it...did they...?"

"It was consensual," I say, guessing at what he's having trouble asking. "It was unexpected and unplanned but there was no force. I could have left."

Could I have? The way Victor grabbed me, the way he held me down...I switch off the question of whether they would have let me leave with difficulty.

"I should leave," Jason says stiffly.

Even though I don't understand why he's here, something inside me doesn't want him to leave. "You don't have to."

"Do you need me to stay?"

"Need you? No. But I wouldn't mind you being here." I gesture to the couch. "I think I am going to have a shower. I won't be too long. Do you want something to eat?"

"Why don't I make you something? I'm sure you haven't eaten tonight."

"Do you cook?" I ask with surprise.

Jason shrugs and I notice how broad his shoulders are. "I'm good with eggs."

"I have eggs."

He nods curtly. "Go have a shower and I'll make us something."

Us. It's been a long time since I've been an us.

I shower quickly, and efficiently, wanting to wash the fingerprints off me. But I don't let my mind wander to Julian and Victor. As soon as the water hits me, I push those memories away.

I think about Jason.

The fact that he's in my apartment cooking me dinner. I push away the humiliation of him hearing/seeing/being a witness to my interlude with Julian, and let the soft haze of happiness ease over the intensity of the sex, like one of those weighted blankets helping with anxiety.

Knowing he's here soothes me.

He puts me at ease, and that's difficult to do. My past relationship with Ethan was full of competition, regret and disappointment. Looking back at the two years I spent with him, I wonder if I was ever comfortable.

I'm comfortable with Jason, even though we've never taken our friendship out of the office.

After I shower and dress in a worn pair of jogging pants, I realize we've definitely taken the friendship out of the office and into the kitchen. Jason stands at the stove expertly flipping an omelet, the remnants of a cut-up red pepper and my package of ham on the counter beside him.

"I helped myself to what I could find in the fridge," he says as he slides it onto a plate and sprinkles cheese on the top.

I eye the omelet, not realizing I'm hungry until the smell hits me. Then I glance at Jason. "I didn't know I had an apron."

His shirt is covered by a full apron covered with lemons and limes. Jason is so tall that it's like he's wearing a child's apron.

"It was in the drawer," he says without a hint of apology. "Eat before it gets cold."

I sniff appreciatively. "It looks amazing. Thank you. Did you make yourself something?"

"I ate at home."

I push away the papers and books covering the tiny table and sit down. Rather than joining me, Jason clears up the counter, sweeping the bits of pepper into the compost bin under the sink. He seems very comfortable in my kitchen.

"You clean too," I say, taking the first mouthful of egg. "That's always—this is amazing," I interrupt myself, covering my mouth. "Really, really good."

"I'm good at eggs," Jason says. "And you had a lot of them in your fridge."

"I eat a lot of eggs," I admit, devouring the omelet as quickly as I can. "It's easy when you're cooking for one, plus it's a good source of protein." I hunch my shoulders when Jason glances at me. "Not that I'm all that into healthy eating these days but after years of competing, it's hard to get out of the mindset of protein good, carbs bad."

"Do you miss it? The competing, not the actual snowboarding. I can only imagine it was a very heady experience to accomplish something like that."

"It was the best time of my life," I confess. "I miss it every day. And not the physical-ness of the sport, even though I miss that too. But the *winning*. It was something else."

Jason nods and fills the sink with water. "You don't have to do the dishes," I protest.

"I need to leave a clean kitchen."

"Obviously, I don't." My cereal bowl is still on the counter, along with my coffee cup. I'm so glad I rinsed my bowl so that Jason wouldn't see the soggy remainder of my Froot Loops.

Jason adds my bowl to the soapy water. "I don't mind. I like cleaning for you."

"For just me or for anyone with a messy kitchen?"

"For anyone. But especially for you."

"Thank you," I say softly. I keep quiet as I finish my omelet, each bite melting in my mouth. Jason makes quick work of my dishes, leaving them sitting clean and rinsed on my drying rack by the time I stand with my empty plate. "And thank you for cooking for me. That was really sweet."

He takes my plate without meeting my eyes. "I'm not usually called sweet. Nice, but not sweet."

"I always call you sweet." I wonder if I should dry the dishes but then a yawn splits my face.

"You should get to bed," Jason says as he washes my plate before unplugging the sink. The water empties with a gurgle.

"I was going to watch some TV," I say. "If you want to."

He meets my eyes. "Do you want me to stay?"

"I do." There's no hesitation in my voice. I want Jason to stay, to spend time with me. Regardless of what I was doing an hour ago, I want Jason here.

As a friend. I've pushed Julian into the back of my mind, but my body is still too exhausted to consider anything else right now.

"I have beer," I offer when Jason doesn't respond.

"Are you trying to bribe me?"

"Is it working?"

He chuckles. "I'll take a beer."

Cold bottles of beer in hand, we settle on the couch and I pick up the remote, landing on the first movie I find. An uncomfortable silence drifts between us and I wonder if I was wrong asking him to stay. I might want him here, but does he want to be here? Is he staying out of obligation? Is he thinking about what I did tonight—disgusted by my behaviour?

He has no right to be disgusted. It was my decision, my choice.

Even though I'm not sure it was the right one, it was still my choice.

"I don't know what I'm supposed to say," I confess after the silence becomes more awkward than uncomfortable.

"You don't have to say anything," Jason says so quickly that I know he's thinking of the same thing I am.

"I think I need to explain."

Jason turns to me, tucking his leg underneath him, and resting his arm on the couch behind me. For a moment I'm tempted to curl into the space he offers. "You don't have to explain anything. I'm not here to question your decisions."

"Why are you here?"

"I don't know," he admits. "But I find myself wanting to be here."

"Even after that? After I—with Julian and the other—"

"That meant nothing to me," Jason interrupts.

"Oh." His statement sends a sharp stab of pain through me.

"I mean, it shouldn't," he adds. "We're friends."

"Friends," I echo.

"So, as your friend, I shouldn't be bothered by what you do in your spare time, or who you do it with. Right? That's what friendship is. No jealousy. No feeling like I have a right to judge."

"I guess not. I mean, no. There shouldn't be any jealousy. If we're friends. It's silly."

I've often thought jealousy is one of the worst of the emotions. It makes no sense, to be envious of someone's appearance, good fortune, or special person at their side. In all the years I competed, there were odd moments of envy, but after giving myself a sharp talking to, I would force myself to be happy. If someone had an achievement I was reaching for, I should just work harder to get what I wanted. Make my own luck.

I know this is a good way to look at things. Healthy. Mature.

But for more than a moment, I want Jason to be jealous of Julian.

Jason is quiet for a few minutes, and I don't know if the conversation is over or if he's thinking of what he wants to say. He often thinks carefully before he speaks so I don't want to break the silence.

"It did bother me," he finally says.

A spark of happiness flickers in my chest. "It did?"

"I didn't like them touching you. I didn't see it, but if I did..." he shakes his head. "I wanted to be the one touching you."

"Oh." I'm not sure how to respond to that. I might need about a month of thinking before I come up with the proper answer. But Jason isn't finished speaking.

"That goes against what I said about us being friends. You're not supposed to want to touch your friends in such an intimate manner."

"I guess not." Emotions dance through me, from happiness to fear, from excitement to anger.

Not now. Isn't it enough that I want Jason to be here? I don't have the bandwidth to deal with anyone more tonight.

"What I'm saying, is that I think I'd like to be more than friends."

Chapter Fifteen

CALLIE

I'M SETTLED ONTO MY couch with my tried and true remedy for a sleepless night—popcorn and a Disney movie when my phone buzzes beside me.

The cats are curled up beside me and Olaf, my giant of a cat gives the phone a disdainful glance.

I'm surprised to see Brienne's picture flash on the screen. It's only been twenty minutes since we said goodbye at the bar.

"What's up?" I ask, pointing the remote at the television to mute it. My Disney obsession is my business and no one else's.

"Eli was at my building when I got home," she says in a rush.

I groan. I'd worked so hard on her tonight. "Oh, Bri." And then, "Why are you calling me?"

"Because I told him to leave!"

"Before or after?"

"Before! He'd still be here if I let him stay. But I didn't. I told him what we talked about—that my pussy liked him but my head thought he's a bad idea for me."

"You told him that?" I laugh.

"Not in so many words."

"So you didn't say pussy?"

"I did! You'd be so proud of me, Cal!"

"I am proud of you! You've made all women-kind proud of you tonight. Now, tell me exactly what happened."

As Ariel explores her underwater world on screen, I listen as Brienne gives me an in-depth recap of her confrontation with Eli. I am proud of her, but I can't help rolling my eyes when she describes what her female parts thought about the whole thing. This was a long time coming. Women all over the world have spent too long with their Mr. Wrongs—me included—but Eli was a special case. Other than his roving dick, he was really perfect for Brienne. And there's no doubt he loves her, but I knew it killed her a little bit every time Eli had been with another woman. I don't know if it made it worse or better than he never tried to hide his dalliances with her.

"Are you going to give Cooper a try now?" I ask when she's finished. "As good a time as ever, now that Eli is officially out of the picture."

"We'll see," was all she would say, which is as good as a promise for Brienne. After I said goodbye for the second time that night, my smile remained on my face. It would be fun at work to watch things progress with Brienne and Cooper.

It might be interesting to see if I can speed it up a little bit.

But thinking of work invariably got me thinking of Michael, and the smile slides off my face. Almost three weeks without a word. He stayed with his girlfriend and is too guilty to face me.

Or ashamed.

Or—and I hate myself for the number of times this had popped into my head over the last weeks—maybe he doesn't feel the same way.

Maybe he hadn't enjoyed it.

"No," I say aloud. How could any man not like fucking me? I've even had a gay guy get into it once, so fascinated by my breasts that he barely noticed when I slid onto his cock. A few pelvis tilts had finished both of us off and he had had a smile on his face for the rest of the night.

How could Michael not have picked me?

I shift on the couch as the storm raged on screen and Ariel dove into the water to save her true love. That's what hurts so much. That a man would pick someone else over me. Maybe Michael hadn't been in love with me—yet—but there had been time for that.

I'm very loveable. "I am," I say as Jafar meows in disappointment and hops off the couch.

Then why can't I find someone to love me?

I literally push away the loneliness and the uncertainty with a wave of my hand. I don't need to be thinking of that. It's bad enough that I'm home alone with my cats, singing along with Ariel. To get into why I can't find someone to love me will only make a bad night worse.

It's not a bad night. Brienne made sure of that.

She's a good friend. But why, I have to wonder, in all the years of our friendship, have I never told her about Devon?

Devon, my husband.

Devon, the man I fell madly in love with when I was eighteen and planned on spending the rest of my life with.

He was perfect for me; quiet to my loudness, reserved to my exuberant nature. But he matched me every step in the bedroom.

We married when I was twenty and had four perfect years together. And then he met Ashley Adams and fell in love with her.

Or at least I think he did. I'll never know the true story, never know who she was or what she meant to him because they died in a car accident. Together.

My biggest regret in this world is never knowing what my husband was doing in a car with another woman the night he died.

By the time I recovered enough to start asking questions, eight months had passed, along with any witnesses to their relationship. If they were having an affair, they certainly hid their tracks well.

I'll never know why he picked her over me.

Which is why this thing with Michael bothers me so much. "It irks me," I say to Olaf as he kneads my thigh. "I don't like to be irked."

I need to stop letting Michael irk me.

I need to push him out of my heart just like I did with Devon all those years ago.

As I finish watching Eric fall in love with Ariel, I work on convincing myself that I'm not in love with Michael.

Chapter Sixteen

JASON

S ADIE DOESN'T SAY ANYTHING. I wait for a moment, another long one, an excruciating, never-ending ten seconds.

"I see." I stiffly pull myself off her couch. "Maybe I should go."

"No, wait. Jason," Sadie says as she grabs my hand.

I stand by the couch, but can't look at her. Suddenly, it all became so perfectly clear. Sadie is the woman for me. She's smart, attractive; we have everything in common, we're already friends. I find her extremely attractive...

The list goes on and on.

"Don't go." Her voice is quiet but serious. "Not like that. You can't throw that on me now, not after what happened."

"I said I didn't care what happened."

"But then you did. And that's fine—it's nice, actually."

I glance at her with confusion.

"Can I at least think about all this? Because I've had Julian chasing me for weeks and I want to make sure I'm not just running from him to you. I don't want to do that to you."

"I don't understand. Do you have feelings for him?"

She shrugs. "I don't know. I honestly don't. I've had sex with him twice now so my heart tells me that I should have feelings for him."

"Are you listening to your heart?"

"It's pretty loud right now. But I don't know if that's because..." she trails off, unable to meet my gaze.

"Because of the intense sexual encounter you just experienced with him," I supply.

"Kind of, yeah. I might hate the guy tonight, after all this," she falters again.

"Pheromones, I would imagine. Things may feel different after they wear off."

"Sure. And they will wear off, but I don't want to say anything to you until they do. I've got a really bad track record with relationships and I don't want to mess up anything with you." She squeezes my hand. "You mean a lot to me."

"But you're not sure if I'm in the friend or more-than-friend category."

Sadie smiles grimly. "I don't trust myself right now. I shouldn't say anything. I shouldn't do anything."

"You're exhausted. I'll go."

"It might be nice if you stay," she says at the same time. "We could watch whatever this movie is for a bit."

I contemplate her offer. I don't have anything else to do, and I am worried about her. Sadie is always so colourful and exuberant but the episode with Julian has drained her.

It's driving me crazy that I don't know what happened in that conference room because I've been imagining scenarios since I first heard her scream. Can I stay here without asking questions? Without demanding she tells me everything?

I don't think Sadie would do well with demands right now.

"I'll stay," I tell her grudgingly.

"Good." Her smile is her regular smile, warm and sexy, and I'm embarrassed to admit my heart stutters at the sight of it. I'm also embarrassed to admit that I've never looked at her the way I'm looking at her now.

I'm not sure how or why, but things are different now.

I'm going to kill Julian Donovan if I find out he hurt her in any way.

I drink my beer and try to keep my gaze off Sadie as onscreen, Picard and friends save a planet. Gradually I relax into her couch, enjoying the comfort of the fabric as well as her closeness.

It's more of a loveseat, so it's difficult for two people to lounge without some part of their body touching. Sadie fidgets; she starts with her long legs propped up on the coffee table, before shifting to curl them up underneath her. She leans against the armrest, she sits upright.

"You really can't get comfortable, can you?" I ask, setting my empty bottle on the table.

Sadie laughs self-consciously. "I've never really noticed before, but I always sit on that side. It's like I'm the princess with the pea under the mattress over here."

I immediately stand up. "I'll move. You sit here."

Sadie grabs my arm before I can take a step to her side. "No, wait. Stay. Maybe I can sort of lean against you?"

"As a pillow?"

"Like a sexy body pillow," she counters.

"Is that a body pillow that's considered sexy, or a sexy body?"

Sadie frowns. "What's the difference?"

"I have no idea." I sit down stiffly, all my earlier relaxation vanishing with her sexy comment.

"Maybe if you sit with your legs out," she suggests demonstrating what she wants. "Or maybe like this."

Sadie positions me with my legs outstretched diagonally and balanced on the far corner of the table and tucks herself into my side, leaning against me.

I take a deep breath and put my arm around her and she cuddles against me with a contented sigh. "You could have just told me you wanted to cuddle."

"I didn't know I did," she admits. "I don't know what I want tonight."

"Did you want them?" I ask in a strangled voice. "Julian and his friend?"

"I've always liked the idea of two men," Sadie says after a moment's pause.

"But...?"

"But with Julian..." I feel her head turn towards me but I don't look down. "It's like he's trying to outdo himself. Like he's competing with someone. Tonight, with both of them, they were both competing. Who was making me come more, who was—"

"Please don't give me details," I interrupt.

Sadie stiffs against me. "Sorry. I'm sure you don't want to hear this."

"I do. I have no trouble listening to your thoughts about the evening. But I'd rather not have details about how many times they pleasured you with their hands or mouths, or how many times they fucked you." I pause and swallow the resentment that swells. "It will only arouse me."

"It will—pardon?"

"Arouse me? Sexually excite me."

"I know what it means, but really? Hearing me talk about it would turn you on?"

"Has turned me on," I correct. "Thinking about you and them is enough to do that, but hearing details would make it uncomfortable to sit with you like this."

"I guess so. It's kind of gross thinking—"

I crane my neck to look at her. "There's nothing gross about it. You can do whatever with whoever you like. But if you tell me about it, it will excite me and I'll find it challenging not to kiss you."

"You don't want to kiss me now."

"I think, Sadie, I will always want to kiss you, regardless of how I may feel about you. But if I were to kiss you, one thing would lead to another, and I think you have had enough of that tonight."

She gives a bark of surprised laughter. "Maybe."

"When it happens with us, I'd rather it not happen when you're exhausted."

"When." She speaks so softly that I think I've misheard her.

"Pardon?"

"You said when. When it happens. Implying that we're going to have sex."

I frown. "Do you think differently?"

Her laughter is a rumble as she leans against me. "You're so different, Jason."

"Thank you for not saying strange. I've got that all my life."

"Even if I said it, I'd mean good strange. Weird in a good way. I like it."

"Do you like me?"

Sadie sits up and with several quick moves, ends up in my lap, her arms looped around my neck. "You found me having sex with two men and you're asking if I like you? Most guys would have run out of here with their tail between their legs."

"I have no tail."

"No, you don't." Sadie smiles and I wonder if I'll ever get tired of seeing her face light up. "And I'm glad because I'm sure it would take away from your fine ass if you had a tail sticking out of it."

"You think I have a fine ass?"

"I think a lot of things about you."

"Do you think you're still interested in women?"

She stiffens with surprise again, and I have a moment's regret because I don't want her to move. "You don't beat around the bush much, do you?"

"There's really no point."

"There is sometimes," she corrects. "But I guess not now. Neither one of us has anything to hide. Or do you?"

"I had sex with Callie," I offer.

"I know."

"I know about you and Alma."

She winces. "I'm not sure what to say about that."

"Which is why I asked if you're still interested in women."

She cocks her head, looking into the distance. "Women—I'm not sure. Alma—definitely not. How's that?"

"I'm fine with anything. It's your life and I have no say in it."

"But if we..." she trails off uncertainly. "Wouldn't you want a say in it?"

"I'm not one of those men who think they live to control women. So you don't have to worry about that. And nothing will happen tonight."

"No, because—"

I put a finger to her lips before she can finish. "Not because of anything you're going to say. I'm sure you scrubbed their fingerprints off in the shower, so I'm not worried about that." And I'm not. Even though when she smiles, I feel a little pang at the thought of another man's cock in her mouth, but I might feel that regardless of when it happened. No, the Sadie sitting in my lap is a different Sadie that I drove home from the office. And she's definitely different from the Sadie of yesterday.

I wonder what Sadie she'll be tomorrow.

"Nothing will happen tonight because it's not our time. I expect it will be, and soon, but not now."

"Ok." Her arms tighten. "Can I tell you something?"

"You can tell me anything."

"I've never believed in regret. I think it's worthless to regret something. People should just accept and move on."

"I agree."

"But I regret being with Julian tonight because I'd really like to kiss you and see what happens and now I can't."

I run my thumb over her lips, that wide mouth curled up in the faintest of smiles. "I'd like that too, but it will happen. Besides, when it does, it'll be sure to exhaust you in different ways, and I don't think you could handle that tonight."

Her smile widens against my thumb. "I think you're right."

Chapter Seventeen

BRIENNE

I LOOK FOR CALLIE when I get to the kitchenette the next day. She's always been my source of encouragement, always ready to give me a kick in the ass to do something. And this morning, I'm ready to do something.

But no Callie, only Delia and the ever-present Carl laughing together. And Cooper.

My stomach tightens when I see him. I may be ready to do something, but I'm not sure what exactly I'm going to do. And whatever it is, I'm nervous.

Cooper's smile is hesitant, tentative. I don't blame him. Caught up in the mess of my love life, I haven't exactly greeted him with open arms.

But I smile widely at him, and his expression transforms. Eyes widen, smile deepens; his whole face changes. It's very cute.

He's very cute.

Taking my smile as encouragement that it is, Cooper steps across the room to me. "Morning."

"Hi, Cooper."

"Hi, Brienne."

I notice Delia's sideways glance, her smile that she can't hide.

"How was your evening?" he asks. I can tell he's trying to sound casual but fails miserably.

"Good. I went out for drinks with Callie."

"Ah. The ears of mankind must have been burning."

I laugh nervously. "Not all mankind. Also, I didn't have sex with my soon-to-be ex-husband."

"P-pardon?"

I take a deep breath. "You asked what I did last night and I told you what I didn't do. I didn't have sex with my ex."

Cooper blinks at my frankness. "Actually, I asked how your evening was, but hey, elaboration is always a good thing. Is it also a good thing that you didn't...uh...not engage in non-marital relations with the soon-to-be-ex?"

Another deep breath. I've gone this far, and even though I want to run out of the room with embarrassment, I hold my ground. "I think so. I mean, it would have been good, but it wouldn't have been a good thing to do."

"I see." Now Cooper takes a deep breath. There's a lot of heavy breathing going on between us with nothing to show for it yet. A myriad of emotions flash across Cooper's face and for a moment I think he's going to be the one to run.

I laugh. "You really don't, do you."

"Not really, no." He smiles ruefully. "But I'm happy that you're happy. And that you didn't have sex with him. Am I allowed to say that?"

"You can say anything you want," I say in a low voice, aware Delia is doing her best to overhear our conversation. "I think you should be, especially when you consider the reason for me not having sex with him."

His eyes narrow with confusion. "I assume it's because he's your soon-to-be ex-husband?"

I wave my hand. "That too. But it's really because I want to have sex with you."

Now Cooper's eyes practically bug out of his head. "Now?"

I give a delicate shrug, smiling when Cooper's jaw drops. This is fun. "I was thinking of some time in the future."

"In the future," he parrots loud enough for heads to turn towards us. "Us."

"Is there a concern with that?"

"No!" Cooper drops his head and I'm rewarded by a flush of embarrassment along his jaw. "Of course not. That's fine. Great."

"Great." I make a move to rejoin the conversation but Cooper grips my arm.

"You can't leave me hanging here."

I open my eyes wide. "I can't? What would you like me to do to help you...hang less?" I ask, improvising widely. I burst out laughing. "I can't do this anymore."

Cooper's face falls quicker than a barrel going over Niagara Falls. "You can't? This wasn't—you don't want..."

"I'm not used to making the first move with guys," I confess, my face heating up more than the water in the Tassimo.

"But you are making a move?"

"I was trying to."

"Thank god." Cooper shudders with relief. "I thought you were joking and I didn't think I could bear it if you were."

"Really?"

"Really. Keep going."

"I can't now."

"So start again."

Chapter Eighteen

SADIE

I FELL ASLEEP IN Jason's arms last night.

It was nice, at least it was until Jason woke up in a panic around four a.m. He leaves in a rush, his sleep-encrusted voice listing reasons why he shouldn't have fallen asleep with me. I let him go without argument but couldn't fall back asleep after he left.

He likes me.

The big question is—do I like him? In that way.

When I was curled up on my couch, leaning against his firm and surprisingly muscular body, I liked him. I liked him a lot. But when he left my apartment and I crawled into my bed that felt cold and lonely, I let my mind drift to Julian and things got confusing.

It's just sex with Julian. I know that. But I like the sex with Julian.

Even the sex with Julian and Victor. It was intense and it left a bit of a bad taste in my mouth the way Julian assumed I'd go for it, like greasy fingers after eating too many potato chips.

It was too much. I had too many chips with Julian. Even though it was a brand new flavour for me, it was too much.

But I liked the chips.

After an hour of lying awake, turning myself on with the memories of the night before, I have a cold shower and go to work early.

I walk because I left my bike locked up when Jason drove me home.

He was so sweet last night.

Neither Alma or Agatha is at their desk when I walk in. The only one around is the caretaker rummaging in the supply closet that Alma had initiated me in.

I stop myself from looking in that direction as I take the stairs, afraid of meeting Julian in the elevator again.

I'm not sure what to say to him.

I'm not sure what to say to Jason either.

Julian is offering sex, and good sex. Is that all I want? Jason is offering much more. At least I think he is. In the light of day, I need clarification to what exactly he wants. A relationship? I'm not good at those, and I don't want to damage the friendship we already have.

Julian, Jason. Julian, Jason. Their names echo through my mind as my shoes click up the stairs.

The kitchenette is dark at the early hour, but I turn on the lights and find my freshly washed mug in the cupboard and set about making a much-needed cup of tea.

Then I go to work. At least I try to.

Two hours later, the office is full of morning conversations and the usual attempts at procrastination. I've managed to finish two assignments and respond to all of my outstanding emails, but I haven't come to any conclusion about what to do about my love life.

Or my sex life, because it's clear that's all Julian is offering.

Is that all I want right now?

The question pops to the forefront of my mind whenever I lose focus on my work. I've had a relationship and it didn't end well. I've never had the passionate intensity that Julian is offering.

Heart or pussy. It sounds crass, but that's what it's going to come down to.

Callie stops by my desk with her usual smile, but her eyes are tired, the mirror image of me. If I didn't have so much on my own mind, I would drag her away and demand to know what's up. Instead, I follow her to the kitchenette, neither of us speaking more than usual greetings.

The kitchenette is full of people—Delia and Carl with Abby, and Brienne and Cooper shutting out the rest of the group with their whispered conversation. I give them a surprised smile, happy Brienne seems to be getting it together with Cooper.

Jason stands next in line for the Tassimo, his cup in his hand. His eyes light up when he sees me, and he holds out his hand.

Does he want to hold my hand? Here?

"Give me your cup?" he says. "You look like you need it more than I do."

Callie has joined in the laughter around Delia so I stand with Jason. "I couldn't fall back asleep," I mutter as I give him my cup.

"I apologize for leaving so abruptly," he says in a low voice. "I'm not used to sleeping in a new place. Or not a bed."

"I'm sorry I fell asleep."

Carl steps away from the Tassimo with a smile, the aroma of his coffee tickling my nose. Jason selects two chai tea pods and feeds the machine. "You must have been exhausted. I shouldn't have stayed so long."

He won't look me in the eye. What has happened? Where did the sweet intimacy of last night vanish to? Even the way Jason is standing is stiff and formal, nothing like the way he held me last night.

He's changed his mind.

There's no sense in deciding between Julian and Jason because Jason doesn't want me anymore.

I glance around the room, suddenly self-conscious. Do people know what I did last night? Has something been said about me? A sick feeling rises in my stomach and I want to snatch my cup back from Jason.

"It's fine," I say stiffly.

He looks at me quickly. "Are you alright?"

My phone buzzes before I answer. I don't usually take it with me, but this morning I was checking Facebook as Callie collected me and shoved it in my skirt pocket. I pull it out with surprise.

It's Julian.

I breathe in through my nose and Jason narrows his eyes as I stuff it back into my pocket. "You're not going to answer that?" I shake my head. "You don't usually have your phone with you. Expecting a call?"

"No. Not that I know of." Now it's my turn to avoid Jason's gaze.

"It's him, isn't it?" Jason asks in a low voice, sounding so casual and off-handed that I wonder if I dreamed last night.

"It doesn't matter."

The room falls silent as Michael walks in. It's the first time I've seen him away from his desk in weeks. Giving him a nod, my gaze directs to Callie, who has fallen silent.

Things aren't good there.

"It matters because he's still your boss," Jason points out. "You'd better go see what he wants."

Things aren't good here.

I glance at him with surprise, shock and disappointment. "Fine," I mutter. "If that's what you think I should do. That's what I'll do." Not waiting for my tea, I stalk out of the kitchen.

Chapter Nineteen

CALLIE

It's been a while since Michael has been in the same room as me.

Under the same lights. Talking to the same people. Breathing the same air.

His lips so close to mine that it's like we're sharing the air between us.

Well, shit.

Apparently, I wasn't as good at convincing myself to fall out of love with him last night.

Especially when he smiles at me as if nothing had happened between us.

Like his head had never been between my legs. Or like he had never pushed me against the wall and fucked me like both of our lives depended on it.

Maybe it's a good thing that he's pretending. Because I can too.

"Morning, Callie," Michael says after he's greeted by Abby, Delia and Carl. He looks right at me when he says it, not like the cowardly eye avoidance he's been practicing for weeks.

"Nice to talk to you," I say. "I thought for a while there that you'd forgotten my name. But then I thought—how could *you* forget *my* name? I seem to recall you saying it a lot a few weeks ago."

The kitchen falls silent because my voice carries, especially when I'm not being quiet.

I'm tired of being quiet about Michael.

"Time for me to get back to work," Carl says with forced joviality. With a rueful smile, he picks up his mug and heads for the door. "Coming, Delia?"

"I should get back to work too," Abby says, giving me a worried look. "Callie? Need some chocolate?"

"Not at the moment, no. But thanks, Abs," I say brightly, turning my hard gaze back to Michael.

"I have to make my tea," Jason mutters. His shoulders hunch uncomfortably. I saw Sadie storm out so I don't think this is all because of me.

No matter. Jason knows what's going on. So does Brienne, who is still huddled with Cooper in the corner. With a wink, I turn my shoulder to Brienne. "I wonder if Delia ever told Carl we caught them," I muse. "That morning in the kitchen. You remember, Michael, don't you?"

"You told them?" Michael gasps, his face draining of colour.

"There aren't any secrets in this place. Is there, Jason? You know everything."

"Not what's happening with the two of you," Jason says, giving us a confused expression over his shoulder.

I smile. I knew Jason wouldn't leave. He likes information too much.

"It's no big mystery. After weeks and months of flirting and intense eye play, we hooked up. Only I thought it meant something, when in fact, it really didn't. My bad."

I kept my voice light, my tone even like I couldn't care less.

I was done showing Michael that he hurt me.

"Callie, it wasn't like that," Michael says urgently.

"No? What was it, then?"

"It's...complicated."

"Complicated. Of course, it is. That's what happens when you screw around on your girlfriend, something that I frown on. More than frown on. In fact, it's been years since I've made the mistake of being with a man with a significant other. It's a deal breaker for me. But if I recall correctly, you said things were over with your girlfriend."

"I said things weren't good," Michael mutters. Jason forgets about his tea and his gaze rockets between me and Michael.

"Implying that you wouldn't be together much longer, is that right? When I'm kicking myself for doing something stupid, I like to know exactly what I've done."

"It wasn't stupid."

I cock an eyebrow. "Oh, no? Sure feels stupid."

"Callie...I'm sorry."

"Again, just to make sure—what exactly are you sorry about? Lying to me? Fucking me? Fucking me like it meant something?"

"I'm not sorry about that."

"But lying to me? Are you sorry about that? Or is that not a lie, and you really broke up with her but still don't want me." I regret the words as soon as they leave my mouth. That makes me look weak like I care, and I don't. Not anymore.

Maybe a little.

"It wasn't a lie, not really. Things had been bad with Liana and I didn't know how much longer I wanted to be with her, but then after you and I..." he swallows audibly, and I feel a surge of hope that he really does care about me. "After what happened, things got better with us, and I thought I'd give it another try."

"Another try," I echo. "Did you tell her about it?"

"I did." It's the first time Michael has met my gaze during this conversation. His eyes are purple-shadowed, tired. I wonder what happened between him and his mystery girlfriend.

"What'd she say?" I shrug. "Just curious."

"She agreed to marry me."

"What?" I can't hide the shock on my face, the lurch my stomach gives as if Michael suddenly kicked me in the shin.

It would have hurt less if he had kicked me.

I breathe deeply through my nose, once, twice. "You're getting married?" I ask, enunciating my words carefully so there's no mistake.

"I'm sorry, Callie. I should have told you."

I can't show him how this affects me. I can't let him know how much it hurts.

Even though it does. It really hurts to think of Michael married. I may not have wanted to marry him, but I hate the thought of him with someone else.

Pulling up all my considerable willpower, I give an off-handed wave. "Why? It's no business of mine. Congratulations." I turn to Jason. "Did you know about this?"

He shakes his head with bewilderment. "First time I'm hearing this."

Jason and Michael are good friends, so it seems Michael is keeping a lot of secrets. I'd feel sympathy for the distance between them if my heart wasn't crumbling into dust.

Not crumbling. Not dust. Michael is not worth it.

I take another deep breath through my nose, hoping my nostrils aren't flaring like a bull.

"We haven't made any official announcement so maybe keep it to yourself, if you don't mind," Michael says apologetically.

"Don't worry, I definitely won't be going around talking about how the guy I was mooning after is now engaged. No, I think I'll keep that little tidbit to myself as long as I can." As much as I try, I can't keep the bitterness out of my voice.

"Callie," Michael implores.

"You say my name so *well*," I say. "I really thought you forgot about me."

"That's not possible," he says.

"No, it's not," I agree. "But you'll only have the memories. Unlike some people." I turn to Jason, praying my voice won't quiver until I get out of the kitchen. "Jason? I heard we got a shipment of sandbags down in the equipment room. I know that's a lot softer than cement mix, and I wondered if you'd like to go try them out with me?"

I chance a glance at Michael's face and I'm satisfied with what I see.

"Uh, me? Sure," Jason says, quickly. "Whatever you want."

"Whatever I want? That sounds like fun." I set the cup I'd been clutching on the counter. "I think I'll save my tea to drink later. Bye, Michael. Have a nice day."

And I sweep out of the room with Jason on my tail.

Chapter Twenty

JASON

I'M NOT SURE WHAT happened in the kitchen.

One minute I'm making a chai tea for Sadie and then she runs out to meet Julian. I was excited to see her, curious about what would happen in the light of day. I felt that we had really developed a connection last night, despite the lack of physical intimacy.

I had really wanted to kiss her.

Did I say something? Do something to offend her? Because when I woke up this morning, she was snuggled up beside me, the television still playing a Star Trek marathon.

I had to go home before the hardness in my pants embarrassed me more than I had already done.

When I left, I thought Sadie had given up on Julian. Or I thought it was over between them.

At least I hoped it was.

But one simple text and she goes running.

He must be exceptionally talented.

Sadie's departure had sent me into turmoil but instead of running after her, I got caught in the drama with Michael and Callie. I should have gone after Sadie, but instead, I was roped into office gossip. And now, I'm following Callie to who knows where.

What am I supposed to do now?

Chapter Twenty-One

BRIENNE

PART OF ME WANTS to ignore the exchange between Michael and Callie in the kitchen and focus on how good Cooper smells. The other part of me can't.

When Callie walks out—really, it's a saunter or a sashay, and it gives me all the feels. For Callie to be able to turn on her heel and walk away from Michael with Jason in tow is beyond impressive. Unless she somehow managed to perform a heart transplant on herself after I got off the phone with her last night, she must have been hurting over Michael's cavalier announcement of his upcoming marriage.

I want to be Callie when I grow up. But now I have to check on my friend.

"Just a minute." I turn away from Cooper but he grabs my arm.

"What's going with them?" he hisses.

"Nothing—now."

"But there was something. You know the new office policies—"

I pull away. "I have to see if she's okay," I say. "I'll be right back."

I brush past Michael in my haste to get to the door. "Brienne," he calls in a pleading voice.

"Congratulations, Michael." I hope he hears the sarcasm in my voice. I prefer more of the passive-aggressive style of conflict rather than Callie's in-your-face bravery.

"Callie!" The door to the stairwell has already closed after them and I stand in the aisle between the wall and cubicles, wondering if I should go after her.

Jason is with her. Which means...

Maybe I shouldn't go after Callie after all. She might be okay on her own, or at least with Jason.

Before I can head back to the kitchen, Cooper catches up with me. "That seemed intense," he says. "You obviously knew about it."

"Not really," I admit. "I didn't see that coming. Michael is engaged."

"Which Callie is clearly upset about. And Jason went to console her."

"Something like that."

Cooper nods. "We should get back to work." He reaches around me and pushes open the door. "After you."

Callie is long gone because I can't even hear her footsteps on the stairs.

"What was all the sneaking around in the stairs the other day?" Cooper asks. I'm conscious of the fact that he's behind me and most likely—maybe—watching the way my skirt curves around my ass as I climb the stairs.

I hope it looks good.

"There was no sneaking around," I retort in a prim voice that masks my inner thoughts.

"There looks like there was sneaking around."

I glance over my shoulder and stop on the stairs. "There wasn't. I can't talk to you when you're behind me."

"But I like being behind you," he says with a cheeky smile.

"Ha ha."

"But seriously, what was going on? I feel like I'm always playing catch up here, trying to figure everyone out."

"Don't bother," I say as I turn to face him. "There's stuff that's better you not know."

"But I want to know everything about you."

"You sound like a stalker."

"Is that a good thing?"

I laugh which then fades into a sigh. I don't remember the last time a man was so obvious about his interest in me. I had always danced around Eli, waiting for him to drop scraps of affection, usually doled out in a sexual nature. And Ian—

I still don't know what Ian thought of me. Or whether he did at all.

"I don't think you need to stalk me."

"What do I need to do?"

"Do whatever it is you're doing," I say slowly, sliding my hand up his arm and feeling the cotton of his dress shirt. I wish his sleeves were rolled up. I've always thought Cooper has a surfer vibe, with his lanky frame and touselled blond hair and I'd like to see his arms, tanned and muscular. I'd like to feel them slide around me. "And wait for me."

"Wait for you to do what?" he asks. His blue eyes stare intently and I lean closer, mesmerized by his lips, his scent surrounding me. "Brienne?"

At the sound of my name, I blink and rear back, losing my nerve. Instead of answering, I start up the stairs again, my heart racing.

Cursing myself.

That was the moment. That was our moment. He had been the perfect height and it would have been nothing for me to reach over and—

I trip on the stairs.

I stub my toe on the concrete step and pitch forward, my hand still holding my coffee cup and unable to catch me. But a strong arm grabs me around my waist so that only a tiny slosh of coffee spills out of the cup.

"You okay," Cooper breathes into my ear.

"Yeah." I turn, his arm sliding around so he still has a hold of me. "Just—"

I'm conscious of how close my mouth is to his. How soft his lips look, the twinkle in his blue eyes. The—

I kiss him.

I don't mean to, and neither of us expects it, but when I lean in, his mouth is welcoming, like a beacon drawing me closer and it's there, so I take it.

Soft and surprised, but Cooper recovers quickly. But it's only a moment before I pull away.

"I'm supposed to wait for you to fall?" Cooper asks breathlessly, the eagerness in his expression combining with the hunger in his gaze to give me warm tingles.

I turn to face him fully, forgetting about my coffee until I slide my hands around his shoulders. "I already did."

I kiss him again.

His lips are warm and soft. He tastes sweet, like cotton candy. I sink into his mouth, made dizzy by his cologne and the way his hands caress my back. My world shrinks to hands and mouth and tongue, the tingling sensations Cooper creating in me the only way I can tell this isn't a dream.

I want to sink down onto the stairs, pulling him over me, under me. All around me. I want to—

Neither one of us hears the door open, even though it's only a few feet away. Or, if Cooper hears it, he makes no move to stop kissing me. But then the soft tap of heels breaks through, like a background noise when I'm trying to fall asleep. And then a cough, a clearing of a throat.

It's Cooper who pulls away this time, slowly, reluctantly. Like he's annoyed. When my eyes unglaze, Delia and Carl stand behind us on the stairs.

"If you don't mind, we need to pass to get back to work," Carl says politely, a hint of a smirk on his face.

"Sorry," I say, and move closer to the railing. Cooper steps with me but makes to move to remove his hands. This isn't over yet, then.

Delia doesn't try to hide her smile as she steps around us. "About bloody time," she murmurs.

"I know," I whisper.

As soon as they're gone, I smile, waiting for the kissing to resume. But Cooper leans his head on my shoulder.

"I can't do this."

"Can't do what?"

"Can't do this with you."

"Excuse me?" I pull away as far as I can while his arms are still around me. "What's going on?"

"Would you maybe be interested in hiding this?" Cooper asks, pleading expression on his face. "Just for a bit?"

I push him away. "Why would I want to do that? Do you have a girlfriend? Oh, god, are you *married*?"

"No, no, nothing like that," Cooper soothes, reaching for me again. I dodge his hands, backing against the cool wall, my arms folding against my chest.

How could this have gone so wrong so quickly?

"Look, Brienne, I like you. I really do. I think you're amazing, and it's clear that I've been interested in you since I stepped foot in this office. But I'm also interested in keeping my job."

"What's wrong with your job?"

"Only that it might be in danger if I start dating you?"

Chapter Twenty-Two

SADIE

I MEET JULIAN IN his office.

I know what I must look like—my heart is beating quickly, my skin flushed like I ran all the way.

Which I didn't.

My eyes are bright and I caught my lip between my teeth as I stand before Julian's desk.

Would I like him to fuck me on that desk? The wood biting into the front of my legs as he bends me over it. The papers and Mont Blanc pen swept away as he lays me on my back, pounding into me like he did last night.

His mouth between his legs, his hands—

"How are you this morning, Sadie?" Julian asks, cutting through my reverie.

"Fine, thanks," I reply like he has no idea what I sound like when I come.

"Sleep well?" There's a hint of a smirk on his handsome face, but he keeps his eyes downcast.

"Is that really an appropriate question?" I ask.

His eyebrow raises, and he gestures to the chair before his desk. "Sit down, please."

Is he *firing* me?

There's no reason for me to think that there is anything negative about this meeting, but that's where my mind goes. And it goes there *fast*.

But Julian says nothing like that. And keeps things professional as he gives me instructions on a press release, something I am fully capable of doing myself.

My eyes glaze over as he drones on about market research and branding. Finally, he steps around his desk and leans against it.

I sit before him in the uncomfortable chair and lean back because the waistband of his pants is at my eye level.

I could reach out and grasp his hips, pulling him closer so I could unfasten the belt, slowly unzip...

"One more thing, Sadie." His voice slows to a drawl and when I meet his gaze, I know exactly what he's going to say. "About last night."

"Yes?" I keep it polite like he didn't give me one of the most intense sexual experiences of my life. I sound like it means nothing.

It should mean nothing.

Tell the clenching in my nether regions that.

"I enjoyed myself. Very much. As did Victor."

What am I supposed to say to that? Callie would come up with a quick retort like *of course, you did,* or *I'm not surprised.*

"Yes?" I repeat and Julian lifts an eyebrow.

"Did you enjoy the evening? Did you enjoy meeting my friend?"

"Technically, it wasn't an evening. I'd call it more of an interlude."

"Whatever you like to call it."

"An interlude. Or a rendezvous. But that sounds more romantic than it was. There was nothing romantic about it."

"Do you need romance, Sadie?"

My mind flashes to Jason holding me in his arms. "If I do, I don't think I'm going to get it from you."

His mask slips and he frowns. "You sound upset."

"I'm not upset," I say slowly. "And yes, I did enjoy myself."

"Good." The smile is back, making him look like the cat that swallowed the canary. "I have another friend who would like to meet you."

My heart stops for a moment, then speeds up like I'm excited. Am I excited? Last night was...it was a lot. Do I want a repeat? Is that all he wants from me—a willing and eager body, ready to do exactly what he wants?

Of course it is, Sadie—are you stupid?

"Do I have any say in this?" I hear myself ask.

"I'm sorry?"

"Do I have any say in meeting your "friends?" Because last night I sure didn't. There I was, and there you were, and there was somebody else, who I didn't even know, and put his cock in my mouth, and in other places. A few other places. And I admit I was into it. It was good. It felt good. I enjoyed it." I pause to collect my thoughts.

"I didn't like it when it was over."

"Did you want to continue? Did you want *more*?"

It's the emphasis on *more* that gets me standing, no longer sitting subservient at his feet.

"Whether I wanted more or less, is a non-issue, really, because you never asked exactly what I wanted. You just assumed I'd be into it."

"But you were."

"I was. And I'm not going to go into consensual or anything like that, because, yes, that was consensual. I submitted to everything you wanted, and it was good."

I wrap my arms around myself, wanting a shield for my next words because a big part of me is ready and willing to ask when I'm going to meet his friend.

"It was very good," I continue. "But it's not going to happen again. I'm not about to be a play toy for you like I was with Alma. I'm a person, and I have feelings and opinions. Not just a body."

"I didn't realize I hurt your feelings."

"You didn't, because I have no feelings for you. And that's the problem."

"I don't understand."

"I don't want to be a plaything. I don't want casual sex in your office, whenever you want it, with whoever you want to bring in. Even though it was good," I say with a shiver. "I'm not that person."

"Are you sure about that?"

"Very sure. Or, maybe I wasn't but I'm very sure now. I liked the experience, I don't regret it, but I don't want it anymore."

Julian slides a hand around my waist with a possessiveness that raises the hairs on the back of my neck. "Are you sure about that?"

"Very sure," I say forcibly, stepping to the side so he can't touch me. Because my lady parts still really want him to touch me. "I want a relationship, Julian, but even if you were capable of that, I wouldn't want it with you."

"That's unfortunate."

"Unfortunate or sad? Because if you say unfortunate, it makes me wonder if I should be afraid for my job."

"What are you saying, Sadie?"

"I don't know, Mr. Donovan, what are you saying?"

"I'm not saying anything, Sadie. I think you're overreacting. I think you're overreacting about everything, actually. I have no problem if you're interested in a relationship with anyone. It doesn't have to affect our friendship."

"But it would. I'm not that person. I thought I could be. I thought this casual office-place sex would be exciting and hot, and it really was. But now I'm done with it."

"That is too bad."

"Not really, no. Because I think a relationship would be better. It can be hot and exciting too, and that's what I'm looking for. I should really thank you, Julian, you and Alma, because you're the one who steered me into thinking like this. Sex with strangers and other people can be really good, but I need to find out if sex with someone you care about can be better. I think it will be." I head for the door.

"I hope you find out, Sadie."

"I'm about to."

Chapter Twenty-Three

JASON

I HAVE NO IDEA what to say to Callie.

It had been obvious Michael's announcement had hurt her deeply, so it was obvious that her propositioning me was only to get back at him. From the expression on Michael's face, I knew it had worked. He may be engaged but it will be a while before he's over Callie.

I should know.

A few weeks ago, I would have been over the moon at the thought of another chance with Callie. The memory of our time together has been stored neatly away for cold, winter nights. She's a sexy, sensual woman with a sex drive higher than most men.

I'd almost call her insatiable.

And that's okay with me. It had been a good thing. But now, after last night...

Sadie.

I don't want to be with Callie.

I glance around, worried that I'd said that out loud. But no, Callie still walks beside me, with her Cheshire grin and her blonde hair bouncing as well as her luscious breasts. How could I not want her?

I do want her. I want to do everything to her. I'm a man, aren't I?

But I want to be with Sadie more.

Callie opens the door to the cavernous equipment room and peers in. "Coast is clear," she says brightly.

I know Callie well enough to realize the smile is forced. She wants to be here less than I do, but I know her well enough to know she's not going to be the one to back out.

I step into the room, my mind spinning like a hamster on a wheel trying to come up with something to say, something that won't hurt her more than she's already been hurt.

Michael is my friend, but even I acknowledge that he's a dick.

"So? Where shall we?" Callie asks with a smile that's heart-breaking in its beauty. My cock twitches at the sight of it. One time wouldn't hurt. It might make her feel better. Sadie will never know. Sadie wouldn't even care. She's back to running after Julian Donovan—

"Jason?"

I turn to Callie with an embarrassed expression, caught trying to talk myself into having sex with her.

Unbelievable.

"Uh, maybe..." I begin to flounder right away. Wouldn't it be easier just to bend her over the pallet one last time, seeing that sweet ass and those big, beautiful breasts?

"What's the matter?"

"Huh? Oh, nothing. Why would anything be the matter?"

Callie cocks a hand on her hip. "Because you're not salivating at the thought of seeing me naked again, are you? Something is off."

"It's not you," I say in a rush, flashing on an explanation that's nothing but a stroke of genius. "It could never be you. But you know, I've heard rumours of Julian Donovan setting up security cameras in the office. I didn't think he'd put them here, but look." I point to the far wall at the box attached to the wall, painted the same dreary gray, and sit almost flush to the wall. "There's one."

"That doesn't look like a security camera," Callie argues. "I thought they were those dome things."

"These are new. More discrete." I improvise wildly. "I read an article online about how people nowadays have become so used to seeing them that they can't blend in anywhere. This new kind—"

"I don't care right now," Callie says with a wave of her hand. "What I care about is why Julian is watching everyone."

"It's definitely unsettling." I grab onto the lifeline gratefully.

"Especially considering what goes on around this place." She stares at the camera. "That gives me the creeps knowing he could be watching us. I'm not opposed to being watched, but I would like to be consulted about it first, you know."

"Of course. And then there's the question of legality."

"It's illegal to film employees? You think?"

"Well, I'll have to check with Abby, but," I trail off at her grin. "You were joking."

"I was joking."

"Were you also joking about wanting to have sex with me?" I ask hopefully.

"I take it that you're not so inclined as you were last time," Callie says with a rueful smile. "I get it."

"No, you don't." I grab her arm as she turns towards the door. "You can't, because I really don't understand it. I should be at your feet at the thought of getting with you. Salivating, as you descriptively call it."

"And you're not. No worries. Everyone has off days."

"It's not an off day. It's because of Sadie."

Callie frowns. "What about her?" she asks sharply.

"I don't know."

"What don't you know?" Callie's voice raises dangerously, protective of the younger woman.

"I spent the evening with her. Not like that," I say quickly as Callie's eyes widen. "I'm not sure what I'm allowed to tell you."

Callie cocks a hand on her hip. "You might as well tell me everything because I'm heading to Sadie's desk as soon as we're out of here. Without you seeing me naked," she adds.

"Thank you," I tell her gratefully, then shake my head. "I can't believe I just said that."

"Neither can I. Now, on to Sadie. And make it fast before I really start to worry."

"There's nothing to worry about. At least not from me."

"You're not helping, Jason!"

"I had to come back to the office last night, and she was here. With..." I trail off, raising my eyebrows.

Callie covers her mouth with her hand. "Julian and Alma?"

"Not Alma, but there was another man involved. Sadie was...I don't think it was her choice. No, that's not right," I hasten as Callie's expression darkens. "I don't think she was expecting such a...a scene. She seemed a little off. She ensured me that it was consensual."

"I'm going to go talk to her."

I grab her arm again. "Let her bring it up, please," I beg.

"I know how to deal with Sadie. She's like my little sister."

"I know. She looks up to you. Which means she may not be as forthcoming with how she feels about what happened. With all your adventures..."

"Is that what you call them?"

"I'm not sure how to say it without sounding offensive, which isn't my intention."

"I know, Jason. But Sadie—"

"—seemed to be fine this morning. But his interest in her is a little disconcerting. Not that she's isn't a beautiful woman," I add hastily. "But..."

"What should we do?"

I like that she uses *we*, that I'm not alone in my concern for Sadie. "Let her come to you," I suggest. "You know she will. Just let her do it on her own."

"What am I supposed to do in the meantime?"

I gesture to the equipment room. "I hear voices in there. And I doubt Julian has thought to put cameras in there. You might find a way to pass the time."

Callie shakes her head with a smile. "You surprise me, Jason. And you better be good to Sadie."

"I will be. If she gives me a chance."

After I leave Callie, I rush up to Julian Donovan's office, my heart hammering with the possibility that I'm too late.

The door is closed.

I spend an agonizing few minutes staring at the door, wondering what's going on in there.

Imagining what he's doing to her.

Is there anyone else in there? Did Alma join them? Will he leave her drained and exhausted again, twice in less than twenty-four hours?

How can I possibly compete with him?

My thoughts spiral darker as the minutes tick by. I can't hear anything, but is that a good sign? Maybe Sadie is—

The door opens. Sadie stands before me looking tired but pleased with herself. And no different than when she ran out of the kitchen earlier. No mussed hair, unkempt clothes.

There definitely hasn't been enough time to pass to have things reach an intensity of last night.

"Jason! What are you doing here?" Sadie hisses, with a backward glance at Julian's office. She closes quickly.

"I wanted to make sure you were all right," I say stiffly.

"Why wouldn't I?"

"Well, because of last night—"

Sadie smiles and it's the most beautiful sight I've ever seen. "It wasn't like that, Jason. Not at all. It was just a meeting."

"Just a meeting," I parrot. "I thought you might..." I trail off, unable to find the words that don't make me sound like a possessive stalker.

"I thought it didn't bother you," she says coyly.

"It does." I take a deep breath. "Callie wanted to...you know...and I didn't because I couldn't stop thinking of you. I want you to stop doing...you know...with him, not because I want you to, but because you can't stop thinking of me. But I need to know if you even think of me, or think of doing...you know...with me, because if you don't I think I've really embarrassed myself." I glance at her, feeling unbalanced as if the floor is steeped and I'm about to fall. It's not my best moment or my most eloquent speech. With more time I could have perfected it but it was a moment and I needed to say it.

Sadie steps forward and reaches up to cup my chin. "I've never seen you when you're not perfectly shaved," she muses, rubbing her fingers along my jawline.

"I was a little out of sorts this morning," I admit.

"So was I," she says with a smile. "Because I was thinking of you."

And then she moves closer and rises on her tiptoes and then Sadie kisses me.

I pull away as soon as her lips touch mine, hating the expression of confusion on her face, but I have to make sure. "You didn't?"

"No."

"You're not going to?"

"Never."

"But you ran to him?"

"Because you told me to!" Her face scrunches with frustration. "This morning, it seemed like last night didn't matter. Even though nothing happened, I still felt...it mattered to me."

"It did to me too."

"Then why were you so...I don't know. Cold, this morning?"

Now it's my turn to frown with confusion. "I was myself this morning. I offered to make you tea. I've never done that before. To anyone. To give up my place in the line is pretty big."

Sadie's shoulders relax and a smile brightens her face, like a sunrise. "You were yourself and I was in my head. I'm glad that's all it was."

"Me too, even though I'm still confused. But if you're happy, that's all right. Are you going to kiss me again?"

"Would you like me to?" She doesn't let me reply but presses those lips against mine again. Those lips that taste cool and sweet and delicious, just like I imagined. And holding her close to me, my hands on her waist, her back, in her hair—

I'm dizzy with the thought of having her in my arms.

I don't hear the sound of the office door opening, but the voice breaks rudely into my haze of Sadie. "What's going on here?" Julian says loudly.

Sadie jerks away with a guilty expression on her face. Then she lifts her chin defiantly. "I'm seeing about that relationship thing."

Julian looks between us, his eyes cold and calculating. "That's fine, Sadie, but I forgot to tell you that due to recent charges against several employees, there is to be no fraternization between Hever employees."

My heart stops but Sadie laughs. "That is the most hypocritical thing I've ever heard you say! You had no problems fraternizing with me last night."

"This is a new rule, in effect today. There will be no relations between employees if they want to keep their jobs."

She laughs again, and while I'm proud to see her stand up to Julian, I want to pull her away because I need my job. Or at least I'd like to keep it. "That's bullshit," she says, her own voice hard. "And I'd like to see you stop us."

She takes my hand and pulls me away. I glance over my shoulder to see Julian staring after us, an unreadable expression on his face.

This isn't good.

As soon as Sadie pulls us into the stairwell, she stops with another gasp of laughter. "I can't believe I did that!"

"Neither can I."

"I'm going to lose my job."

"It seems like I might too."

She stands on the stairs above me so that we're almost the same height and wraps her arms around my neck. "No, you won't. I'll make sure he doesn't do anything to you."

Before I respond, she kisses me again, and I let all my worries float away for the moment.

This is good. This might be worth it.

Chapter Twenty-Four

CALLIE

I CAN'T BE MAD at Jason for leaving.

It's been a while since my little tryst with Jason on the pallet of concrete bags, but in my mind, it had been well worth a repeat. Knowing that he's got a thing for Sadie, I shouldn't have even put him in the situation. But I need something and someone to take my mind off Michael.

He's getting married.

It hurts more than it should. And that's what makes me take a *Fuck you* approach. There will be no pity parties from me, no woe-is-me moment.

I pause outside the equipment room, hearing the echoing voices inside, and the growl of a truck starting up. Michael is getting married three weeks after we had sex, sex that meant something to me.

Maybe a little moment.

But then I harden my heart like only I can do and take a stroll through the room.

It's been weeks since I visited the bottom floor, where the construction workers hang out between shifts. They come in tired and dirty, after driving those huge machines and doing all sorts of manual things that I would never be interested in, but somehow gets me excited thinking about it. I mean, who wouldn't be excited thinking about a man who can command a twenty-ton tracked excavator?

I know I do.

I don't have anyone in mind when I go for my wander. I don't have any*thing* on my mind, other than I'm looking for something to do to for about twenty minutes which will leave me with a smile on my face that would last the rest of the day.

I see Greg right away.

He's one of the dump truck drivers and sometimes runs the concrete mixers. He's not my type—I'm sure he's someone's type, but I haven't heard anything about him and anyone else. He's big and burly and gruff and kind of a grouch but the man has magic fingers.

We met about three years ago; I was feeling lonely; there was alcohol involved and a lot of laughter.

There was no laughter after, and Greg cured whatever loneliness I might have been feeling.

Greg has a cup of coffee in his hand standing outside of a group of men sitting at the table. I catch his gaze and he nods his grizzled head. His beard is fuller now than ever, a reddish brown colour that's lighter than the close-cropped hair on his head. He looks like he belongs to a biker gang, and I know he does drive a motorcycle, so it might be possible. "Callie," he says as I sidle over.

"Greg." I match his somber tone.

He turns his back to the group which effectively blocks me from their view. "You looking for someone?"

I glance over his shoulder at the other men and dismiss them with a sniff. "What if I'm looking for you?"

Greg glances around the vast equipment room, full of backhoes and Bobcats and all sorts of handheld tools. Another small group of men stand in the far corner recapping someone's escapade with raunchy laughter. The whole area smells of grease and dirt and men. It's one of my favourite places in Hever.

Why did I get involved with someone like Michael when these guys are so easy and fun?

"I'm on a break," Greg says with a shrug.

"Were you looking for me?" I ask.

Only now does he smile, his surprisingly full mouth snaking up among the beard. "Callie, I'm always looking for you."

And it's that easy.

I don't understand how some women are always moaning about never meeting men. It's because they're looking at the wrong ones. If a man isn't an asshole, you can always find something attractive about him. It's the personality and passion that draws me to a man. I don't care if his beard needs grooming or his abs are hidden under a twelve-pack of beer.

Sometimes Mr. No-so-Perfect is exactly what you need.

Greg sets down his coffee cup and follows me into an alcove across the room. There's no door but it's stacked full of shelves which makes it easy to hide from the rest of the room. And there are no cameras in sight.

Of course, I have to be quiet, but I can handle that.

I position myself in front of a shelf full of power drills and begin to unbutton my blouse.

"How've you been?" Greg asks.

I pause, my fingers hovering over my cleavage, noting the way Greg is caught between my reveal and a sincere interest in the question. "Do you really want to know?"

"Sure. I mean, it's been a while."

I shrug ruefully as I continue to unbutton. "I'm not sure if office gossip gets down here, but for the last couple of weeks, I've mooning over Michael in engineering. He's got a girlfriend, and that's always been off-limits for me. You don't have a girlfriend, do you, Greg?"

"Who'd want me?"

Leaving the last of my blouse buttoned, I slide my hand down his barrel-like chest, down his plain white T-shirt that's beginning to strain at the seams. Greg is a very big guy, tall and broad and muscular, which is another reason I find him attractive. If I wanted him to, he could throw me over his shoulder and carry me around for the rest of the day. Not many men can do that.

Michael certainly can't.

My hand slides under the waistband of his pants like it has a mind of its own and I find his cock, already semi-hard.

It's another reason I went looking for Greg.

I give him a ravishing smile. "Right now, *I* certainly want you."

Greg grunts and grabs a handful of my hair and pulls it to expose my neck. His beard tickles as he nuzzles the sensitive skin under my ear. "You've always been a good one. What'd this guy do to you?"

"I was so good," I say as I begin to stroke semi into hard. "I kept my distance for so long. I really liked him."

"He's an idiot," Greg growls, his mouth still on my neck, his hand pushing up the hem of my skirt.

"And then one thing led to another and we ended up taking a tumble early one morning."

"A tumble, huh? Do you remember our tumbles?" I spread my legs as his fingers push under my panties. There's no finesse, no subtly with Greg. He's a pussy man. He's told me himself. He's *shown* me himself. He's—

I gasp as a finger arrows in on my clit.

"That's why I'm here," I tell him breathlessly.

There's no build-up, no gentle exploring. Greg's going for the gold and I'm ready to hand over the family fortune.

"What'd this guy do to you? Not a good tumble?"

I'm not embarrassed that I'm more turned on by the thought of bad-mouthing Michael while Greg is finger fucking me than I am by the actual finger fucking.

Greg slides a second finger inside me as his thumb wrecks havoc with my balance. I grab his shoulder with a hand to steady myself as he rubs my clit with a steady rhythm.

Michael, who? Nope, this is better than bad-mouthing anyone.

My other hand is working on hard to rock hard.

"It was—good," I sigh, my muscles clenching in response to Greg's hand. "Too good. But then—really good."

"So you said."

"No, you." I lean back against the shelf and settle my foot on a box on the floor to give him more access. "Don't stop with that."

I feel his smile against my neck.

"After we...you know," I continue, my eyes half-closed as the sensations start to build. "He stops talking to me."

"Arse." He slides his fingers out of me and almost gently caresses my clit before jamming them back inside in a move that makes me gasp.

"Exactly. I knew he had a girlfriend, but he said...he implied..." I bite back a moan. "I don't remember what he said."

"It can't be important."

"No. But after, he stopped talking to me. Stopped...looking at me."

Greg lifts his head and looks me full in the face. "Who could ever stop looking at you?"

I stifle a moan of gratitude as well as pleasure. "I have to stop...thinking...about him. No more."

"More of this?" Greg thrusts his fingers inside me, his thumb relentless against my clit. I push my head into his shoulder and moan aloud. "No thinking about him now."

"No. No, *no no no*...oh god!" I come with a gasp, my hips bucking against his hand as the sensations coursed through me.

"Bet whatshisname couldn't make you come that quick," Greg says with a satisfied grin.

And that's the most important reason I wanted Greg. If all I wanted was a quick come, he would never insist on more. He told me once that he gets more enjoyment out of bringing a woman to orgasm than anything she could do to him.

But that wasn't all I wanted today.

"Nope. He definitely couldn't." I grin back and quickly unzip his pants, freeing his thick cock that winks up at me. "Now it's your turn." I move to bend down to take him in my mouth, but Greg stops me with a hand on my shoulder.

"No."

"No?"

"Do you have anything?" he asks in a low voice, his fingers, now gentle, still between my legs.

I widen my eyes. "Why, Greg, do you want to fuck me?"

"As good as a blow job would be, yes, Callie, I want to fuck you."

He doesn't have to ask twice. I pull out the condom I'd hidden in my bra and suit him up quicker than anyone has even slid a condom on a cock that is already twitching at the gate.

And then he's inside me, with fingers still stroking to bring me back up to speed, and the other hand hiking up my knee.

"Oh, wow," I breathe, my hands clutching at his chest as Greg thrusts gently. His cock is so big that I have to stretch to accommodate. Serious excitement is mandatory with Greg to keep the initial pain to a minimum.

Nothing hurts now, not even my heart. It's like my pussy needed a good dose of cock to overthrow the heartache.

"That's...nice..." I whisper.

Greg rears back. "Nice?"

"Nice is good." I bite my lip to stifle the cry that threatens to escape. Those fingers...I'm almost ready to come again and Greg hasn't even gotten going yet. "It's fucking amazing."

"As long as you're happy," Greg mutters. At that moment, I erupt again, this time catching his shirt between my teeth so as to not cry out.

"I'm really happy now," I say with a weak smile.

Greg slides his hands under my ass, supporting me as he thrusts. And thrusts. And thrusts, quickly leaving me breathless from his strength and accuracy.

I feel my eyes begin to roll back in my head and I clutch his shoulders. Why didn't I come to find Greg sooner? He's making me forget my own name, let alone Michael's. I think I should—

The sound of voices breaks through the heavy breathing. I open my mouth to say something, but Greg's fingers tighten on my ass as he quickens the pace. Maybe he's heard them too. Maybe—

"—HR thinks it's our best recourse," the voice says.

It's Julian.

Apparently, he's finished meeting with Sadie.

It's not easy being fucked so thoroughly and eavesdropping on a conversation at the same time, but I do my best.

"The harassment charge will not disappear, and I'm afraid there will be more," Julian says. I don't recognize who he's speaking to, and I miss the response because Greg does something with his hips that takes my breath away.

This is so good, this is so good, this is so fucking *good...*

"We lost the last few bids, so the engineering team needs to be readdressed anyway," Julian says.

"Fuck you," I breathe into Greg's shoulder.

While it sounds like Julian and friend are coming closer, Greg is making no signs that he's close to his endgame. Never before have I wanted a man to come so quickly, but I also want to eke out another orgasm for myself. I reach down to give myself a helping hand.

Greg mutters something unintelligible and I assume he's finally getting closer. I rub my clit, forgetting about Julian other than hoping he stays away for a few more minutes.

...so good, so very good...

Greg stiffens and he comes with nothing more than a sharp intake of breath. His final thrust tips me over the edge and I close my eyes as shudders rack my body. Greg holds me, still moving slowly inside me like he can't bear to stop.

"...shut it down. We have to sell the company," Julian says, as clearly as if he's standing beside me. I hold my breath until my throat is ready to explode.

"The boss is right there," Greg whispers in my ear. Ever so slowly, he slides his hands off my ass and takes a step back.

"I know," I mouth. "Whatever happens, thank you for this."

"What's going to happen?" Greg mouths in return.

Chapter Twenty-Five

BRIENNE

"**Y**OU WERE SERIOUSLY HAVING sex and Julian was right beside you?" I cry with astonishment.

Callie had called an emergency meeting for after work at the same bar we had been at last night to tell us about what she'd heard in the equipment room. Sadie, Jason, Delia, Carl, Abby and her husband Ben are now crowded into the same booth we'd sat at.

And Cooper. He's right beside me, his firm thigh tucked beside mine.

As soon as drinks are served, Callie wastes no time in telling us about her rendezvous. She didn't tell us *who*, but she isn't shy about giving other details. Cooper stares at her open-mouthed, clearly not used to her stories.

Like always, it sounds like she had a fun time and there's no mention of Michael. And from the way Jason hasn't moved from Sadie's side, it's clear that Jason wasn't her mystery man.

When did that happen?

Seeing them together and hearing about Callie's sex-escapades makes me super aware of Cooper beside me. We haven't talked since our make-out session that morning, which means we haven't talked about our make-out session.

We also haven't talked about how he thinks he's going to get us fired if we take things further. That should possibly be brought up at this little meeting.

Cooper sets his pint glass back on the table and his arm brushes mine. Are those goosebumps? Am I getting goosebumps because his arm brushed mine?

I catch his eye and he smiles. Everything inside turns to mush.

How much do I like my job?

I wrench my attention back to what Callie is saying. I'm sure it's important, but all I want to listen to is the beating of my heart after Cooper kisses me again. The way his lips fit against mine, how his tongue—

"—selling the company," Callie exclaims.

"What?" I gasp, tuning in at the right moment.

"I heard Julian say he was selling the company," Callie repeats.

"Are you *sure*?" Abby leans across the table.

"It sounds like you were a bit busy," Ben adds with a grin.

"I might have been, but I'm sure about what I heard." Callie's expression is grim. "He's selling us."

"Well, that's...I'm not sure what that is," Cooper says with a glance at me.

"It's pisser, that's what it is. And for him to say there are problems in the engineering department is only going to make it harder for us to get another job."

"Bubalo Construction is getting all the jobs," Ben offers. "I know they're hiring, so I'll tell the guys to get their names in now before this news hits. Are you absolutely positive, Callie?"

"That's what I heard," she says firmly. "Is there any way to confirm it?"

We all glance at Jason, who nods. "I can do some digging. I know there have been a few board members around lately. This deal might be why."

"Did Julian say when?" Sadie asks in a sad voice. "Because I met with him this morning and he didn't say anything about this."

I can only imagine what she's feeling. Not only was she involved with Julian, but with his wife as well, and neither of them thought to mention this news to her. In their defence, it could be a last-minute decision, but Julian seems like the planning type to me.

"End of the quarter is next week," I muse. "This would be the time to announce something like this. He'd have to find a buyer. There's no sense telling us if it's going to take months to find someone to take it over. We'd all be long gone and that would hurt the bottom line."

"I'd like to hurt his bottom line," Delia says in a menacing voice, which makes us all laugh.

Nothing is resolved except that there are a lot of bad feelings towards Julian and Hever Construction in general. There are quite a few bad words thrown around. When we're getting ready to leave, Callie makes us all promise to report back if anyone hears anything.

"I'm heading back to the office," I say to no one in particular as we solemnly file out of the bar.

Sadie whips her head around. "You're not going there after hours. Not by yourself."

"It's fine Sadie," I assure her. "No one is going to bother me."

"Really? After five o'clock, things happen in that place."

"Are you going back?" Jason asks her.

"No, I'm not," she says firmly. "I'm never working extra hours again."

Why does Jason smile so widely at her words?

"I left my book in my office, so I'll head back with you," Cooper says, trying for casual and failing miserably.

"I think that's a good idea," Sadie says. "You always want to have your book."

Cooper follows me to my car. "You don't mind driving me back, do you?" He doesn't wait for my response but hops in the passenger side as soon as I unlock the door.

"Did you really forget your book?" I ask suspiciously as I pull out of the parking lot.

"Do you think I'm lying to you?" he asks with a grin. "Do you think I'm using my forgotten book as an excuse to spend more time with you without seeming to spend more time with you?"

"If they're selling the company, then no one should bother about who is dating who?" I can't keep the hope out of my voice and Cooper's smile widens.

"At least something good can come of it."

My foot hits the gas a little too hard, getting us back to the office in record time flat. Anticipation builds within me, countered by my internal naysayers who keeps telling me nothing is about to happen.

He's getting his book.

I'm getting—actually, I have nothing to get. But something is drawing me back to the office and I had a wild hope Cooper would want to come back with me. So this is my way of making something happen.

The office is still open but there's no one to be found as we make our way up to the accounting department. When we come up the stairs, Cooper veers off. "Let me grab my book and I'm good to go."

"Ok," I say, anticipation sinking fast. This was a mistake. Callie said Julian is watching the employees—why would Cooper want something to happen here?

Why would I?

Cooper finds me a few minutes later at my desk, staring across the room. "Are you okay, Brienne?"

"A lot has happened to me here," I admit. "Thinking of it gone—I honestly couldn't care less about the company, and I know I'll find another job. But the parts of me that changed, that's what I'll miss."

"Like what?" Cooper leans a hip on a neighbouring desk.

"Like I was married when I started working here and now I'm divorced. Or, almost divorced."

"Yes, the infamous Elias Ford."

I smile tightly. "That's a good word for Eli."

"Doesn't sound like you're regretting it. Splitting up, I mean."

"No, I should have done it a long time ago. It's just—changes things, you know. I'm a divorced woman now."

"Scandalous." I like the way Cooper smiles at me, teasing, but not making fun. Like he understands. "So what else? What happened in that office over there?" He gestures to Ian's old office. For some reason, Cooper was given a different office when he started, on the other side of the floor. Ian's office is still empty, but full of memories.

"Why do you say that?" I hedge.

"From the way you're staring at the door."

I shrug. There's no sense of hiding things. "The controller who had the job before you. Ian. That was his office."

Cooper nods. "I heard things about him."

"Most of them are probably true. He wasn't the nicest guy."

"A bad boy. Is that your type?"

"Not, dangerous un-nice, just not friendly. Cold. I wouldn't say he's a bad boy, just an ass."

"Good, because if a bad boy is your type, I really don't think I have a chance."

I glance at him with a smile, my stomach tightening. "Do you think you have a chance?"

Cooper smiles, warm and sexy and all the anticipation I felt driving to the office comes rushing back.

Maybe. Just...maybe.

"I hope so," he says slowly. "But maybe you should tell me about this Ian and all the stuff that happened in his office."

"I'm not sure you want to know all that." I'm surprised when Cooper takes my arm and leads me to the office. It's empty, save the generic furniture. My eyes are drawn to the desk; the simple office desk that changed so much for me. "Why are we here?"

He drops my arm, but his hand strays to the small of my back like he's comforting me. "Obviously whatever happened in here had an impact on you, so let's see if we can make you forget it."

Cooper's hand is warm and firm and his finger splay against my back, moving slightly, rubbing. "It didn't...not much..."

"But something happened between the two of you?" I nod, unable to say anything, hoping this isn't a game-changer. Maybe he won't want anything to do with me. "I'd like to know."

It's the way he says it and tells me this is really going to happen. And the expression in his blue eyes. Interest, yes, but hunger. It's the way Eli looks at me when I'm on the couch. It's the way Cooper looked at me in my dream.

"Do you really?" I ask archly.

"I really do. I like being told stories. I think you might have a good... story."

Something explodes inside me and I bite my lip to keep from smiling. "What do you want to know?"

"This Ian. What did he do first?"

My mind races back to that one night with Ian—at his cool smile, the memory of watching him with Agatha making me excited even as I shivered with fear of the unknown. "He told me to undress."

"You took off all of your clothes?" I nod, unable to look at Cooper. "What would happen if I asked you to undress?"

I hesitate for a split second, sucking in my breath with an audible hiss. And then I stand before the desk and begin to unbutton my blouse.

Suddenly the fluorescent lights on the floor switch off, leaving it bathed in a yellow glow. I clutch my blouse and jump behind the desk so whoever is out there can't see me.

"It's okay," he soothes. "No one's there. The lights turn off automatically. I'll turn this one on." He fumbles with the light switch by the door.

"Leave it off." There's enough light from the safety lights for me to see the outline of Cooper, see his smile and his eyes. There's enough light for him to see me.

The darkness gives me an extra boost of confidence.

"Whatever you want," he says, moving around to the far side of the desk to face me again. I take a deep breath and begin to undress again. Cooper watches open-mouthed, his eyes turning dark with desire. "Do you like to be told what to do?" he asks hoarsely.

"I like it that you asked," I whisper, my fingers fumbling with the last button.

"Can I help you with that?"

I shrug the blouse off my shoulders. "I can manage on my own." I like the way he looks at me, his eyes all by devouring every inch. It would be nice for him to undress me, but then I wouldn't get to watch him watching me.

I slowly unzip my skirt, enjoying the way his gaze trails down my bare stomach. I've never had a man look at me that way. I knew Eli wanted me from his gaze, but there was always a smugness to it like I was expected to do certain things. That he knew I would bow to his needs. It would be good, always good, but he was always in charge.

With Cooper, I sense disbelief in the way that he looks at me like he's amazed to find me here with him.

It's a heady sensation. That this man, this big beautiful man with the eyes I can drown in and the mouth...I'm still excited by the memory of the way that mouth felt against mine.

I'm excited by the thought of him now.

I kick off my skirt and I reach around to unclip my bra, covering my breasts with teasing hands as it slips off my shoulders. I decide to leave my panties on for now. My pale skin glows in the dimness.

I stand practically naked before him and I'm as comfortable as if I'm wearing my flannel pyjamas.

"I want to see," Cooper says in a strangled voice.

"Say please," I order, caressing my breasts. I tug at my nipples and Cooper's eyes widen.

"Is that what he did? Did he ask? Did he beg?"

Would Cooper beg for it? The thought makes things turn to liquid. "I don't remember what he did," I lie breathlessly. "I like that you asked."

"Can I see your breasts?" Cooper asks obediently and I drop my hands, the cool air pebbling my nipples. "Can I touch them? Please?"

I nod once. Cooper drops into the desk chair and rolls it before me. A sigh escapes as his hands find me. Warm and gentle and big.

I drop my gaze. Is everything about him so large?

I've never been considered well-endowed and have spent many insecure moments wishing for a chest like Callie's. But Cooper's touch makes me believe my breasts are works of art. He caresses, he worshipped, he teases—and that's all before he bends his head to them.

My quick intake of breath prompts him to raise his head, his mouth dropping open-mouthed kisses on the sensitive skin around my nipple.

"You like that?" His tongue flicks out to brush my hard-as-rock nipple.

"Yeah," I say with a shaky breath.

"What else do you like?"

"I'd like you to do more with your mouth."

I feel his smile as Cooper presses that mouth under my breast. "I'll get there," he promises. "I'm having fun here."

"Then, by all means, take your time." I grasp his head with both hands and gently tug his hair until his lips close over my nipple.

"You're demanding," Cooper complains, turning his attention to the other breast.

"I guess so."

I think I like being demanding.

Cooper spends long minutes on my breast, licking and sucking and caressing, his fingers become more demanding, his mouth more adventurous. I can't help but wonder if this will be the time I come with only nipple play. But finally, when the ache between my legs is becoming unbearable, I tug his hair. "More," I whisper.

"More, what?" he asks, obediently lifting his head.

"More of you touching me. You touching more of me." I'm not demanding. I never ask for what I want, trusting my partner to give it to. I may be enjoying myself, but asking is new for me and I'll need some practice.

Cooper looks up at me from between my breasts, his hands running up my torso. "What did he do next?" His thumb flicks my nipple and a jolt of wanting answers between my legs.

"I don't remember."

"No, you do. I know we've deviated from the plan, but let's try again. I want to know what he did." My cheeks heat as I drop my gaze to the floor. Cooper takes my chin in his hand and makes me look at him. "Tell me, please."

"He—I...he made me lie over the desk," I say quietly. "And then he spanked me. While he used his mouth."

Cooper won't release my gaze and his hands haven't stopped touching me. Now they slid over my ass, still wearing my brightly coloured cotton panties. "Did you like it?"

"I'd never—it was the first time."

"That you were spanked? I hope it wasn't the first time anyone tasted your pussy, because I have to wonder about the men in your life."

The corners of my mouth turn up. "First time for a spanking. Slapping."

"I've never done it," Cooper admits, kneading my ass, his fingers working closer and closer to the warmth between my legs. "I might have to work up to that. Is that okay?"

"Okay." I gasp as a finger wanders into my heat. "Okay."

"I would like to taste you."

"Okay," I repeat, unsure if I can manage another word.

"Is that all you're going to say?"

"Maybe." Another finger has wandered in, the two stroking my sudden wetness with languorous speed.

"Do you want me to ask permission?"

"O-kay," I say hesitantly. This is why I never want to be in control. I don't want to waste time on me making decisions. I want

Cooper's mouth between my legs *now* and I want him to make me come. Then I want him to fuck me.

Why all this talking when we both want the same thing?

Cooper stands and settles me on the edge of the desk. Then he returns to his chair and wheels it forward.

"Brienne, can I take off your underwear?" he asks in a low voice, his fingers running up my legs with a delicious tickling sensation. When he reaches my hips, the fabric of my panties thwarting his progress, he dips his thumb under the elastic and tugs it down.

"Yes," I whisper.

"Would you like me to do it...slowly?"

Is slowly the same as ripping them off? "No."

"You want them off right now. Right this minute?"

"Yes."

With a smoothness that brings a smile to my face, Cooper lifts me off the desk, while somehow sliding off my panties. It's a quick move to yank them all the way down my legs. "Is that better?"

"Much."

He spreads my legs with a questioning look, and his fingers trail up my legs at a quick pace without giving me a moment to answer. And then he brushes my pussy with his knuckles before slowly sliding into the wetness.

"Can I touch—?"

"Yes!" I cry.

Cooper chuckles. "Well then. Someone's impatient." And then he replaces his finger with his tongue and I sigh with relief.

Teasing flicks of his tongue. Soft kisses on my inner thighs. Cooper takes his time getting to know my pussy and I endure for as long as I can before I'm forced to grab at his hair.

"What's wrong?" he asks in between flicks of his tongue.

"More," I whisper.

"You want more from me? You don't want me to take things slow?"

"It's been slow enough."

Cooper chuckles as he kisses my clit and the sensation makes me cry out. "You like that? Tell me what you like Brienne."

"I like that," I gasp.

He slides a finger inside me. "Do you like this?"

"Yes. Both...together." I close my eyes as he adds another finger and begins to thrust. Gently at first but enough.

"You are demanding."

"I like it."

"So do I."

He bends his head again, circling my clit with a lazy tongue before sucking on it. When I cry out, he does it again.

And again.

And again.

His fingers thrust harder, faster, and I lean back on my elbows, spreading my legs. His teasing aroused me more than I thought and now when things have speeded up, the sensations are running wild through my body.

I realize I'm pushing his head further between my legs, wanting him to take more, more of me. All of me.

He tongues my clit quickly, relentlessly as his fingers bring me closer to release. "Do you like this?" he asks breathlessly.

"Yes," I moan.

"Do you want me—?"

"Shut up and just *do* it!" I cry.

He's still laughing as I come, crashing over the edge with a long, drawn-out cry of pleasure.

"Did you like that?" he asks, a huge smile on his face.

"Fuck me now," I beg, reaching for him.

"I'd like that very much."

Somehow there's a condom and then Cooper is fucking me, fucking me hard and fast with his hands on my breasts as I lay on Ian's desk with my legs around his waist. Fucking me like a man reaching for his own release. His thumb settles on my clit a moment before I erupt again, this time crying out his name as he comes as well.

It takes a moment for my heart rate to settle, to realize where we are. Still buried inside me, Cooper pulls me to him, cradling me against his body.

"I think we should take this out of the office," he says into my hair.

"Yes, please," I say, winding my arms around him.

Chapter Twenty-Six

CALLIE

J ULIAN MAKES THE ANNOUNCEMENT at the end of the next day.

But by the time the email pops up on everyone's computer, the news has already spread. Resumes have been updated, shared, and commented on. There is a feeling that we're all in this together, that the enemy is the Board of Directors headed by Julian.

It's been an interesting last two weeks at Hever.

I always thought I'd spend my last days at the office in an orgasmic haze. Despite my best efforts to be fair and inclusive, there are a few of the guys at Hever that I haven't had a crack at, whether it be by missed opportunities or lack of interest.

My interest, not theirs. Jason is the only man who has ever turned me down, and considering what's been happening with him and Sadie these last few weeks, I'm perfectly happy with his no.

It might have been weird otherwise.

They've morphed from friends to lovers in no time flat and it makes me smile every time I see their heads bent together, talking about Jason's new security venture. Romance might not work for everyone, but I think they're going to be just fine.

The same goes for Brienne and Cooper. *She's* been walking around in an orgasmic haze these last few weeks, and while I'm happy for her too, I admit to being a little jealous. Cooper has never been my type, but he's perfect for Brienne.

It makes me wonder if there's someone out there that's perfect for me.

Thank You!

Thanks for reading Office Plays—The Collection! And that concludes my Office Plays trilogy

But never fear, there are more steamy books to be read! How about spicy swingers? Or an unconventional romance between a married couple? Sign up for my newsletter to find out more and learn about my characters, and me too!

Also, stalking is welcome (The nice kind please!) I'd love it if you'd keep in touch on Facebook and Instagram. Watch for me on Tiktok soon! for my newsletter and find out more

And I'd love it if you could take a minute to post a review of Love After Hours, either on Goodreads or Amazon. This would help other readers fall in love with Brienne, Callie and the rest!

Here's a quick link to Amazon where you can tell others what you think about Office Plays. Thank you! I really appreciate it.

One last thing—Callie has become one of my favourite characters,
so you haven't heard the last of her!
More Callie:
Check out
Room Service
The second book in the Adults Only series

And then, you'll be ready for
Fantasies Book Club!
Callie

Thanks again for reading!
Anna xo

About the Author

ANNA ELLIS LIKES TO writes about happily married couples having sex with other happily married couples. There's no werewolves or vampires, shapeshifters or tentacles involved - just good, old-fashioned sex. And maybe a little tying up. Or a spanking or two.

In the **Husbands and Wives** series, follow new neighbours Jacey and Dominic as they learn to navigate the slippery sidewalks of suburban swinger lifestyle. Being a good neighbour has never been so much fun!

Her series, **One**, returns to the swinger lifestyle with three married couples looking to spice up their marriages.

Her **Office Plays** series takes you to the workplace to meet the most excitable group of office employees you would ever want to work with. They give coffee breaks a new meaning.

The series **Touch** is an unconventional love story about a woman who falls in love with a man...and his wife. All nine books are available now, *Touch*, *Caress,* and *Embrace.* Each has three separate points of view from Kenna, Iliya, and Del.

Adults Only follows Morena and Lorde, who run a B&B especially for swingers. The four book series includes characters from other series—Jacey and Dominic from **Husbands and Wives**, Callie, from **Office Plays**, and Iliya from **Touch**. While you don't need to read the other series first, it would improve your pleasure!

And her latest series, **Fantasies Book Club,** brings back a few favourites as a book club reads dirty stories that seem to mirror their own lives.

Anna also writes women's fiction/chick lit under the name Holly Kerr. If you're looking for something a little less steamy (but still hot!) check out her books.

Visit Anna at or Facebook

Or visit Holly at

They'd love to hear from you!!

Happy Reading!

Husbands and Wives

Making Friends
The Husbands
The Wives
New Neighbours
Joe & Jacey

Interludes
Interludes II
Interludes III

Melissa
Paige

Touch

Touch
Touch – Iliya's Story
Touch – Del's Story
Caress
Caress – Iliya's Story
Caress – Del's Story
Embrace
Embrace – Iliya's Story
Embrace – Del's Story

Adults Only

Shared Accommodations
Room Service
Late Checkout
No Vacancy

Office Plays

Lost Weekends

Office Plays
Secrets and Lies
Love After Hours

One

One Summer
One Week
One Night

Fantasies

Gemma
Emmy
Callie
Nia
Malcolm

Peek-a-boo